Sisterhood of the Stones

The Complete Series

L.A. Boruff Lia Davis Lacey Carter

Onyx Interruptions

Formatting by L.A. Boruff

Citrine Wishes

We hereby dedicate this book to Mari Hinton. May you find ALL the luck in your life, and a bit of gorgeous jewelry wouldn't hurt, either. <3

Chapter One

No Island Wedding Is Too Good For My Daughter

"WHAT DO you *mean* you don't have a suite available?" I controlled my voice, barely hinting at the shock and outrage that simmered underneath the surface. "I confirmed the reservation online days ago, double-checking that it was a suite." Now the man behind the desk was trying to tell me none were available.

Breathe, Cami. It'll all work out.

I'd already reached my breaking point before arriving. My daughter had been piling on the pressure. She wanted, *needed,* everything to be flawless. Her need for perfection—a personality trait she'd developed the moment she'd started talking.

Everything was going wrong, which made her text me a million times an hour.

Not really, but it felt like it. Maybe a hundred times an hour was more accurate.

To make this whole trip worse, I was going to have to spend the next week hanging out with my ex-husband, and whatever bimbo of the week he brought as his plus one.

I felt like a kettle shaking on the stove, ready to scream at any moment.

Thou shalt not commit murder. I'd reminded myself of that since I'd first begun to plan this wedding. In reality, I didn't have a murderous bone in my body.

That's what hitmen were for.

"I'm sorry," the clerk said with a little shrug, but he didn't look the least bit sorry. "But, if it's any help, the father of the bride has already checked in…" He had the good sense to cower a bit. "But it was in one of the suites you reserved."

Snotty little hotel concierges who messed up room reservations were unfortunately included under the umbrella of not killing folks. I couldn't punch him in the throat either. Out of deference to the commandment, there was nothing I could do without ending up in a foreign prison and on Santa's naughty list the week before my daughter's wedding. Gritting my teeth, I forced myself to lean away from murder and more toward dirty looks.

Peering at his nametag, I tried using the clerk's name and making sure my voice was very nice. *Arthur, Front Desk Manager.* He was just trying to do his job. "Arthur, I had three suites reserved." I held up three fingers. "What happened to the others?"

He looked down his long nose at me, sniffed, and looked at his screen before tapping on his keyboard. "I can check."

Oh please, find my room.

Arthur sighed. "The bride's father, Mr. LaCroix, and his companion took the Presidential suite, and the bride will be in the honeymoon. One Mrs. Jolene Hollingsworth, the groom's mother, assured us that the third was meant for her."

I put my hands on the desk and leaned in a little, the desire to explode washing over me. "I did everything I was supposed to do, and you gave my suite to that witch? I'm sorry that she pulled one over on you, but no, you need to fix this. Even if it means tossing that awful woman out on her butt." I'd booked a regular room for my future son-in-law's mother. She could move her skinny butt to that one.

He pasted on a fake customer service smile. I understood that smile and had used it many times in my life. I still wasn't fully mad *at* Arthur. He'd been duped. Then he had to get all snooty and said, "Perhaps you should've booked a fourth suite."

No, perhaps this little snot shouldn't have given a suite to the woman I hated most in the world, the woman who had been my nemesis for years. The woman whose name was on a regular room, not on a suite. Jolene Hollingsworth had treated me like I had the plague when Jean-Luc and I were in high school and then overruled every single one of my suggestions at every PTA meeting in the twelve years our kids were in school together. She was a gigantic first-world problem, and I wanted to throw her into the ocean and never look back.

Except I wouldn't do that. I was a lady.

The resort itself had sentimental value to my daughter, who'd insisted that we book her wedding ceremony at the hotel where her father had brought us when he'd won his biggest hockey trophy. Well, his *team* had won anyway. I honestly couldn't understand why this place was so important to her, at least important enough to plan a wedding at.

But to be fair to her, we had some wonderful family memories here. Memories of a father and daughter playing in the surf, swimming in the sea, collecting shells which she still had years later. To me, that vacation had been the beginning of the end of my marriage, so coming here was a little more painful than it was pleasant. Those memories, so happy for Loralai, were old wounds for me.

"I simply don't have another suite available, Ms. Danes-LaCroix," he finally said, looking up at me with annoyance.

This hotel was three city blocks long and had wings that branched off in each corner, making me wonder if he was being honest. Of course, seventy-five percent of it was under construction, so I couldn't very well call him a liar and know for *sure* that I was the one walking the high road.

Still, I drew my shoulders back, because there was no way I'd be sleeping on the beach when I'd planned everything perfectly for this trip. "Are you *absolutely* sure? I booked two suites for the Lacroix-Hollingsworth wedding party. One was for me, and one was for Jean-Luc, the bride's father. I checked to make sure everything was right before I even got on a plane, so there has to be a mistake. I implore you to check again." It had to be a simple mistake; one they could rectify. Probably. Although, if his attitude was anything to go by, this would require a state order and a paper signed by the king of all the land.

I wanted to believe that there might have been a *biggest nemesis and future-in-law* exception to killing and forgiveness, but until I knew for sure, sticking to ugly glares, eye rolls, and wishful thinking seemed to be my only option. Besides, I was pretty sure that if anything happened to her, I'd be suspect number one, and my daughter would be right there, telling them I ruined her wedding.

So, no killing for me. But this *would* be handled.

A chill rolled through me, and for the first time, the clerk looked a little uneasy as I leaned in even closer. "We're here for *my* daughter's wedding. You gave away the rooms *I* reserved under *my* name. What do you bet that if I speak to upper management your life will get a lot more complicated?" I followed my words up with a smile that made him step back.

Arthur huffed a little, patted his dark hair, and then cleared his throat. "Let's see if we can't find you somewhere to stay." His fingers flew over the keyboard.

I glared at him. "I thought you just told me that there's no other suite available because the hotel is under construction."

He finally stopped typing and smiled. This time, there was no missing the smugness in it. "Yes. That is true." He swiped a key next to his computer, and then pushed the room key across the counter. "But I did manage to find you a room. It is the one we had initially booked for Mrs. Hollingsworth. Third floor. Room 302. And, again, we're *very* sorry for the inconvenience."

"You won't make her move out of my suite?" I gritted my teeth and tried not to clench my fists.

"We can ask her, but if she says no, it is hotel policy to never force a guest to move." He blinked a few times. "If it helps, I truly am sorry."

A room. Not a suite. Whatever. I could live with it if it had a bed and a hiding place from the mess I was diving into. A place to recharge before facing the music.

I took the key with a quick snatch. "Just an FYI, you should tell your hotel manager to put the fact that more than half of your resort is under construction on your website." He opened his mouth, and I cut him off, "And not give away a room booked under someone else's name."

Before he could answer with some other smug remark, I turned around and marched off, hoping the rest of this trip would go more smoothly. This had to be my big bump in the road, right?

Turned and pointed at him. "One more thing. Take my credit card off of the suite you gave Mrs. Hollingsworth, the groom's mother. I'm not paying for her room. That wasn't in my contract.

Now that I had arrived at the hotel for the week-long wedding festivities, there were a thousand or so things that required my attention. Things like the problem with the dress. It had been sent over from a custom designer in New York. It was *the* dress. Loralai had spent months hunting it down, going to bridal shops all over the States and even Paris. She'd finally found it, and the darn thing cost my ex-husband fifteen *thousand* dollars.

Except, the dress they delivered wasn't *the* dress. Instead, what had arrived was a wad of fabric, a giant, shapeless tent made of lace and satin. Not only that, but it was the wrong lace, the wrong satin, the wrong accent color, and the wrong veil. Did I mention that it was about eleven sizes too big? In short, it was wrong, wrong, wrong.

Everything was wrong.

The flowers—imported from Costa Rica—died en route.

Then we had the cake baker who'd lost a finger in a drug deal gone bad. It hadn't been *his* drug deal. He was just a wrong-place-wrong-time kind of guy. His innocence didn't change the fact that he could no longer make the cake. On this whole island, there wasn't another baker who could make a three-tiered, buttercream masterpiece like the one Loralai had picked out. At least, that was what Loralai had told me before I got on the plane.

I was the mother of the bride, I ran a successful wedding planning business, and I could figure out how to solve these issues without stressing my daughter out more during her big week. Unfortunately, being in a foreign country and an unfamiliar place meant I needed a local expert to help me.

As the elevator doors dinged, I steadied myself, stepping out into the lobby and heading straight for the concierge desk.

Arthur saw me coming, but I didn't break eye contact as I marched across the large, beautifully decorated lobby and then came to stop at the desk. I smiled at the shady little desk clerk and tried my best to start over with him. I had enough enemies around here within my own family, both new and old. I didn't need any more. Even if the temptation to drag him across the counter was still there despite the time I'd taken to refresh myself and calm down.

Instead, I made myself smile sincerely, because I was Camille Danes-LaCroix, and I didn't resort to violence. *Yet*. "Can you tell me how often the ferry comes from the mainland?"

Ferry was a generous description for what was essentially little more than a fishing boat, but I didn't have another argument in me, nor did I have the desire to make the distinction that would surely start said argument.

"It comes at 9 AM, 1 PM, and 5 PM. After the flights land." He sounded bored, but it was probably information he gave many, many times a day. "Also, here are your messages." He handed me a couple of pieces of pink paper. One was stained with something that looked like coffee with barely legible writing and the other had a wad of gum stuck to the corner.

Do not punch this idiot. Do not punch this idiot.

I held up the one with the coffee stain. "I don't suppose you know what this says?" I was trying to maintain my nonviolent stance, but he rolled his eyes, and my fist clenched.

"It says that the band has to cancel. The lead singer is afraid to fly."

I peered down at the stained paper. If that's what it said, it was in a different language, but I wasn't here to teach a penmanship class.

Besides, now I had to worry about finding a new band that sang eighties, long-haired, power ballad rock because that was what my ex-husband had promised our daughter at one of the seventy or so planning meetings my beautiful little bridezilla had demanded.

"And this one?" I didn't want to touch it, so I pointed.

He removed the piece of gum from the corner of the paper and put it somewhere under the counter. Hopefully in a trash can. Without even looking at the gum-stained counter, he smiled and said, "It says Romando can't bake a three-tier wedding cake on such short notice, but he can get you three hundred donuts by Saturday if you pay for their transport from the mainland." He pushed the slip back across the counter at me.

The message was fine with me. Jean-Luc was paying for the whole shindig, and Loralei *loved* donuts, so maybe it had all worked out for the best. At least with that one aspect of this nightmare wedding.

So far.

Thinking of the devil, Jean-Luc walked up, smiling, his arm around a teeny bopper in a bikini. Seriously, she was half his age, and *hopefully* over eighteen. She looked younger than Loralei.

He hadn't changed much in the years we'd been apart. He was still tall, with a head full of thick blond hair, and eyes that turned smoky when he was angry, excited, or in the throes of passion.

Part of me missed those days. The smarter part of me could never forget the hell he'd put me through. Hell that made those smoky eyes of his turn my heart into steel rather than melting it, like they once did. And beside him? Some girl who was hopefully in her twenties, wearing a string bikini with a see-through cover-up over it. Like a flimsy shift made her blend in perfectly in a lobby of fully dressed people.

But I held in my sigh. I'd psyched myself up for this. I could handle it.

I could.

Jean-Luc grinned. "Hey, Cami. Looking good."

No. He looked good, which was entirely unfair. If karma was real, he'd look like a sick walrus right now, not almost entirely the same, save a few more wrinkles, and a tiny bit of gray weaved into his golden locks.

I, on the other hand, looked like a forty-something-year-old mother who'd been through twelve years of PTA meetings, a cheating husband, a tragic divorce, and a year of loneliness since her divorce. His sincerity sucked. The effort was nice, though, so I patted his arm. For all his cheating ways, he wasn't without his good aspects.

"Thanks. So do you." My hard feelings about our marriage were somewhat softer these days. As my mom always used to say, wasting time hating someone was like poisoning yourself to make your neighbor sick. While I could never bring myself to like my ex, I no longer hated him.

"How are things so far?" He spoke with an optimistic tone as if he was sure that it was all taken care of. That figured. He'd been more of a figurehead at the meetings about the wedding. And a check writer. That much I appreciated. My wedding planning business was successful, but nothing like Jean-Luc's fortune.

He didn't want the long answer. Jean-Luc *never* wanted the long answer, but I wasn't his wife anymore. It wasn't my job to protect him from reality. Baby Barbie tried to move between Jean-Luc and me, but I wasn't having it. If she wanted to be the pretty thing he spoiled, then she should already know her job was to stay quiet and out of the way, *not* act possessive of a man I wouldn't take back for the disappearance of all cellulite on my butt.

"I have to find a short-notice baker or bakery, but so far, no luck. The lead singer of the only band our daughter wants for this wedding is suddenly afraid to fly, despite already taking your three-thousand-dollar deposit." It wasn't the whole answer, but it was close, and much to my amusement, Barbie was just about snorting steam out of her nose.

"Well, I'm sure my Jean-Luc and I can figure it all out," she said, her squeaky voice immediately grating on my nerves.

"And how will *you* fix this?" I asked her, unable to take my eyes off the huge fake eyelashes blinking slowly over her angry eyes. The things looked ridiculous. Like black butterflies desperately trying to escape captivity.

She opened her mouth, then closed it, because we all knew there was nothing she could do to help. But still, she crossed her arms over her chest and gave me the dirtiest look she could manage.

I didn't care how she felt, and Jean-Luc grinned, completely ignoring his angry date. That's how he was in any and all situations, happy and relaxed. It would take an act of God to shake the smile from this guy. That, or a sudden shortage of women who liked athletes with French accents.

"Cami, babe..." He slid his arm around me and tugged me close. I got a big whiff of his CK One and smiled. I'd grown, moved on. Having Jean-Luc hold me this way didn't make me want to vomit anymore. That was quite a milestone for me. It wasn't at all romantic when he held me now. He was just a giant child in a man's body. One of those bodies they put in magazines for men's cologne, but still, that's all he was. I was no longer young and stupid. I knew the horrors of marrying a man who would never grow up, so being held close to him was just nothing. Mildly irritating at worst. "Why don't you take a rest, sweets? I'll fix it all."

I had my doubts he could do anything at all to improve this situation, but the idea of letting him take over for me for a little while was tempting. I didn't care if he fixed anything. I just needed to regroup before Loralei and Noah arrived in the morning. If that meant my ex would have to pretend to be a father and a grown-up for a little while, all the better. Heck, maybe he'd even get more done with his clueless attitude and checkbook with no limit. "Are you sure?"

He grinned again. "*Mon Amour*, I would love to do this for you." He kissed my cheek and whispered, "Maybe later you can thank me."

I sighed on the inside. Was he suggesting that he wanted to cheat with me, the woman he had already cheated on? Of course, he was because he was Jean-Luc.

I wanted to ask him if there was trouble in paradise, but I wasn't a blind woman. She was shooting him daggers with her eyes, and he was his usual oblivious self. I was used to him. She was new.

She was so angry he might need protection from her. I could probably flatten Barbie without breaking a nail—I outweighed her by thirty years of Dunkin Donuts and Olive Garden dinners, but I wasn't in the mood. He was on his own. Which meant if she went nuclear, he might withdraw his offer of help.

It was wise to nip the flirting with me in the bud. “No.”

Jean-Luc couldn’t help himself. The man flirted, even in his sleep. It was what he did, and he couldn’t turn it off. But if he wanted to pretend to handle some of the wedding details for a while, I was more than willing to let him do that.

I nodded to Mr. Save the Day and pulled out my to-do list. It included headings and numbers and the issues involved. After taking one of Arthur’s pens and scribbling a few things to the list, I had the bakers, the band, the dressmaker, the florists, and my mother’s flight information to deal with. “Do not lose this paper, Jean-Luc.” On second thought, I walked back to Arthur. “Could you make me a photocopy of this?”

His smirk was less of a smirk and more of a grimace. He snatched the page away and came back a second later with a copy that I checked. It was kind of dark but otherwise would do. I thanked him and walked back to Jean-Luc. No way was I giving him my original, so I handed over the copy.

“*Mon amour*, I will handle all of these things, and you will have a relaxing day on the beach.” He eyed me, and I smiled.

“Thank you.” It was easy to be gracious when I expected so little.

In an effort to decompress, I headed to the market set up near the pier the cruise ships docked at and tour boats launched from. It was a local glory, set up on the boardwalk with tents and stalls full of Caribbean wares, foods, crafts, and other local finds. I took my time browsing, hopeful Jean-Luc wouldn't handle much more than a fancy umbrella drink and the waitress who brought it to him. I only needed a break to clear my head and then I could dive into figuring out the details.

Leaving Jean-Luc in charge was a risk, and if history had proven anything, the problems would likely double, but undoing his mistakes never took long. He couldn't make it any worse than it already was. The man never put in enough effort at anything except hockey to make much more than a minor faux pas. Besides, when he made things worse, he usually fixed the situation by throwing more money at it, and maybe throwing money at some of these situations might work.

Who knew?

No matter what happened though, I needed a moment to process that the Caribbean Knights Hotel and Resort—a.k.a. Caribbean Knights Hellhole—which looked so good in my memories, was now rather ramshackle. Like all island buildings, it had been worn down by years of salty island air and moisture and decades of traveling abuse. Essentially, by time. I just hoped that when we pulled this wedding together, it would look the way my daughter had imagined. Otherwise, we were all in for a world of trouble. That was just another thing I'd have to find a way to handle. Hurricane Loralai.

I walked in and out of tents and stalls, looking at shell necklaces and teeny tiny totem poles. Finally, I found a tent I could have stayed in for hours. It wasn't huge. The saleswoman didn't have more than four or five tables set up, but she had an inventory I wished I could have afforded to relieve her of.

The tables were simply decorated, covered with plain cloths, and carefully displayed boxes, each box intricately carved. The open ones each held some sort of jewel, and they came in every color and shape imaginable. It was intoxicating. But there was one that called to me like a siren's song. Begging for my attention. Whispering my name.

The wrinkled woman behind the table with the money box wore a bejeweled headdress over a long, black braid hanging loosely over one shoulder. Her bright green eyes seemed to glow but that was probably an effect of the Caribbean sun—like the white sand, the crystal clear waters, the honey-colored skin of my ex-husband's new bimbo—Barbie or Babette or... Sue. Whatever.

The box I wanted looked as if it belonged in a museum behind glass. It was intricately carved. Solid. Old. Not like my grandma was old. This thing was *old* like it probably took a ride on the ark. Old Testament old. There was something about this box that spoke to me, and it wasn't the intricate carvings on the lid. They didn't make any sort of picture, more a geometric design. I loved it.

I fumbled with the clasp and chuckled at the silliness of it. I couldn't even get the darn thing open. The woman behind the table watched, not at all inclined to help, yet here I was, ready to whip out a month's rent to buy it. I checked the price tag. Month and a half.

"Where did you find such a thing?" I asked.

"I found it washed up on the beach." She shrugged like it didn't matter. Then she smiled and waved me in closer as if we were sharing secrets now. "Back when pirates roamed the seas." She looked out at the water. "It is said it belonged to the greatest pirate of all the years, Captain Renegade Remington who pillaged from port to port." I listened to her thick accent, deciphering what I could, imagining what I couldn't. Her long braid hung over her shoulder, the headdress catching the sun, and she reached over to tap the box.

However, it was mine now, so I pulled it away. "Pillaged. Sounds intriguing."

She narrowed her eyes at me. This wasn't a woman who liked interruptions. I clamped my lips together and she continued.

"One night a horrible storm raged across the sea." Her voice changed. She'd told this story before. Probably had it on a script somewhere, but I dared not ask. "The captain battled waves a mile high, and the crew jumped ship in fear. But he saved his beloved ship."

I could've listened to her talk all day, listened to her talk about the pirate captain. I was picturing a certain sexy bad-boy pirate captain from one of my favorite movies, and he was worth picturing.

She glanced at me. "Renegade brought that ship into port at Pararey Island, but he lost his chest of treasure in the storm. It fell overboard." She shook her head and made a clicking sound with her tongue. "His crew returned, the way cowards often do, but they didn't believe Renegade. They thought he was trying to cheat them and there was a mutiny." She widened her eyes and dragged her hand across her throat.

"They killed him?" Oh, no. I loved history and things that had a story attached to them. Plus, I had plenty of time to stand and listen to the story of the box and whatever was inside it since Jean-Luc was *handling* everything back at the resort.

"Made him walk the plank." I pictured the pirate again, hands up, stutter-stepping backward as his men prodded him with the tips of their foils and daggers.

"You think this was part of that treasure?" I asked in awe.

She nodded. "Although I can't prove it. Yes, I suspect it."

"Can this price be negotiated?" I blurted out, which was *oh* so subtle. This woman knew darn well she was about to get paid whatever she wanted.

She told me the price with a cocked brow, which was the price on the tag, and I foolishly didn't haggle. I just handed her the money and walked out of the tent, clenching the box, knowing I was being silly.

Still. No regrets.

When the sunlight hit my face, a peaceful, hopeful feeling surged through me. I didn't know what it was, but it took my breath away. Maybe it was the sun or the fresh scent of the sea. I couldn't have said for sure, but whatever it was carried me back to the hotel and lasted up until the minute that I walked into the hotel and came face-to-face with my ex-husband and his girlfriend. They were dripping all over the tile floor, obviously fresh from the pool. Bitsy or Buffy, whatever, was young and blonde, beautiful in that way young people always were, meaning unmarked by time. I hated her for it. Just a little.

Jean-Luc stared at me. "Oh, sweets. You're back so soon." Translation: he'd not made a call, not resolved a single wedding-related thing.

Surprise, surprise. I hadn't expected much from him, so he didn't let me down.

Chapter Two

Bimbo Babette, My Ex, and a Jewelry Box

I TOOK my box and headed back to the registration counter where Arthur acknowledged me with a smarmy smirk as I waited my turn to speak to him. Maybe I'd wronged him in another life. Not that I was the kind who necessarily subscribed to such an idea, but there had to be a reason he'd instantly hated me. Well, other than the name-calling. And the insinuations that a sloth would be better and faster at his job.

Or had I actually said those things or only think them? I couldn't remember anymore.

There were two women ahead of me asking about island attractions. Arthur took his sweet time explaining how to find the snorkeling guy and the swim-with-dolphins guy and the horseback-riding guy. Then he handed them a map of the island with said attractions marked and highlighted. He could've just done that to begin with. I took a deep breath and decided not to let Arthur get a rise out of me.

The lobby was big, open, and airy with a counter on one wall halfway between two doors, and an open wall on each end. The oversized fake palm trees in the corners hid speakers that played electric drum music at every moment of every day. There was a mural on the ceiling of an underwater landscape of coral and fish. The floors were travertine tile, and the furniture was wicker with brightly printed cushions, clustered in seating arrangements from one side to the other, but none too near the open doors.

It was in all ways a pretty place that screamed *vacation*. Only, this was the furthest thing from a vacation for me and all the decor just reminded me of that. Although, dealing with all of this was more than worth it to see my daughter walk down that aisle. To see her happy. But I would have to be all business from now on to make that happen.

I'd wasted an afternoon roaming an island market, doing nothing to solve the problems of my day, and what was left of the afternoon and evening *wouldn't* be spent finding any of the people I needed to talk to. It was too late now, they'd all closed up shop. Tomorrow it would have to be. Unfortunately for me, I'd left my beautiful daughter's wedding mishaps in the incapable hands of her father, and that was on me, not on anyone else. What in the world had I been thinking?

Not to say that Jean-Luc was a bad father, it was more that he was inexperienced at handling matters on his own. Or, well, matters *of* his own, so it had been extremely silly to leave things in his hands in the first place, but this was where we were at. It was annoying, but I could handle it, and everything would work out.

I was back on the case, renewed, refreshed, and ready to tackle whatever problems the wide world of wedding planning threw at me. First, I had to deal with Jean-Luc because he was striding towards me from the spot where I'd left him with Daisy or Delilah or... Jane. Their bare feet slapped against the cool tile, and I inhaled a calm, steadying breath, mentally preparing myself to deal with them.

Buffy was draped over his six-and-a-half-foot tall frame like she was trying to use her left boob to tattoo herself onto his arm. Not that I didn't understand. Every few minutes, it seemed like, Jean-Luc was replacing whatever girl he was dating with a new one. This woman was probably desperately hoping that if she clung all over him, he wouldn't get distracted by the next shiny pair of boobs.

Unfortunately for her, that was impossible. Jean-Luc sought out young, pretty women like a horny-seeking missile. No matter what she did, he'd be replacing her soon.

Not that I was bitter about it.

Okay, maybe a little bit.

Since our divorce, and possibly since even a month or so after we'd met, Jean-Luc's taste ran more toward young and nubile than anyone who would be considered age-appropriate.

The good news was that he was good to Lor. He had paid for college, this wedding, and anything else she had needed that I couldn't afford. Of course, that didn't give him a free pass to flaunt all things young and bikini-clad in my face, but it meant I didn't want to punch him in the face at *all* times. Just on occasion.

I rolled my eyes at the thought. I was the one who'd agreed that he could bring her along. Lor had asked me specifically if I minded, and I'd said no because Jean-Luc wasn't the kind of guy who could make it for five days without getting laid. No way was his lay going to be me. Not under any circumstances.

He came to stop in front of me and flashed me an apologetic look. "I didn't get to the, uh, wedding tasks, not yet."

"Yeah, I noticed," I said, because what else could I say? What did he *want* me to say?

He shrugged apologetically as if he thought I'd actually expected him to do anything with regard to the wedding. "The beach was calling to Brit. Do you forgive me? I tried to help, but..." He smiled that old endearing smile that I always used to fall for. "I promise you, Cami. I gave it a good try." Oh, sure he tried.

Jean-Luc smiled and hung his head. Sheepish and ashamed was a familiar look and one he wore as well as any others. "I made calls."

I nodded because this was actually the very best he could do. "Thank you."

"It was exhausting." His knees bent as if he was going to collapse, but then he stood tall again and smiled. "I don't know how you do it, Cami."

"Yes, making calls is exhausting. All that hold music..." Arguing with him did me no good, but mocking and sarcasm had seen me through some hard times. It was my go-to move, especially when I was feeling a little jealous that he was still looking young, living the life, and I was here feeling like life had left me behind.

The box shifted, and I almost lost my hold and sent it tumbling to the floor. It was old and probably delicate. I couldn't let it be destroyed just to talk to them.

I lowered my hand to secure it, but Bambie leaned in and asked, "Where did you get that?" There was such admiration in her tone, a giddy sense of pride washed over me. Again, this was mine, my precious, and I didn't want anyone touching it. Especially not Biffy.

"I got it at the market on the boardwalk. Some famous pirate lost his treasure, and legend says this might be part of it. They had a bunch more. You should check it out." And by that, I meant she should check it out alone. I certainly wasn't taking her to see it. Then I followed her gaze. She was staring at my box. Lusting. Longing.

Seriously? She already had my ex-husband. By God, she could have him. But she wasn't getting *one* more thing from me, and certainly not the box I was holding.

I looked at Jean-Luc. "I have to go."

He nodded. "Okay. I really tried to help, Cam." His words are almost a whine.

"I'll take care of it, don't worry," I said because I just want to get out of there. And, luckily for me, his phone rang, and he forgot all about me and the work he hadn't done.

As soon as Jean Luc left, I walked to Arthur's desk. In my nicest voice, I tried to start over with the guy. "Hello. Hope you're having a good day. Room 302. Any messages?"

He pushed a black curl off his forehead and smiled, and I had hope that this time he might be the kind of clerk who answered without snark. Granted, we'd started off on the wrong foot, but I'd taken the smaller room and assumed that would be the end of the attitude.

Boy, was I wrong.

He grinned. "No messages." He was a little too delighted to tell me I had zilch. Almost like he was hiding something.

"Nothing from the florist?" I narrowed my eyes, and he narrowed his right back, but he smirked as he shook his head.

"Dress designer?" My eyes couldn't have narrowed any further without closing completely, but it wasn't like I needed to see to know this little snot was still smirking.

This time he added a snippy little, "Nope."

"Cake baker?" I could be specific.

He looked at me again. "Ma'am, *no* messages." This time, his voice was stern and he drew the word no out so that it could've had about sixteen syllables instead of just one.

"Thank you. Please contact my room if that changes." I nodded because if his words hadn't put an end to our conversation, his tone certainly had. At that moment, there was no reason to do anything other than go to my room and try to open my souvenir.

I waited at the elevator bank and stepped inside one of the cars when it opened, and it rapidly filled. I hadn't even known there were this many rooms available in the hotel thanks to the construction, much less this many guests. At least not in this wing of the place.

It didn't matter to me if this was the most populated resort on the island and my bad luck meant that every single guest decided now was the *exact* time to pile into the elevator, because they weren't my focus. I couldn't stop looking at the box, even as a man next to me jostled my arm. It was just lovely and special in a way I couldn't explain. In my life, I'd had so few things like this. Any extra money always went to my daughter or to bills. I'd refused any money from Jean-Luc in the divorce, and we had split custody, which meant no child support on either side. He did spend more on Lor than I could, and I appreciated that. He'd told me a while back that he'd put the money he'd offered me in the divorce in a trust for our daughter. That was nice.

"That is a lovely trinket box," the man next to me said, then lifted his hand to run a finger over the intricate carvings on the lid.

"Thank you." I held it closer to me, not really sure why I felt so protective over a box I couldn't open. There was something inside because it called to me.

Maybe I had finally lost my mind. I blamed the stress of everything that happened since I arrived.

I looked up at the man. He was tall and dark, with a slight mustache the same deep shade as his hair, and a smile like sunshine. If not for the box, I would've been intrigued. Might've even been willing to invite him back to my room to show him a good time. Rather, to let him show me a good time. It had been a *long* while since good times had been had, and I missed them. I hadn't let loose and slept with a man since the end of my marriage. By the time we'd separated, two years ago, Jean-Luc and I hadn't been intimate in a good year.

That made it three since I'd had an orgasm I hadn't given myself.

I chuckled at the thought. Not because it was funny, but because between this guy and the box, *one* was coming to my room with me, and it wasn't the *good time* one. Although, the box was okay. It probably wouldn't disappoint me the way a man would.

When the door swished open, I exited without a second thought about the man, then walked to my room, my mind focused back on the incredible item in my hand. The clasp on the box was useless. Or tricky. Or I was too dumb to know how to use it. But if I could figure it out without breaking the box, I would, because it had been too damn expensive to break.

Setting the box on the bed, I stared at it. Then I knelt on the floor and looked at it at eye-level, feeling oddly awed by the item I'd purchased in a way I never had been before. Material things didn't usually matter much to me, but this box felt exceptional, almost magical. Maybe that older woman's story had planted silly ideas in my head, but I was trembling with excitement as I reached out to the box.

Nothing except a big letdown happened when I reached out to touch the clasp.

I'd half expected it would open and a light would shine down on me while the angels sang an aria. The lack of light and angels signing wasn't nearly as important to me as the fact it did nothing. No light. No aria.

Nada. And a whole lot of it.

Over the next hour, I tried everything to open the box, everything from prying it to getting nearly getting desperate enough to bang it against the table, to staring at it, hoping some sort of magic in the world existed and this thing would just break open at my will. It did not, but now I *needed* to know what was inside it. And by needed, I meant *really freaking needed*. There wouldn't be sleeping or bathing or eating until I discovered what treasure was so securely hidden inside.

I sighed because I'd spent a month's mortgage on a box I couldn't open or even see inside. As much as I didn't want to admit it, I was disappointed in myself for not resisting the urge to impulse purchase this box.

But I wasn't giving up yet. I just needed a break. A break that didn't involve going downstairs and dealing with people I didn't like.

Not knowing what else to do, I walked to the bathroom to wash my face, splashing water on it, trying to feel more like myself or something. I wasn't really sure. Looking in the mirror didn't do much for my morale. New lines and wrinkles, as opposed to the old ones, had now appeared on my face. Probably from the stress of, well, everything. I pulled my skin back, and for the second I held it there, I looked like the old me, the young me.

Once upon a time, I'd been nice to look at, nice enough to get a guy like Jean-Luc—and young. I'd been blissfully and ignorantly young. Years and stress had taken their toll. I wasn't that woman anymore. "I wish I was still her," I muttered. I wished I was still beautiful, but sometime after my divorce, I'd given up on wishes. Turning away from the mirror, I let go of my skin, shut off the light, then fell into my bed dreaming of pirates and their booties.

The treasure kind, not the rear-end kind.

Chapter Three

A Jewel and a Tale

THE NEXT MORNING, the sky was a little bluer, and the smell of the ocean air blew through my window along with a breeze that comforted my warm skin. The dreams of the Pirate Renegade were vivid, and I wished for a second that I knew that kind of passion in my waking hours.

My bed was a tangle of sheets and a fluffy white down blanket. One of my seven pillows was crumpled under my head and my hair was a mass of knots, but I smiled because even my dreams of late had been kind of dull. This one had been fully erotic. Hot romance novel erotic. *Spank me with your sail rope, Captain* erotic.

Usually, I woke up before the dream ended, but not this time. The dream had come to a, um, natural conclusion, one in the toe-curling category. It'd been a long time since *anything* on me curled.

There'd been a time when Jean-Luc and I broke beds, countertops, and tables. Once, the neighbors had called 911 and the cops had come rushing over to break up one of the best nights of sex I'd ever had. That was back when I was blissfully and ignorantly young. When I was beautiful enough, and he couldn't keep his hands off of me.

Jean-Luc had lit my fire back when I was naïve enough to appreciate the kindling, but in the two years we'd been apart, the passion well had run dry. Wishing for passion was a big, fat waste of time, but that didn't stop me from dreaming, apparently. If I was, prone to wishing, which I wasn't, I would have wished Jean-Luc not to be so handsome. Maybe for him to get a case of facial warts. A mole on his nose. At least a receding hairline. But he was perfect and aging like time was his best friend.

Any of those things might have made it easier for me to get through this last two years and the next few. Maybe I should've wished that he'd never cheated on me in the first place. Or that he still loved me. But I didn't. It would have been pointless. If I was going to do any wishing, I'd go with some that had a snowball's chance in Hell of coming true, like Brad Pitt falling for me or becoming the Queen of England.

Pushing those thoughts aside, I sat up in the big king-sized bed and looked over at the wicker table next to my bed.

Holy freaking crap. The box was open. Inside, there was a jewel, a yellow stone, on a chain that sparkled like it was infused with sunshine. I didn't know stones well, but if I was guessing, I'd say citrine.

Scooting to the edge of the bed, my hands shook as I reached out. When I touched it, the most exquisite burst of feeling rumbled through me. A feeling of being *alive*. My body trembled, and my muscles turned to mush. My heart throbbed with what I could only think was joy. Unbridled, unfocused joy, so powerful it took my breath.

I'd never been so alive. The incredible feeling only lasted about ten seconds, maybe as much as twenty, and then the world went black.

I couldn't be sure how much time passed before I woke up again, or maybe it was the first time I was waking for the day, and the last bit I remembered was a dream. The sky was still blue, the sun was still shining and the curtains were still blowing in the breeze. Either way, I was on the floor beside the bed in front of the table where the box sat still open, the stone shining, sparkling.

Rubbing my eyes, I tried to make sense of why I was on the floor. I looked at the table again, but now the box was closed. I scooted over toward it. This time, I flicked the clasp open as if it had been this easy all along. Shaky but careful, slowly pulled the jewel and its chain out.

I still wasn't sure whether I was awake the first time or it was a dream, maybe even a premonition. I was pretty sure I'd been awake because the powerful feeling surged again. This time it didn't knock me out. Instead, I stared at the stone and watched the jewel as if it might speak to me. Not in the metaphysical sense, but in the audible sense.

When it didn't, I held the damned thing up by its chain, letting it swing in the breeze. Nothing.

Electricity still buzzed through me, except it was manageable now. When I put the heavy stone over my head and let the chain dangle around my neck, the sweetest warmth flowed through me. It must've been quite some pirate who rescued this jewel from its owner. Kind of made me wish I had one. A pirate. I already had the jewel.

Either way, I was glad I'd gotten it. Whatever this feeling was, it was nice, even if it was all in my head.

I felt pretty as I walked out of the room an hour later, like I was shining brighter. Shining at *all*, actually, instead of just feeling like the blob that time forgot. Which was absolutely perfect timing, because the real work could start now. My daughter was due to arrive any time now, and I couldn't wait to see her.

Taking the elevator down, I practically bounced on my heels, thinking of Loralai. Even though nothing was ready, I was confident I could make her wedding day special. Maybe exactly the way she pictured, but incredible all the same.

When the doors opened, I hurried to the lobby to wait for her. Finding a spot to sit and observe, I sighed and let my sundress spread out on the chair. It was a soft blue color, with little yellow flowers on it. When I'd packed it, I wasn't sure how comfortable I would feel wearing it. But this morning, it felt like just the right choice.

Glancing around the lobby, I realized it was even more beautiful than I'd realized before. At some point they'd put out some violets in terra-cotta pots and lilies in glass vases, so now the place looked like a rainforest. I loved it. I loved every part of this day.

There must have been some kind of magic in the necklace. At least some calming mojo, because the issues with the wedding didn't seem so big anymore. I could bake a cake if need be, and if not, I could make cupcakes. I'd once been a PTA queen, a baker extraordinaire. It was why Jolene had hated me even more once our kids were in school than she had when we'd gone to school together. Well, that and she was still jealous that her now-husband Randy and I had dated before I'd started seeing Jean-Luc.

Still, while Jolene had tortured me when we were in high school together, the way she tortured me changed once our kids were in school. When we were younger, she'd ruined my stuff, started rumors about me, and made my daily life hell. As parents, she'd purposely left me out, made frequent snide comments, and had a way of making me feel like I was an inch tall. As an adult, at least I could escape her.

I walked to the front desk. "Good morning." I greeted my not-so-favorite clerk with a smile, combating his snarkiness with a chipper good humor.

"Good morning, Ms. Danes-LaCroix." He emphasized it and added a grimace. It made me think that he thought my hyphenated last name was pretentious. It certainly was, and it was a bonus because every Barbie Jean-Luc had dated in our time apart hated that I still used Jean-Luc's last name, but I didn't need this little twerp's attitude. I ignored it, although my smile was less genuine now.

"I was wondering if any of the bakers I called," last night I'd left messages on the voicemails of ten, and I only needed *one* to say yes, "might have left a message for me at the desk?" I couldn't say whether or not my room phone had rung. I'd been knocked out for part of the morning. And my cell got zero service out here.

He turned to the computer, checked his screen, then looked at me again. "No ma'am. As I've said, if there are messages left for you at the desk rather than on *your cell phone*," For someone who was paid to answer phones and take messages, his tone indicated that he had a certain bitterness about it, "I will certainly make sure you get it." Under his breath, he added, "even if I have to hire a skywriter."

Of course, that wasn't true, but I didn't dare call him on it or I would never get any messages from him. Actually, I didn't dare do more than wish one of those darned bakers would just call. Before I even finished the thought, the phone rang and as I was about to walk away, he held the receiver out to me.

"It's Renault. One of the bakers." He handed me the receiver. His eyes narrowed, and he looked at me like I'd just turned the phone to cheese. "How did you do that?"

I took the receiver. "Yes, hello?"

"Ms. Danes-LaCroix? You wanted to speak to me?" He had an accent almost as thick as Jean-Luc's, but I'd spent years deciphering half-mangled English, so I was practically an expert. Plus, I could speak French, although it sounded way less French than when Jean-Luc spoke it.

"My daughter's cake baker for her wedding in three days cut off his fingers."

"Ah, *oui*, purr, purr Pierre."

Ok, so the story had spread. And *poor, poor,* Pierre's finger was being mourned island-wide. "Yes. I need a cake for Sunday evening." I crossed my fingers. *Please, let Renault be available.*

"Of course, of course. I can be on a plane in an hour."

I wanted to jump up and down in excitement. One item on my list was fixed. Bonus points that now I wouldn't have to bake.

I went back to the desk and reserved a room for Renault on Jean-Luc's tab. Not a *suite*, because the witch and the other guests already had them all booked, but a regular room. If I could handle one, so could he. Even though the fancy chef probably wouldn't like it, but I'd make sure Jean-Luc left him a generous tip.

Now, if I could just get a florist in line, life would be all well and good. Except for the dress. I glanced at the phone again, wishing it would ring, then jumped back when it did. Even Arthur shot me a side-eye as he answered the phone with his normal greeting, then narrowed his eyes and handed me the phone wordlessly.

"Miss Danes-LaCroix? This is Patty from Patty's Pretty Petals. We're located just across the sea from the island." And she said all that without taking a breath. "I'm returning your call."

I cleared my throat. I didn't have the same word-per-minute speech count, but I was willing to give it a try. "My daughter's wedding flowers died en route from the mainland. They were Cattleya orchids."

"Yes. I have Cattleya Orchids."

My jaw dropped. This had to be the luckiest five minutes of my life. "Would you be able to get them to the island for Sunday morning? We need one intricate bouquet, three—erm four"—Bella could have one too since Jean-Luc was paying and I was feeling great—"corsages, and three boutonnieres." I held my breath, wishing I could knock on wood.

"Yes, of course."

Do not do a happy dance. Do not do a happy dance.

"Could you make them with white lilies, a lot of green, and no baby's breath?" Loralei hated baby's breath.

"Yes, yes. That was on your message earlier. No problem."

I'd been efficient, but specific. I hadn't wanted to waste her time. "I will fly them over in a refrigerated casing. My husband has a helicopter. Sunday by noon."

A helicopter? The perfect flowers? Refrigerated casing? It wouldn't be cheap, but Jean-Luc had said many times that he didn't care, all he wanted was for our daughter to be happy. This would certainly fit the bill. She'd never even know that just yesterday her wedding was falling apart.

"Oh, yes." Wishes came true, these flowers were proof of it. "Thank you so, so much." And because I was in a mood, I added, "I don't suppose your husband has a 1980s cover band?"

"How did you know?" Her voice was dry. She was probably teasing. There was no way in the world he really did. "Hank! Hank! Pick up the phone. Someone wants to talk to you about the band!"

Barely able to believe my luck, ten minutes later, I had a deal on flowers and a band who would play everything from Billie Jean to Xanadu. I couldn't wait to see what a garage band that specialized in Elton John and Bon Jovi would bring to the table. How? How had this happened?

Everything was falling into place. But as Jean-Luc and Marianne or Ginger or... Alice—I really needed to learn her name —sashayed out of the elevator, I rolled my eyes. She'd traded the teeny tiny bikini for a teenier tinier one. All of her surgical enhancements were on full display. She adjusted when one spilled over the bit of string holding them in place, then looked at me and smiled like the boob *accidentally* fell, but we all knew it wasn't an accident. She just wanted me to know how perfectly formed and perky her boobs were.

I was probably paranoid though. Why would anyone be that insecure and... creepy?

At that moment Loralei blew into the hotel like a hurricane draped in island silks and a wide-brim hat, with a camera crew following her and her new fiancé on her arm. Her face lit up as she walked and the wind seemed to blow her hair like she was in a real movie.

She wasn't. The camera crew was simply a very expensive and exclusive videography company Jean-Luc had hired to capture the week for Loralei's future memories.

I wasn't complaining.

Chapter Four

Here Comes the Bride

My beautiful daughter was glowing, and like everyone else in the room, I couldn't take my eyes off of her. Loralai had inherited the best parts of me and Jean-Luc. His eyes. His full lips and high cheekbones. His long eyelashes. His height and athletic build. My hair.

I didn't understand how the cameraman she'd brought along could look at anyone but Loralei, and yet his camera was aimed at the bikini bimbo on my ex-husband's arm. I grunted at Jean-Luc, staring pointedly at the situation. He leaned down to suggest something in Bunny's ear that either infuriated her or she was trying out her acting chops and the first emotion to be seen was anger. Her face rippled into lines of sheer rage as she wheeled away. He shot me a shrug.

Loralei wore a fur stole over a sundress and, like an old version of Zsa Zsa, shrugged it off and onto the floor. Noah, the groom, bent to pick it up and shook his head. My girl had a big chunk of her father's flair for the dramatic.

Our daughter breezed toward me, air kissed my cheeks like she'd just traded her US citizenship to become a proper Parisian. I laughed at my own thoughts, which came out too loud, and everyone stopped and looked at me. I held up an *I'm sorry* hand, and they all turned back to their prior interests. Noah looked at Loralei. Jean-Luc watched his bimbo stomp away, and I looked at the camera, smiled, and waved like the queen of the dorks that I'd become.

Once upon a time, back in the day, I'd been one of the cool kids. My husband was a pro athlete, and I was the wife everyone wanted to be around. I'd planned the best parties. I'd served the best booze. I had the best-looking husband. There was no better fairytale than that of me and Jean-Luc LaCroix. His name even sounded like something out of a story.

But then the rumors started to circulate, and I couldn't stay with a man who cheated on me. It didn't matter that I'd thought our life was a fairytale. Knowing the truth meant realizing that our fairytale had never been real. Now, I was just the former wife of a former hockey legend, and the phone had stopped ringing right about the time the ink on the divorce papers dried a year ago.

"You look beautiful, honey," I told her.

She smiled. "So you do. That color really suits you. The fresh air has been good for you."

My cheeks heated. My daughter loved many things about me, but it was rare for her to compliment my looks.

She looked after her dad's retreating bimbo and wrinkled her nose. "He brought her? Ugh." We'd known he wanted to, just hadn't been sure he actually would. Loralei wasn't a fan of any of the women her father dated. For a while, I'd tried to chalk it up to her wanting his attention for herself, but then I realized she saw the exact same thing I did. Jean-Luc's taste in women ran to trashy. Neither of us wanted her wedding pictures tarnished by fishnet stockings and a corset top. But I'd hired the photographer, so I could make the requests. "I could ask him to make her leave."

That would make me the bad guy and cause a Jean-Luc-Cami rift. No one wanted that. We did much better as parents when we got along.

She waved my words away. "She's fine. You'll handle her, and Dad would've ended up with a woman at the wedding either way. I'm just glad it's not with one of my guests." This meant I was going to keep my big mouth shut about baby-sized bikinis on Dolly Parton-sized breasts and deal with it.

"Absolutely! Your wedding is going to be amazing, with or without her." I pasted on my fakest smile and hoped she bought it. "The baker is going to be here today to start the cake and the flowers are going to be here Sunday morning. *And* I found a band." That was the two-cent update. I only hoped it was enough to distract her from the dress.

"Can I see my dress? Is it here?" Her eyes sparkled in excitement.

Well, so much for that hope.

It was a one-of-a-kind *Dionne*, all right. Or it was supposed to have been. It was more like a six-sizes too big tent that would swallow my daughter as well as half the island. I didn't want to tell her that I hadn't been able to get Dionne on the phone. I wasn't going to be the one who crushed my daughter before I exhausted every available option to fix this mess.

I had to admit that without Dionne, there was no possible way to keep this unsavory truth hush-hush. I had to tell her. I had no choice.

As I was about to break the bad news, I took her hand in mine and smoothed the veins on the back side with my free hand, there was a great commotion in front of the hotel, and out of a stretch limousine—looking like she'd just come from Coachella—stepped *the* woman herself.

It took a second for her coat—we were on a tropical island and this was the second bit of fur I'd seen so far—to unfurl behind her as she moved into the openness of the hotel lobby, but she was here, *Dionne*, designer to the stars. Along with her fur, Dionne wore Chanel sunglasses and Louboutin shoes, yet she didn't look at all out of place. Rather, she looked like she owned the place.

I held back an eye-roll because I couldn't afford to insult the woman when she'd come to save the day.

"As soon as I heard about the mixup, I flew in straight away to make the dress of..."—she looked at me—"your darling daughter's dreams."

Of course, she had. Dress designers always flew straight to the scene of the crime to right the wrongs of their shipping departments. But I wasn't about to look a gift horse in the mouth. She was here, whatever the reason. I didn't care, as long as my daughter got the dress of her dreams.

Dionne turned and spoke to Arthur in her I'm-the-master-of-my-own-destiny voice as she said, "Take me to the garment!" Then, she stuck her finger in the air and swished it in a small circle. An interesting choice, for sure.

The weasel of a man snapped to attention, far more polite to Dionne than he'd ever been to me. He led us to the room we had reserved for Loralei's wedding stuff.

Noah, seeming to realize he shouldn't see the dress, reversed course. "I'll go oversee our luggage."

Jean-Luc, however, gave our daughter a hug as we walked, a grin on his face, probably because he'd forgotten all about the disaster of a dress.

My daughter cast me a confused glance. "Why does she need to be here?"

I tried not to give away just how bad her current dress was. "The dress had a few issues that I'm sure she can fix."

"Mom…?" She didn't look at all happy.

"It's all under control," I told her, then waited for the bomb to drop.

We followed Arthur to the room. He held it open for us, and our party swept in like we owned the place, even though my heart was racing. It took a few full seconds for Loralei to realize exactly what she was looking at, then her eyes went wide and her face contorted. Not only had she seen it, she knew the disaster that she was looking at.

"My dress! It's all wrong."

"But Dionne is here now to fix it," I said in my most chipper voice. "That's a comfort, right?" I hoped so, anyway.

Loralei looked at Dionne, who winked in assurance. "The dress is going to be exactly what this beautiful bride wants. If the great Dionne says it…" She might've been a bit full of herself, but there was no denying her talent. I did, however, question the competence of her shipping department. "…you have no choice but to believe it." That she believed it was enough, and even Loralei applauded as if she'd just heard George Washington himself speak.

I glanced at Jean-Luc and mouthed at him. "Did you call her?"

He shook his head, then pointed at me with his eyebrows raised.

I shook my head back at him. I also hadn't called. I mean, I had, but I never got further than her very full and somewhat abrupt voicemail box. It hadn't even let me leave a message. Perhaps her shipping team had informed her of the error. I didn't know, but I was grateful she'd come.

"Is there anything I can do to help?" I felt awkward, but I was asking both the designer and Loralei.

My daughter shook her head. "No, you can go ahead and go. I'm going to do whatever I need to get the dress adjusted, and then I think Noah and I will spend some time together, exploring the island." I smiled at her. To be young and in love was beautiful, and I liked Noah. I liked the way he looked at her and cared for her, the way he loved her in spite of the fact she was a little bit spoiled and a lot over-loved.

I liked him a *hell* of a lot more than his mother.

Loralei gave me a quick hug and smiled. "Tomorrow, I promise, I'm all yours!" I savored every second of the hug. She was going to be married. That could only mean less time spent with dear old Mom.

Dionne clapped her hands. “The dress is going to be spectacular!”

All I could think was from Dionne’s lips to the fairy godmother’s ear.

Chapter Five

My Very Own Pirate

I WAS on an island that was once one of the most romantic places I'd ever been, and I had no one to socialize with. At least no one I *wanted* to socialize with. This made me a woman who needed a stiff drink. If I had to drink alone because I didn't have a social circle of my own, well, there was nothing I could do about that.

I'd thought that I was over all of the Jolene stuff. I hadn't even seen the woman since graduation, but it took until this minute for me to realize that she and I were going to be connected for the rest of our lives. It hit hard, so hard, in fact, that I *really* wanted to drink, and I didn't care what drinking alone said about me.

I walked out of the resort and headed down the beach to the bar set up near the pier. There was something to be said for the sound of the waves rolling in, lapping against the sand, and the salty taste of the air. It was calm and peaceful, but also thunderous and chaotic with the people on vacation everywhere along the beach.

Right now, I just wanted to take it all in.

There was also something to be said for frozen drinks in tall glasses with freshly toasted coconut on top, a sugared glass rim, and a slice of pineapple hanging off the edge. The menu made it look gourmet, and I ordered one, then sat on a stool at the end of the bar.

At the end nearest to me, and stuck in the sand, a tiki torch burned and several more in a line led down to the water's edge. The torches didn't provide light or mosquito protection. They were purely aesthetic but I liked that someone cared that much about the vibe.

Mmm, the drinks were even more divine than I remembered. They tasted nothing like liquor and everything like a dream I once had. Maybe a dream about sexy pirates who could blow my mind? Yeah, dreams like those. Dreams that could only ever be a fantasy, but that I was happy pretending could happen, either way.

Drinking slowly, I half floated through the dream I'd had last night and half continued to take in the landscape, while flagging down the bartender for another drink, here and there.

He was more than accommodating, probably because his bar was nearly empty due to it not even being late afternoon yet. Either way, I felt content. Five o'clock somewhere, and all that. I even felt a little hopeful for a better future as I watched the couples walking hand-in-hand on the beach.

After a few minutes considering the bar's thatched roof and bamboo ledge, and a couple of sips of my newest drink, a voice, deep and warm and divinely Scottish said, "Excuse me. Is this seat taken?" The most delicious accent slipped into each word.

Was someone asking me if this seat was taken? It was barely past noon on a Monday, and there were no seats down the long row taken except mine. Of course, this seat wasn't taken, just like all the others. So why sit next to me?

I was on my third tall, frozen drink, so that was likely what made my brain a little slower. I turned, ready to say yes, when my breath caught. The man was beyond gorgeous. Tall, dark, and chiseled, he was dressed in pants that had a flap in the front rather than a fly. Said flap was secured with two gold buttons on each side, and his shirt laced up over his chest. He wore a bandana around his forehead. Damn if he didn't look as if he'd just escaped a Disney movie.

I held up my glass in salute. "Yo, ho, ho."

He chuckled. "And a bottle of rum, if we're lucky."

Oh, yeah. He took my words to an even weirder place and left them in a holding pattern there. I liked this guy, even though I didn't know him. I was like that with people sometimes, we either clicked or we didn't, and this guy and I were clickety clacking.

"Sit on down, and I won't make you walk the plank!" I patted the stool next to me.

He laughed and sat, barely giving me time to move my hand.

I stared at him for a second. A man so beautiful and so oddly dressed was hardly seen in a life like mine. So hardly seen, in fact, I looked at the bartender to make sure he also saw a pirate. I had to make sure he wasn't an illusion. The bartender looked at him, too, so I wasn't crazy. I reached over and touched his arm. He smiled and laid his warm hand over mine until I withdrew.

Well, wasn't that something? It seemed that my wish for a pirate had come true. How often did something like that happen to a gal like me? The answer was never. It never happened. Probably was a dream right now. Or an alcoholic hallucination.

Not that I was disappointed.

"Nice night for a pillage." Oh, sweet daylight. *I* was the dork that was making it weird. Too late to take it back now, so I smiled and went with it as though being a dork was the most natural thing.

His laugh was as intoxicating as the coconut rum. "I've already done all the pillaging and plundering I'm required to for the day." He grinned, set his hat on the bar in front of us, and held out his hand for me to shake. "I'm an actor at the resort theater. We're doing a production of 'Pirates of Pararey.' I'm Captain Renegade."

Of.

Course.

He.

Was.

"Maybe I could take in a show while I'm here." I meant it to sound sultry, but it came off a lot more like creepy. My temptress days were a long time ago. I cleared my throat. "I mean, the show sounds great." He hadn't even told me what it was about. How could I know if it sounded great? I sighed. "An actor, huh?" I grimaced and shrugged, then shook my head.

He grinned, seeming not to mind one bit that I was acting like a weirdo. Luckily for me. "Yeah. The play tells the story of Captain Renfro Renegade Remington, a great, great, great uncle of mine, actually. He's famous because he lost a bunch of treasure to a storm at sea, and his crew mutinied." Like I didn't know what treasure was, he clarified, "Jewels and coins. Near the island, apparently. When he refused to take to the seas to plunder more riches, his crew..." He made the same slicing motion with his thumb across his neck that the old woman in the market had made. He gave me a look, maybe checking to see if I was listening or if I believed him.

“I heard his story when I was down at the market.” I pulled the jewel out and showed it to him. “This came from a woman who claimed it was part of Renegade’s treasure.”

He cocked his head, staring at it. “Captain Renegade was killed. His men thought he was holding out on them so he didn’t have to share his treasures.” His voice, his accent, enchanted me.

There was something about his smile that sent my pulse into overdrive. I waved to the bartender and ordered us both a drink. Then I looked at him because I very much liked looking at him. “Why are you wearing your costume right now? Are you late for a matinee or is this part of the show?”

He smiled and it was like the sun came out. Actually, it did, from behind a cloud, but the light I was talking about came from within the pirate, like some magical source of illumination. I was sure of it.

Or possibly I was already drunk. I wasn’t a frequent drinker, so three tall frozen island drinks had probably gone a long way.

“I just finished a dress rehearsal. I wanted to come to get a drink, and now I get to have one with a beautiful woman.” The way he said it made me *feel* beautiful..

"It's flattering," I smiled. "I mean, I'm flattered." Which was his intention, no doubt. Meh. I didn't mind that I didn't truly believe him. It was enough that he was saying it. "Sadly, it's been a long time since anyone's bothered to really look at me, and even longer since anyone's flirted. Jean-Luc says it's my personality. He says it *gets lost*. Then there's the invisible stop sign that is my clothes, at least according to him." Booze made me chatty, and I might've said too much, rambled when rambling words weren't necessary. My skin was on fire, but I certainly liked looking at Mr. Pirate. I stood and waved the bartender over. "A bottle of your finest rum for me and the pirate king."

The bartender nodded, but the pirate chuckled. "That's a different play." I could've fallen into that smile, swooned even.

"What's your name, Pirate King?" Had the world ended right then, I would have died happily staring at him. Probably rudely staring, but I didn't have it in me to care.

"Not wholly a coincidence, but it's Remy." I couldn't make words to answer, to tell him who I was. He waited for a second, then asked, "And you, my bonnie lass, are...?"

I giggled, and immediately hated myself for it. "Not wholly a coincidence, but my name is Bonita." I said it like Bow-nee-tahhhh.

He brought my fingers to his mouth and kissed my knuckles. "It is very nice to meet you, Bonita." He mimicked how I'd said it, but in his accent it sounded exotic and sultry. Boy, I liked it, even if it wasn't my name.

"Nice to meet you, too." And I meant it.

"And what brings you to Pararey Island?" He smiled again and my stomach did a cute little somersault that would've made a gymnast jealous. I hadn't felt these kinds of tingles in about two years. It was unsettling, but not unpleasant.

"My daughter is getting married here on Sunday." It wasn't nearly as lame as I made it sound. It was joyous for her. I didn't want to think about faulty dresses and bakers with missing fingers, or dead flowers, or the fact that my ex-husband and his teeny bikini girlfriend were probably upstairs doing the deed.

Right now, I wanted to concentrate on Remy. I was going to do whatever I had to do to make sure he was concentrating on me.

"I've always heard that wedding planning is stressful."

That was an understatement, but there were a thousand things more interesting than my whining that wouldn't make my head ache.

"But you don't seem stressed. You look peaceful, serene. Did I mention beautiful?"

I giggled again because it had been a while since anyone other than Lor cared about more than raising my stress level. Even longer since anyone had called me beautiful.

Twice.

Honestly, I wasn't drowning in self-pity, but I might've been horny. It had been a while, so I couldn't be sure that this buzzing inside me wasn't the alcohol, but it made me want to put my hand in his lap and fondle his gold buttons.

"Tell me, how does one become part of the Captain Renegade theater show?" Really, I just wanted to hear his voice.

He turned his body toward me, his elbow on the bar, and rested his face on his hand. "I live on the island."

"Really?" I mirrored his pose and put my chin on my palm, facing him.

"In a yurt."

"A yurt? That's a fun word." Much more fun as a visual. I pictured a teepee kind of thing.

He nodded. "It's a tiny house." He shook his head. "Words can't do it justice." He took out his phone and showed me a picture. It was shaped like a canoe that had been cut in half and stood on its end. It had a small glass door he probably would've had to crawl through because no way was he walking through it upright, and wooden walls. "It's got a kitchen, a bath, and a bed." He spoke the last word as if an invitation with raised eyebrows to make it a question.

"Is it far?" I wasn't saying yes.

Yet.

He smiled and looked down into his rum. "It's a walk."

The walk wasn't what caused my hesitation. I wasn't the kind of woman who picked up men in tiki bars. I also wasn't the kind of woman who walked with them back to their yurts.

"Ask me again later." I also wasn't the kind of woman who wanted to say no to this guy.

"You can count on it."

On Captain Renfro Renegade Remington's honor, I hoped so.

Chapter Six

What Have I Done and When Can I Do It Again?

WITHOUT AN IMMEDIATE MEMORY of how I got there, why I was naked, or how I got that way, I woke, head throbbing, sun streaming in the window of my room. I remembered drinking... so much drinking. I seemed to recall doing a wild rendition of *Modern Major General* I'd learned during a high school production of *Pirates of Penzance*, but I couldn't be sure if that was a memory or nightmare.

I did have a quick flash of sudden remembrance—sitting at the bar with my hand on his arm, his other arm around me, a kiss. Oh, no. I'd kissed a man I only just met. That wasn't me. It couldn't have been more out of character for a woman who hadn't kissed a man in years. Literal years.

Trying to recall everything, I went through the night. We'd walked to my room because his was too far. Ohhh, no.

I had flashes of vivid memories—a tongue in my mouth that wasn't my own, fumbling with those gold buttons, giggling some more.

When I reached behind me, without looking, I prayed to feel a nicely unwrinkled, cold sheet. Not as much because I was embarrassed about having slept with a stranger, but because I had no lucid memory of said stranger. It was like I dreamt it.

Remy.

Okay, a couple of slight memories existed. Hot, steamy memories.

I laid my hand on some decidedly warm skin, a hard chest. A smattering of chest hair. And lower, a ripple of muscle. Lower yet... *Oh, dear.*

Okay, maybe the memories were coming back as more than flashes. Other folks spoke about having photographic memories. Mine were pornographic. My skin flushed with heat again.

Oh, double dear.

Remy took my hand and kissed first my knuckles, then my palm, moving to the inside of my wrist before I found the gumption to pull away. To be horrified at my own... wantonness.

I sat up in the bed, too fast, making the room spin. The result was a wobble, and when I tried to catch myself, I grabbed a piece of his upper thigh as well as something else. He sat up beside me and laid his hand on my back. My *naked* back and the skin-to-skin contact was enough to make me want more of his skin touching mine and in better places. I hadn't realized until that moment how badly I'd missed a man's touch.

Maybe I'd realized it earlier, but this time I was in my fully rational mind. It only half mattered to me that this man was a stranger.

I shouldn't have been excited by that. It was wrong. Yet it didn't feel wrong, quite the opposite actually, which should've been a warning flag.

It wasn't.

When I looked at him, I was only semi-prepared to ask him to leave because we didn't know each other. I should've told him that this was a mistake. For Pete's sake, I didn't even know his last name. What would my book club say?

Pfft. Probably they would've cheered me on, but no way could I ever tell them about Remy—even his name was dreamy—so it was a moot point.

If he'd said his last name, I'd forgotten. Or maybe it was his last name? The self-recriminations were only barely being held at bay, so I couldn't think about the fact that I didn't even know his name for sure, or I would probably shame myself further by hyperventilating and passing out.

Also, I couldn't be a hundred percent sure, but I thought I'd told him my name was Bonnie. It'd been funny at the time because he'd said something like I was a bonnie lass.

His Scottish accent had made the bonnie lass comment decadent. I'd always loved Jean-Luc's French accent, but a Scottish lilt made my body warm, and I looked away to keep myself from jumping on him and starting up round two. Or three. Hell, for all I knew, it could've been round ten.

The clock ticked beside me, loudly, like a drumbeat inside my head. I looked back and cursed, like, as it turned out, a sailor.

"Oh, no. What did I do?" When I looked back at him now, he wasn't smarmy or smug, and I wasn't sure why I'd thought he would be. He had a pleasant smile, which made me want to drink all of him in. His dark hair was a little messy, he had a bit of a five o'clock shadow, and a jawline that most men would kill for. In all ways, he looked like a handsome man who had been deeply satisfied.

Why had I thought he'd be behaving otherwise?

All the romance novels in the world, and I'd read my fair share, hadn't given me an accurate picture of the morning after. In the books, there was always a hot, soapy, sexy shower scene. A lot of kissing, getting dressed only to get undressed again, then getting dressed one more time in front of each other, as if saggy breasts and an ass making a rapid descent toward my knees weren't part of the scene.

Nowhere in said novel was it mentioned that there would be an inordinate amount of wrestling over the sheet, more than a few surreptitious glances around the room for undergarments, and in all my years, I'd never read about a single one-night-stand where anyone worried as much about gravity as I was at the moment.

But we were both sitting up now with our backs against the headboard, and I had tugged the blanket up over my boobs. So, that was something.

"Have you ever heard of beer goggles?" Remy asked suddenly.

I didn't care what kind of accent he asked in. Hopped up on hormones and Caribbean rum, I'd thought he was perfect. Now he was a couple of syllables away from losing all that luster. A smarter woman would have stopped him. A smarter woman would've put an end to this line of questioning before it ripped out the last shreds of self-worth she had. She would've strutted to the bathroom and refused to come out until he was gone.

I wasn't her. I was prone to taking my medicine no matter how bad the taste, and he was my Robitussin. I was powerless to end this before it picked up steam.

"I believe I've heard of them." My voice was soft, but bitter anticipation dried my tone.

"Well, I was worried you were looking at me through beer goggles last night and that as soon as you laid eyes on me this morning, you'd send me on my way." The tips of his ears turned a very endearing shade of pink.

Welp. Okay. That took a turn I hadn't expected, and I might've fallen in love with him right then. "*You* were worried?" I looked at him and smiled. "Have you ever seen *you*?"

He laughed. "Yes, but I've also seen you and you're far out of my league." His skin flushed again. "Thank you for the hours of passion."

I melted as several passionate memories surfaced. I was supposed to be at a luncheon right now with my daughter, her fiancé, and his mother. But instead of rushing out the door, I stayed in bed and kissed the man I'd spent the night with. At this point, why not?

We got in a few more passionate embraces before I finally rolled away, taking the sheet with me and leaving him gloriously and beautifully exposed. I looked back when I got to the bathroom door. My heart palpitated and my stomach fluttered. This guy was perfect. And I wanted to linger.

I hurried through getting ready, taking a quick sponge bath with my favorite perfumed soap, and dressed in the sundress I bought specifically for this luncheon. It hugged my boobs and pushed them up where they belonged but had a flowy skirt and empire waist. The pretty dress was a great deal better than the one I'd worn the day before, and definitely showed and hid the right parts of me. I felt pretty.

After a quick touch-up of my makeup, which looked far better than I would've expected, I walked out of the bathroom. Remy was dressed and sitting on the bed. For goodness' sake, this man was as inviting in clothes as without them, but I only had a couple of seconds to spare for appreciation before I had to race out and run down the hallway from my room to the elevator. I used those couple of seconds to mentally undress him, but it wasn't quite the same. I sighed out loud. "I have to go."

"I know."

This kind of awkwardness was never in books. "Thank you for last night."

He grinned down at me. "No. Thank *you* for last night." He slid his hand into my hair again and nudged me to him. His fingers massaged my scalp. "I had a wonderful time." Then he lowered his head and kissed me softly, stirring an ache in my belly.

When he pulled back, he tucked my hair behind my ears and smiled. "Should I go first?"

He was right. The last thing I needed was someone to see us leaving together. "I could take the stairs."

“Or I could.” He was right again. He could. At the door, before he opened it to let me walk out, he kissed me one more time and said, “Thank you, Bonita.”

I giggled, a habit I promised myself I’d quit. I kicked cigarettes years ago. I could kick the giggles. But for now, I looked up at him. “Thank you, Captain.”

I walked out of the room and down the hallway to the elevators. When I looked back, the door to the stairs was swinging shut. I stepped inside the elevator, not bothering to look around. But then I looked up and into the mirror.

Oh Lord, Jean-Luc. With the *child*. Because the goodness of my morning couldn’t last. That would have been way too much to ask.

Chapter Seven

The Reason I Hate Elevators

I HAD to endure this because he was my ex-husband and my sometimes friend, and we were here for our daughter, a daughter who'd survived our divorce and come out a shining star. Besides, it wasn't like I hated him. For the most part, I loved him, even after things had gone south. I didn't like his choices, didn't like his lax standards for marital fidelity, and didn't care for his new car or his new women. But he'd given me my daughter, and for that, I would be forever grateful.

So, I said, "Good morning," as graciously as I could. I glanced in his direction, but for all they knew, I was saying it to both of them.

"Morning," the Barbie woman said, running her hand down his arm in a possessive way.

I had to work really hard not to roll my eyes.

"How did you sleep?" he asked, his eyes darkening as if he knew exactly how I'd slept.

I hoped I wasn't blushing. "Fine."

He was still looking me up and down like he was trying to figure something out. Once in a while, I got a case of residual shivers when we were in the same place at the same time. When I could smell his cologne and see the flecks of steel gray in his blue eyes, but now, I was shiver-free. That didn't stop him from staring. And smiling.

"What?" I finally asked as the elevator slowly made its way down. I'd just had a pretty good morning, despite the hangover headache, and I wasn't in the mood for any version of French judgment that he would come up with. He had a way about him, a demeanor that spoke to his strict upbringing, but he was a double-standard kind of guy. He was probably about to tell me to get a sweater to cover my "naked shoulder." Which would have made him a hypocrite since the woman-child was wearing yet another version of a bikini with a sheer wrap around her hips.

He flashed his Jean-Luc girl-getting smile. I'd seen it a thousand times yet it still made my stomach flutter. Usually. Not today. Interesting.

"That color"—coral—"suits you." But the voice, specifically his accent, had surprisingly little effect. Must have been from the hours of sweet nothings whispered in a beautiful Scottish accent that had dulled the attraction. Or maybe I'd just needed to get laid to get all the way over Jean-Luc. I didn't know. Heck, I didn't care. It was a relief to not care.

Next to him, Bimbo Buffy scoffed and shook her head at me. "Whatever." She rolled her eyes, and I saw it in the mirrors from three different angles.

Once, I'd been as belligerent as her, but the humiliation of a cheating husband who hadn't bothered to hide it had eaten away at that confidence. I didn't want her to suffer the same humiliation, but hopefully, she would outgrow her unkindness.

Then Jean-Luc looked at me again. His big blue eyes went wide, and he sucked in a breath. "Is that a *hickey* on the back of your neck?"

No way. It couldn't have been. I hadn't had a hickey since college, but I couldn't deny it with any degree of certainty because I didn't make it a habit to check out the bck of my neck in the mirror.

"What are you talking about?" Barbie turned to look, and now they were both staring at my neck. With all the heat rolling through me, my skin tone had to be about fifty shades of *oh frick*.

I knew Jean-Luc. I knew what he was thinking, and what that smile meant. I knew what every one of his smiles meant. Every glance and practically every thought he'd ever had. He stood in that elevator with his plastic play toy next to him, and he was remembering. He was thinking about the first hickey he'd given me. I wasn't throwing stones. I'd just climbed out of bed with someone else, and here I was remembering the same thing.

God, those had been some days for us. He'd just scored his hundredth goal. I think he was twenty, and I was eighteen and we'd celebrated. All night. Too bad the next night he'd celebrated with someone else, but that was a different kind of memory. Not one I cared to think about, especially with both of them staring at me like I'd brought the plague to the island.

Instead, I needed to get my head into this moment. To focus on what his parted lips and his cocked head and wide eyes meant. He was incredulous that some other man had given me a hickey. "Cami!" He practically whined my name. "You're here for our daughter's wedding, not to bed every cabana boy you can get your dainty little hands on."

My hands were anything but dainty, and they hadn't itched to slap him this much since we'd first separated. That probably wasn't the part of the conversation he intended me to focus on. "He wasn't a cabana boy. He was a *pirate*, if you must know." I had no intention of explaining what that meant. Let them wonder. "May I remind you that you're here with your newest girlfriend? How many have you had since we divorced? Four? Five?" I scoffed. "Not to mention, how many did you have while we were married?"

Barbie stared at him, anger rolling off her in waves I could almost see. Jean-Luc was losing his mojo. I doubted that he'd ever been in an elevator with two women who were this unhappy with him.

"Where is your sense of decorum, Cami? Babe, I'm so disappointed." He clicked his tongue and shook his head. Anger flared in my stomach. I used to love when he called me babe, but I'd outgrown that too.

I lowered my voice to a dangerous level. He was on very thin ice. "Jean-Luc, you brought your midlife crisis along as your plus one. You don't get to lecture me about *decorum*." I mimicked his accent on the word. "You don't get the high road pass on this one." It was satisfying, but for good measure, I added, "Worry about your damn self, okay, *babe*?"

A pointed look at the woman-child said everything my words didn't.

In the bedroom, my ex was proficient, exciting, and incredible. Anywhere sex wasn't appropriate, Jean-Luc had no idea how to deal with women. If we hadn't had such intense chemistry that had kept us mostly in the bedroom when he was home, I might've noticed his lack of interpersonal skills. But I'd been too busy appreciating the ripples and planes of his finely tuned body and how he'd used it to make mine sing. At first.

It was probably the same draw Baby Buffy felt for him.

He continued staring at me, she was staring at him, and I was busy trying to see this *alleged* hickey in the mirror-door without *looking* like I was trying to see it.

I was embarrassed, and it made me act out. "I wish you knew what you lost and how badly you hurt me. I wish there was justice in the world, and I wish you could see what a pig you really are." Heck, I'd turn him *into* a pig if I could.

THEN, blessedly, the elevator doors swished open, and I was out of *the* most uncomfortable situation I could have ever imagined finding myself in. Honestly, I would've never guessed this would be my morning.

Why was I allowing my ex-husband to make me feel bad about my one-nighter? I was an adult with needs. Sure it might have been a little reckless, especially at my age, but I had fun and felt beautiful. No one was harmed. Quite the opposite.

I was already late, so a quick stop to the bathroom wasn't going to hurt. Not time-wise anyway. Although, even if there was a hickey, and by Jean-Luc's reaction, I had no reason to believe there wasn't, I'd left my bag and makeup upstairs.

I walked into the bathroom, my hand over the back of my neck like I had an ache or an itch. I twisted around and looked in the mirror, and oh, hello. I had the Orion's belt of red marks on my neck. Two small red dots in line with a smaller third on one side—the side Jean-Luc hadn't been able to see—and a much larger starburst mark on the side he had.

Perfect.

Chapter Eight

I Should've Skipped Lunch

I WAS ONLY about ten minutes late by the time I finally arrived. I'd had to go back for a scarf because no way was I letting the glare of this hickey blind my daughter. I wanted her respect, and to my way of thinking, a scarf would accomplish that. There'd been a wait for the elevator, of course, and I had to pick the right scarf.

When I got back to the room and Remy wasn't there, in my bed, waiting for me—of course, I'd known he wouldn't be since he'd left when I did. I was more depressed than I wanted to admit. I didn't really have time to indulge in such silliness. My lack of time was a boon, or I probably would've raided the mini-bar. Instead, I knotted the silk so that it hid the mark at the back of my neck, tucked my new yellow stone down into my cleavage, then dashed back to the elevator. The stone wasn't really visible with the dress, but I liked wearing it.

The restaurant was below the hotel. It had no walls to the outer side, where the waves rolled peacefully onto the beach. There were umbrellas in lines along the white sands. Being a smaller island, it was well-staffed and well-visited.

Stopping just out of view of the others, I took a deep breath. Jolene was there. Darn it. She hadn't aged nearly as bad as I'd hoped. If karma existed, it had unfairly spared her. She still had long, dark hair, big dark eyes, lashes for days, and a sense of style that made me feel frumpy. The only difference was that even with plastic surgery, her butt and boobs weren't nearly as high as they once were, her stomach was rounder, and the face job and botox hadn't been able to beat back all of the wrinkles on her face.

However, having her age better than me I could handle. It was all the negative feelings that rose up when I saw her. Remembering the day I'd started my period, and she'd screamed it out for the whole classroom to notice. Or the day she'd dunked my sweater in the toilet. Or the day she tripped me, and I'd ended up covered in my lunch. And then there was the rumor she'd spread about me being a prostitute. So, yeah, I hated her.

For my daughter, I'd endure anyone. Jolene. Jean-Luc. Barbie. All of them.

I sat on the side of the table that had a view of the beach, next to my daughter. She smiled, took my hand under the table, and gave it a squeeze. Lor was so ready for this wedding, and she held Noah's hand across the table. I was happy for them. To see her smile like this, to be so in love, was all I'd ever wanted for her, even if I wasn't quite ready to let her go.

Thinking of her moving out made me tear up. I didn't care that she was twenty-one and starting her own life. She would always be my baby girl. Letting go was hard, but tears would only leave me with a matching pair of mascara tracks down my face. That wasn't going to happen. Especially not with Jolene here, looking like she traveled with Julia Roberts's hair and makeup team.

"This place is so beautiful," my daughter said as one of the camera crew fitted me with a microphone attached to the top of my dress. They were trying to be very professional about the whole thing, but it was really annoying. How were we supposed to eat with microphones on us?

"I see why you wanted your wedding here." Noah responded, but his gaze was on Lor.

Damn. My daughter was in love with a man who loved her just as much. They had no idea how lucky they were. "It really is the perfect place."

Lor looked at her soon-to-be mother-in-law and smiled. "Jo, I am so glad you guys decided to make the trip." At first, she and Randy, her husband, had been content to watch a live stream of the ceremony, but Jean-Luc didn't want Noah, who he really liked, not to have his family with him. So, he'd included their airfares, hotel stay, and return flight in the budget for the destination wedding.

"I felt terrible leaving all the planning to your poor mother."

I could sense a dig coming, and I waited for it because, from the moment I'd met this woman, it'd been one dig after another. "But she's already handled everything so beautifully."

That was it? She hadn't even been the least bit snide. Before I could thank her, Lor smiled. "That's my mama. Give her a project and stand back and watch her go."

Tears threatened to fill my eyes, but I blinked them back. "Thank you, honey."

As glad as I was that Lor was happy with the results of all the planning, I also didn't want to tell her about the mishaps. They were handled, so there really wasn't any reason for her to know.

"I really wanted to be able to help you and Noah. But the store"—she owned a boutique back home that sold high-end kitchenware and 'cooking' clothes for 'the woman who wants to look hot while taking care of the family'—"has been so busy, I haven't had time for anything else. You remember how it was before you landed Jean-Luc?" I'd been a junior in High School when I landed Jean-Luc. She grimaced. "I'm sorry. You never did work, did you? Just did the mommy thing." She huffed out a breath. "I so envy you that."

And there it was. The dig I'd been waiting for. She'd been hanging onto that one for a while. Probably saved it specifically for when the videography cameras were rolling.

Noah shook his head and muttered, "Jesus, Mom."

And because my luck was limited to meeting a strange man and getting lucky—in the very best sense of the phrase—a breeze blew through the openness of the restaurant and my scarf rubbed against the microphone. The sound guy shook his head.

One of the women came over. "Ma'am, can I ask you to take your scarf off?"

I BLANCHED and held onto the scarf like I was a passenger on the RMS Titanic and it was my life preserver. "But it's part of my..." I would've finished with *outfit,* but Lor was looking at me with her, *please don't embarrass me,* look, accompanied by her, *Dad wouldn't do this* sigh. I worked the knot loose, wishing I'd covered the red marks with makeup instead of trying to save time by using the scarf.

Reluctantly, I tugged it away. At least the big hickey was on the opposite side of Lor. I knew the exact moment Jolene got a big blue eyeful of it. I also knew the exact moment she decided to point it out to my daughter, or maybe question me about it. Her face lit up. Oh, come on. I wished, just this once, for the space of one meal, she would just shut up. Not speak.

Jolene had just been about to tell Lor about my hickey, but then she sat back and cocked her head. Mercifully, she didn't say a word, and I was careful to keep my daughter or her fiancé from seeing the evidence of my wild night.

"Mom, do you have the itinerary for Thursday?" We had activities planned for the wedding party.

I rooted through my bag for the printed sheet of paper. When I finally found it, I pulled it out. "You guys are booked for snorkeling in the morning at nine, then lunch, then there's a round of golf for the guys, and you ladies have a spa afternoon planned." I'd booked it all online and my copy of the itinerary had the confirmation emails attached. Hers had the confirmation numbers.

"Daddy paid for all of that?" She was misty-eyed.

I nodded. "He said his little girl is only getting married once." And he'd said it through teary eyes. Then he'd said he wished he'd only gotten married once. I couldn't be sure who he meant, so I hadn't replied. I'd thought I was his only marriage.

Not my circus. Not my Jean-Luc.

"Friday, you have the morning free, then rehearsal at three, then dinner with all the bridesmaids and groomsmen and family."

She glanced at me again.

"Saturday, we have family coming in at all times of the day, so you'll be busy with that. So many cocktail hours. And a night tour of the island for some of the guests." I nodded like a cocktail hour was a big trial, but I was looking forward to it. I loved playing hostess. Most of the time. "And then Sunday..." It was the big day. "Hair and makeup are all lined up and then it's just a matter of 'I do' times two and you're married."

She squeezed Noah's hand and smiled at him. "Can you believe that at this time next week, we're going to be an old married couple?"

He grinned back and pressed his forehead against hers. They were cute and so in love. The kind of couple other couples wanted to be. "I've been waiting a very long time to make you an old married woman." Aw, he said the sweetest things.

They stared at each other for a few minutes, then Loralei turned to me. "There's some kind of pirate-themed theater here. I thought we could all go to it tomorrow night?"

I choked on my water, but I nodded and continued coughing when I tried to speak. "That sounds lovely," I finally managed. But the last place I was going to go was to that theater. I would fake an illness if I had to. No way, no how.

I tried another drink and this one went down the right tube. I smiled at Lor, then glanced at Jolene. She was still blessedly silent, and for that I was grateful.

I'd sown a wild oat while I was on the island with a very handsome man, and I'd enjoyed myself, but now, I had plenty of things to worry about without adding the Pirates of Pararey Island to my to-do list since I'd already *done* their captain.

Although, if I was extremely honest, I wouldn't have minded doing him again. Once or twice.

Chapter Nine

All The Dirty Details

After a blissfully quiet—and by that I meant Jolene was quiet—lunch, massages were already booked for Loralei and me. If there was one thing I needed right then, it was to have my muscles kneaded in the most therapeutic way possible by someone named Henri or Fernando or Vincent.

When I went back to the room to get ready and to douse the hickey in concealer, I looked at the bed with a sigh. I still couldn't believe I had a one-night stand. Honestly. Remy was the kind of guy women like me dreamed about sleeping with. He was tall and dark, handsome in ways most men weren't. And suave.

A rose sat on the pillow with the note, written on hotel paper torn from the pad on the desk next to it, with the signature of Captain Renegade and an X and O behind it. This guy was so perfect he'd left me a note when he skedaddled. And a rose. Although he could've only taken it from the arrangement on the table inside the room, it was the thought that counted. How hadn't I noticed it when we'd first left together, or when I'd come back for the scarf. Although then, I'd been in a hurry and hadn't paid too much attention.

If I hadn't had a date in years, it had been decades since anyone left me a note with Xs and Os in the signature line. Later, I was going to do some serious daydreaming. Fawning, at the very least.

I showered, then looked at myself in the mirror. At forty-plus, I exercised. I took the occasional spin class, and I was avid in yoga. I watched what I ate—usually as I scooped it onto the fork and stuffed it into my face—but it was the effect of years that I couldn't escape. I could if I was willing to pay for injections and peels and procedures, but to my way of thinking, there was a point to aging, a purpose, and I wanted to do it as gracefully as hair dye and teeth whiteners allowed. Plus, all that stuff was expensive, and I had much better ways to spend my money.

For a moment, though, I wished to be as beautiful as I'd felt with Jean-Luc when we'd been happy. Maybe it hadn't been happiness at all, maybe it was only the peace that ignorance had given me. Or maybe it was that he'd made me believe I was happy, and I'd believed it because I'd wanted it so badly. I'd wanted the family and the hot husband that made all the other wives envy me.

I looked at the clock blinking on the bedside table. I didn't have time to be standing around making silly wishes for youthfulness. Loralei was waiting for me. I dressed and dabbed the makeup on my marks so that they weren't as obvious.

When I walked into the massage suite on the main floor of the hotel, Loralei was already there. She looked at me, then looked again. It was the kind of double take that made me look behind me to make sure there was no one there. Then I glanced at her. "What?" Maybe I had a booger.

"Mom, you look radiant today." *Radiant* was a word I liked. It meant good things. Probably meant I didn't have a booger. She continued heaping compliments on my praise-deprived psyche. "So pretty."

I smiled. "Must be the island air."

She'd always been the sweetest girl, kind beyond measure, happy. A girl, woman now, like Loralei deserved the world handed to her. Jean-Luc and I had agreed on that point a long time ago.

"I don't know, Mom. I'm only this alive after I get..." She pursed her lips and wiggled her eyebrows at me. "Lucky."

I shook my head and covered my ears. “No, Lor. No.” Even as she laughed, I continued. “No. No. No. No.”

She laughed. “Did you, er, get, um, lucky?”

I wasn’t answering that. Not that I couldn’t lie to her. I just didn’t want to.

After we changed, she went to one table, and I stretched out on the other. As the big-handed female massage therapist set warm rocks in a line along my spine and started finger-poking my muscles, kneading and manipulating, I moaned. My body needed this. My *soul* needed this. When I moaned a second time, the sound brought forth a flood of memories.

Good memories. The erotic kind of good that made my body flush, made me think and be grateful. I sat up. The rocks slid down my back, clinking to the table and rolling to the floor with soft thuds against the carpet.

Lor looked over at me. “Mom? Are you okay?” She had that worried-her-mom-was-losing-it scowl on her face. There was nothing I could do to erase it.

No. I was most definitely not okay. There was one memory that had escaped my mind upon waking that picked now of all times to surface. I probably had a handprint on my ass. And if that was the case, I’d also let Pete the Pirate or Captain Hook or whatever he’d called himself do things Jean-Luc had begged me to do and when I’d refused, had started doing it with every other woman on the planet. No wonder Jean-Luc smiled so much.

My entire body flushed with heat. Now the massage therapist had taken several steps back and stared at me. My breasts were exposed and heaving because the memories weren't only vivid, they were potent. Mouthwatering. Desire seeped through my blood. I recalled every moan, every touch, every ab muscle. The reverence with which he touched me. Sitting here half-naked with this kind of total recall was almost creepy.

Loralei sat up, holding her towel around her as she moved to hand me mine. I took it and covered up, then tilted my head at the masseuse. "Oh, my God. I'm so sorry. I didn't mean to..." I couldn't be sure of all the things I'd done to ruin this massage, and I probably wouldn't be allowed to book another, but I remembered the entire night, and that took priority over everything else. I remembered what my night with the pirate had been like.

"Sorry, I think it'd be better to do a massage another time," I managed to blurt out, then jerked my towel around myself and rushed for the dressing room.

Loralei walked in behind me. "Mom, are you okay? Is it too much being here? Is it heat exhaustion? Did I put too much on you with planning the wedding?" Her face was pinched, and it wasn't a look a bride was supposed to have in the days preceding her wedding.

"Gosh, no, honey. I just had a moment." How else was I supposed to explain it?

"Are you sure? You look flushed."

Yep I probably did. I had visions of a gloriously naked man lying in my bed running through my head. I was imagining said man's come hither grin, the crook of his finger, the kiss that led to the... Oof. The memories were delicious. My body was one mind-movie scene away from purring.

Instead of saying yes, as I should have, I turned and looked at Loralei, and like I'd forgotten who she was, who *I* was, I blurted, "I haven't been with a man in a very long time."

One of the great things about Lor was that she wasn't the kind of girl who was going to blanch or hide. We talked about things. So many things. Things I needed to know, things I didn't want to know. But we'd always talked the way I'd wished I could've talked to my mother and couldn't. But I'd never really told Loralei my secrets, just accepted hers. It worked for us. Or it had until now. Now I was about to hyperventilate.

"It's okay," she told me. "Let's get dressed and then we can talk."

Talk? I wasn't usually the one talking when we shared, but maybe the topic would be something else. I didn't know what I wanted, but I dressed quickly, and so did Lor. She headed back into the massage room, probably to give some kind of explanation about our absence, but I practically bolted for the beach, not knowing if I wanted to be alone or to talk.

After a few minutes, she sat beside me on a bench just past the boardwalk and asked, "Was not being with another man your choice?"

I didn't know what to say, so I didn't say anything for a second before I managed, "Not exactly. Just after everything with your dad, and I don't know."

She widened her eyes. It was her—*I have a brilliant idea that you're probably not going to think is so brilliant, but trust me it is*—look. "I could set you up. Noah's friend Marco's dad is single. He's a little hairy, but he's single." She said it again—single—in case I missed it the first time. I didn't.

"He's *hairy*?"

She shrugged. "Not like... he has a beard and last summer when we were swimming at their house—a barbecue—when he took off his shirt, I had a strong urge to wax his back, but he was nice. Likes wine."

For some reason, I didn't want some hairy single dad, but not because there was anything wrong with hairy single dads. My brain was just still focused on my night with the pirate, and what this all meant. It seemed I was going through something unexpected, and I wasn't sure how to handle all of it.

I shook my head. "I'm fine." After all, I'd had more sex last night than I'd had in years. I wasn't quite desperate enough to have to Nair my date before I boinked him.

Loralei laid a hand on my shoulder. "Mom, there's no reason you should be alone. There are men out there who would love you. Daddy shouldn't be the only one getting his groove on. You're beautiful and young, still vital, whatever that means." We both laughed, but this wasn't a conversation I wanted to have with anyone right now. Not while visions of Renegade's sugar plum still danced in my head.

Right now, I wanted to find the captain and go a few more rounds in my bedroom, but I didn't want to tell my daughter that. "Come on. Let's get out of here before that masseuse presses charges."

As we walked through the lobby, Arthur stopped us. He was holding a crossbow and wearing gloves. "Excuse me, ladies. But the restaurant is closed this evening, and we have reluctantly had to cancel your dinner reservation."

Words like *plague, disease, e. coli* flittered through my mind. "Why?" If I needed to book a new caterer, I needed to know ASAP. Or a medical professional. A poison control center.

"There is a *pig* running loose on the property." He jerked the cord back, put the bow close to his face like he was sighting it in, then released the cord. The cord snapped free, and I imagined that scene in Robin Hood with Costner standing in front of the fire as he let loose his arrow. He was showing off in front of guests. There had to be a rule. “A pig. It’s been years since we’ve had wild boar here.” He shook his head. “Very dangerous. Tusks…” Another head shake. He pointed at the beach and pretended to shoot. It was then I noticed the quill of arrows slung across his back.

“Is there anything we should do?” *Tusks. Dangerous.* His words. They inspired a bit of a tremble in my normally steady hands.

“You should make accommodations in town for dinner.” He looked left and right. “If you need help, leave your names at the desk and a member of the hotel staff will contact you to assist.” It sounded reasonable enough, but I couldn’t stop looking at the crossbow. I didn’t know the kind or the model or even the genre if there was one—it was a crossbow. I didn’t need to know much more than that—but I couldn’t stop staring.

“I’m sorry, but are you planning to shoot the pig?” Poor Wilbur.

Arthur looked at me as if I’d sprouted a third eye, and his forehead pinched. “Of course. No swine running loose in this hotel shall survive my wrath. None that snort and wallow in mud, then drag it through my carpets.”

When he took his weapon and ran off, Loralei turned to me. “Wow. That’s, um, something?”

“Yeah.” I nodded, still watching the beach.

"Mom, would you mind terribly if Noah and I have dinner in our room?" She smiled, probably because she thought she was letting me down. "There isn't going to be much time after tomorrow when the guests start arriving, and I want to be with him one last night the way we are right now before things get hectic. Is that okay?"

"Of course." I couldn't refuse her. I could manage for a night without her. I'd certainly seemed to manage last night. I didn't say that, of course. I just smiled and nodded, letting her go, something I was only just learning how to do. I hoped I never got good at it.

Chapter Ten

Out Here On My Own

I USED to wish that Loralei would stay little forever. I used to hope she'd never face a cruel world or those middle school girls once they figured out they had the power to separate into cliques. Mean girls who always had a mean leader. I didn't know how I would deal with that hurt for her or how I could teach her to deal with it. She was always soft-hearted, but soon, my Lor found her power. She made me so proud. She was always kind, but never let anyone hurt her either. I'd made the perfect kid, and of course, I took all the credit.

Now, I loved the woman she'd turned into. I loved that she was still kind, that she wasn't afraid to ask for what she wanted, and that she'd found someone who complemented the best parts of her and still loved the worst. I was a lucky, lucky mom.

As I walked through the lobby, baby Barbie came storming toward me. It was one of those moments where I looked around for a place to hide, didn't find one, thought I should look again and... nope. There she was, glowering up at me.

I really needed to learn her name, but since she looked like she was about to explode—red, tear-stained half grimace—and the explosion was far too close to me. I smiled and hoped she wore herself out quickly. I hated scenes. Worse though, half-exploded, tiny, part-plastic woman would clash with my sundress.

When she was still about thirty feet from me, she pointed and yelled, "Murderer!"

I looked behind me because she sure as heck wasn't talking to me. Except there was no one behind me. Nothing but open air and ocean.

My mouth fell open. I was having another moment. A shocking one. More so than the last. Every eye in the place that wasn't mine was on me. They were probably all here waiting to see if Arthur had nabbed himself a swine, but boy, did they get a lot more than they bargained for today.

I sighed. "What in heaven's name are you talking about?" There was no telling what lunacy this woman-child had dreamed up.

She crossed her arms and shot me a potent glare. "Jean-Luc is *missing*."

Missing was a new take on checking out other island honeys but I didn't think she was in the mood to hear my opinion. Plus, she was still sputtering. "And he *has* been since we ran into you at breakfast. I know you're hiding his body. I want it back."

I cocked my head, completely confused, and she huffed again.

Hiding his body? Obviously, this child knew nothing about Jean-Luc. We were on our second whole day at the island. Which meant I hadn't had time to plan and carry out a murder. However, it also meant that Jean-Luc had ample time to find an island honey or hotel honey to spend some time with.

It wasn't that he was a dog. He just had so much—no. Maybe it was time to admit it. Jean-Luc was a dog. A pig. A man who let the little head do all the thinking and the big head was just there to keep his ears separated. He was a ladies' man.

"He's probably found a, well, a friend." She didn't look like she was equipped to handle the raw facts about her boyfriend. Although the truth was that very likely he was naked right about now.

She punched a fist to her hip, and her nostrils flared. "He isn't that way with me." For the effect she probably knew she'd get out of me, she smiled—maybe it was a smirk—and tilted her head. "Don't you want to know how I know?" I didn't. But she wasn't inclined to care what I wanted anyway. "We're having a baby."

On my life, I had no idea. She couldn't have shocked me more if she'd shot me. I also tried not to react because there were a lot of people watching, and I didn't need this kind of attention. So, I nodded, opened my mouth to congratulate her, then snapped it shut and walked away instead. Nothing I could think of to say would be appropriate. Plus, everyone really was staring.

I wished health and happiness to all of them. Well, most of them. I wasn't quite that good of a person. I couldn't stand there with her. Nor did I have the energy to argue with and remind her that Jean-Luc and I also had a child and he'd still cheated. Repeatedly.

Getting out of there was for the best.

I made a beeline down the beach for a while. There wasn't really a way to think *around* this. My twenty-one-year-old daughter was going to have a baby brother or sister. It was a new life, and I should've been happy because I was that person, a happy person who was genuinely happy for others. Usually.

At the moment I wasn't that person. I was something else. Confused. A broken resemblance to my former self who resented that Jean-Luc had found such happiness with someone else. I was pissed, if I was being honest.

When I made it to the tiki bar at the far end of the beach, I slid onto a stool. The bartender was the same guy as yesterday. "Do you want rum or a pina colada?"

"Ah, how well you know me." Probably I should've been ashamed. I wasn't.

"Drinking alone tonight?" As if I had placed the order, he set a glass of rum with ice and a sprig of mint onto the counter.

"A little alone." When he gave me a pity frown, I narrowed my eyes. "It's a choice."

"Beautiful women should never drink without someone to adore them." The compliment was nice. I sipped slowly, wishing I had some distraction from all the thoughts going around in my head.

Once upon a time, I thought Jean-Luc and I would be together forever. Then after we split, I'd thought Jean-Luc might settle down. Even though, by then, I knew it wouldn't be with me. I was sad for him that he hadn't. I was sad for me that he hadn't been able to find enough in me to make him want to. And immediately, I was angry at myself. Men didn't change for women.

Like a gift from the sea or the gods or from whatever angel looked out for simple women drinking alone, Remy slid onto the seat beside me. "Feel like some company?"

"Yes." I *very much* felt like company. Naked company would've been better, but this was a little too public for that. "I feel like I should tell you my name isn't Bonnie."

Tonight, he wasn't dressed in his pirate attire. Instead, he wore a pair of jeans that looked like they'd been made for his long legs and a polo that hung from his broad shoulders. He looked nice. "All right. What should I call you?"

"Cami. My name is Camille." He smiled and I shook my head. "I might not be much for company right now." I grinned because how could I not grin at Remy? Especially with our dirty memories running through my mind, distracting me from the other thing.

"That's okay because sitting quietly with a pretty woman is just the thing my morale needs." He leaned in closer, and I got a big whiff of his citrusy cologne. "And my reputation." A tingle shimmied its way across my skin. "Maybe, if you could be so kind as to just smile at me every once in a while so the natives think we're together, and I'm charming and handsome enough to get a beautiful woman to smile at me, I would be forever grateful." His warm breath against my skin was such a bonus.

He cocked a brow. "If I happen to call out Bonita"—what his accent did for me. It made me want to swoon, especially when combined with the eye wag that changed the meaning of *call out*—"it still means you."

He was charming. I liked him, and I smiled just because I wanted to smile at him.

"What's happened to make you sad?" Oh, no. If he could see that I was sad, I wasn't doing such a bang-up job hiding anything. I'd always thought I was good at masking my feelings. Turns out, I wasn't.

"My ex-husband, Jean-Luc, is dating a woman who I'm convinced is the same age as our daughter, and I just found out that they're having a baby." I chuckled. "If that doesn't sound pathetic..." There wasn't much else to do but laugh at myself and shake my head at the ridiculous emotions bubbling under my skin.

He looked at me. "Jean-Luc sounds like the kind of guy who knows which color crayon tastes the best." When I smiled and looked down, he curled his finger under my chin and nudged my head up. "Tell me, do you envy the people who've never met Jean-Luc?"

I thought of all the heartache I would've avoided had I never met him, but then I thought of Loralei. "I don't regret meeting him. I regret loving him. I regret being so young when we got together, not seeing the things about him I could've avoided." He nodded along as if he understood. "But we're mostly friendly now. *Mostly* on good terms."

His fingers ran from my chin along the front of my throat. "What about you? You have a past you would rather not talk about?"

"Mm-hmm." And now that fingertip was working its way back up my throat.

I didn't spend an extra second thinking about Jean-Luc or whatever woman Remy had waiting for him to forget about me because he turned on his stool so he sat facing me, and I looked at him. "I'm glad you met Jean-Luc, too, because if you hadn't, you wouldn't be on the island right now, smiling at me." And then his finger dipped lower and he pulled the silver chain from under the collar of my shirt. "Pretty."

"I got it at the market on the boardwalk and the woman said it's part of Captain Renegade's treasure." *His* Captain Renegade. "But I told you that last night."

"My treasure, then." He grinned softly and looked into my eyes. I was a goner. I didn't believe in love at first sight, but I had a bad case of lust. I recognized it and desperately wanted to give in to it.

Being with him was the freest I'd ever felt. It wasn't about being Loralei's mother, which had kept me occupied since Jean-Luc and I split. It wasn't about Jean-Luc or hating him or missing him or trying not to feel anything for him. This was a hundred percent about me and Remy and nothing else.

"Remy, would you like to go for a walk on the beach?" I smiled and thought I might never want to stop smiling, then added, "With me." Like there might be some confusion

"Oh, you didn't mean with Zack?" He nodded to the bartender, grimaced, then turned to give me an up-and-down. "I guess you'll have to do."

"I guess so." If he played his cards right, I would've been very happy to drag him into a dark cove and *do* him. Again.

Chapter Eleven

A Date With The Police and a Pig on The Beach

THE MORNING WAS QUIET, and I basked in the comfort of my bed for a moment. Storms had rolled through last night, and with the pig still running loose, and Arthur on the hunt with a weapon I'd been assured he was qualified to use, I'd opted to stay in my room after Remy walked me back to the hotel.

I'd held his hand as we walked. We'd taken cover beneath a rocky overhang during a surprise rainshower and laughed, hugged. We might've even kissed a few times. To have someone's undivided attention, even for just those few minutes, had been glorious. If I was the kind of girl with an addictive personality, this was certainly the type of thing I could get addicted to.

When it became clear we were going to either have to stay under the cover of the rock wall or make a run for it, we'd kissed once and ran back to the hotel. Inside, he walked me to the elevator, kissed me until we reached the third floor, walked me to my door, and then kissed me goodnight. There was something decadent in the way he kissed. Like ordering dessert even on a diet. It was that kind of thing. Mouth-watering. Delicious.

The morning was a luxury of thoughts of him. A host of *dear-diary* memories.

While I would've loved to stay here and think about nothing other than that man, my mother's flight was due to arrive this morning.

Loralei and Noah were off to get her, but I was to meet them at the boat dock with all the pomp and ceremony my mother expected on such an occasion because she was the matriarch of the family. She'd lived longer than anyone, tolerated more, plus, as she reminded me at every opportunity, she would have to tolerate *that rancid Frenchman* for as long as she stayed. Secretly, she loved him, but out of loyalty to me, she pretended to hate him. I loved her for that. Still, I knew she still sent him birthday cards and a Christmas check. To his credit, he never cashed them. He did have *a few* good points.

A very, very few.

The phone next to the bed rang, and I looked at it like I'd never seen a phone before. This was a relatively new phenomenon since I'd been waiting for calls a-plenty and none had come through. "Hello?" If I sounded surprised or unsure, it was because I was.

"Ms. Danes-LaCroix, it's Roman from the front desk." I hadn't met Roman yet. I'd begun to think Arthur did it all around here. "Your mother has left a message stating that she's very dissatisfied with the flight you booked for her. She's had to share with..." He paused. "Ah..."

"That's okay. You can skip that word." It would be derogatory, and it didn't take a rocket scientist to figure it out.

"Oh, it's not that. I just can't read what I wrote." He chuckled. "She was actually pretty funny. Anyway, she said your father and that horrible Jolene's mother have done nothing but discuss golf since the flight left Arizona." He added a huff that eerily mimicked my mother's. I had to hold in my giggle. My mother had the same relationship with Jolene's mom that I had with Jolene. "She said that they almost came to blows over a three-year-old golf game." Another huff. "And that is the end of the message."

"Thank you, Roman. And I apologize." I felt like after a message like this one, and what I knew he'd gone through, and had to listen to before he could write down said message, an apology wasn't out of line. Probably I should have sent him gifts. Or hard liquor. Tequila was a good option in a situation like this.

Mothers. As much as we love them, they're hard wired to drive us crazy.

By the time I rolled out of bed, into the shower, then got dressed and made myself presentable, I was ready for Mom. I'd wrapped and put the necklace in its box on the dresser since it didn't go with this dress. I had my hair pulled away from my face. She liked to be able to see a person's soul through their eyes and apparently hair interfered. I'd tried for flawless makeup, but settled for meh. When I was almost done, the phone rang again.

"Hello?"

"Ma'am, it's Roman again."

I clamped my mouth against an *oh Lord*, instead settling on "What can I do for you, Roman?" Undoubtedly, I would be apologizing again soon, but first I wanted to hear why.

"Your mother called again. She said to tell you she will speak to you when she gets here about the following..." He paused, and I wondered if he was considering mimicking my mother's snooty tone. "Your inconsideration at having her on the same flight as that horrible Sumner woman, your inability to talk your daughter into a wedding at a church. She hopes that your ex-husband has been told to be on his best behavior because your father can't tolerate foolishness, and if you've booked her on a return flight with those horrible people, change it now before she gets here." He sucked in a deep breath. "And there was something about having the wedding on an island with terrible cell phone service."

These were things that were out of my control. I had no idea, when Loralei booked the flights, that my mother would be with Jolene's parents. It was ironic, though, since my mother's mantra since high school was that I should ignore Jolene's bad behavior.

She was probably singing a different tune now.

She was going to be in fine form when she finally stepped off the dock onto the sand. I already knew it. She wasn't usually this bad. Annoying? Sure. Horrible? No. Jolene's mom must've been a beast on that flight.

"All right. Well, thank you, Roman." I hung up and sat down on the edge of the bed. Maybe two bottles of tequila and a big bottle of rum.

As I was just about ready, I took one last look at myself in the mirror.

Lovely. My dress was wrinkled. Mother would have a fit. I yanked it over my head and went to the dressier clothes in the closet.

And of freaking course, while I stood there with no real clothes on, there was a knock at my door because the devil who managed these kinds of details saw a bra and panty opportunity. I threw on the hotel robe and answered because I had no idea what was waiting for me on the other side.

"Oh. Hello." Cops. Two of them, holding out badges in wallets. Their uniforms were remarkably similar to Anywhere, USA's police uniforms. Blue and generic. They didn't wait to be invited in, either, they just walked right past me into my room. My dress was still in a puddle of wrinkles on the floor, and the room looked like I'd only just crawled out of bed. "Ms. LaCroix?"

Seemed to me like that was a question they should've asked before they barged in, but I crossed my arms and nodded. "Yes?"

"I'm Detective Lawrence." He nodded at the woman beside him. "This is Detective Molly Rothel. We need you to come with us." The same cop spoke, and I stared him down. He was possibly my age, but looked so much older. He had a bald spot at his forehead, a comb-over that didn't hide it, and bags under his eyes that could've carried groceries for a family of five.

"Come with you?"

"To the police station on the mainland."

"Oh, geez. What did my mom do?" I was picturing every manner of bad old lady behavior. Maybe she'd kicked a flight attendant and had been taken into custody by the air marshal, or she'd taken to stealing the bags of other passengers and got caught, or something alcohol related had happened. I had too many guesses. I hoped none were right. She was kooky enough for any of them to be a possibility.

"That's an interesting question. What did your mother do?" The other cop spoke, a woman with a bun so severe her eyes pulled into tight slits because of it.

"Nothing. I just assumed." I was going to stop talking now. "Why do you need me to come to the police station on the mainland?"

"A report's been made. Your husband, Jean-Luc LaCroix, has been reported missing. We need to ask you a few questions." She stared at me through her permanently narrowed eyes..

"He's actually my *ex*-husband." I shrugged because these detectives didn't appear to like being corrected. She scowled, and it screwed with my psyche. Made me nervous. Therefore, I bumbled. "If you need to talk with me, shouldn't you just do it now?"

"We can discuss that at the station." The male detective nodded to the closet. "Get dressed."

I didn't tell them I'd been trying to get dressed when they interrupted me. I was in a robe. They were detectives. If they couldn't do that math, it wasn't my problem.

Instead, I grabbed a pair of jeans and a t-shirt from the open suitcase and walked into the bathroom. I could've probably climbed out the window onto the balcony, but I would've been stuck there and it wasn't likely that I had anything to worry about anyway. Not having an alibi might have been a problem, but somewhere in this hotel, there had to be a camera that caught me going into my room or through the lobby.

They allowed me to get dressed in peace. I took a couple of seconds to consider where Jean-Luc could be and what in the absolute hell he was doing staying out all night, so his frantic and delusional girlfriend called the police.

After I dressed, they brought me by boat to the police station, leaving a group of officers behind to search my room for evidence. The good news was they didn't cuff me. The bad news was everyone saw me walking out with two police officers.

There went my reputation.

There wasn't much in my room but some clothes, a book I'd brought to read on the plane, and the trinket box. No smoking gun there. Not that there would be a smoking gun anywhere. Jean-Luc was misbehaving and worrying his new woman. No gun necessary. Unless she was the vengeful type.

At the police station, the detectives stuck me in an interrogation room very much like the ones on cop shows, but on TV they looked a heck of a lot bigger. This was little more than a closet with a one-way mirror.

While I waited, I counted the ceiling tiles, concrete bricks of the wall, and was just about to start on the floor when Detective Lawrence came in smelling like cigarettes. He sat in the only other chair in the room.

True to every cop show in the history of cop shows, Detective Molly Rothel walked in next, shut the door behind her, and leaned one shoulder against the wall. She had a file tucked under her other arm and one ankle crossed over the other. She was purposefully casual and yet didn't quite pull it off. There was no mistaking her animosity.

Lawrence opened his folder, pretended to read from a paper, then slammed the folder shut. He would be the bad cop in today's exercise. "Did you want to kill your ex-husband?"

"No. Is he dead?" I'd seen enough Law & Order to know to answer simply and not embellish. He ignored my question.

"How would you do it if you did kill him?"

I was actually a little surprised he didn't tell me he'd be asking the questions here.

"What?" The question was ridiculous. Even the dumbest murderer on TV would never answer that one.

"When was the last time you saw Jean-Luc?" This time Rothel asked.

I sighed. "At breakfast yesterday. Actually, it was in the elevator when I was on my way to eat with my daughter, just before breakfast." I amended with a shrug. "*Our* daughter." They looked at each other as if my quick correction meant Loralei might have been the reason I offed Jean-Luc. "Do I need a lawyer?"

Lawrence laughed. "Not unless you're guilty." Bad cop answer. The Law & Order writers would've been shaking their heads.

Rothel leaned in. "Where did you go after you got off the elevator? And where did Jean-Luc go?"

"I don't know where he went. I wasn't especially concerned with him. He was with his girlfriend." Fair was fair. I would've bet a month's alimony that I was here because she'd told the Keystone Cops that I'd killed Jean-Luc.

"Britney Harlow?"

Oh yeah. That was it. Her name was Britney. I nodded like I'd known her name all along. "I went to the restaurant." There would be witnesses—the waiter, my daughter and Noah and Jolene—and hopefully video.

Of course there was. Lawrence handed me an iPad, queued a video, and hit the play arrow. It was my elevator ride with Jean-Luc and Barbie, erm Britney, and then after a few seconds, the doors whooshed open and we all left the elevator. Britney stormed off in one direction, I left in another, and Jean-Luc followed me. The next video showed me going back into the elevator a few minutes later and coming out with a neck scarf.

“Where did you go between the time you left the elevator and came back?”

Well, I had a hickey—still do—and I wanted to hide it from my kid, so I went back to the room for the scarf. “I went to the bathroom, and then I wanted to go back to my room real quick for a scarf.”

“To cover up the evidence of an altercation?”

It happened less than a day ago. I would’ve still been wearing the scarf if any evidence existed. “No.”

“To cover up that hickey on your neck?” Lawrence pointed to the spot on the back of my throat. “Did your husband see it and fight with you about it?”

“*Ex*-husband.”

“Right. Maybe he didn’t want to be an ex-husband anymore.”

I chuckled. “Oh, for sure. That’s why he brought his gorgeous girlfriend to our daughter’s wedding.” I hoped they understood the sarcasm was real. But in honesty, he’d pitched reconciliation more than once and more than once I’d reminded him he would have to forego his extracurricular dating. That usually ended the reconciliation chatter pretty quickly. “She’s pregnant, you know.” I was talking too much and there wasn’t a person in this room who didn’t know it. Their objective would be to keep me talking. My strategy would have to be shut the hell up. If I could.

"Did that upset you?"

"Of course not." So that might've been a lie. A fib. Something of the tiny little variety.

"Did your hickey upset him?"

"You'd have to ask him." And now I was cocky, probably more so than I should've been.

"A lot of times women get roughed up by their former spouses and then the former spouse ends up dead in a barrel at the bottom of the cove." Her words made me wonder how many bodies they'd found in barrels, but I didn't have the nerve to ask. I'd been taught to respect the law and its enforcers.

"Quite the imagination. I couldn't stuff Jean-Luc in a barrel. Have you seen the size of the guy?" He wasn't tiny. He had muscle and sinew and more muscle. And all that weighed a lot more than I could lift without the aid of a forklift.

"But you've thought about it? Or you have experience with such?"

Of course I'd considered killing him. He was my ex-husband for a valid reason. He'd hurt me. He'd hurt me enough times I had fantasized about his death. I sure as hell wasn't admitting that to these idiots.

"I'm an American citizen. Do I need a lawyer?" Those things weren't hugely connected except that all other countries thought Americans were very litigious. This was a whole different kind of situation.

"You don't." Rothel nodded down at me and smiled. "There is no lack of rumor about Jean-Luc LaCroix. The tabloids say he has a woman in every city. We're checking now to see if we can find him using traffic cameras."

I hoped they found him and when they did, they'd better give him what-for, for worrying everyone. Certainly a night in jail, so long as it wasn't Saturday night to ruin Sunday's wedding, wouldn't hurt him.

"If you run across him, don't mention his girlfriend is pregnant. He might not know." He'd been so happy when he'd found out I was pregnant with Lor. I didn't want them to deny him that moment with Brittany.

"But you do?"

I nodded. "She told me when she accused me of hiding him from her."

We seemed to be finished now. They both left the room then a uniformed officer came in. "Ma'am, I'll see you back to the island, now."

Why couldn't they have asked me those questions back at the hotel? I stood and followed him out to the pier and the boat they'd brought me here in.

He smiled. "We didn't find any evidence in your room, although we did confiscate the sheets and blankets from your bed for testing."

Heat flushed through me. I was mortified. I didn't know if housekeeping had changed my sheets since I got those hickeys, as well as a number of other things I'd done that night. I couldn't bear the thought of DNA testing. As a principle, it was fine, but when it came to my… secretions…oh, geez. My thoughts were grossing me out, but I didn't have a choice so I did my best to hide my heated reaction.

He took me back to the island. Needing to decompress, I walked down the beach from the dock toward the hotel. There was a sign that said the beach was closed, no reason given, but I was walking, not swimming or lying in the sand.

As I walked, I noticed the pig zigging and zagging like it'd had too much to drink and was in a big hurry to get away from whatever was chasing him.

Arthur appeared down the beach, running hell bent for leather. Or hell bent for pig skin. Unlike earlier, he had his crossbow loaded with the bolt sitting on the track and the cord pulled taut. I stood and held up my hand in the international sign of surrender or the old west sign for *don't shoot*. I whirled around looking for the pig and saw the clerk coming for me. With the pig hot on my tail, I ran behind a rock. The pig came to a halt with me. He stood near enough to rub his snout against my leg.

"Hey, Porky. Hit the road." I shooed him, but he stood firm. "Go on. Get lost, Wilbur." I could imagine the headline. *Woman killed by madman chasing pig.* I sure as hell wasn't going to stick around and wait for it to happen. I ran for it and the pig tore off after me. We were kicking up sand, and now I understood the zig and the zag. There was nowhere to hide. No matter how I thought of it, this did not have a good ending. I was being chased by a pig that was being chased by a crossbow-toting maniac hotel manager. Maybe I should've listened to the signs saying the beach was closed after all.

I ran up the ramp to the lifeguard station and hid behind the building. The pig joined me again, and then Arthur, so there were three of us running around the perimeter of the lifeguard shack.

I ran down the plank of wood and into the sand. I was flailing and screaming because this pig was still chasing me, or so it seemed. I was fast though, I ran to the empty tiki bar and hid behind the counter among the tiny fridge and a lot of bottles of tequila and rum.

Nope. Not fast enough. The pig ran in after me, snorting and squealing.

Hold on a second. Just one second. That snort sounded French.

How did a snort sound French? I don't freaking know! It just did.

"Jean-Luc?" The pig snorted again and nodded his big head.

This was a total oh-shit moment. I was talking to a pig. *Hiding* with a pig who may or may not have been my ex-husband.

"It can't be you. This isn't possible," I whispered.

The pig gave me the saddest look I've ever seen on a pig. Not that I'd studied many porky facial expressions.

"Is it? Is it you?"

The pig nodded again.

Okay, maybe this was just a pig that could nod. "Do you have a tiny dick?"

Hoo, man. I would have never thought a pig could look so offended, but this one did, as he gave a very angry snort and shook his head.

It was official. I'd lost my mind. "Did you turn into a pig?"

Another nod.

"And you came after me because?"

He inched closer, then set his head down on my knee, making the strangest whimpering sound.

"Damn it. You want me to help you figure out how to be human again?"

Another awkward nod came, followed by the pig scooting closer and almost cuddling with my knee. Because, of course, pig or human, Jean-Luc expected me to save him. That was the other thing, as impossible as it was, as insane as it was, I actually did think this was my ex-husband.

I needed a drink. I slapped a twenty onto the counter over my head and pulled a bottle of tequila from the rail, ripped off the shot stopper with my teeth, and took a swig.

Oh, frick. How was I going to tell Lor that her dad had gone full-on Porky? And what about Barb, er, Britney?

These were tequila thoughts. Tequila is the only thing that had a chance of making sense of it all. Fortunately, I was in a good place for that.

Chapter Twelve

The Truth or Not the Truth, That is the Question

I SNUCK into the hotel via the back of the building and ushered the pig into my room, shutting the door firmly behind me.

Oh, dear. The room was trashed. Clothes had been thrown from my suitcase, which was lying on the floor. The mattress was askew. The drawers were open and lopsided. Even the hangers in the closet had been thrown on the floor. The cops thought I'd killed my husband, but I was pretty certain he'd been turned into the pig he'd been since the moment I'd met him.

It wasn't wholly his fault. He hadn't asked to be born with that face, and he hadn't asked to be worshiped by women who loved sports. Nor by me or our neighbor Chandra, our housekeeper, our dog sitter, or most of the women who'd been in our social circle.

Those things probably didn't negate the fact that I'd now absconded with said pig who went straight for my suitcase and pulled out a pair of my panties. I snatched them from his mouth and bristled when someone knocked at the door.

Instead of opening it and letting the person in, I looked at the pig. "Shh." I put my finger to my lips. He got that old familiar gleam in his eye, further enforcing my belief that this was indeed Jean-Luc. I cocked my head. "Look Piglet, unless you want me to call fake Legolas, Fakolas, and let him turn you into bacon for tomorrow's breakfast buffet, you *will* be quiet in here." I snatched a second pair of underwear out of his mouth. "And leave my panties alone, piggy perv."

I walked out of the room to find my tearful daughter standing in the hallway with her future husband, my mother, and Jolene... oh, and her camera guy. Loralei rushed into my arms, her voice filled with unshed tears. "Daddy's missing."

Behind my daughter, my mother watched us. I smiled at her, noting that she wore white dress shoes with heels, which were completely impractical for a beach, and a white dress with blue flowers on it that fell just below her knees. Her pantyhose were a shade lighter than the rest of her skin, and she finished the look with a white hat with a little blue flower on it. Her short blonde hair curled under the brim of the hat.

A completely ridiculous outfit for the beach, but she'd have fit right in with English nobility enjoying a tea party. My mom had always kind of been that way. Even for a relaxed Sunday afternoon, she wore nice clothes with stockings. Maybe that had been a little more normal in her day and age. At least that's what she'd always claimed.

"Where could he be?" my daughter asked, a sob exploding from her lips and drawing my attention back to her.

Patting her back, I tried to soothe her like the perfect mother. Or like me, the not-perfect mother. I hoped she wouldn't notice that I hadn't spoken. I hadn't spoken because I couldn't believe telling her that the police thought I'd killed her father would make the crying better. I wasn't positive I could keep from blurting out that I had in fact, instead, turned him into a pig.

My mother gave me a look, and it wasn't a good one. It was half grimace, half disappointment. She knew something was going on, but if I gave her a thousand guesses, no way in hell would she ever get it. I was never going to tell her or anyone else because I didn't have the faintest idea how to accessorize a straitjacket. I barely believed it myself. How could I explain it to anyone else?

Then there was the *why* and the *how*. Nothing made sense right now.

"Look, sweetie, I'm sure the police are going to find him." *Liar, liar, pants on fire.* "He's probably just found a new..." There was no real delicate way to say it. "A new *friend.*" I couldn't be more delicate than that. Or more honest.

She sniffed and stepped out of my arms, back into line beside her fiancé and my mother. "I know. I know that you're probably right, but I'm still freaked out and worried."

"Listen, I'm going to shower the police station off of me." Probably, I should've softened the statement with a joke. No one moved, but four mouths dropped open. "They brought me in for questioning to see if I knew where Jean-Luc might've gone off to." I chuckled, and the babbling commenced. "You know. They had questions. They thought I might've had answers." The shrugging was out of my control. "I didn't, of course, have answers." I rolled my eyes and shrugged again. "You all know Jean-Luc and he's kind of..." I wagged my finger beside my ear. "Crazy. Impetuous, really."

"Mom?" Lor's brow pinched. She looked almost as uncomfortable as I felt.

At last my babbling ceased. "I'm—thank you for stopping me." I looked down. "Mom. I'm so glad you made it."

She nodded. "Yes." After a second, she tilted her head. "Police station?"

Possibly a bad memory or two had been replayed. In my younger days, after the first couple times Jean-Luc had cheated on me, I'd gone a little wild with alcohol and more than once disturbed the peace outside of whatever hotel I'd thought he was in. Thankfully, I'd grown out of it quickly.

I shrugged. "Okay. Shower, then I'll meet you all downstairs for lunch."

"It's dinnertime." Now we were back to a disapproving grimace. I'd never realized how much my daughter mimicked my mother. Even though she bore a stringent resemblance to Jean-Luc, she had my mother's expressions down pat.

"Fine, dinner, then."

My mother, the one and only Penelope Danes, put her hand on my arm. "I could stay with you."

"No." I said it too fast and had to soften it. "Mom, no. Go enjoy the kids. I'll be along as soon as I can." I looked at her. She was almost eighty years old and still spry. On any other occasion, I would be relieved to see her, mostly happy for the diversion. If only I didn't have Porky in the room waiting for me.

"I'm going to clean up. I'll be down to the lobby as soon as I can." Provided I could figure out a plan to keep Jean-Luc LaPork hidden in my room. As far as pigs went, he wasn't so easy to hide.

I walked back into my room when I heard the elevator doors open and close again. Jean-Luc was in the middle of the bed, on his back, legs in the air. I didn't know what he was trying to say, but I wasn't amused.

I looked around. My bag with my passport, house keys and favorite perfume, lotion, and hairpins was missing. At least, I couldn't see it anywhere.

For giggles, I wished I knew where it was. Then it came to me to look under the bed. I knelt on the floor, lifted the bed skirt for a quick peek. I expected to bear no fruit, but there it was. Beside it was the intricate box with my necklace inside.

After grabbing the box, I slid the bag out and sat back on my heels. Okay. Not so bad. I wished. I looked. I found. Not like it had slid out from under the bed on its own. Weird, though. Just not super weird.

Not like my ex being a pig weird, at least.

But... what if? My thoughts started churning as I put the necklace safely in the top drawer of the dresser. I had made a few wishes over the last few days that had come true, now that I thought about it, starting with all the wedding stuff falling into place, and then my sexy pirate. Hadn't I also made a wish about my pig ex?

Okay, I was officially losing my mind, because there was no way my wishes were coming true. And yet, I'd kind of already accepted that my ex was a *literal* pig, hadn't I? So, farting wishes wasn't out of the question.

Still, I should probably test this new theory rather than just confirming it because I'd quickly found my bag under my bed. I had to make a super weird wish or I wouldn't feel right about anything else. Ever.

In that vein, like a fool, I wished the room would clean itself.

Then, because I almost didn't want to see the magic happen, I closed my eyes for a second, waiting to pop one open because I didn't hear anything happening. Except, I did hear stuff happening. Opening my eyes, I could only stare, open-mouthed. The mattress shifted onto the foundation, my clothes floated through the air, folding themselves as they did, and placed themselves ever so neatly into the suitcase that was now sitting, not at all askew, on the little bench at the end of the bed. The drawers closed, and the hangers took their place on the closet rod. Porky had, at some point, moved to the foot of the bed, and he was happily lying on cushy bedspread.

I was wrong about the last time being a holy shit moment. *This* was the holy shit moment. The holy shittiest of all the holy shit moments.

"Holy shit," I whispered.

Indeed.

Chapter Thirteen

This Little Piggy Went to Market

JEAN-LUC WAS A PIG. Not in the metaphorical or metaphysical sense. For a half of a hugely maniacal second, I smiled. Once upon a time, he'd told me he wanted to be a pastry chef. He'd gone from baker to bacon. I sobered. I couldn't be *sure* it was him, I hadn't seen him change from human to pig but even so, I felt like I was pretty dang positive.

So what had changed in my life that might lead to magical wishes coming true?

The answer came easily: it *had to be* the necklace. It was the only magical thing in my life right now, and things had started changing for me around the time I found it. Not just around the time. The moment I arrived back at the hotel, my luck had changed.

Oh, and there was also its interesting background full of pirates, storms, and murder. *Sweet sweating summertime.* It was a magical necklace.

This was as crazy as life got. If ever I wrote my memoirs, this would be the chapter that sold it. Again, I laughed because a title came to mind. *This little piggy went to market.* None of the girls in my coffee club were going to believe this. Hells bells, I didn't believe it and I was living it.

I didn't know if it was true, though. Okay. Okay, maybe it wasn't. Honestly. I stared at myself in the bathroom mirror and splashed a little cold water on my face. How could it be true?

The stone.

But that was ridiculous.

Like the baker, the florist, Jolene, at lunch. The freaking hotel room cleaning itself!

Those were coincidences. I'd wished someone would call. They had. I'd wished Jolene would shut up. God, that had been a great lunch. The hotel room I couldn't explain, except maybe I'd hallucinated it because of the unusual amount of alcohol I'd consumed since arriving at the island. I never drank that much, and never drank hard liquor. I'd had more than my fair share of tequila this week.

I had to try one last time. *I wish Jean-Luc wasn't a pig.* And I waited, rocking back and forth on my heels.

Maybe I had to ask specifically.

"I wish Jean-Luc was not the pig that is currently trying to eat my bra."

Certainly, that was specific enough. But again, nothing happened. And my frown came from deep in my soul. Why in piggy hell wasn't this working?

I certainly wasn't going to find the answer in this hotel room. I only knew of one place where I had even the slimmest chance of figuring it out.

In lieu of a leash, I wrapped a scarf around the pig, then opened the door and peeked out. The last thing I needed was the psycho Robin Hood to come in hot with his crossbow locked and loaded. I had to get back to the market and find someone to tell me how to turn my ex-husband back into a man.

Since it wasn't like I could take Wilbur into the elevator and out the front door, I walked him down the hallway to the stairs. Trying to take a pig down three flights of stairs, when it didn't want to go, exercised muscles I didn't even know I had. Not unlike trying to pull a truck out of mud with raw body strength. It took me twenty minutes to get the pig down the steps and out of the hotel's back door, a far cry from the mere minutes it had taken to get him up to my room.

As we walked, my gaze darted back and forth to the shadows and the sunlight. We gave the hotel a wide berth so as not to be seen from the open lobby and walls of windows. Then, as soon as we were clear, I ran, dragging Jean-Luc behind me. It was a slow trip. He was a lot faster when he was being chased by the rabid desk clerk, but we finally made it to the boardwalk. I was sweating like… Well, suffice it to say, I was sweating. We'll leave it at that.

I looked in all the tents because I couldn't remember specifically where hers had been or what it looked like. She wasn't there. Not anywhere. The woman I'd bought the box from was nowhere to be seen. I checked again, then asked one of the women in the other tents.

"Have you seen the woman with the braid who sells trinket boxes?"

She cocked a brow.

"She said they were from Captain Renegade's treasure."

She looked at me like I had three heads. "It's against our laws as well as the sea god's to sell Captain Reny's treasures."

Against the law? And a sea god? "Okay, I must be mistaken. Thank you."

That didn't stop me from going into another tent. The man inside looked at me, stared for a second. I supposed it wasn't every day a woman and her silk scarf wearing pig walked into his pop-up store. "Do you know a woman with a long braid who had a tent somewhere over here? She sells trinket boxes with jewels inside."

This guy was old, and he looked like he aged ten years as we stood there. "I don't know who you're talking about."

Oh-ho. Yes, he did. He was a horrible liar.

"Shoo, now." He waved his hands at me, and I moved outside his tent. The man exited behind me and closed the flaps. Moving on, I asked in several of the other tents if anyone had seen her. If they had, no one was willing to say so.

I walked into the last tent, repeated my story and the woman looked at me. "Did you buy a box?"

"Yes, yes, I did." It wasn't quite an admission of anything magical, but I had hope.

"Was there a golden jewel inside?"

I nodded vigorously, Jean-Luc snorted and nudged me with his snout. "Yes."

"I don't know anything about any golden stone that belonged to Captain Renegade." Her eyes darkened and she turned away from me. I wasn't stupid, and I hadn't been drinking. "Or any other color stone." It was funny that she'd mentioned the golden color specifically.

Which, of course, meant she knew quite a lot about all the stones.

She moved around her table like she was going to leave, but I moved between her and the flap, and my porcine pal did his part to get in her way, too. We danced side to side in our respective positions, and then she looked up at me. "You have to go."

I shook my head. "I need to know about the stones." I only knew about one, but she'd mentioned others.

With a sigh, her shoulders dropped and she glared at me. "If I tell you, will you go away?"

I nodded with one eyebrow up.

"The stones are imbued with power. Citrine is for wishes. Blue is for special sight, and black is to pause time." A wishing stone, a special *sight* stone? There's no amount money I wouldn't give to own the one that stopped time. Although I had to wonder how it worked. How could it possibly work?

I wouldn't have bought into such cockamamie bull stuff, except for the fact that I'd seen the aforementioned *citrine* stone in action.

"Where are the others?" Maybe it would be worth my time to find them, if I had such time. Which, after the wedding, I would have in abundance.

She sighed as if I was the one taxing her nerves. "They were all lost at sea. But they would be very valuable to those who hold the power of the three."

It was more than I could wrap my brain around. I needed a minute. Or a month. I needed to figure out if I believed it. But of course I believed it. I'd used the wishing stone to turn my husband into a pig. *Ex-husband.* My brain was going in circles.

The power of one was probably sufficient, but if my overwhelmed brain was following what the woman was telling me, the power of three could end the world. Or rule it. And who didn't want to rule the world? Maybe that was me being dramatic. I didn't know any more.

What was more, I didn't actually *want* to rule the world, even if I could. It was too much pressure. This one stone was more than enough pressure. Strangely though, I also didn't want anyone else to rule the whole world. If it was even possible.

Why would I think it wasn't? I'd seen my room clean itself. I'd stopped doubting that Jean-Luc was the pig currently oinking his way through the tent, sniffing and nibbling as he went.

"Have the other stones been found?" Not like I was going to let go of mine, or go looking for the others myself, but when I looked up, she was gone. Out of the tent like a flash of bejeweled pink pashmina and mauve hair accouterments.

If what she'd said was true, I'd used the stone to turn Jean-Luc into a pig. I should've been able to use it to turn him back.

I wish Jean-Luc was back to his normal self. I looked down at my portly porker and waited a second. Jean-Luc probably hadn't turned into a pig in a split second. It had probably taken at least overnight. Just to be sure, I reached for the stone. Maybe I had to be holding or touching it.

But when I reached for my throat, all I got was a handful of skin. It was gone. The necklace wasn't there.

Chapter Fourteen

Help! My Magical Stone is Missing!

WHEN I WAS YOUNG, I'd always thought of myself as the character in a book or a play. All the people I knew were the cast. I'd always imagined that the story of my life was being written as I lived it. I just never knew if I was the one making the decisions and the writer was documenting them or if the decisions were being made by the writer, and I was just the subject. If it was the latter, the writer was toying with me. And they were mean.

I felt again for the chain, hoping I'd just not felt it for a moment, that it had blended into my skin. But it wasn't there.

It was okay. I knew where it was. Not the time to panic. I'd taken it off earlier and put it in the dresser, but then the room had cleaned itself. I hadn't been physically touching when I'd wished for that. I hadn't even been looking at the necklace. Did that mean I didn't need to be wearing it for it to work? Just being near it would make wishes come true? I wasn't sure. I wasn't sure of anything at this point.

I rushed back to the hotel, or to be accurate, rushed as much as I could while I was half-dragging the pig behind me. He wasn't a pig of the small, *carry-in-a-tiny-purse* variety and by no means could he possibly have been the the runt of his litter. Or whatever a birthing of multiple pigs was called. This guy was huge, probably enough to feed an entire town, if one was so inclined. He'd make a lot of hot dogs, in any case. All that meant hiding him was easier said than done. I was merely fortunate that the lobby was mostly deserted, thanks to the crossbow-toting hotel manager and I could walk through mostly freely. Still, I kept a watchful eye pointed in each direction.

Not really, but I darted my gaze around. A lot.

I was close. *So close* to being clear of the lobby when I ran smack into my mother and daughter. And by *ran into*, I mean I had to duck behind a fake palm tree because they were coming straight toward me. They passed, and I waited a few seconds before I dared look up.

I thought I'd done it. I was a mere feet from the elevator, so close to safety, but then, like it was the battle cry of disappointed mothers everywhere, I heard, "Camille." The only person who ever called me that was the person who chose the name.

She peeked through a palm frond with a cocked eyebrow and a thin line in place of her lips. “Camille, what in heaven’s name are you doing?”

Obviously, I couldn’t tell her the truth. *Gee, Ma, I found a magic necklace that’s part of a pirate’s booty and used it to turn JL*—in my head, I sometimes called him JL—*into a pig, and now I need to run.* I didn’t think that was going to fly with my mom. I also didn’t think it was wise to let go of the leash.

Instead, I leaned in, waved her closer, and lowered my voice to a whisper. “I’m trying to save this pig from being shot by the manager.” No telling where that shifty little weasel was hiding, and I couldn’t risk it.

“Why on earth would the manager be trying to shoot a pig?” Wasn’t that the question of the day?

Which made the answer, “Because he’s in the hotel.”

“Why did you bring him into the hotel?” It was a vicious circle of unanswerable questions. Not that they were questions without answers. I just couldn’t provide said answers without, again, being a fresh candidate for the crazy house. Not that I needed yet another piece of evidence that I was losing it.

Fortunately, my mother had a soft heart when it came to animals and stupid ex-husbands. No matter what I did, or what he'd done, she loved Jean-Luc.

My skin heated as I stepped out from beyond the cover of my fake palm tree, looked at Lor and Noah and then at Ma. I just needed to get this little piggy up to the room, put on the necklace, and change him back.

I was amenable. I wholeheartedly believed the necklace was the key to returning Jean-Luc to normal. As much I thought his being a pig was divine retribution for the bevy of babes he'd bedded during the course of our marriage and after, I didn't think he was going to be able to walk Lor down the aisle this way. She didn't deserve to suffer because her father was... well, a pig. Literally and figuratively.

I was only partially hidden behind the palm tree. Suddenly my super-sized ex-husband started snorting like he had a hairball. He pawed the end of the scarf like he'd only just discovered his hooves could have another function. He was trying to break free, so even half-hidden was a stretch.

This was the moment Remy chose to walk past. I would've waved or said something that would have drawn all the attention I'd so far been able to avoid, but his head was down. I had a sliver of luck right now. Remy was speed-walking to the exit.

The jacket he wore was a bit worn out, but who was I to judge? I was currently wearing a fake palm tree.

Then, like the drill sergeant she was, Ma looked around then snapped her fingers at the portly pig, and somehow, some way, he stopped struggling. She moved to stand beside my daughter and future-son-in-law. Then as a group, like a little portable wall, they side-stepped shoulder to shoulder, hiding me and Jean-Luc as we made our way to the elevator.

Once we were inside, the cameras would see us, but there wasn't anything I could do about that. I had to hope that no one was monitoring them at this particular moment. If they were, I'd have to explain, but I wasn't crossing that bridge yet. One crisis at a time.

When the doors opened, I walked down the hallway like it was absolutely normal to take a large pot-bellied pig into a hotel room.My mother walked in beside me, but I couldn't worry about her judging me right now. To be honest, this wasn't the time to worry about anything other than putting on the necklace and wishing Jean-Luc would come back.

I went to the dresser where I knew, beyond a shadow of a doubt, with a hundred percent certainty I'd put the necklace, opened the top drawer, and I could've swallowed my tongue. It was gone. No jewel, no chain, no glowing *citrine* stone. The box sat empty in the drawer.

I pulled out all the empty drawers, looked behind the dresser, underneath it. Under the bed, in the closet. This was DEFCON-1, the worst-case scenario. Jean-Luc was going to remain a pig and not be able to walk our daughter down the aisle. Not upright or without a leash, anyway. And the tuxedo would look absolutely ridiculous. Lor would be devastated. Our grandkids wouldn't learn French swear words. I would end up telling the folks in my nursing home a crazy story and they would put me on psych meds for… Okay, no. I calmed myself, took a breath, and tried to will my heart not to explode. We were in dangerous territory. I looked down at the pig. *Oh, Jean-Luc.*

I'd never been sorrier. More ridiculously sorry.

No, no. I looked over my shoulder at my mom as all of my systems were shutting down. I couldn't breathe. This was what dying felt like. Had to be. If not, my heart had certainly stopped beating, so I would be dying shortly. Or hyperventilating. And I needed to pee, not that peeing was relative, just coincidental to the timing.

Dying or not, only one fact mattered at the moment. The necklace was gone.

Chapter Fifteen

Everybody's a Suspect

I COULDN'T BELIEVE THIS. It was gone and Jean-Luc was still a pig. The sum total of my day, of my most recent days, was un-freaking-believable. No one I ever told this story to was ever going to say, *I believe you.* I was living it, and I couldn't wrap my head around it.

I looked at the night table next to the bed where the box sat, taunting me. The damned thing didn't look so remarkable now. The carved top wasn't as lovely as I remembered it from only this morning. On the off chance that there was enough residual magic in the box, I walked to the table, picked it up, and wished for Jean-Luc to appear.

Nothing happened.

I stomped my feet and pounded my fists against my legs. The pig stayed a pig, despite my tantrum.

Ma looked at Lor and Noah. She breathed in deeply and her nostrils flared, so I assumed I was in trouble. It was usually what it meant, anyway. “Go to the buffet dining room and fill some plates and bring them in here for the pig.”

Of all times for Mom to haul out the take charge attitude, I was beyond grateful for this one. I appreciated her attention to detail. Of course the pig was hungry. He was a pig.

I needed to find the damned necklace.

Again, I checked all the drawers, my suitcase, and the closet. Then I looked under the bed. In the bathroom. I even opened the toilet lid. It wasn’t anywhere. I called down to the desk. Demanded to know if anyone had been in my room. I always left the do-not-disturb sign on the door, but I’d also been at hotels where the signs weren’t always observed by housekeeping if no one was in the room. I hadn’t run out of fresh towels since I arrived.

“Hello, Ms. Danes-LaCroix. How can I help you?” Arthur. I could tell it was him by the nasal disapproval in his voice.

I took a slow, deep breath. “I’ve had the do not disturb sign on my door, but I need to be sure that no housekeeping person or anyone else entered my room today.”

The snotty desk clerk wasn’t likely to change his attitude thanks to the accusation I was leveling. “I can assure you, Ms.

Danes-LaCroix, no one violated our policy by disrespecting your wishes."

I couldn't let this go. Jean-Luc's life depended on it. "Well, then, I need to report a robbery. Someone has been in my room."

"Yes, madam. The police searched your room."

"My necklace is gone. It was there after they left, but now its not. It's very valuable, and it's missing. I know I saw it after the police searched my room. I took it off this morning and now it's gone!" I was getting frantic.

"Ms. Danes-LaCroix, we have cameras outside in the hallway. It might show your door."

Convenient. While it might show anyone who walked in my door, it would also show me leading a pig, a *wanted* pig, into my room on the no pet floor of the no pet hotel. It was a chance I'd have to take because I needed this damned stone back, and I needed it back as soon as possible.

"I'll be right down."

My mother looked at me, then at the pig. "Go. I'll stay here with him." I didn't give Mom enough credit, it was clear that I was going to have to make this up to her. Tequila wouldn't work for her. I'd come up with something.

I nodded and gave her a quick hug, then dashed out. I had to find the necklace. Whoever stole it was getting a very special wish when I got it back. I went straight to the counter and there he was. Arthur nodded then waved me around the counter, then to the office behind. He looked around like he was expecting someone to come and stop us, but no one did and we walked in. "Please, have a seat."

I sat and waited for him to boot up the security computer. He called up the camera for the floor three hallway A. I knew that because the video was marked. I also knew that there were three hallways.

I was in room 302, which was in hallway A. There was no video. He rewound until he found the moment a hand reached with a can of paint and spray painted the lens.

"Shit." I hadn't meant to speak out loud. This was bad news. Someone had done this on purpose. "Were any other rooms entered?" We couldn't tell from the video, but maybe someone called down from the desk.

He shook his head. "Not that I know of. And I've been working all day. Surely someone would have reported beside you."

"What about the elevator? Wouldn't there be footage from inside? We could match the times and maybe determine who did it. If they were in the elevator a few seconds before the spray paint?" I pointed at the screen, hope burning in my heart, then I looked at him, and the light inside of me died.

He was sheepish. "Regrettably, those cameras haven't functioned since the hotel opened." He paused and stared down at the hand on the computer mouse. "I realize that to you, it must seem like quite the oversight. Regrettably, there have been a great many things to care for since I took over from the original manager."

"Of course." If I was a nail-biter, I would probably have no nails left. That was neither here nor there, but the lapse was robbing me of a detail I wanted and needed. Someone's life depended on it. Arthur's excuse and the fact that the cameras didn't work despite the validity of said excuse didn't solve my problem.

"What was taken from your room?" He pulled out a piece of paper and a pen. At least it appeared he was going to take this seriously.

"A jeweled necklace that was in the bureau drawer. Nothing else." He wrote, and I stared over his shoulder, reading. He had terrible penmanship. "It's citrine." In case it mattered or I needed to identify it later, I wanted the color documented. Plus, I liked the fact that I knew it was citrine.

"In thirty-eight years, there's never been a robbery at the Caribbean Knights Hotel and Resort." Great. He probably thought it would make me feel better, safer. It did not. Absolutely it did not.

"So this is strange, right?" It made sense in my head.

He nodded. "Quite odd." With a click of his jaw, he clammed up like words were his second language. He'd given me all the help I could've hoped to get from the hotel and if nothing else said it, the abrupt end of our conversation signaled that it was time for me to go. That was fine with me.

He stood and pushed his chair back extra hard, so it hit the wall behind him. Actually, probably not that hard since the room was the size of a small closet, but the sound was so loud I startled. His smirk said he'd noticed.

Dejected, I trudged back to my room. I had to go back there and tell my mother I was no closer to finding my necklace and getting the pig out of my room and back to his normal self, and this wasn't a conversation middle, or high school, or even college, had prepared me for, and no amount of therapy would ever let me forget.

I had no firm proof that anyone had been in my room except for the fact that my necklace was missing, so everyone was a suspect.

Chapter Sixteen

Even the Man of My X-Rated Dreams

I COULDN'T GET out of the formal, four-star restaurant on the mainland dinner with Lor and Noah because Jolene and her family were going to be there. With Jean-Luc gone, Loralei needed some family on her side of the table. Even distracted, I was better than nothing.

Loralei apologized for Jean-Luc's absence. Noah's mother smirked and my mother glared, but other than that, everything was going along fine until my mother spoke directly to Randy, Jolene's husband, and the boy I'd dated in high school. We'd gotten along fine until he'd gotten a load of Jolene. After he met her, he dumped me on my "pancake shaped" ass. Yes, he'd used the words "pancake shaped" to describe my ass.

That was years ago. So many. I got over it when I met Jean-Luc. The heartache that had been Randy had only lasted about a minute for me. The jealousy for Jolene had lasted over two decades.

My mother continued her quiet chat with Randy while Jolene huffed and puffed, her face turning almost the same color as the merlot in her glass. Mom continued chatting quietly with Randy.

I knew my mother. She'd hated Randy when we were kids. He was snotty, arrogant, *gorgeous*, and had a motorcycle. He was all the things a mother wanted to keep as far away from her teenage daughter as she could. High school hotties, though, were nothing compared to athletic, blond, French boys. She was doing this purposely to get under Jolene's skin. And by the looks of it, it was working.

Man, sometimes I really loved my mom.

My mother and Randy laughed, Jolene fumed. Loralei and Noah only had eyes for one another and the other guests were interspersed at tables around us. It was honestly going better than I'd hoped, and when we made it to the dessert portion of the meal with no issues, I took it as a sign that I could escape. As gently as possible, I excused myself, kissed my daughter, and snagged some leftovers for the pig before I hopped on a boat back to the island to go back to my room.

When I walked in, Jean-Luc snorted until I handed him my leftovers wrapped in a foil swan, after unwrapping them, of course. He ate most of the food in one bite while I sat beside him on the floor. When he was finished, he plopped down on the mat of blankets Mom had "borrowed" from an unattended maid's cart.

I ran my hand over his fur, patted his belly. I could've sworn he winked at me. "I'm so sorry about this, Jean-Luc."

He snorted twice and scooted his body around to lay his head on my lap. Same old Jean-Luc. I turned on a streaming service and leaned back against the bed until my mother came in. She, too, had a foil swan and Porky-Luc switched allegiances, which was fine with me.

Leaving my mom to babysit the oinker, I showered, then crawled into bed.

Sometime after Mom crawled into bed beside me, it started. The portly pig began rooting with his snout along the carpet, snorting at every quarter hour, as if he was aware of and was watching the clock. No matter how we begged, or threatened, or cried, he wouldn't stop the noise or the rooting.

In total, I managed barely an hour of sleep, but that hour had been full of vivid images of Remy, in and out of his pirate garb. I was in the middle of stripping him out of the pirate garb in a lovely ten second dream when it occurred to me that there was a reason I wasn't actively seeking him out. My subconscious was called on. It answered. Reacted. Produced a memory I didn't want. It wasn't a naked memory. It was a verbal thing. While I liked Remy's voice, I didn't like that the memory came during my single hour of sleep.

It was one I couldn't avoid. Remy, the man of my dreams, had commented on the necklace. It wasn't like he'd commented solely on it. He'd seen it and remarked that he was a descendant of Captain Remington, the renegade, himself. Probably innocent. But my-middle-of-the-night, sleep-deprived brain continued depriving me because it replayed the comment over and over again.

I'd seen him making a beeline out of the hotel. With my own two eyes, I'd witnessed it.

Didn't it just figure? The first gorgeous man I'd met since Jean-Luc, the first man who'd looked at me like I was desirable and seductive, might also be a thief. Honestly, all I really knew about him was that he was an actor. A starving artist, maybe. Being an actor certainly didn't speak to fabulous wealth or riches. It wasn't like he was Brad Pitt slumming it on a Caribbean island at a resort's tiny theater. I didn't know the value of the stone in the necklace, but it was a good size, probably worth something. If the price was based on weight, it would be worth a lot, and then take in the ability to grant the owner all their wildest dreams... The darn thing was priceless.

A man like Remy, who lived on a resort island and had a job as an actor in a theater production that had been written by no one, acclaimed by no one, might have appreciated the value of the stone. Maybe he needed the money it could bring.

Then again, it could've been Arthur. He certainly wasn't breaking the island's bank with his robust paychecks. Somehow I doubted it was him.

There were suspects a-plenty, and as I lay there waiting for the next quarter hour snort from Jean-Wilbur, Jolene and Randy popped into my head. Mom told me last night that the rumor was that Jolene and Randy were experiencing financial difficulties. The rumor made sense, considering Jean-Luc had purchased their plane tickets and was financing their accommodations on the island.

Then there were the police who'd come into my room and searched. Maybe one had decided to return a second time, found me gone, and then went in any way. I hadn't asked the weaselly little Arthur if he or any one of his staff had seen any cops lingering.

This mystery needed to be solved, and fast. I had wedding responsibilities today that required an entire functioning of my psyche. I had breakfast with Loralei, Noah, and the arriving guests in about an hour. There was nothing left to do but shower, get ready, and get to it. So I did, and then I immediately started the day.

I dutifully greeted them all, then nibbled a slice of avocado toast as one of the bridesmaids dominated the conversation with the harrowing tale of her boat trip to the island. "The boat trip was treacherous. We had a captain named Skip. What kind of captain is named Skip?" Oh, she wasn't nearly finished. "He had an eye patch like he was a pirate. An actual pirate." She was so excited, like I could blame her. In my experience, pirates, fake or not, were incredible... except when they were filthy thieves. Again, I didn't have a spare moment to think about him. Well, beyond that minute, anyway. No more minutes thinking of Remy.

After breakfast, we had a dress fitting with Lor so that her bridesmaids and my mother—and me, although I wasn't allowed to act as if it was the first time I saw it—could see the finished product Dionne had created in the two days since she arrived.

The weight of these tasks, to my daughter, wasn't small. Loralei's happiness for the rest of her days would be measured by how these moments played out. Whether or not everyone oohed and ahhed. Whether my mother and I teared up. Whether or not the girls fawned. These were the events that she was going to remember for the rest of her life, cherish even.

Even knowing that, I had to find the necklace. I had to turn her father back into her father before Lor found out.

I waited until the dress was zipped into its bag and the girls were off for spa treatments before I marched off to do the rest of my tasks. Unfortunately, it was nearly evening by the time I was finally finished with enough of my list to be able to run back to my room to take my pig for a walk.

Man, I hoped pig Jean-Luc knew how to use a toilet...

We walked along the beach, and this time, he didn't pull or fight the scarf. He just strolled beside me. As we were walking, I talked to him. We'd been friends once. "You know, I'm happy for you and Britney." Happy-*ish*, so it wasn't a total lie. It was an embellishment, but as soon as Jean-Luc was a bi-ped again, he would thank me for my effort. "You kind of have to appreciate the irony of this situation." Irony was a nice word for my wishing he would turn into a pig.

"I mean, I can't count the number of times I've called you a pig over the years." It had been one of my favorite words throughout the divorce when we'd been fighting over the house and he'd brought his women—one day he'd come in with one on each arm—to our divorce negotiations.

"You hurt me, Jean." I pronounced it John even though he liked when I drew the J out. "So much. And even though my heart was broken, I was so sad to lose you." These were the things I'd never said to him because I couldn't stand the idea of him looking at me with those big blue eyes. He was sensitive, and cried easily. He also fell in love like it was a sport.

"I blamed you for all the nights Lor went to bed sad because you didn't call after your games. She watched them all, and just wanted you to call so she could say how proud she was that you were her dad." Those had been some tough nights.

"Since you retired, though, you've been great. Stellar, actually." I could sugar-coat it any way I wanted, but we both remembered. "I've been able to forgive you, and I'm starting to move on. I'm sorry I turned you into a pig." That was the worst part. The worst thing I'd ever done.

When we got to the edge of the beach where it met the rocks that extended upward into cliffs, he flopped down in the sand, and I sat beside him. Once, when Loralei was young, when Jean-Luc and I were still trying to work things out, we'd sat on this beach together, stared out at the sunset, and watched the waves roll in. This wasn't quite the same thing.

When the sun sank and the moon rose, we stood, and I dusted the sand off of both of us, then headed back to the hotel. Before we were within sight of the building, an arrow whistled past and ricocheted off the rocks behind me.

I knew exactly what the hell was going on, and I was pretty sure I knew *why* it was happening. I climbed out from behind the rocks, hands in the air, and left the pig hidden. "Whoa, whoa, whoa! I'm a resort guest! Stop!"

Pepe le porker was making a horrible, keening sound and when I looked down, blood seeped from the porky bacon portion of his rump. "Get over here." I looked at Arthur. He hadn't moved. "You shot at a guest. That is some seriously bad press."

"I shot at the *pig*. I didn't see you. Your black shirt camouflaged you in the rocks." His voice wasn't so arrogant now, or cocky.

"Well, you got him. Happy?" I was not. "Now you're going to have to help me get him back to the hotel." When he opened his mouth to object, I held up my hand. "You shot at a resort guest." That was going to be my ace in the hole for the rest of my stay. "You could have killed me. So, you're not going to argue, you're just going to help me save this damned pig!"

I made him do most of the work carrying my little piggy because, while Jean-Luc was lithe and athletic when he was upright, as his pork counterpart, he was compact and weighty. Awkward to carry. Plus, there was a hole that was seeping, so there was a certain amount of ick factor to consider.

I'd turned him into a pig, then let him get shot. This was not a day I wanted to commemorate with a memory, but I doubted it was one I would ever forget.

"I need this job." He said the words quietly as he huffed beneath Jean-Luc's hefty body.

"I know." Why would he stay at a place he so hated otherwise?

"I wouldn't have shot if I'd seen you." He glanced at me as he navigated around a rock in the sand. He was trying. That had to mean something. "I'm sorry."

I nodded. "Just help me save him."

The man lifted a brow and glanced at me like I'd lost my mind.

"He's docile. Probably someone's pet. I'm an animal lover."

He sighed and lowered Jean-Luc to the ground. “I can’t carry him more. I promise. I’ll be right back”

Before I could argue, he took off toward the hotel, and I checked my watch. He had ten minutes before I stormed the beach—the hotel, actually, but I was feeling a bit dramatic. I was going to hold him to his promise, because no way was I telling Lor I’d not only turned her father into a pig, but I’d also gotten him shot. Those were the kinds of things good mothers didn’t say. I might not have been a world wonder, but I was a good mother, and since I didn’t have a whole lot of other things going for me at the moment, nothing was going to tarnish that image.

Chapter Seventeen

To Believe or Not to Believe? That is the Question

A few minutes later, Arthur raced out of the hotel pushing a luggage cart along the path at a semi-dangerous speed. One stray rock or broken piece of path and he was going head over cart, or maybe he would just land on it. It was one of those dome-style gold ones that they used when a guest came with more than a couple of bags.

Somehow, we had to get Jean-Luc from this spot on the sand to where the cart was.

The path was a long way and Jean-Luc was heavy. My back was killing me. I looked at Arthur. "We could drag him?"

"He'll get sand in his wound." I didn't want to remind him how my pig had been wounded to begin with. I tried to look at this from a logistical point of view. "Can we move the cart through the sand?"

"Maybe empty, but not with Babe laying on it."

"A pig reference? You haven't earned that right."

He looked slightly chagrined. "I got the cart."

I shrugged. It didn't matter to me.

"We could bandage him first."

I didn't know what that would accomplish, nor did I think we had that kind of time. My little pig was losing blood. Finally, Arthur looked at me like he wished he'd shot a pig belonging to a sturdier woman if he was going to have to carry it thirty yards to the cart on the broken path. And he was going to have to do it quickly.

When there was nothing left to argue about, I took two of Jean-Luc's legs and he took the other two. That woke him up and he began to squeal. With some struggles and miss-steps we finally loaded poor hollering Jean-Luc onto the cart and wheeled him back to the hotel.

His wailing and keening turned to a shorter, quieter whine. Before we dared go inside, Arthur went in and got a blanket, draped it over Jean-Luc, and then rolled him in the front door and through to the kitchen.

I stopped him before he made it to the prep table. Jean-Luc wasn't tomorrow's breakfast and if he reached for a knife, so help me, we were out of there.

Instead, he pulled a cell phone from his pocket and dialed. "Not really the time for a personal call, Wyatt Earp," I said, eyeing him.

He rolled his eyes at me in a show of attitude I didn't appreciate, but then he spoke. "Dr. Willowby, it's Arthur from the hotel. We've had an incident." He listened for a second. "An arrow." Then he listened some more. "Accident, but we need your help." He nodded like the person, doctor, on the other end of the phone could see him. I wasn't one to judge since I was holding a pig's hoof. I waited until he hung up and nodded at me before I breathed.

"Thank you, Arthur."

He nodded. "I'm sorry I shot him." He looked down at his hands. He had some of Jean-Luc's blood on them and he wiped them on a towel. "Dr. Willowby is a human doctor, but he'll know what to do."

I nodded, and he went to the back door. Thankfully, the kitchen was closed tonight since they were still hunting for my little piggy. We were alone. No explanations needed.

I checked the time seven or eight times before Willowby arrived twenty minutes later. He had Einstein's hair, a doctor's bag, and a white coat. That was official enough for me.

"Where's the patient?"

Arthur pointed to the table where I was now holding a towel over Jean-Luc's wound.

The doctor wasn't as shocked as I expected. "That's a pig."

This wasn't his usual patient, but he wasn't running screaming away. It was a little comforting, but I was worried. Jean-Luc was asleep now, breathing much slower. "Can you save him?"

"You want me to work on a pig?"

It wasn't like I could tell him who the pig was or why it was so important, so I only nodded. Pleaded with my eyes, first to an unimpressed doctor, then to Arthur. "Please?"

He glanced from the doctor to me and back again. "Look Doc, this isn't just any pig. This is a show pig, and she's his... owner. And I'm the one who shot him. Accidentally."

"Art..." Willowby sighed in concession, checked the wound and gave me a wink, which was neither a yes or a no, and didn't do much to make me feel better. "The arrow went in and came out. Without an x-ray I won't be able to see if it damaged anything."

"Is he going to die?" The strain in my voice made it softer. I couldn't help it. Everything was spinning out of my control.

"No, no. He's going to be fine."

Before he could do much more than lay his hand on the fleshy pink skin, Jean-Luc squealed, jumped off the rolling cart and ran out of the kitchen.

Willowby looked at me and shrugged. "My usual rate for a house call is five hundred an hour."

I cocked an eyebrow. Loralei wasn't the only one who'd learned a trick or two from my mother.

The doctor sighed. "For you, I'll lower it to three hundred." I stared harder at him, narrowed my eyes, and he corrected again to, "Two-fifty."

Arthur, apparently trying to broker peace in a room where there were more knives than people, smiled at me like he wasn't the reason this had all happened. "We can charge it to your room." A second later, a pointed stare in his direction, he sighed. "Or the hotel could pay for it."

I nodded. Now I had to find Jean-Luc, again, and the necklace, and whoever took it. I didn't really have time to argue about who was paying for what, exactly.

I turned to Arthur, because, heck, he owed me more than one. "Can you get any staff you trust to help find J– the pig?"

He sighed. "Of course, and I'll be searching too."

Darn right he would.

As I walked out of the kitchen and through the lobby, the sun had already set.

I stopped short. Remy was at the front desk. At this point, I had no other real suspects, and I felt foolish. I'd let him into my room. Showed him the necklace. I wanted the damned thing back, so I stomped over to him. A woman on a mission, one who had the audacity to think she could actually sniff out a thief. If he happened to be one, anyway.

Too bad the only thing I could actually sniff out was a divine cologne that smelled like bergamot and citrus with just a hint of lavender. I took in a big lungful and tried not to swoon. The effort was taxing.

"Where is my necklace?" I didn't bother with a greeting.

"Excuse me?" He turned and looked me up and down. Every inch of my skin burned in the wake of his gaze. His smile was slight. I was windblown with a smattering of pig blood on my shirt, and I possibly smelled either like the salty Caribbean air or like a pig. I was nose-blind to all of it now.

To his credit, he didn't wrinkle his nose, so I didn't step too far back.

He hadn't answered my question, so I repeated it. "Where is my necklace?"

This time, he didn't smile at all. "I came here looking for you, but I couldn't remember if you're in 302 or 304. They act like your room number is a state secret. I'll have to get an MI-6 designation to get it."

I didn't know what to think. He sounded adequately frustrated for having to deal with the staff at this place. But I couldn't trust anyone right now. "I saw you yesterday, leaving the hotel."

He shook his head and reached for my hand. I pulled it back so he had to drop his arm. "It wasn't me." When I crossed my arms, he reached for me again. This time, I took a full step backward. "I was on the mainland. You can ask anyone."

No. He was lying. I was certain it was him.

He laughed and there wasn't anything I could say because the sound was rich and deep, a sound that, since I'd first heard it had haunted my dreams, haunted meaning I woke up aching with need.

"Let's go get a drink and we can talk about it." How was a girl supposed to resist a guy like him? He was tall and dark, even the way he stood was yummy—feet apart, square with his shoulders, no slouch, no slack, eyes dark and lovely. I didn't *not* want to, but what if I was wrong about him? What if the feeling I'd been thinking was a gut feeling was nothing more than lust?

When I glanced behind us and saw staff members racing around the halls, I figured there was more than enough manpower looking for Jean-Luc. At least for the five minutes it'd take me to have this conversation, hopefully find my necklace, and make a wish to both heal Jean-Luc and turn him back into himself.

Therefore, I might want to get a drink with this man under any circumstances, but I wasn't doing it right now so I could swoon at his feet. I was doing it because I was the only one who knew about the necklace and what it could do. Getting it back should be my priority, and their priority should be finding Jean-Pork.

We sat in the lobby, and without even a moment to take a breath, Britney walked up, although walked probably wasn't the right word. *Stomped*. *Stalked*. She was mid-tantrum so *walking* didn't really describe her stride accurately.

She crossed her arms and stared at me.

Remy, too, looked at me. "Friend of yours?" Silly question, since no way could the look on her face be interpreted as friendly. A blind man could've seen the anger.

To him, I said, "Not so much." To her I said, "What do you want, Britney?"

"I want to know where my... where's Jean-Luc?" She was one sniff from a full tantrum.

I sure as all goodness couldn't tell her I'd accidentally turned him into a pig. "The police are working on it, and I'm certain they'll be in touch soon with good news."

She glared and pointed at me. "You know, he might have cheated on your old, saggy self, but he wouldn't do that to me."

I didn't remind her that one day she would be old and saggy too, or that once upon a time I'd been hot just like her. I had other fish to fry. "Okay."

"Bitch," she muttered, then stalked away. Remy didn't ask what all of that was about, and I didn't offer. Again, big fish and all that.

The encounter had put me off-kilter, defenseless, and so I looked at him, wished it wasn't so even though I knew in my heart it was. "Remy?"

He glanced at me. "Yes?"

I didn't want to ask, but at the same time it was the only question I needed answered. "Did you steal my necklace?" I blurted it in a big huff of breath. "I know it was you I saw in the lobby yesterday. Either that, or you have an identical twin, and you probably would've mentioned that." When I paused, he nodded. "It had to be you. No one else has been in my room."

He sighed. I'd hurt him and whatever anger he spewed I deserved, but I braced myself anyway. "Except the police and housekeeping and who knows who else?"

I felt almost ridiculous enough to not bring it up, but not so ridiculous that I didn't. "No one else is the direct descendant of the pirate who stole it from whatever witch or fairy or voodoo priestess—"

"What?"

"—imbued it with magic that would turn my husband— "I stopped because nothing good could come from finishing that sentence. Plus, if I was wrong about him, I sounded crazy enough without adding portly porcine. Remy's eyes flashed, and he glared.

He looked at me, and it was clear I'd made an error. In this minute, probably in several before it. Of course, it stood to reason that the first man who'd looked at me in the last three years was a thief. Why else would he be interested if not to get his family heirloom back? I wondered if he knew that the gem was imbued or injected or cursed. Whatever it was.

When he shook his head, the disappointment settled into the lines of his face, in his frown, in his narrowed eyes. "I have my own money, Cami." There wasn't any way to pull this moment back from the depths. "I don't need your trinket, and I'm sorry you think I would stoop so low."

He stood to walk out as Arthur stepped in. He hurried to my table, and then whispered, "The pig has been found. He's in your room, with your mother, and the doctor has been able to stitch him up. The doctor says he'll be fine."

Without thinking, I rose to my feet and hugged him. He was stiff for a second, then when I was about to pull away, he hugged me back.

We separated, and I smiled at him. “Thank you so much.”

Things were looking up. All I had to do now was find the necklace.

And then the police walked in.

Chapter Eighteen

Lost and Found

THE DETECTIVE from the mainland was back, and he was making a beeline right for me. "Ms. Danes-LaCroix?" When he said it, I suddenly realized the mouthful I was forcing on others. I didn't really care, but it was the first time I'd actually noticed. "I need you to come with me."

Oh, no. We were three days from Lor's wedding. I couldn't spend them in jail.

Three. Days.

"Am I going to be brought back to the island this evening?" The stutter was from fear. I couldn't help it.

He looked at me and smiled, then nodded. "To be frank, I think what I'm about to show you is going to put an end to all of this drama." I had a pig downstairs that probably would've begged to differ, but I relented anyway. It wasn't as if I had a choice.

I stood and walked beside him outside. "So, this visit is a good thing? I'm not going up the river?"

"Up the river?" he asked.

I had no idea where the reference came from. I only knew it was relative to jail. If I got out of this without heading up the river, I could search it online and decide if it was a statement I would use again if ever I turned my ex-husband into a pig or any farm animal again.

Right now, we were walking down to the dock. Their police boat sat at the edge, bobbing in the water. I'd taken more trips on and off this island in the last few days than I had anywhere else in ten years.

This wasn't my place with Jean-Luc and Lor anymore. This island would be Lor and Noah's place now. Where they vacationed on their anniversaries and brought their kids to snorkel and swim with turtles and dolphins and any number of wildlife creatures. Me? I probably wouldn't come back. The thought made me a little sad.

Before I could wallow, we'd reached the end of the dock and Detective Lawrence stepped into the boat, then reached to help me in. I didn't know where Rothel was. Lawrence seemed to be taking this task on his own. He walked to the front of the boat and started the engine with the little button. "Put on your life jacket and buckle up, please."

Hmm. Last time, they hadn't offered me a life jacket. Once I was buckled and belted, he hit the throttle and we raced across the water, under the moon now, and I lamented my losses. Jean-Luc. Remy. My wishing necklace. Somehow, those things all fit together, I just didn't know how.

He stopped the boat at the seaside dock of the police station, and this time, Lawrence climbed out and then helped me out and onto the small pier that led to their offices. Instead of pushing me into their tiny interrogation room, they showed me to a hallway with a door that was controlled from inside a small room enclosed by what I suspected was bulletproof glass. The man inside the booth smiled and nodded at the detectives and then a loud buzzer sounded and a piece of metal slid against another—a door lock unclasping. It was like every clichéd cop shop in the history of American television.

The hallway was long, with cinderblock walls on either side and a floor that was shined concrete with cracks in the paint. This was a hallway that saw a lot of use. Had been walked many a time. And damned if I had any idea what the hell I was doing here.

I was sandwiched between Lawrence and Rothel, who'd just come up behind me, and they weren't taking their time getting us to wherever we were going. We were practically running. Rothel moved around me to stand in front of a heavy door made of steel with a little glass window. Lawrence stopped, and it felt as if they were setting me up for a grand kind of surprise. “Is someone going to jump out and scare me when we walk in there?”

Rothel’s eighties bangs were blocking the small glass window, and she smiled. “You’re going to love this one. I promise.”

“Pardon me, I’ve had one promise too many this week.” I smiled though, because what else could I do?

“Tuesday afternoon, we made an arrest. A disorderly conduct arrest.” Oh, okay. I could see where Lawrence was going. I tried to look around Rothel. She shifted and smiled.

“I appreciate all the suspense, but open the door.”

Lawrence chuckled. “He won’t give us his name.”

“You don’t do fingerprints?” This was why I agreed with the initial assessment of them as the Keystone cops.

“This isn’t CSI TV. It takes time.”

I rolled my eyes.

“Could you just tell us if this is your missing ex-husband?” Rothel nodded her head and Lawrence reached to the side and turned the knob.

She moved so I could see inside the cell and there he was. Jean-Luc sat on the floor with his knees drawn to his chest. He stood when the door opened. His clothes were dirty, and he didn't have shoes on, but he smiled. "*Amor*!"

He rushed toward me and pulled me against him. Oh, boy, did he smell. The pig version of him hadn't smelled so horrible. "I was terrible to you, *amor*. A pig. Will you ever forgive me?"

Of course, I would. But first, I probably had to bail him out of jail first. I turned to Lawrence. "What do I have to do to get him out of here?"

"Pay a fine."

"A fine." I didn't have my purse, and I assumed he didn't have his wallet. "Okay. I'll have to go to a bank. How much?"

"A thousand American dollars."

Of course it was. It couldn't be something cheap. Leave it to Jean-Luc to be expensive. "All right. I'll get it and come back. Is there some sort of water taxi I can get to the island and back?"

Rothel smiled. Then laughed. Then covered her mouth with her hand.

"Okay. I'm guessing not." I pulled my phone from my back pocket. Or I would have, but I didn't have my phone. I hadn't brought anything. The resort was all-inclusive except when it was closed for pig shooting, in which case they gave out vouchers for off-the-island food. I had no service out on the island, so my phone was in my suitcase.

I had money, but it was all in my suitcase in my room with the injured pig I'd thought was Jean-Luc. Boy, was I going to have a story for him later.

And then it occurred to me that the reason Jean-Luc still clung to me—not in the literal sense, but in the *after every breakup he showed up at my place* sense—was because we were the only ones we shared our stories with. Now he had Britney, who would probably love to hear his stories.

For months we wouldn't speak, couldn't be in the same room without me bursting into tears and Jean-Luc hip checking the furniture in anger. It had been a long road to where we were right now. Apparently, we were still a work in progress. There were going to be grandkids and birthday parties and we were going to be doing it all together, whether we liked it or not. But we couldn't do it this way.

Jean-Luc finally let me go, and I moved back.

"I have a baby on the way."

I nodded. "I know."

"My daughter is getting married this weekend."

"Yeah, but she's young." He was a man having one of those midlife crises that had been brewing since he'd turned thirty and had to reevaluate his life. It didn't hurt me to try to make him feel better. "I'm going to call my mom and tell her to set the pig free and then bring some money to the mainland."

"Set the pig free?" His brow pinched, and I shrugged as I dialed the phone Lawrence handed me.

Yes, that is... if the pig was still there. I didn't know if now that Jean-Luc was back, the pig was just a regular pig, or if there had never been a pig. Maybe it had just disappeared and been replaced with my ex. I'd have to do a little magic if I ever got that darn necklace back.

Then I remembered when I first discovered that Jean-Luc was turned into a pig. I'd brought him to my room, which was a mess from the police going through it. I'd wished the room to clean itself. Then I wished that Jean-Luc wasn't the pig currently eating my underwear. After that, I couldn't think of a specific time the pig had acted like Jean-Luc again. Not like he had before then.

"I'll explain later." In short sentences that didn't convey any of the feelings and emotions. We had to redefine our relationship, fix it so that he could get on with his life and I could get on with mine. I had soul searching to do so I could figure out why I couldn't move past my very dysfunctional relationship with him.

I dialed the hotel and Arthur answered.

"Arthur, it's Cami." After our adventure with Willowby and the baconater's bum, which was going to be the name of my memoir if I ever wrote one, Arthur and I were on a first name basis. "Can you ring my room?"

"You betcha, big C."

Later, we were going to have to talk about our pet names for one another, but right now, I had to talk to my mother.

She answered on the first ring. "Camille?"

"I need a thousand dollars, and I need you to bring it to the police station on the mainland." Just so there was no disproportionate frowning about having a daughter landing in jail during her granddaughter's wedding celebration, I added, "It's for Jean-Luc."

"You found him." In the background, the pig snorted.

"I did." I nodded. She still had the pig. It was just a pig now. Had it been all along?

No way.

"Also, you can set the pig free, Mom. He's safe. Just make sure you're more cautious of him." If I lived to be a thousand and had a million dollars to bet with, I would've never put money on that sentence coming from my mouth.

"Set him free?" She sniffed. "I thought..." She sniffed again.

"Mom?"

"I thought he was my grandmother's gift."

Grandmother's gift? Was that a thing? "I'm going to need a little more."

"Well, I always wanted a pig." Now the sniffing was real.

"How are you planning to get him home?" Where in her one-bedroom apartment, on the fourth floor of her seniors-only apartment building, did she plan to keep him?

"I was thinking of staying on the island."

"On the island?" Where the hell was she going to live? A yurt? "What, are you getting a place on the beach?" I pictured a house with a view of the waves, with a kitchen and a living room, indoor plumbing. Open, airy, lots of windows.

"I got a job that I'm really excited about. Plus, the pig is the sweetest!"

The surprises kept coming, but Jean-Luc stood next to me still smelling none too fresh, and now he'd put on his snooty Frenchman scowl. I turned away from him and hissed into the phone. "What?"

"I'm going to work at the hotel with that lovely boy, Arthur." I had to be hearing wrong. My mother hadn't had a job since before I was born. Maybe not even before then. It wasn't a time I knew much about.

"Um, Mom, we're definitely going to talk about this later." A long talk. "But right now, I need the money here at the police station."

"Yes, yes. But, the pig?"

I had to hold back a laugh. "You can keep him as your, er, grandmother's gift." Seriously, whatever made her happy.

"Wonderful! Now, let me get Arthur to watch JL, and then I'll be on my way." She clicked off like the conversation was over. It certainly was not over. Not by a thousand miles was it even close.

She called the pig JL. She named the pig, who she didn't know had ever been the real Jean-Luc, after the man.

Freaking awesome.

But right now, I had little choice but to sit down and wait. So, I sat beside the real Jean-Luc. "You're having a baby, huh?"

He nodded, solemnly. "I'm having a baby with a child."

Yeah, he was, but I held that thought back and the giggles, and simply shrugged. This wasn't a conversation I wanted to have. "You did it once before, and that turned out okay." I added a smile and nudged his shoulder with mine, because there was a young mom and a baby to think of. "Come on. Britney's a nice girl." It almost burned to say. "She was really worried about you. She even called the cops and made them question me for killing you."

"No kidding?" He laughed, looking genuinely surprised. "Did you tell them all the ways you wanted to kill me?"

"No, some of them are pretty elaborate, and it would've been just my luck that you ended up getting yourself killed, and then I would've been suspect number one."

We understood each other, and we had the same sense of humor. "If it makes you feel better, I spent last night on the beach pouring my heart out to a pig that got shot in the ass by a rogue Robin Hood."

He laughed and slid an arm around me. "Same rogue who put those hickeys on your neck?" I shook my head, and he sobered. "I saw them and went a little bit crazy."

"I noticed."

"I was jealous."

"Jealous? You have Barbie, erm, Britney." He'd chosen her from the giant Barbie army of women he'd been with in the years we'd been apart.

"Yes, and she loves me, but you, *mon amour*, you are my *mon trésor.*" His treasure. A little bit of me melted. Jean-Luc always knew all the best things to say. That was how he'd managed to amass the previously mentioned army of women. Thinking on that one put an end to the melting.

Speaking of treasure, I still had a necklace to find. The urgency of it was a bit less now. Still, I wanted to get it back, and I was in the perfect place to inject myself right into the investigation.

There was no word from the detectives on the wishing stone, so Jean-Luc and I caught a ride back to the hotel with Mom, who had commandeered the resort speedboat and was captaining it like *she* was the descendant of Captain Renegade.

"Tell me about the pig."

I laughed and studied Jean-Luc. Did he not remember being a pig? Because I was still sure he had been until I'd wished he wasn't. I decided to play along. I looked a little less insane that way. "You wouldn't believe me if I told you." When he nudged me and made his puppy dog face, I relented. "Fine. I bought a jewelry box at the market on the boardwalk and there was a stone inside. It came with this great story about a pirate and wishes. Anyway…"

He slid closer, wearing his *I'm going to kiss you now* face. And then he leaned in, breath all hot and moist when he said, "I miss you so much, Cami."

In my haste to get away, I slid across the back of the boat. Slid too far to be exact, and then I was falling, tipping.

And then I was in the water.

Fortunately, we were almost at the hotel. I could see the dock in the moonlight when I bobbed back up.

Like he was my own personal little mermaid, Jean-Luc jumped in after me, despite the fact that I was an all-American in high school swimming and he preferred his water frozen and with metal blades on his feet.

He slung his arm around my neck like he was going to put me in a sleeper hold and dragged me against him. Now we were swimming away from the dock. I turned in his arms and instead of saving me, now he was grabbing my ass. "Jean-Luc!" I shoved him away. Ugh. He went under. I pulled him up by his shirt collar and dragged him back to the dock. When he was safely on dry land—well, dry planks—I climbed up beside him. "You really tried saving *me* in the water?"

"I really do miss you, Cami."

"Oh, sweetheart. You didn't miss me when you had me." I wasn't being mean. He was who he was. Maybe we could be friends now, and the past didn't matter anymore. We had Lor and that was enough.

He nodded. "I'm glad I have you."

I smiled. "I'm glad you're not an actual pig."

"I'm scared of this baby thing." His voice was soft as he not-so-casually changed the conversation, and there was no mistaking the honest fear. "I'm too old. It's why I went to the mainland in the first place."

"To drink and be disorderly?" When he nodded, I laughed. "*Babe*, it's too late to be scared, and age happens. Go with it.

You're a great dad to Lor, and you're going to be a great dad to this kid, too." Jean-Luc was as confident as any skater when he was on the ice. He could shoot and score, check and weave. Off the ice, he needed reassurance. I could give it without costing myself anything.

He laughed, and it was kind of bittersweet to me. Maybe part of me always thought that there was some off-chance that when we were old and gray, we could sit in our matching rocking chairs and watch the grandkids run onto the porch.

"*Amour*, I can't take care of a baby. I didn't have to with Loralei. You did it. Britney wasn't meant to be hands in."

"Hands on."

He nodded. "*Oui*. I can't take care of a baby. I don't even know how you managed to arrange all this wedding stuff. I had to make one phone call, and it took every ounce of energy I could muster. It was you who made everything fall into place."

Thanks to a magical wishing stone.

"Well," I struggled to find the words. "Think about it. Now you aren't busy with work any more, so you'll have more time for your child. And Britney is young and full of energy, so she'll probably figure it out quickly and be able to keep up with the kid."

He didn't seem any happier.

My thoughts spun. "If that doesn't work, Jean-Luc, you're forgetting that you're rich. You can just hire people to help you." I hadn't really thought through the idea before I said it, but the excitement in his eyes told me everything I needed to know about what he thought of the idea.

"Of course, my Cami. That's it!" he hugged me like I'd just save his life.

No, I wasn't a fan of rich people pawning kids off on nannies, but this child could do worse. It would be fine.

Chapter Nineteen

I'm an Idiot

Jean-Luc and I were less drippy by the time we trudged into the lobby.

Jean-Luc stopped me just outside the doors. "Thank you for talking me off the ledge."

"You have no idea the effort." I wiped my brow and smiled. "Not so long ago, I would've happily given you a shove right off of it."

He glanced down and chuckled, just a little, before he looked up again. "I hope we can become friends."

"We've both grown, and I don't have to flaunt all the things I know. Anymore." Instead, I gave him a hug and a shove toward the elevator. "Go. Fix your relationship."

When I gazed up at the moon, I thought of Remy. He was an island adventure if ever there was one. If I was sad about anything, it was that I'd blown that right out of the water. I would never see those eyes half-closed after a kiss that had made them darker. Even though I definitely saw Remy fleeing the hotel, and my gut still whispered something wasn't right, I believed him when he told me he hadn't stolen from me.

I'd made the mistake of believing liars before. It was just that Remy seemed different. Perfect for me in a way that Jean-Luc never was.

Like I'd summoned him with a thought—a power I could only wish for a stone to give me—he called out to me. I sighed and turned, looking for the source of Remy's voice.

The moonlight or the light from inside the hotel caught a glimmer of plastic wrapped gold in his hand. I gasped. My necklace. He did have it.

As he approached, he held it up by a strip of red at the top of the plastic bag. When he got close, I could read the side. It was marked *evidence,* also in red lettering.

He held it up, smiled, and showed me his badge. I ignored the necklace for a second and took the badge in my hand. "What?" My heart froze. What did this mean? Had he slept with me to find this necklace for some kind of police thing? Had it not been real at all?

He nodded. "I'm a special investigator hired by an insurance company to find the treasure."

My mouth fell open, and pain pierced my heart. "You used me?" I whispered. I'd thought he'd liked me for me. Boy did it hurt to find out he hadn't.

He shook his head and held up his hand. "No. Cami, I swear. It's coincidental. All of it. I didn't use you." He took his badge back and put it into his pocket. "I swear to you, that first night we drank together, I had no idea we were going to get tangled up in all of it. I didn't know you had this stone. I didn't even know it was in necklace form. I've been on the trail of Renegade's treasure since the stones were found and put in a museum." Oh man, he was cute when he was apologizing. "They were stolen, and I tracked one of the women we suspected to the island."

"So, none of this was true?"

Pain flashed across his face. "It absolutely was. There was just a lot more to the story."

My heart still ached. I didn't understand what was true, what was him, and what was just part of the chaos. "Are you really a descendant of Renegade?" Not that it mattered. It was just an interesting piece of trivia I'd use in my stories later when I finally got it all organized enough in my head to tell.

"Yeah, yes, I am. My name is Ethan Remington. I'm a direct descendant of the famous pirate. He would be my great-great… maybe another great-grandfather." He shrugged. "Probably how I got the job." It was certainly an ice-breaker, and he looked the part, too. Like a rogue. The kind of guy mothers warned their daughters about. The kind who looked good on the cover of romance novels. "Anyway, I never took the necklace. When I stomped away from you earlier, it was because I noticed the chain of the necklace hanging out of one of the clerk's pockets."

"Which clerk?" I didn't want it to be Arthur. Mom would be so devastated. Arthur and I had come to an understanding. We were buds now. I called him Art. He called me Big C.

We were going to work on it, anyway.

"Dudley, I think." He held up his hand to about the height of his shoulder. "'Bout this tall. Curly red hair." I didn't recognize the description.

"There are some unfortunately named clerks around this place." It wasn't Arthur. No mistaking his hair for curly or red. Thank goodness.

Remy smiled at me, and all thoughts of desk clerks and pirates faded. I was here with a real-live man who liked me, who had piercing eyes and gentle hands, who tilted his head and slid his fingers into my hair and left his palm against my cheek. "I couldn't break my cover."

Instead of going for the big kiss, he pressed his lips against my forehead and then backed off. I wanted more, but had too much pride to ask.

"I understand." He handed me the plastic bag.

"Can I open it?" Last thing I wanted was to end up on the wrong side of the cell door. He nodded. "So, have you been following me?"

This time, his nod was accompanied by a little smile. He led me to the seats in the center of the lobby and waited for me to sit before he took the seat beside me. "Not because of my job, but because..." He paused, and it worked for him. I was hanging on every word, waiting for whatever he was going to say next. "I like you, Cami. I didn't really count on liking you so much." He took the necklace and waved his finger for me to turn. "I wanted to know you better." He brushed my hair out of the way and his fingertips against my skin made my heart thump about twelve times faster than usual.

Maybe it was a line, but Ino one had looked at me or touched me the way Remy had since Jean-Luc.

He smiled. "Would you be willing to get to know me and let me get to know you? At least while I'm on the island. Until we both have to leave?"

"I have a wedding in a couple of days, then I'm back to reality, to being the ex-wife of Jean-Luc LaCroix and the mother of a daughter who isn't going to need me nearly as much." Despite my excuses, he still looked hopeful, and I liked him a lot more for it, so I couldn't help adding, "Maybe. But you have to make up for not being truthful with me."

He grinned and grabbed my hand. Maybe he wouldn't be the next great love of my life, or maybe he would, but he could definitely be the great love of the next three days. I moved in closer and slipped my arm through his. "I almost bought into that whole wishing stone business. You know, the tale about the stones granting your greatest wishes."

He smiled, and I wanted to fall into it. I was too old for this kind of attraction. But I felt young. I felt pretty. I felt...

"Maybe you should give it another try."

"Maybe." A smart girl wouldn't make another wish for as long as she lived.

"Can I walk you to your room?" Who wouldn't like a guy who looked at a woman who'd just crawled out of the sea like she was the most desirable woman in the world? I sure as heck liked him. A lot.

I nodded. "Oh, yeah."

We walked toward the little bank of elevators and stepped in side by side when the doors whooshed open. He waited until the door was shut and then he backed me into the corner and pressed his lips to mine just the way I'd desperately been wanting him to.

Chapter Twenty

Going to the Chapel and...You Know the Rest

I, Loralei Marie-Christine, take you, Noah Webster Collingsworth, for the rest of my life, through good and bad, with all the love and respect and devotion one person can have to and for another.

The wedding was beautiful, far exceeding my expectations. I looked at Jean-Luc. He was dashing in his tuxedo, but if there was one garment a man like Jean-Luc was born to wear, it was a tux. Even more so when he was happy. When he looked at Britney, he was happy in a way I didn't remember seeing him when we were together. Maybe he *would* be able to make it work this time. I hoped so. They could all grow up together.

Beside me, Remy shifted, and I couldn't believe my good luck. The last three days, not doing them alone, all the fun and friendship and sex, were definitely going in the memoir. They were the kinds of things a girl wanted to look back on in her old age and remember.

He'd been a lovely companion, and my mother loved him. Almost as much as she loved Jean-Luc. Actually, more, possibly. It would've been something to strive for, anyway, if life and Virgin Air wasn't sending me home to resume my dull and mostly lonely existence.

Mom sat beside me on the other side with Arthur, and she leaned in, "She's gorgeous, Cami. You raised a good girl."

I didn't need help missing Lor already or loving her more than I already did. But Noah had a look in his eyes that was so beautiful it brought tears to my eyes. He loved her the way I always hoped she would find someone to love her. I couldn't have been happier for her. My heart was so full.

By the time we walked off the beach for the celebration after the ceremony, I was ready for a night of dancing in the hotel banquet room. And I was dressed for it in a gown that made my eyes look bluer, and my boobs like they were in the vicinity of where they'd been when I was twenty-five.

For tonight, since we were still on the island, and technically since I had a legit claim to the necklace, I was wearing it. Every single time I wished for Remy to ask me to dance, he did.

When I wished for him to take a walk with me on the beach, he took my hand and led me to the edge of the water.

"It was a good night, Cami." His lips were warm when he brought my hand up for a kiss.

He was so right, but it was our last night, and I wanted to make it perfect since I was out of here first thing tomorrow afternoon. "Yeah."

"What time's your flight tomorrow?"

"Flight leaves at one." Those were the saddest words in the English language. "Are you sticking around longer?" Didn't sadness make me eloquent?

He didn't answer. He just looked at me. Turned me so I was standing in front of him, and he could thread his fingers through my hair and pull me in close. "Stay a couple more days."

"Maybe," I told him, and it felt like I was always saying that now. *Maybe*, because no was too painful. Because what my heart really wanted to say was yes to him, always. Every time.

When I wished for him to come back to my room with me, now that Ma had her own, he whisked me to the elevator and upstairs.

We made the night one to remember.

The first kiss was a brand of his lips against mine. The second made my clothes disappear, and it was a long time before I could do more than thank the stars that we met.

I almost wanted to wish this night would never end, but I wasn't taking the chance of getting stuck in some Groundhog Day kind of scenario while I was wearing the necklace.

I couldn't just take the necklace at face value. I had to test it out. Middle of the night. Sexy man in my bed. Yet, I couldn't stop myself. I had to do it. I walked into the bathroom, still wearing the necklace, and smiled in the mirror. I wished for Jean-Luc to find a way to make things work with Britney and that they would have a healthy baby. And I wished for Loralei and Noah to know nothing but happiness and contentment in their lives, whatever they chose and wherever they went. For myself, I wished for a life of adventure, and if the necklace wanted to throw some passion into it, I was here for that, too.

Speaking of passion… I watched Remy walk into the bathroom, naked and smiling. There wasn't much I liked to do more than watch Remy walk anywhere naked. The bonus was when he wrapped his arms around me, hugging me from behind.

"What are you doing awake?" Not that I was complaining. His nakedness and my nakedness were getting cozy, and I would take every opportunity I could get.

"I got a lead on another one of the stones. Your braided mystery lady showed up at a flea market in Connecticut." He paused long enough to kiss my neck. "I'm going to fly out tomorrow."

"Oh." I sighed. I was glad, in the most extreme and opposite way a person could be glad, that I hadn't canceled my flight out.

"It's the blue stone. The *seeing* stone." He widened his eyes, and he said it as if he wasn't quite buying the whole power of the stone thing.

If he expected optimism, there was going to be one very disappointed and quite naked pirate descendant in my bathroom. I couldn't fake it that well. "Nice." I should've said more.

It wasn't like I was going to stay on the island while he flew out and left me behind. We were both leaving. He probably expected some sort of Cami diatribe, since I said a lot of words throughout most days. It wasn't often I was silent.

"It's a good lead." I couldn't imagine why he would speak and then kiss my neck like he was. I didn't know of a woman anywhere who would be able to maintain even a single conscious thought.

"I'll bet." My voice was a full octave higher.

"Come with me." And his roving hand has found its target area. I sucked in a shallow breath and held it.

"With you?"

“Mmm.” He moaned against my throat, and his tongue traced a lazy circle at my throbbing artery. “Come with me. I don’t have a French accent, and I’m not a professional athlete. I eat carbs. I sometimes dress up like a pirate and take silly jobs on the side of my real job. I’m not rich. I’m not famous. But the thing is, nobody cares when I have a good day or a bad day.”

“I care.” I turned in his arms. “In case you’re taking applications for the job.”

“Are you applying?” He dragged his mouth from my chin to my jaw. “Please be applying.” He kissed the soft hollow under my ear and I was in serious danger of melting. There was about to be a puddle of Cami goo on the floor.

“I could get you a reference from a ridiculously tall, French-accented, professional athlete who tossed me to the side and made way for you to have me.”

He tugged my earlobe, and I could’ve swooned. His breath was hot and delicious, and his fingertips were massaging my scalp, and it was a lot of sensations to undergo at one moment. “I love that guy. Remind me to send him a gift basket.”

“A good gift basket could solve world peace.” I could barely speak. Being witty was more than I was equipped to be.

“I bet you make a good gift basket.” Our conversation skills devolved, and it was an hour or more before we could chat again. He kissed me and pulled me close, so I laid my head on his chest. "So, do you think you could come to Connecticut?" I didn't answer right away, and he stroked my back. "We could find the stone woman, then maybe take a ride in a convertible through that place they always show on TV with all the leaves."

I didn't have a lot of obligations. I sold the house a couple of years ago. I had a car. An apartment. Not much else. I'd stopped taking weddings while I planned Loralei's. The business was busy, but there was certainly nothing that required my immediate and speedy return to the heat of the Arizona desert.

"There's a maple syrup festival in Connecticut I've been dying to see."

"Maple syrup, you say?" I gazed up at his smile.

He nodded. His grin was as incredible as any I'd ever seen before. Probably ever would again. And Heaven help me, I wanted to see more of it. Much, much more of it. "I wished for an adventure."

"Well, if you go with me, it'll be an adventure."

There really wasn't much to think about. Except... "Do you still have the pirate outfit?"

He smiled, and that was about all the promise I needed.

Now the real adventure could begin.

Sapphire Omens

Chapter One

Delilah Bradbury Loses it at Association of Actors Awards

On one of its greatest nights, Hollywood lost a superstar. Not to death, but to her own recklessness when, during her acceptance speech for the Best Actress award, Delilah Bradbury leaped from the stage and pounced on her longtime BFF, Shara Hewitt. Security quickly separated the combatants, but not before Bradbury ripped out half of Hewitt's extensions. Punches were thrown, designer dresses destroyed, and once again, The Association Actors Awards has made a spectacle of itself. - National Inquisitor

It had taken exactly three tequila shooters, ten seconds, and a few snarky headlines about a flop of a movie for me to become a Hollywood laughingstock. Add that to four ex-husbands, with the last divorce still raging 3 years after the split, and I was tabloid TV's walking wet dream. My meltdown at the awards had made national and international news. The headlines had gone wild. "Delilah Bradbury Goes Postal at Association Awards." "Bradbury Outburst: Another Humiliation in a Storied Career." "Delilah Goes Down in Flames." I had a scrapbook full of them. As technology had moved on, I'd even become a meme.

It'd been beyond humiliating. Embarrassing wasn't nearly a strong enough word for it. In the end, it kept me from working in the entertainment industry for the last *ten* years. Now that I'd hit my forties, I was completely unemployable. At least in Hollywood, which was all I knew.

My career had been going so well. I'd worked with all the big names. I'd worked with the Richards, a Bruce, a Brad, a couple of Bobs, although one had insisted I call him Robert. The other Bob went by initials. There was a Joe, a Julia, a Val, a Betty, a Meryl, and a Sandy. There were the young'uns—Channing, Tom, Drew, and a beautiful young lady whose name was changed because it was too unique to keep her publicist happy. Such was the biz.

A string of A-listers, and I had dirt on *all* of them. Including who'd kissed whom, who was full of bad behavior, the drunken fights, affairs, drugs. Hollywood's truest stories from one of its own. Since nobody wanted to hire me, I'd done what I had to do to survive.

After struggling for five years after my awards show meltdown, I'd done the unthinkable: told all their secrets. I'd written a tell-all book.

Boom! Instant bestseller, for about a month. They were on to the next drama. For the next five years, I stretched my book royalties. Bought a smaller house. Pfft. Small, my butt. Crackerjack boxes were bigger. I let the cars go back and started taking the bus. I hadn't even had a new pair of sneakers since all of this started. I began shopping at bargain basement discounters for clothes, and only when I *had* to have them.

All that added up to me being super skeptical when I received an invitation after so long being forgotten. It was suspicious. It was probably a mistake. Maybe a joke. Despite the fact that this was almost certainly not real, I opened the gold embossed envelope with the thick cream-colored paper and stared for a second.

A thousand thoughts rumbled through my mind, but disbelief led them all. It was an invitation. An *invitation* popping up in my mailbox in a Crackerjack house so far from Hollywood...suffice it to say it was a bit of a shock.

It couldn't be real, but a little part of me wondered. What if it was? Could I ever be invited back in? That would be beyond my wildest dreams. I'd pretty much given up on even dreaming about it.

There was only one way to find out. Pulling out my phone, I called my former manager, Lou. He wasn't an agent. Mine had dropped me before the first punchline, but Lou was a friend. I hoped so, anyway. He was the closest I could get to a friend still in the industry. Calling him made sense to me.

"Yo, Delilah!" Lou had a smoker's rasp from the two packs of cigarettes he smoked a day, but it never tamped his enthusiasm. Shoot, I was grateful that at least *someone* was happy to hear from me. That didn't happen often anymore. Mostly because I didn't contact a lot of people, especially from my old life.

"Hey, Lou. I just got an invite to the big red carpet next month. The awards. Is it legit?" We never spent time on niceties. In my opinion, people spent too much time on asinine conversations that neither party cared about, the *hellos* and *how dos,* the *how're the fams*, and all the other ridiculous bits like that. Plus, both Lou and I were viewed by others as exactly the opposite of nice. Maybe we were viewed that way because we were *unwilling* to participate in the act of niceties. It didn't matter. Perception was what it was, and one way or the other, we shaped it as much as we were shaped by it.

"*You* got an invite?" It was at this very show that the meltdown heard around the world had ended my career. An involuntary shudder rolled through me, as it did any time I thought of that day. It really was cringeworthy, even for me. Maybe all the therapy I'd put myself in the last few years had helped me see the error of my hot-headed tempest ways.

"As a presenter." I read closer. Scoffed. Someone at the Association of Actors had a twisted sense of humor. They wanted me to present the lifetime achievement award to Shara Hewitt—my kryptonite, my nemesis, the reason husband number four had become *ex*-husband number four. The source of the emotional upheaval that led to my award show disintegration.

"For whom?" He rattled off a few names of actors I'd worked with, ones far more worthy than Shara Hewitt. Actors with distinguished careers.

I could barely hear him for the bubbling sound of the blood boiling in my ears. "That... that *bitch*! That hussy! That piece of sh—harlot! Shara Hewitt." My mama, God rest her soul, would've washed out my mouth just for the tone of voice. Mama hadn't suffered much bad behavior, but she hadn't heard anything yet. Nor had she ever been subject to anyone like Shara. A woman so bitter, so unlikeable, so vicious that she was... oh there weren't words for how horrible she was.

He laughed. Laughed! Lou had the audacity to chuckle, several times. "Oh, man. That's priceless."

Frowning, I refrained from reminding him he was supposed to be on my side. I couldn't blame him, but it hurt just the same. Even after all this time. Her betrayal still stung.

"They think I'm going to stand on stage with her, kiss her cheeks and not kill her? She stole my husband." The arrogance of The Association to even think I would consider this invitation was shocking. Absolutely not. Heck to the no. A big, fat not-a-chance cherry on top of the *you've got to have your head up your butt* sundae.

It didn't matter that I had a new man. That I had a *better* man. That after all this time I knew my marriage with husband number four would've ended with or without Shara's interference.

This was about principle. And, maybe, if I'm honest with myself, a little about how much that night hurt me and continued to haunt me for longer than I would've thought possible. It had been traumatic.

It was ridiculous that they'd even asked.

Lou, on the other hand, wasn't so highly principled, apparently. "Hmm." My senses sharpened. I didn't like the sound of that little noise he'd made. It sounded a heckuva lot like he was about to side with the Association. "You should do it." There it was. He said it.

"Don't *hmm* me, Lou. I'm a hundred percent *not* doing it." Adamant was the word best fit to describe my resolve. He was out of his ever-loving mind.

"Let's not be so hasty, Dee." He paused, and I couldn't speak with my mouth hanging open and my brain fuddled because he was agreeing with whatever idiot on the awards team had hatched this plan. "This might be worth thinking about."

Or it wasn't. Definitely wasn't. "No."

"Just hang on a second."

I waited, but if he'd been in front of me, I might've killed him. My fists were clenched and ready for battle even as he softened his voice and tried for the cool, calm placating tone I'd heard a thousand times before.

"What if this is about mending your fences? This could be your chance to rebuild that burned bridge. This could be your chance to walk it all back."

Walk it back? "She stole my husband, Lou. That is the ultimate best friend betrayal. How do *I* walk that back?" She'd *taken* him before I'd been ready to give him away. More than that, she was supposed to have been my friend. The only thing worse than being betrayed by your husband is to be betrayed by your best friend at the same time. The same time.

"Delilah, how long has it been since you worked?" Now he was trying to be all reasonable.

I scoffed. I didn't want to discuss that.

"Dee, sweetheart, think about it. This could open doors. Go. Show them you're above it. Forgive. Forget." He sucked in a deep breath. "Finally move on."

For all his fine words, all his gentle cajoling, the thought that brought me closer to accepting was that I wasn't likely to get another chance to throw a drink in her filler-enhanced face. It was a thought that hadn't come from him at all but from the blackened depths of my own heart.

Of course, I was right.

So was Lou because Lou was always right. Career-wise, anyway. He was the reason I'd had so many primo jobs in my career. The reason I'd worked with the big names. Had the stories to tell. I'd told them. I couldn't think of anyone I'd ever worked with who might want to work with me again. I'd sold them all out to the highest bidder. Also, none of the new guys would want to work with me either. Not after I'd written the book.

I spent a second picturing the theater where the award show was always held. Dolby theater on Hollywood Avenue in the Ovation shopping mall. On a normal day, that place teemed with people, sightseers, and celebrity watchers. This night would be a normal day on steroids. I would have to eat crow in front of a crowd.

I'd been silent long enough, so he tried again. "Think about how much you like being all dressed up and fawned over. Couture. A makeup and hair team." He was speaking my language. Actually, my former language since I couldn't afford any of those things anymore.

"It's been a while." It was a grudging admission, but it was an admission. However, I had a nice quiet life now.

"The goody bags. You remember those?"

Yeah, I did.

Lou's voice was far too smooth as he said, "What was it last time?"

Over the years, The Association had made it a point to go all out. I'd collected an iPad, a Tiffany bracelet, Dior perfume, a Burberry coat, and the year I won, a Birkin bag. They didn't skimp. That was the curious thing about this invite. I'd disgraced them. Made a mockery, a YouTube spectacle of their big night in front of the world. Live TV had the tendency to be unable to resist a scene, especially one that exhibited exactly how unhinged a woman scorned could be.

Darn it. I was just curious enough to want to find out why they wanted me back. "You make a good point." The Birkin bag had made a couple of car payments back in the lean years. Maybe I'd get something good if I went. "RSVP me."

I could overcome. I could be the bigger person. Not literally. Shara was a foot taller, and she'd been surgically enhanced to the point of deformity. "And Lou?"

"Yeah, sweetheart?"

"Put me down for the steak." I hung up the phone and walked into the kitchen to stare at Repo Ron. "Dust off your cowboy boots, darlin'."

He glanced up from the newspaper and arched one eyebrow.

"We're going to a party ."

Chapter Two

Delilah Bradbury Shops at Local Flea Market

Ten years after her spotlight abruptly burned out, Delilah Bradbury was spotted this week at a flea market near her Massachusetts home, wandering the aisles with a hunky mystery man, maybe looking for that perfect vintage piece to wear to a comeback on live TV. Could said comeback save the ratings for an ever-failing Hollywood award show? –National Inquisitor

Repo Ron's real name wasn't Ron. It was Nicholas Pontchalac, and he was an old creole soul, but I either called him Nicky or Ron. His family called him Nicholas and never anything else. He called me *cher*, *bébé*, *mon trésor*, and sometimes he called me *araignée,* which meant spider, because I was going to be the thing that killed him one day.

I didn't even know if he knew my name for certain beyond what had been on the work order when they sent him to repo my G-wagon. I was pretty sure that had been the last time he'd called me Delilah. Also, the first and only time anyone had held me while I cried. He'd taken the car but then had come back with a dozen roses and a card.

It'd taken me a week to call him. Another to get the courage to ask him out. We'd been together ever since. I never would've met him if I hadn't been ousted from Hollywood, so there was always a silver lining to every sad story. I'd lost my career, but I'd found a wonderful man.

Plus, he loved shopping. Flea markets. Malls. Discount stores. Boutiques. I'd never met a man before him who didn't bitch about trying on clothes. My theory was that he didn't have a bad look. He kept his hair long—to his shoulders—had mastered a man bun and was blessed with a metabolism that meant he could eat *all* the carbs and gain none of the weight. He didn't work out, he just had one of those badass, real-man jobs. It was hot. Many days he came home glistening with sweat. Many days came that I washed his back and loved every minute of it.

Today, we were shopping at a flea market set up in downtown Rochester, New York, where we live. Nicky had family here, and I'd been dying in LA. One of the beauties of Rochester, beside Lake Ontario and the Genesee River High Falls, was the Charlotte Flea Market. It was a treasure trove full of goodies. I hadn't bought a lot of jewelry or clothes since I left

Hollywood—my jewel budget had taken a hit—but no way was I going to the Association of Actors awards with a bare neck or naked ear.

Nicky and I strolled the aisles and checked the tables. He stopped and stared, motionless, speechless until he said, "*Bébé*?" and pointed to an open box that displayed a necklace with the most beautiful blue stone. "It match*es* your eyes." His accent dropped some of the ending sounds, and he spoke like there was a race to get the most words out in a second, but I loved everything he said. Even his fibs–like this one–sounded melodic.

If only I had eyes as blue as the stone. It did match a stunning blue sequined dress I'd never got the chance to wear before getting the old Hollywood boot. It was the last relic of my days there, and I'd never been so happy I kept something as I was that I kept the dress. I'd nearly sold it several times but hadn't been able to bring myself to do it.

I walked closer because the thing was calling to me, singsong saying things like *buy me, buy me, buy me*. Maybe it was singing to me or maybe it was just my imagination, but the words sounded as real to me as Nicky's voice.

The old woman behind the counter had a long black braid she kept flipped to the front over her shoulder, and her eyes were the color of darkness, with pupils so big I couldn't tell if there was a color around them at all. She looked up at me and smiled, her nearly black eyes sparkling. "It suits you."

"You see, *chér*? Nicky don't lie." He smiled, and for a second, I stood there just seeing him, really seeing him, and thanking the heavens he was the one who had come for my car and not Repo Rick, the real Ron's brother. Repo Rick had stopped growing at four-nine but was packed with the muscles of someone twice his size and an attitude of someone bigger than that. It wasn't Rick's height that put me off, though, it was his personality. I preferred the softer, more understated qualities of Nicky's.

I checked the dangling price tag. "It's a lot of money, Nicky." Despite the cost, I'd never had such a deep, burning desire to own anything before in my life.

Nicky whipped out a stack of bills and handed them over to the woman, who smiled and nodded as I picked up the box with one hand and hugged Nicky with the other. Tonight, he was getting a thank you he wasn't going to forget until *at least* next week.

As we stood there, he started to take the necklace from its bed of black velvet, but I said, "No. It's too special to wear just walking around."

"Just for a minute, *chér*. I want to see it on you." As soon as he clasped it around my neck, something surged through me, overwhelmed every muscle holding me, and I fell to the ground. It was like I'd been shocked with power of some sort. It might've looked like a faint, but it felt like all my bones had melted to liquid. Then... lights out.

Chapter Three

Delilah Bradbury Rushed to Hospital–Overdose Suspected

Delilah Bradbury was rushed to The University of Rochester Medical Center this morning after an apparent overdose at the flea market where she'd been shopping with a mystery man only a few hours earlier. She is now listed in stable condition. – National Inquisitor

When I woke, I was flat on my back, yet moving and looking up at a frantic Nicky. I lifted my head to figure out why I was moving flat on my back. Nicky walked beside me as men in blue uniforms rolled toward an ambulance. He held my arm in both of his through the covers with the box to my necklace tucked under his arm. "*Lord, please let mon amour être bien.*"

I hadn't seen his lips move, but I was disoriented. Weird. "I'm okay, Nicky." I wanted to brush his hair back so I could see his face, and he could see mine, but my hands were tucked into the blanket.

Instead, I waited until he was on the seat beside me in the ambulance and smiled at him. "I'm fine. This is silliness." He closed his eyes. In times of trouble, Nicky relied on his faith. I tended to rely on alcohol and Nicky and the occasional Xanax. I closed my eyes, too, and let him do his thing. Over and over Nicky's shaky voice asked for my good health and that I would be well. Again, I wanted to comfort him, but I couldn't move.

After they wheeled me into emergency, unstrapped my poor arms and lifted me onto another bed, they took my information. We had to wait a good thirty minutes, then the doctor came in. "Miss Bradbury." He stopped, looked up at me, and smiled. "Delilah Bradbury, the movie star? In my ER?"

"That's me." All the old insecurity and apprehension from right after the *smackdown heard around the world* came rushing back to me because I was about to be recognized. This guy didn't look like he was the right age to remember the me I was before I went ballistic on TV, so I wasn't sure where this was going. I also wasn't sure I'd be able to stop myself from bolting out of there in a panic.

The doctor's face reddened, and he went full-on fangirl. As he spoke, my heart warmed. I'd forgotten how much I liked being recognized for the bits of my career I'd had before I'd humiliated myself on live TV.

"Man, I loved you in 'Two Parts Romance.'" It was a movie from the peak of my heyday. I couldn't remember the working title, but it hadn't been Two Parts Romance. What sounded like a chick flick wasn't. It was action. A half-witch baker who was trying to make love potions to help the lonely accidentally made a nuclear bomb. It was supposedly badass enough to blow up the world. Five governments came for her. The hero decommissioned all their armies with witty one-liners and fists of fury while I'd followed him in some sleek leather bodysuit. It had made me look like a dominatrix fresh out of her lair to follow a dude around the world so he could save it while I posed and primped and looked pretty.

Because of the names attached, mine and the hero, the thing had been a box office smash, and it had catapulted me to super-stardom.

The movie had been pretty cool. It had a killer love scene. I'd been allowed to fire a missile launcher. It was a pop-culture cult thing now. Probably the reason my frat boy doctor even knew about it, and not enough about me otherwise that he was able to be excited to meet me.

I looked at him and nodded. "Thanks."

"I can't believe it's you." Dr. Phi Beta Kappa—unless they were of the white-haired variety, all doctors these days looked young—shook his head and smiled at me. "I've wanted to meet you for... as long as I can remember."

I looked at Nicky who smiled and nodded encouragingly. He was all too used to the other kind of fan, the ones who were rude and judgey.

"It was total horseshit, what happened to you." Oh. He knew. Okay. Dr. Frat looked honestly offended on my behalf—eyes narrowed, and lips twisted in a scowl—and such support bolstered me in a way that was so ridiculous. Having one anonymous person on my side meant nothing, not really, but man it gave me confidence. "She stole your husband." He shook his head again. "How people didn't recognize that was...?" More head shaking. This time of the vehement and furious kind. After a second, he looked at me, shifting gears. "Back to your health. Have you been drinking?"

That was a shift I wasn't quite prepared for. "No, um, no. Not today and I'm not hungover from yesterday either, I didn't drink that much."

"Drugs?" He cocked an eyebrow like he probably thought he knew the answer and was watching to see if I would lie.

"Nope." I was one of the few in Hollywood who hadn't even dabbled, though the tabloids certainly had blamed drugs for my meltdown. They'd been wrong, but since when did they care?

"Last menstrual period?"

Hmm. These days women tracked with apps. I'd always been afraid of hackers and my menstrual cycle showing up in the pages of the Inquisitor or one of the other magazines that had taken such pleasure in documenting my decline.

"I don't know exactly." I glanced at Nicky as though he might've been the kind of guy who kept track, but he only looked away like the question was too embarrassing, and he thought I might have been embarrassed for him to be in there while I answered.

The doctor cocked his head. "A guess? Months, weeks, years?"

Years, really? While I hadn't indulged in the big Botox craze that had swept my generation, I didn't look *that* old. I was age appropriate. "A monthish?"

He nodded. "Do you feel safe in your home?"

Probably not a question he meant to ask in front of the person I lived with, but I nodded because the sooner we finished, the sooner I could go home. I had some thanking Nicky to do. "Very safe."

The doctor nodded. "All right then. We're going to take some blood, do a scan, and check to see if this was a fluke or something that needs to be addressed."

I shot another quick look at Nicky. This wasn't the first time I'd ruined his day, and it probably wouldn't be the last, but that didn't mean he had to be joyous about it.

Bless him, when the doctor left, he stood and came to the bed, still holding the box. Now the necklace was inside. He'd taken it off of me back at the market.

"How are you feeling?" He stroked his finger across my eyebrow and then down the side of my face to my jawbone.

"Stupid, I feel stupid." I didn't know what had happened back in that tent, but thinking it was the necklace was probably one of my more insane thoughts.

"*Tu es belle, bébé.*"

I looked over at Nicky. His mouth was closed in a hard line. I hardly looked beautiful. I couldn't remember the last time I'd glammed my makeup or really blew out my hair, but Nicky made me feel red carpet ready every day. Without Nicky, there was no telling where I would've ended up, and I loved him for the little lies like this one that he told.

"*Je t'aime*, Nicky." I knew enough French to be dangerous, but I knew how to say *I love you* in a lot of languages. The sentiment, though, was true in all of them.

He responded with a whispered, "*Te amo, bébé.*" The kiss was soft and sweet, like a thousand others, but today, he lingered, cupped the side of my face, and stroked my skin. If I hadn't already been in love with him, this kiss would've done it.

A nurse came in to take my blood and ruined the moment we were having, but I already had every part of him etched into my mind, probably onto my heart, so her needle didn't matter. All they would find was that he was in my blood. He sat beside me on my bed, holding me close until they came back so they could wheel me to another room for a scan.

The scan was quick, and when I returned to my room, Nicky stood and smiled down at me. “What did they say?”

I grinned so he wouldn’t worry. He was a really laid-back guy —so much so that I liked to joke that he should have a recliner strapped to him—and I couldn’t remember ever seeing him quite so concerned—brow pinched, wrinkles lining his normally smooth skin. “They said I’m fine, and you shouldn’t worry.”

“I’m *concerned*”—the word sounded strange coming from him—“because you blacked out.” He was holding the necklace box, tracing his finger over the intricate carvings in the lid. He lifted his head and stared at me. “If I lost you, *cher*, I would lose my heart.” When he laid his hand on his chest, I reached for him and smiled when clasped his fingers around mine.

“I’m not going anywhere.” I hoped not, anyway.

It happened. The moment I’d dreaded, even though I didn’t think it would ever actually come to pass. A moment that I’d actually had nightmares about. “Maybe you’re pregnant.” I scanned his face for any sign of how he might’ve felt about it, too. His expression was blank. I couldn’t tell. Now I really wished I could hear inside his mind.

"I don't think so." I continued watching him and continued trying to assess whether or not he cared. I couldn't tell, and it was killing me. This was part of the problem with dating someone younger, someone who didn't have an airport's worth of baggage trailing behind them. "Do you want kids?"

His expression stayed like an unmarked slate. "I don't think I've ever thought about it until right now."

"Right now, what do you want?" My entire body tensed while I waited for an answer.

"I want you to be well, *bébé*." He moved to sit beside me again, and I inhaled a big whiff of his cologne. "Only that."

That wasn't true, and I knew it. My heart knew it. How could I ask him to give up the chance to have a child?

"*Bébé*, please don't make *un probléme*." His stormy gray eyes pleaded with me, and when he tilted his head and cupped my cheek again, I was angry that he'd implied I would.

A problem? "It *is* a problem, Nicky. I'm too old for babies. I missed my optimum window of time." If I tried to have a baby now, there would be complications and probably bed rest. Expensive testing. I would be almost sixty-five before the kid graduated high school. *Sixty-five*. Until now, that number had seemed abstract. Far away. Now it stared me in the face, and I didn't care for it. I couldn't believe I was about to say what I was about to say.

Before I could find the words, he held up his hand. "*Je t'aime*, Delilah. *Je t'aime*. Nothing else matters."

I wished that was true, but it wasn't. I loved him enough that I wanted him to have everything he ever wanted in life. I also loved me enough that I wanted me to have him.

He leaned toward me and kissed me, this time with some authority, and if I'd been attached to a heart monitor, it would've been going crazy right about now. "I want you, *bébé*. Only you."

I wanted him. For now, it was enough to keep me quiet.

Chapter Four

The Award Goes To...

Back in Hollywood for a star-studded night of celebration and accompanied by her mystery man, Delilah Bradbury was pure eye candy on the red carpet in vintage Chanel with a stone around her neck as big as the iceberg that sank Leo and Kate. – National Inquisitor

Since the pregnancy scare that had been more scared and less pregnancy, we hadn't talked any more about babies or our relationship. The time would eventually come, but it had been a month. I had to get through this award show first. Those were his words, not mine, because maybe he wasn't ready yet, either. Maybe our goodbye needed one more firm shove before it saw the light. As soon as we addressed this, I'd have to leave him. It would be for his own good, but that didn't mean it would be easy.

We'd flown to LA yesterday on the Association's dime, were staying at the hotel they'd picked and paid for, and today was the day. I was dressed in Chanel with loaner Jimmy Choo shoes, had my hair pulled back, twisted, sprayed, and pinned, and my makeup was flawless.

Being back in Hollywood was surreal, but I'd stepped straight back into the person I'd been as if I hadn't been humbled by poverty and humiliation. I had a room at the Beverly Hills Hotel and a limousine would arrive to pick us up in a matter of minutes.

Nicky in a tuxedo made me look like I was wearing a paper bag. Prada should've been paying him for the way he made the tux look. It was midnight blue tweed with a waistcoat and a high-collared shirt. The pants fit like they were designed with his backside in mind, and I was one glimpse away from panting.

"Aren't you forgetting something?"

He thought I should've been wearing the necklace, but I'd forgotten it at home and had been hoping he wouldn't remember either. With a flourish, Nicky handed me the box and flipped the lid open. "Oh, Nicky. I love that you remembered it. It's perfect with this dress." I turned so he could clasp it, but before he did, he brushed his lips softly against the nape of my neck.

A slow, near moan escaped my lips. We stood in front of the mirror in the main room, which looked like a tornado had come through and unpacked for us. The tornado was me when I had a frantic moment. I hadn't been able to find my SKIMS, but I didn't care.

"I do not deserve you, woman."

He didn't deserve *me*? I didn't deserve *him*. I used to be a terrible person. Now, sure, I was a better person but still not the person I want to be. This man. He had the kindest heart, the best laugh, and a smile that made my heart swell. He was better than I ever could be.

I chuckled a little because I didn't know what woman he thought he had. "I'm the one who doesn't deserve you, Nicky."

In the mirror behind me, his brow pinched. "How did you know I was thinking I didn't deserve you?"

I turned to look at him in case the mirror was misbehaving and telling me something that wasn't true. The mirror was saying he was about to walk out on me. Maybe that was just my perception. Either way, I wasn't leaving it this way. "I heard you say it."

"I didn't say it out loud, *cher*." He smiled and wrapped his arms around my waist, and all the worry eased out of me in a long, slow breath. "Did I ever tell you about the old voodoo woman?"

"Did she tell you that you were going to find a crazy actress who would fall hopelessly and desperately in love with you?" Because I certainly was all of that.

He shook his head and leaned in, so his breath was hot by my ear. "She told me that one day I would meet a woman who knew my heart with her own and could hear my mind." After another kiss, this one left me reeling and unsteady, trembling and wanting, he pulled back. "You sure you want to go to this thing, *cher*? We could stay in."

Let all this makeup and hair product go to waste? As if.

"No, but we can make it an early night. Leave right after I'm off stage." He was a hard man to resist and if he pushed, I would probably agree not to go. Especially since he'd done so much for me, so I'd do anything for him.

Besides, I wasn't sure this was a good idea anyway. I hadn't seen any of these people since the book came out. I'd said some things, all true, but I'd broken the unwritten rule in Hollywood. We generally left all the shaming and smack talk to the press, the tabloid rags and TV shows, and nowadays podcasters. We didn't turn on one another if there was no beef between us.

I'd turned on all of them.

Maybe Nicky was right. Staying in was best.

But no, that would have been cowardly.

Or smart.

Bah! I couldn't decide.

I'd flown all the way out here. They'd put me up in the hotel, and I didn't have the money to pay that back if they decided I'd breached a contract I probably should've never signed.

He looked me up and down as my skin heated under his gaze. He smiled and held out his hand. It was time to go.

When he kissed my knuckles, I had a second thought about staying in, then walked beside him to the door to our room.

In the elevator, Nicky turned me toward him and wrapped his arms around me. "No matter what happens, I'm with you, okay?"

It was like he knew. Like I should've known, probably, but I was so happy in my bubble of bliss with Nicky that he'd built around us these last few years, I didn't respond to his, "*Please don't let them hurt her,*" because with him I felt strong. With him, nobody could hurt me.

Chapter Five

Delilah Bradbury Can Take a Punch!

It's deja vu all over again at the Association of Actors Awards. Delilah Bradbury and Shara Hewitt threw down in a match that made the Gorgeous Ladies of Wrestling look like pat-a-cake. Hair was pulled, dresses ruined, and breasts were exposed on Hollywood's biggest night. Hewitt and Bradbury were whisked away in police cars. No injuries reported. – National Inquisitor

The car was waiting outside the hotel, and we slipped inside before any paparazzi could harass us, then it was off to Sunset Boulevard. I hadn't seen these streets in years. It was funny that they had once seemed so common to me, because now they felt over-the-top. Pretentious and grandiose. Yes, they were colorful, practically dripping in wealth, but they also made me miss my real life back home.

I liked the life I had with Nicky. I loved it. There was something nice about spending a morning curled up together listening to the birds and the traffic. Of walking places whenever we could and getting a good deal when we were out shopping. All of this… it was my past.

Not that I wouldn't step back into it for the money. I'd be a fool not to. That was part of why I was here, after all. Even a short time back in this life could set us up nicely for the future, a future I wished I'd thought about more when buying thousand-dollar dresses and spending money on outrageously priced meals.

Only with Nicky. Not without him. No life, wealthy or not, was worth losing him.

Hollywood Avenue was backed up with limousines and we were in the line somewhere near the middle when my stomach started churning. The doubts set in. None of these people were going to be happy to see me. I was going to be booed off the red carpet.

"I've never seen anything like this before in my life. *Je trouve cela vraiment risible. C'est totalement ridicule.*" He spoke with wide eyes and a soft voice but told me everything I needed to know with his tone alone. That and the words *are ridiculous* and *risible.* They meant just what they sounded like. Ridiculous and ludicrous, laughable and absurd.

This was my world, my old world, and I was showing it to him. I was already off kilter and shaken. I could've done without his criticism, even though I shared it. I knew full well he would be unimpressed by the glitz and glam.

However, I didn't want him to see it through that particular lens. I wanted him to look at me and tell me I belonged here. Or maybe that I didn't. I was knee deep in confusion. The whole day was a blur of mis-shaped thoughts and heart-breaking self-doubt.

From behind the closed window in the front seat, the driver's voice was sharp. He must've been on the phone. *"Celebrities need their adoration."* Then, *"I could've driven Pitt or Clooney, but I'm stuck with this broad. A nobody. Some disgraced has-been I've never even heard of."* We were sitting still. He had to know there was no road noise, not that there was a lot anyway, to disguise what he was saying. "*Delilah Bradbury's Total Meltdown. Back in the early 2000s, a woman rose to such fame she was called the next Meryl Streep, was said to be the American version of a young Judy Dench...*"

He was reading an article from *Weekly Entertainment,* one of those rag-mags that specialized in tell-alls from unnamed sources. I'd been a cover star more than once.

This particular article had run the day after the worst day of my life. I'd read it during a particularly pathetic binge of whiskey before I'd realized exactly how bad the story had become and how far the word had spread. I had most of it memorized.

"*A source close to the* Live Once, Die Twice *actress said that during an outburst where she dropped more than one F-bomb on live TV, Bradbury was hopped up on coke and has been since the split from husband number four, Mitchell Reed, one-time co-star and much younger husband.*" I hadn't been hopped up on anything, and he'd been two years younger. Apparently, I had a type. I tried to stop listening, but the driver's voice wasn't quiet enough for that.

I looked at Nicky. He'd spent so much time defending me and telling me it didn't matter, that now he must've been tired of it because he sat, unflinching, undisturbed by what the bastard of a driver was shouting to whomever he was speaking to.

He glanced at me. "*Cher*?"

His expression said he was worried about me, but because he didn't directly ask about the guy's cruel words, I just gave a smile to reassure him. Otherwise, he might just put this fool in his place, and that's the last thing we needed right now. I was going to sit quietly and pretend it didn't bother me.

I turned to look out the window. Everything was fine. I could do this.

"Whoa. This chick is mental," our driver said softly.

Seriously, was he trying to get a reaction out of me for the press? Well, I'd show him. I wasn't mental. I'd been made a fool by my "much younger husband" and the woman I'd thought was a friend, that was all. I wasn't about to beat my driver with my lovely purse just because he was mumbling about me.

Besides, I knew the truth, even if the rest of the world didn't. At the time, there had been no representation of my side of the story. By the time Lou had decided we should make a statement, it'd been too late. I'd been blacklisted.

"She's lucky that they've let her in this town at all and not stopped her at LAX and turned her around." He laughed like he thought he was untouchable. "She cleaned up good, though. Nice rack, anyway. I wouldn't mind a wardrobe malfunction or two. Probably fake though. They usually are."

Unable to stop myself, I leaned forward and smacked my hand against the window that separated his cockpit from the back of the car. When he lowered it, I glared at him in the rearview. "Maybe you should keep your voice down if you're going to read articles about me and insult me."

"Ma'am?"

Nicky laid a hand on the middle of my back. "*Bébé*?"

Sure. Now he spoke up. Though he sounded more confused than upset, like I was overreacting to the driver's words. I didn't care, and I was too angry to sit here any longer. "Let's walk from here."

I pushed open the door, gathered the hem of my dress in my arm, and slid out. I held the dress off the ground and didn't wait for Nicky to find me. Maybe it was over the top to climb out, maybe I should've just faced the music because of course people were going to talk as soon as they saw me, but my guts ached from the hurt his words caused.

Anybody who said the truth didn't hurt was a big fat liar. It didn't *just* hurt. It stabbed, pierced, and crushed me under the weight. I had blown my life apart without anyone's help, and even if I let my ex have a share of the blame, it didn't mean anything. I'd attacked a woman on live television, broken her dress, and left her hair piece on the stage as I was dragged away. *Forgiven* and *forgotten* were very different things, and I'd been neither.

Nicky's steps quickened behind me. If I wasn't so upset, I would have slowed and let him catch up to me, but I needed a minute. Just one, to walk off the hurt inside of me. After that, I hoped I could turn to face the man I loved more than anything in this world with a smile on my face.

He caught up a moment later and I sucked in a deep breath. "Ten years ago, when—"

"*Cher*, remember our rule. You don't have to explain to me. I know. I understand. And nothing matters before the day we met."

He was right. It'd been my rule, one I'd made when the pain was too fresh, when I hadn't been able to deal. We'd agreed that we both had a past and that neither of us needed to bring that baggage to the table.

Sometimes it was unavoidable, like this whole mess.

As I neared the Dolby, a building I'd been in a thousand times before, I heard the commotion coming for me.

"There she is!"

Darn it. I should have stayed in the car. I shouldn't be out here right now. Getting out to walk was going to be a heck of a lot worse than dealing with one mean driver, and there was nothing I could do to fix this situation now.

"Delilah! Ms. Bradbury! Delilah!" The camera flashes blinded me. Continuing forward and trying not to panic, my foot hit uneven ground, and I was suddenly stumbling. Falling. Aware of the feeling of my heel breaking on my five-thousand-dollar crystal Jimmy Choo's some boutique had given to Lou for me to wear tonight. I gasped as one of my knees struck the ground, I couldn't do a darn thing about it.

As I tumbled, my matching crystal bag slid along the pavement, and the world seemed to stop, spin slower and slower, and I wanted to die. It felt like that night all over again, and tears stung my eyes as the cameras continued to flash. This was my worst nightmare. I wasn't having a second chance at fame and fortune, I was embarrassing myself.

Stunned on the ground, I was about to climb to my feet and start running away, crying like a kid, when strong arms lifted me and pulled me against a hard chest. Relief rushed through me as the cameras continued flashing, blinding me. Not because I was free of this world, but because I recognized more than just the scent of his cologne. I recognized the feel of his arms, the way my head fit perfectly in the hollow of his throat, and the way he cradled me. Nicky. My beautiful, sweet Nicky. My hero.

On a normal day, he didn't have to rescue me from myself or carry me around to make sure I didn't hurt myself. But right now, I was no longer in my safe world. Somehow in coming back here it was almost like I was returning to my old self.

I didn't like it.

A long time ago, when I'd realized no one cared if I cried, pouted, or threw a tantrum, I'd had to look at myself in the mirror and change. That kind of behavior was a luxury that only children and the wealthy had, and I was neither any longer. I'd had to learn to suck it up and deal with what life handed me or what I brought on myself. It had been a hard-learned lesson, but it had also been well-learned.

One I didn't want to unlearn for one night of luxury.

"Nicky?" I whispered.

"It's alright, *cher,*" he said, his voice like a caress. "I have you."

"You always do," I told him, smiling as he held me just a little closer.

As soon as I was inside, still safely ensconced in Nicky's arms, a woman asked my name. She had a strangely familiar voice.

Nicky said, "Delilah Bradbury," in a voice that was surprisingly confident. Almost like he was the only person here foolish enough to think my name held value.

The woman hesitated, probably looking me over in case I wasn't who he said. Then, no doubt remembering that no one would want to be me tonight, directed Nicky. "That way."

I kept my head against his chest, my face hidden, embarrassed and not yet ready to face the world, even though I had to. Even though I hadn't landed on more than my knee, hadn't suffered more than some torn skin, a broken heel, and a small tear near the bottom of my dress, it had ruined the entire evening. At least it felt that way. If I had a minute to gather myself, I could try to pep up a little.

I didn't have a minute. We were already here.

Pulling my face away from Nicky's chest, I blinked out at the world and watched a woman walk in front of us, probably leading us to our destination. She glanced back, not at me, but at Nicky, and as soon as I saw her face I recognized her. Maeve Gallagher, a friend from the old days. She was dressed to the nines with a big coif of teased auburn and caramel hair and a silk dress that draped her body in a brushed sage color that brought out the grassy green of her eyes.

I studied her as she led us backstage. Her spine was straight. Her smile was plastered on. Truly, I wasn't sure yet if it was good to see her, or if she disliked me like everyone else and was just helping Nicky and me right now to be kind to someone who had taken a spill.

Maybe I'd know in a little while, for better or worse.

"This would be a good place for you guys right now," Maeve said, her voice super chipper.

She glanced at me as he gently sat me down on a chair backstage. There was a bustle of activity—people preparing to go onstage for the opening number, which was always its own production outside of everything else that happened during the show.

"Dee, it is so good to see you." I couldn't tell if Maeve was being sincere. But, strangely, it just felt nice to see her.

"You too, Maeve," I said, adjusting my dress and frowning down at my broken shoe. "How have you been?"

Before she could answer, a woman came pushing through the dancers. She was one of the crew whose responsibility it was to make sure nothing happened like what had happened the last time I was here. I knew because she'd been introduced to me earlier in the day. She handed me the necklace I'd apparently dropped without realizing it. "Ms. Bradbury, this must've fallen off when you fell out front."

I brought my hand to my neck, not realizing it had disappeared. I took the necklace from her and held it in my hand. That old familiar electricity surged through me and for a second time, I was lightheaded, but this time, I didn't go down. Didn't even blink before I had myself in check.

"Thank you," I murmured, still holding it while looking down at my dress.

A producer, whose name I couldn't remember, came up and greeted me once more before turning to Maeve and speaking to her in a low tone, while pointing at a clipboard. Probably arranging last-minute things, that I was sure of. If only they could fix my dress.

"I could fix that." A woman said as she walked past. Our eyes locked for one brief moment before she continued walking, and I didn't know if she meant the dress or the necklace. All I knew was that this might be my chance to keep a little bit of my dignity.

"Hey!" I called out to her and pointed so that the producer could stop her, which he did, even though he looked as confused as the woman. "I'm sorry, but did you mean my dress or this?" I opened my hand and the beautiful blue stone sparkled under the light.

"I don't know what you're talking about." She shook her head, her cheeks bright red as she stared down at her shoes.

"As you walked past, you said you could fix it, but I didn't know what you meant." Neither the dress, the necklace, nor my shoe had fared very well in the debacle.

"I didn't say anything," she mumbled, sounding like she wanted to melt into the ground.

I felt torn between not wanting to embarrass her further and feeling frustrated because I knew what I heard her. Arguing though, if she didn't want to help, wouldn't do me any good, so I took a deep breath and accepted that she wasn't going to be the angel that saved me from this situation.

"All right. I'm sorry. I must've misheard," I told her. Although I hadn't, and I knew it.

"Though," she began slowly, "I think I *could* fix your dress. It would only take a couple of minutes." Her voice was smaller now, and she looked at me from under dark, full lashes.

Relief rushed through me, and I nodded at her and smiled. "Yes. I would appreciate that so much."

I looked at my Nicky. "Will you be okay without me for a little while?"

"No," he said, followed by a wink. "I'll live."

"I'll be back as fast as I can," I promised, then turned to the woman who had offered to help me.

"Can you walk?" She was very gentle with me as I stood, and she took my arm.

I nodded. Even if I had to crawl, I was going to do as this girl asked me, so I wasn't walking on that stage with a ripped dress. "I don't know how I'll ever be able to thank you for this."

"Ms. Bradbury, I'm honored." She put her head down and led me to the bathroom that had been transformed into a dressing room. She handed me a robe. They always kept a supply of them backstage in case someone had to change or needed a quick makeup touchup.

I slid the gown off and the robe on. By the time I was done, she had set up a little station of threads and fabric, probably taken from one of the dressing rooms backstage. I handed her the dress with another thank you and walked out of the private lavatory while she no doubt cut, sewed, repaired, and redesigned my gown to hide the damage. This was my time to clean up my knee and pull myself together again.

The show hadn't yet started when she gave me the dress back. "I hope this is good enough."

"Anything was better than how it was," I reassured her, then put it on in a hurry. It was shorter now, just a bit longer than my knee in front but still dragged the ground in back. It covered the bandage I'd slapped over the wound but left my bare feet bare. I was in a $4800 world of debt because the stupid crystal shoe I'd been wearing was destroyed.

Still, the dress was at least a massive improvement. "It's lovely! You're really talented!"

She blushed and hung her head a little. "She's so pretty."

It was an awkward way to compliment me, but not so much that I would forget my manners and call her on it. Instead, I smiled at her. "You're lovely too."

She looked surprised, then went to a wall shelf and pulled a tube of glue from a bin. "I can fix your shoe, too, although I doubt Mr. Choo will appreciate me using gorilla glue on his fine craftsmanship." The woman was self-deprecating and charming. I genuinely liked her.

She turned away, and while she worked, I glanced over at Nicky every few seconds. He'd slipped into the dressing room a few minutes ago, apparently not comfortable being out among the rich and famous. He was seeing all the action from the inside.

"Look at her. So entitled. Has that poor girl waiting on her like she's a queen. A month ago, no one would've spit on her if she was on fire." I couldn't tell where the voice had come from, but there hadn't been much of an attempt to hide the venom and animosity in the tone. It didn't matter that I couldn't see her. I knew that superior tone as well as I knew my own. Shara freaking Hewitt. Her voice was unmistakable.

She walked around the corner of the dressing room, with the world's fakest smile on her face and arms spread wide, coming at me like a harpy with her wings extended for flight.

I pasted on an equally fake smile like I hadn't just heard her call me entitled. "Shara." My voice wasn't friendly, or rude, it was the best I could do.

"I knew you would come!" She gushed into my ear as she pulled me in for a hug.

"Is that the Chanel?" She looked me up and down. "It's as exquisite as I remember." Her brow crinkled and I knew what was coming. Some sort of backhanded compliment about the dress. "I don't remember it being a high-low." She *clearly* knew about the tumble I'd taken out front and was trying to get me to admit I'd ruined the vintage dress.

"I had it redesigned so it was more my taste." I winked at the girl who'd saved me, who was still holding the heel onto the bottom of my shoe so the glue would dry, the same girl whose name I hadn't bothered to ask. I *was* an entitled bitch. Nobody had forced her to help me. She'd done it entirely out of the kindness of her heart and had complimented me to boot.

Here I was, acting exactly as bad as Shara had pointed out I was. I walked over to the unnamed. "Thank you so much for your help." I transferred the necklace to my other hand so I could shake hers.

“I can fix your necklace, too,” she said softly.

“I can’t ask you to do more.” I remembered why I’d come over. “What’s your name?”

“Rachel Willett. Really, I would be happy to.” She eased it from my grasp and as much as I wanted to be able to wear it, I wasn’t sure about letting it go, but what else was I going to do? It felt wrong to relinquish the jewel. Why did it feel like letting my first kid go off to kindergarten?

Not that I knew what that felt like.

I couldn’t thank Rachel Willett enough, but I was sure as heck going to try. I didn’t care who was watching me hug her or who thought I should be fawning over Shara Hewitt coming to welcome me to a party that was mine long before it was hers. Just for clarity, the awards show was mine first because I got famous way before she did, *not* because I was that much older than her. I also didn’t care who’d just said that behind my dang back. Eff ‘em. I didn’t need them.

Beaming at Rachel, I sucked in a deep breath and squeezed her shoulders one more time. “I have to get back to that mess, but I wanted to say thank you. I know you’ve probably had a hundred more important things to do than take care of the hot mess that I’ve made of this day.” This was me being honest, being the person I should’ve been ten years ago.

“Not at all.” Her smile was so genuine, I believed her. Or maybe I just wanted to believe her.

True to herself, Shara just had to interrupt. Why was I not surprised?

"Well, I wasn't sure you would come, but I told The Association I didn't want their award unless they convinced *you* to come and give it to me," Shara said. *"I'm going to choke to death on all this bullshit. The amount of crow one has to eat to get a lifetime achievement award is hardly fair."* This bit was said more softly, but unmistakably Shara.

"What?" My stomach tightened. I should've known she'd had a hand in getting me here. At least she was coming at me here, backstage, and not in front of the cameras on live TV.

"I want to show the world that we forgave and forgot. Mitch thought it was a good idea, too." At the mention of my ex's name, I cringed and didn't even bother to hide it. "Oh, Dee." She pulled me in again, pinning my arms at my side in the process. *"Shouldn't have mentioned Mitch. Don't want this bitch losing her shit on TV. Again."*

"What?" I knew she was ballsy, but the sheer audacity of that statement was mind-boggling.

She pulled back and smiled down at me. "I have to get to the front. I'm presenting first." She turned, lifted the hem of her dress, and jogged to the door before turning back to blow me a kiss. Then she was gone, and I nearly staggered in relief to be out of her presence. There was no way I could ignore the horrible things she'd said for much longer. The awful, insulting, demeaning things that she'd said just loud enough that I'd heard it but nobody else could've.

My blood boiled in my veins. This was about Shara and only Shara. Not about bringing me back to Hollywood. This was about humiliating me. A smart woman would've walked out right then, would've left through the same door I'd been carried in.

I wasn't such a smart woman. I didn't leave. I was here, and I deserved this second chance. I was ready to be seated. The show was about to begin.

I was ready.

Ready, dang it!

Chapter Six

Delilah Bradbury Humiliated at Association Awards

In a throwback to almost exactly a decade ago, four-time winner Delilah Bradbury was once again humiliated on the Association of Actors Awards stage when she apologized to her colleagues for a harsh tell-all she penned in revenge for her ousting from the public eye. As she stated her remorse, Bradbury was assaulted by Shara Hewitt who had her own embarrassing moment on the stage. The Association has since rescinded Hewitt's Lifetime Achievement Award. –National Inquisitor

They'd gone over everything that would happen to me from here on out. There were a couple more commercial breaks before I had to go backstage to prepare for my presentation. A producer would come for me and a seat filler would take my place between Nicky and some up-and-coming actor, so that when the camera panned the crowd, there wouldn't be an empty seat. I'd always been amazed that The Association paid for this, but then I'd learned it was industry standard. And it made sense. It would be odd to look out into the sea of celebrities on one of their biggest nights and see an empty seat. But that's not what was important right now. I needed to focus. Take deep breaths, and focus. Seat fillers didn't matter.

Rachel had my necklace, and I felt naked without it. Weird, because it wasn't like I was so used to wearing it. It was difficult to stay in my seat and not go see if she'd finished.

As I sat beside Nicky, clutching his hand like it was my lifeline, I watched the show like everyone else in the world. Like a regular person, because that was what I was now. It actually took effort to hide the fact that I was in awe of the star-studded audience. These weren't my people any longer, that much was clear.

I watched for the producer, and when she showed up during the next commercial break, I made my way backstage. Nerves bubbled in my belly. Oh, man. I wasn't sure I was going to make it through this without throwing up. If I got through this, maybe, just maybe, it would open doorways for Nicky and me. I started chanting that in my head like a mantra. Something as simple as a couple of commercials or a small supporting role could make our golden years a heck of a lot better.

That was why I was doing this. For us. For our future. Not because I want to be part of this life again.

I looked out at the sea of faces as Rachel handed my necklace back to me. "Be careful. It'll need a new chain, but this should hold until you can get it to a jeweler." She showed me the paperclip clasp she'd fashioned, and I smiled as she helped me put it on.

"It's genius. Thank you again, Rachel." I didn't know much about Hollywood anymore, but tomorrow, Rachel Willett was going to get a big bouquet of flowers from a very grateful former actress.

I laid my hand over the stone and a burst of warmth ran through my body, like magic washing over me. It happened each time I put it on. I brushed the thought aside because it seemed crazy that a necklace could be magical in any way.

Cray-zee.

I aimed a smile at Rachel as Maeve nodded for me to walk onto the stage. It was nice to see a friendly face before going out to what felt like the wolves.

I hadn't gone many feet from stage left when a thousand murmurs stopped me cold.

"Has-been bitch."

"She told the world I cheated on my husband. What the hell is she doing here?"

"Who let the trash in?"

"Buckle up. The bitch is back. I wonder whose career she'll ruin tonight."

I could hear them all, random voices bombarding me as I tried to make it to the microphones at center stage.

Nobody was speaking. At least, nobody in the rows close enough for me to hear their words. The necklace seemed to warm on my chest as I forced my feet to move, one in front of the other.

It felt like magic every time I put it on. And now I was hearing voices. What was going on?

Sucking in as deep of a breath as my lungs would hold, I tried to focus and ignore the voices. The lights were bright, blinding, and I couldn't see Nicky. It was okay. He was out there and that helped me find the courage to keep going and not run for the wings.

I cleared my throat and adjusted the mic height of the one closest to me. I tried to tune out the voices as I waited but they were so loud inside my head.

Holy freaking crow. That's what it was. The voices. They were in my head.

"She has nerve."

"How dare she show up here, after everything she said."

"Who in God's name decided this would be a good idea?"

A script ran on the teleprompter in front of me, but the words blurred as my eyes filled with tears. "I knew this wasn't going to be easy," I said. This was my chance to make it right. I sucked in a breath, a slow cleansing breath I blew out as the world watched me pull myself together.

At least, I tried to. I really did.

"*Please don't let her go off script.*" I didn't have to wonder whose voice that one was. It was a producer, and it didn't matter which one. Maybe it was all of them, I couldn't have been sure.

All I knew was, I had to do this. I owed every single one of them at this moment. "Hello." I sounded shaky and pathetic because I was. "A few years ago, several years ago, my life took a very sudden and unexpected detour."

"*Oh, shit.*"

"*Oh, hell.*"

The chorus of cuss words inside my head overlapped, laid over top of one another in a cacophony of chaos and sound, but I shook it off, and tuned the voices out. "I don't mean that something happened *to* me. It didn't. I'm not talking about what happened here, on the stage, although that was no moment of glory, let me tell you." I widened my eyes because I was an actress, and I knew how to convey emotion with my face. "What I mean is what happened after."

"*Please let them cut to commercial.*" A voice got through my invisible wall. A cameraman who was being directed by the booth–I knew how these things worked–pivoted in front of me, then swung back to aim his lens my way again.

"The book was unforgivable. You were my friends and my colleagues, and I shouldn't have told your secrets, your stories." I shook my head and looked out at the faces near and the ones in the far corners of the room. "If I could take back all the things I said, and I know it means nothing now, but I would. I'm sorry for the hurtful things I said and did during that period of my life."

It was as I finished, as the silence in the room grew to a deafening pitch that I heard the screech. This particular screech was *not* coming from inside my head. With all the insults swirling inside, it was hard to differentiate the one outside, or I might've known to run. Duck at least.

She came from the wings where she'd been waiting for me to introduce her. Shara Hewitt barreled toward me, fists balled, heels clicking and clacking on the stage floor.

"Holy hell!" I bobbed and weaved in one direction and faked her out so I could get around her.

Pandemonium broke out, or it seemed as if it did as the audience jumped to its collective feet and people rushed out from behind the curtains. This wasn't my meltdown. This was Shara's, and she was screaming at the top of her lungs. "You ruined this night for me! It isn't *your* night!"

I zigged, and she zagged. "Shara, what in the world are you doing?"

"I was coming out to forgive you on this stage. I had it all planned and you ruined it!" She reached out, caught a finger in the strap of my dress, and gave it a sharp tug trying to get her finger back. Unfortunately, that strap—which had already survived my tumble out front by just a single thread—gave way, and the worst possible thing happened.

My boob fell out. My ta-ta, bosom, titty. My right knocker was exposed to the entirety of Hollywood and beyond that, through the cameras, the whole freaking world!

I covered my breast with my hand and tried to backtrack. I had to get off this stage. I'd be safe once I was backstage, but I couldn't get away from her. Shara Hewitt went full-on banshee and started screaming, shifting from foot to foot, and blocking me like she was part soccer goalie. We were zigging and zagging and all the while, I could hear everyone's words and thoughts, and I couldn't figure out which was which. The shouting and insulting, cursing and cutting me down.

"*What a joke!*"

"*A couple of has-beens bustin' out the boobies on stage.*"

"*I'm so glad I didn't stay home.*"

"*Gorgeous Ladies of Wrestling this is not. More like Old Grandmas of bitch slapping.*"

Now the people rushing the stage were reaching us, and obviously if the producers knew anything at all, they'd cut to commercial, or this thing was going to be one solid censor beep. It wasn't until the police came that Shara finally stopped screaming and dropped her hands. I ran as fast as I could in these dang shoes.

My beautiful Chanel gown was ruined. It was the least of my worries, but it was my Chanel. My pretty dress.

Maybe I was in shock.

Nicky found his way backstage and slid his jacket around me, then after I put my arms through the sleeves, he buttoned it, so I didn't have to hold my dress up anymore. Once I was decent, a police officer came over. "Ma'am, I need you to come with me. We can do this the easy way or…?" He held up a pair of handcuffs.

With a sigh, I held my hands out in front of me. "In front, if that's okay." He nodded and gave me half a smile. Thank goodness the guy was nice. He cuffed me, searched me, then helped me into the back of an LAPD squad car.

"I'll meet you there, *bébé*." The window was down on the car and Nicky had come out front to call after me.

Flashing cameras harassed me as we drove away. This was going to be a very long night.

Chapter Seven

Delilah Bradbury's Newest Perp Walk–Mugshot Inside

In a turn of events that can only be called disturbing and not fit for primetime TV, Shara Hewitt went on a full-frontal attack, and both she and has-been (more like where's she been) Delilah Bradbury were taken to jail where they spent the night in a holding cell. Bradbury emerged this morning wearing an orange jumpsuit in what can only be termed her final curtain call on an illustrious career that ended abruptly ten years ago after a similar incident on the same stage. – National Inquisitor

By the time we arrived at the police station, the paparazzi were everywhere. My perp walk was recorded for posterity by several rag magazine reporters who had nothing better to do than to follow washed-up and undeserving old me. Or maybe they were there to get photos of Shara, who walked in without cuffs and with a big smile on her face.

After the kind officer handed me off to a female, she uncuffed me then slapped my left hand and then my right onto a scanner. It was better than the old ink pad method from the television. "Nifty."

"Yeah. We're tech giants here." Officer M. Carbon didn't seem to want to engage in chit-chat, so I clamped my lips shut. I'd played a prisoner once in a TV movie, and if this experience was anything like the one we'd portrayed, I was about to have a very ugly night. "Stand there." She pointed to a wall marked with height increments of inches and feet.

I moved into position and then looked at her. She stood behind a large, ancient-looking camera on a tripod that was bolted to steel plates in the floor. "Should I smile?"

While my face was pinched in question, she snapped the picture, and I ended up looking like the fuzzy-headed sister-cousin of Elmer Fudd. I didn't want to imagine tomorrow's headlines. They were going to be brutal.

All the while I heard all the things the officers were thinking. My suspicions were confirmed beyond a shadow of a doubt. I was hearing their thoughts in my head. Nobody's lips were moving.

"*Isn't that the chick from One Night?*"

"I loved her book, but what was she thinking, coming back here? Kind of shocked they didn't all kick her ass."

"It's always the rich bitches with the bad boob jobs." I imagined a head shake with that one and looked down at my bought and paid-for c-cups. There wasn't a bad thing about them. They'd been done by the best.

I tried to tune them out, but the more I tried, the louder they got.

"Come on, princess. I need the necklace." Officer Carbon held out her hand and curled her fingers in and out as I unclasped the paperclip and dropped it into her hand. The voices stopped, instantly. It was the necklace that had made me hear their thoughts. She deposited it into a bag and then handed me a stack of orange fabric. "You have to change."

I sighed. I'd been a model before I was an actress. Nudity didn't bother me, not even a little bit. I started to undress, but she gave me a not-so-gentle shove to a small room, then walked in behind me. I was fine until she snapped on a pair of gloves as I stepped out of my shoes. The words *body cavity search* snaked their way to the front of my mind. Oh, no. Come on.

She took the jacket and stuffed it into a bag. The dress. My Spanx. For anyone who didn't know prior to this, there is absolutely nothing more humiliating in the world than having to take off a pair of Spanx in front of another person. That was coming from someone who'd just had her breast exposed on live television.

She ran her finger along the edge of my underwear, lifted my boobs to check underneath, because apparently, that was a common hiding spot for illegal contraband—who knew?—then nodded toward the orange jumpsuit. She wasn't going to do a cavity search.

I nearly sobbed in relief.

Choking back my tears, I stepped into the rough jumpsuit, snapped the snaps, slipped on the fancy white paper shoes, and followed her to a bench on the wall where I was handcuffed once again to a bar that ran along the wall.

As Shara repeated the same process, I watched them fawn over her. Once upon a time, they would've fawned like that over me. She was the one making the big movies now. It was her name in lights. She was the one revered by the masses.

I had Nicky and that more than made up for it, because I knew the dirtbag all too well who would be picking her up. I'd read for years about the scandals and Shara standing by her man. She was welcome to him.

As I watched them come toward me, I sat back against the wall. I looked good in orange, so I wasn't bothered by the wardrobe as much as I was by the fact that she still looked like a million dollars, and I was disheveled because of her. She'd attacked me and she was the hero.

After she was printed and processed—although allowed to stay in her Mark Jacobs gown and take selfies with each of the cops—they uncuffed me, and we were led to a room with a window in a door that locked from the inside. A sign on the door said holding.

When we were inside, Officer Carbon unlocked my cuffs, even though they'd just put me into a cell with a woman who'd attacked me on live national TV. Shara looked as if she was gearing up for round two.

In my entire life, I'd never been so humiliated. I was in a room that smelled like urine and vomit with Shara as a cellmate. This was a new personal low. I was *mortified*.

She sat on the bench across from me. These were made of what appeared to be concrete and felt like it under my ass. Probably because concrete cleaned up easier than a mattress and judging by the smell, this was where DUI criminals slept it off.

"I asked for a lawyer." Her voice is soft.

I would crawl into a hole and die before I admitted I didn't have the money for an attorney. I ignored her and looked at my nails instead. They hadn't even chipped. Point one for me. They'd been expensive.

"You just had to steal my thunder. This was *my* night." She stared at me and then shook her head. I wouldn't look at her, but I had excellent peripheral vision. "What was I supposed to do?"

She was never going to let it go. I sighed and rolled my head on my neck with as much attitude as I could until I was glaring at her. "I don't know. Maybe, *possibly,* ask someone else to give you your award next time." Why she'd asked me, I couldn't imagine. "Was the whole point just to humiliate me?"

"No." Her brow wrinkled. "I just wanted… I can't stand you being mad at me."

It took me half a second to process what she'd just said. She wanted me to not be mad at her? That made me about ten times angrier. "You shouldn't have taken my husband then." I shook my head. I wasn't even mad about that anymore. I had let it go. I would not sink to her level. "Look, it's done. Whatever." I had Nicky. I didn't need Mitch or to be mad about Mitch. I'd made my bed. Hollywood wasn't my town anymore. "Just next time have Scarlett or Tom give you your award, okay?"

She shook her head. "No, I've ruined it all. There won't be a next time." Her sadness drew her face into a deep frown. It was going to take a while to get over it.

"Just own it." I knew that feeling. Knew it so well. "My advice is just don't write a book about it."

"I read that book." She tilted her head and considered me. "I wasn't in it." She chuckled a little, and I couldn't tell if I should brace myself for another onslaught of fury or if she was just thinking. She lifted her head and looked at me. "I suppose I should thank you."

"Except the stuff about Mitch that hit a little too close to home to be book fodder, the things I knew about you, I knew because we were friends. I didn't want to betray that." It was true. I hadn't been able to spill her secrets. It wouldn't have been right. Those other people hadn't been my friends. They'd been coworkers and acquaintances and all the things I wrote were public knowledge, or at least known by more people than just me. Others could've spilled the same secrets. I'd just been the one to actually put them on paper.

It took her a few long seconds to look away from me before she spoke again. "I shouldn't have screwed around with Mitch. I'm sorry."

I held up my hand. "Hey, no take-backs. You wanted him; you get to keep him."

For the first time in longer than I could remember, the anger was gone. I wasn't mad that she took my husband. I'd definitely gotten the better end of that deal.

Chapter Eight

Buh-bye Chanel, Hello Prison Jumpsuit–The Delilah Bradbury Story

Delilah Bradbury exchanged her vintage Chanel gown, which had already been transformed between the red carpet and the stage, was carted off to the pokey after a bout of fisticuffs with Shara Hewitt onstage last night as the Association of Actors celebrated sixty-five years of glitz and glamor on the Hollywood stage. Celebs turned out in high style to be praised and awarded by their peers. The only damper on this sapphire celebration was the on-stage, live battle between Hewitt and Bradbury which ended in both women being taken to jail as the show saw an early end giving Bradbury fodder for an epilogue for her best seller, Living in Sin: Delilah Bradbury's real-life account of Hollywood – *Helen Hart, Channel 7, Entertainment Times, 6pm edition*

That was an entire night I was never going to get back. A night spent thinking about the fact that I seemed to be able to read thoughts, with the help of a magical necklace, and about the fact that my life was still a mess. Once upon a time, this place had been my home and there was nowhere else I would rather have been, but now, I couldn't wait to get home, to leave this place, because the stars had faded out of my Hollywood skies. It was time to let this all go for good. To do something with my life that gave me the same happiness I had back when this was my home. Funny that it took jail time to make me realize I was squandering my life.

To his credit, when I walked out of my cell and saw Nicky waiting for me, standing on the other side of a counter that had a locked door on one end, he didn't laugh at my ugly orange jumpsuit even though it had the distinction of making me look something like a traffic cone. He was *such* a good man.

Instead, he smiled, wagged his finger at me, and mouthed, "*Je t'aime,*" with a wink.

My mama always said, "Never trust a man who winks." That bit of advice always stuck with me in much the same way as her, "Never leave home without a condom in your purse," and "If a man is going to buy you a drink, make sure it's a top-shelf gin martini," advice did.

Mama must've said the wink thing because she'd never seen a man who looked like Nicky. She had to have meant all other men except for Nicholas Pontchalac. I'd agreed with her that until I met Nicky, it was just smarmy. Yet, he made it look sexy, and my skin flushed with appreciation for this wonderful man who'd come to take me home.

Some cop I hadn't met yet—part of the day shift, I presumed, since he looked refreshed and clean in a way the others with their wrinkled uniforms and haggard faces didn't—handed me my belongings.

As soon as I had the brown bag in my hands, I pulled the red tape off the top and opened the tabs so I could root through it, looking for my necklace. I didn't know what I would do when I found it. The thing made me pretty darn nervous, but some part of me just wanted to know, either way, what it could or couldn't do. My hands closed around the cold stone, and a burst of that familiar *something* shot through me. No, not something, magic.

I stayed on my feet, not because the feeling from the necklace was less than before, but because I was holding myself rigid, protecting myself from it. From the... magic because that's what I was starting to think this necklace had. All those mean things that I'd thought I heard said, they'd been the thoughts of others. Or maybe it wasn't real, and I just loved the necklace, so I just imagined this feeling. Imagined that it allowed me to hear the thoughts of others. If I'd imagined it, then probably I had a brain tumor. This crap was nuts.

As soon as I connected the little paper clip clasp, my head was full of voices that were not my own.

"I can't believe she came back here."

"The Association Awards are never going to be this much fun again."

That one was probably true.

"Why is her necklace being held together by a paperclip?"

Glancing around, I saw no one who could be saying the words, but lots of gazes were focused on me. Officers pretending to drink their coffee. Officers pretending to read a newspaper. None of them were speaking. I was either losing my mind or hearing the thoughts of everyone around me. I couldn't decide which thing I was hoping for.

Since there also wasn't anything I could do about it, I tuned them out in favor of signing my walking papers. It was probably a promise to never step foot in Hollywood again, but I didn't care. I only cared that Nicky was waiting for me. Since I'd met him, he'd been here for me like no one else had ever been before.

A buzzer and a click opened the exit door, and I walked straight into his arms. He hummed. "I always thought blue was your color, but now, I think it might be orange."

"You know what they say, Nicky. Orange is the new black. Maybe it's blue in my case." Only the perfect guy could look at his woman—and I was *his* woman in a way I hadn't been the woman of any of my five husbands—and think her jail garb was attractive. Fortunately, that perfect guy was mine.

"Aw, *bébé*, every color is your color." He lowered his head and kissed me softly but quickly. "Let's take you home." *At least to the hotel.* The thought was his, not mine.

Home sounded grand, and I was ready.

By the time I walked out of the police station, I'd heard a couple hundred different thoughts, and I was starting to get worried about the voices in my head. They were definitely there, and they were definitely in my head, not coming from anyone's mouth.

"There is never a boring day with you." He smiled as he carried the brown bag with my ruined dress and shoes along with the jacket to his tux in one hand then slid the opposite arm around me and pulled me close so he could plant a kiss on the top of my head. "*En l'aimant pour toujours.*"

Nothing made me melt faster than when he spoke to me in French, but I also liked to know whether he was calling me a crazy she-bat who needed to be on medication. If he was saying that, I couldn't blame him, but I wanted to know. I tilted my chin up to look at him, absolutely ready to brace myself for the hurt. "What does that mean?"

He pulled his head back to look at me, eyes narrow, brow pinched and wrinkled, chin at an angle as he considered me.

"I didn't say anything, *cher.*"

"*En l'aimant pour toujours.*" Of course, he didn't mangle it the way I did, but I'd heard him.

His pretty blue eyes opened wide. "It means, 'I'm going to love her forever.'"

"Oh." I couldn't have wiped the smile off my face with superpowers. "Well, in that case, *en l'aimant pour toujours...*too."

He laughed and kissed the top of my head again.

"This place is pretty," he said, "but I miss our home."

I smiled at him. "I miss it too."

He leaned closer to me. "When we get back home, I'm going to make you breakfast in bed."

I snuggled against him. "I'll help." He laughed, because between us he was the cook, by a large margin. I was a bit of a danger in the kitchen.

They'd let me keep the orange jumpsuit because my dress was in such poor shape and probably would've landed me an indecent exposure charge if I tried wearing it outside of the building. I drew more than one second glance as we waited on the sidewalk for our Uber.

There we were, middle of the morning, me in prison particulars and him in a three-piece designer tuxedo, standing as if it was the most natural thing in the world. To our credit, we weren't the most unique couple on the sidewalk. There wasn't a face tattoo on either of us and we weren't skateboarding upside down on our hands.

He held my hand, and I looked up at him. Nicky was handsome in ways I couldn't begin to appreciate enough, couldn't describe without it sounding so cliché. He had golden brown hair that he kept pulled back. Eyes bluer than the ocean. He didn't smell like his clothes were washed at the prison laundry. It was the smile that made me grateful I'd ever met him.

Still inside of my head, where I should've been appreciating the beauty of my very handsome man friend, there was a nagging thought—my necklace wasn't an ordinary gemstone. Not because of the shine. Or the paperclip holding it together. It was the random thoughts of others that I was privy to when I wore it.

I probably needed my head examined, needed to figure out which medications would best help my strange situation and enhance the realization that the thoughts were likely coming from my own head, but since nary a shrink was in sight and our ride had pulled up, I pushed the thought away until we were buckled into the backseat.

Nicky sat with his hand in mine, and every once in a while, he gave a quick squeeze.

The driver earned himself an extra star by not commenting on my clothes, although a couple of times, I caught him looking at me in the rearview like maybe he thought he was driving the getaway car. I wasn't worried about him. His thoughts weren't much more complex than frustration with other drivers as he zigged and zagged through traffic, and lyrics to the song on the radio.

I looked at the man next to me. His thoughts were borderline X-rated—a very specific prisoner-jailer fantasy—and my body warmed next to him. This was too important to let lust deter me. "Nicky, can we try something?"

His eyes were dark with desire, and he smiled down at me. "Anything you want, *cher*." He'd just gotten to the *back me into the wall and rub his hard-on against my belly while he fondled and kissed me* portion of his fantasy.

"Oh, cher, *don't ask me what I'm thinking."* He nodded anyway.

I lowered my voice so the driver wouldn't believe he was driving such a lunatic as me. "Think of something very specific, but wholly random. Something I wouldn't be able to just guess." I wanted to prove whether or not I was blessed with a psychic necklace or if I was just losing my mind and imagining the thoughts of others.

He glanced at me. *Queen of diamonds.*

"Queen of diamonds." As soon as I said it, his thoughts changed.

Your mama's chicken noodle soup. Matlock. When I guessed each time, he nodded and smiled, looking more and more amazed. "No secrets from my *bébé*." He pulled me close again and kissed the side of my head.

"I hope not."

He smiled, his expression some combination between impressed and concerned. "How did you do that?"

"I'm not sure yet. I'm still figuring it out," I confessed, stroking the stone at my throat.

I let him hold me for a second then shifted and removed the necklace. "Can we try again?" I set the necklace on the opposite side of my seat where neither Nicky nor I was touching it. Now my head was silent. I could only hear my own thoughts, boring as they were. I shook my head at him. I had no idea what he was thinking.

He lowered his head so his mouth was at my ear, and he whispered, "I was thinking about peeling that jumpsuit down your body so I can kiss every inch of your skin."

"Wow. That is a lot better than *Queen of diamonds* or *Matlock*." I tilted my chin up to kiss him as the driver's car hit a pothole that felt as if it was big enough to eat the car and the necklace jumped on the seat, nearly going out the window when he swerved to avoid another. I lurched forward and tilted to the side, but my progress was stopped by Nicky's arm, so I didn't end up in the front seat beside the driver when he slammed on his brakes and the necklace slid off the seat, thunked into the backside of the driver seat then kerplunked onto the floor. When I reached for it, the driver took a hard right and the stone slid out of my reach.

Nicky curled his arm around me to grab it as the driver hit his brakes again. I held my breath as he touched it, but it didn't seem to affect him at all.

I held the necklace, staring at it, unsure what to do now. "This is what makes me able to do what I did." I shot a furtive glance toward the front seat, but the driver was preoccupied with traffic.

"You can hear thoughts but only when wearing it?" he asked.

"It looks like it."

"Which might have been part of why last night was so strange?" he asked.

I laughed. "*Partially.*"

There was a moment of silence between us, before he spoke again, "With great power comes great responsibility." He could've been reading me the phonebook in that accent, and I would've tuned in.

"I know, Nicky." I was going to do my best to be responsible, but first, I needed to know exactly what I was dealing with. I had a feeling that my best chance to find out what I needed to know was by making another trip to the flea market.

Chapter Nine

Delilah Bradbury Heads Home–Disappears For Good From Hollywood

In an emotional return to Hollywood cut short, Delilah Bradbury made her bed. Again. Disappointed a fan base excited for her comeback. Again. Was seen at LAX dragging her tail between her legs as she left Hollywood. Again. Buh-bye Bradbury. Anybody know who the hot guy she travels with is?–National Inquisitor

Once we were back home and Nicky was at work for Repo Ron, I started my research with a backward internet picture search of the necklace and got about three million hits. Most were attached to sale ads at either ridiculously expensive prices or ridiculously low. The stones were all deep London blue and all identical because they were trying to match my photo.

The interwebz had let me down, which happened so seldomly that I was at a loss as to how to cope with it. I made dinner, watched some talk-show TV, and waited for Nicky to get home. Some days it seemed like he had a banker's hours, but other days he came home late and tired, and by the time he got here, dinner wasn't more than a few rock-hard bits of pasta with garlic bread that we could've used to play croquet.

By seven, it was apparent that I was eating the chicken alone. After that, I took a shower and got ready for bed, but I couldn't stop thinking about the necklace. It was on the table beside the bed, nestled in its box.

I wasn't the kind of girl who believed in magic, but there was something mystic, extra worldly going on with this thing.

After the eighteenth time I'd made Nicky let me read his mind, he'd made me promise not to do it unless I told him first. It'd been an easy promise to make while he was kissing my neck. He'd unclasped the necklace and it had all stopped.

I'd been almost mindless by then and then our afterglow cuddle had been a *make a promise* conversation. When that was finally over, we'd gone for round two.

The necklace was too fancy, too big to wear around the house, but I left it by the bed because I liked looking at it. I liked holding it. That power surge was quickly becoming an addiction I couldn't live without.

When he finally came home and crawled into bed, I was still awake, still holding the necklace, wondering what secrets I would be able to find. “I want to go back to the flea market.”

“Okay, are you thinking there might be more magic jewelry? Something that might make you disappear or turn back the hands of time?” He kissed me softly and took the necklace to put in its box. “Maybe I can find one that will make your pajamas disappear.”

I grinned. “An easy-access emerald? A Dr. Denton dissolving diamond?” Not that anyone wore Doctor Dentons anymore.

He laughed. “Exactly, *bébé*.”

I waited until after he’d unbuttoned the last button on my top and spread it apart, I kissed him, then curled my fingers in his hair. “You don’t seem to need any help. You’re doing fine on your own.”

We didn’t talk again until the sun was about to rise, after a night of fun, followed by some much needed rest. The first thing he did when we woke up was sit up, grin at me, and say, “Let’s get breakfast and go shopping.”

Smiling right back, I said, “Eating and magic shopping it is!”

I didn’t tell him that this was a fact-finding mission more than a shopping spree. I wanted the story behind the jewel that let me—and I still couldn’t quite believe it—read minds. I wanted to make sure Nicky wasn’t somehow pulling the world’s most elaborate prank, so I had the necklace in my bag, but I couldn't think of how to test him where I would know for certain. I didn't try.

"Are you looking for another necklace?"

I shrugged. "Maybe if one knocks me on my ass, I might pick it up." He'd darn sure better have believed I was going to be putting my hands on every single one.

When he pulled over for breakfast at one of those mom-and-pop diners, I was too excited to eat, but Nicky wasn't so affected. He ate his eggs and pancakes, then went after my omelet. "You should've ordered bacon."

I laughed. "Or you could order enough food to fill you up without having to wish I would've ordered what you like."

He shook his head and grinned the adorable little grin that reminded me of what he must've looked like when he was being naughty as a boy. "The food you order and never eat would go to waste." When he was right, he was right.

"Do you want me to order some now?" I was anxious to go, but it wasn't like the market was going anywhere. I looked across the table. If he wanted bacon, he could have bacon. I flagged down the waitress who was none too happy that I was in our booth waving my arm like a maniac.

"What can I get you?" She opened her order pad and pulled out our check then laid it on the table and cleared away some of our empty plates.

"A couple strips of bacon?"

She nodded. "Sure." She had the traditional Boston accent and a sarcastic smile, but she brought the bacon a minute later and set it in front of Nicky, smiled at him, then walked away. She watched him from the counter, and I was tempted—really tempted—to pull the necklace out and have a listen, but I didn't.

I rose above. Get me a freaking cookie.

When we were finally on our way, he held my hand as he drove, and when he pulled into the parking lot, he looked over at me and smiled. "Moment of truth, *bébé*. You ready?"

Finding out about this necklace had become my single most important goal, a place to focus all of my attention so I could avoid the fact that my career was over, and I was growing increasingly more useless by the day.

"I'm so ready, *bébé*." It made him smile when I tried to mimic his accent. I assumed it was because I did such a poor job, but when he came around my side to open the door for me, he pulled me into a hug. I was holding the purse that had the necklace, so it wasn't my fault I could hear his thoughts. They were jumbled and in French, but I got the gist. *Famile* or family.

That was fine with me. I wasn't scared to make Nicky my family, even though the five other times I'd tried hadn't worked out. I wondered if he realized how bad I was at it. The chicken heart in me wouldn't let me ask. Instead, I walked silently beside him, my hand in his. We were just a couple in love, having a nice leisurely stroll through the tents, both thinking about becoming more and neither quite sure whether it was a good idea to bring it up.

It was a tense few minutes before I could think of anything else. Before my Hollywood exit, I'd fallen in love a lot. A co-star. A camera guy, a stuntman, and with anyone who looked like he might love me for a few minutes outside of the bedroom. Not that I was a harlot or a slut, but in between husbands I'd dated and anybody who'd made it to a second date ended up walking me down the aisle.

The truth was, I'd probably only been in love with the idea of being in love. Why wasn't there a necklace that could tell me if this was the real thing? My own judgment certainly didn't cut it in this area, and I would've paid a whole lot of money for one that could help me out now.

I didn't want to lose Nicky by making this something it wasn't. We didn't need to change anything. I was currently listening to his thoughts which was breaking the one rule he'd set, the promise he'd asked me to make, so I couldn't tell him I was quite happy with the way things were. There was no way I could think of to bring it up without exposing myself for the promise breaker I was. Not that I probably would've brought it up because I was happy with the status quo, and I wasn't jeopardizing it.

While I was happy with everything as it was, and my hand was curled around his, he walked us between the tents and tables and piles of antiques and furniture. It was sunny and seventy out, not too cold or unseasonably hot. Someone was popping kettle corn—the smell was divine.

We walked the aisle twice. The necklace woman wasn't there. Darn it! There wasn't even an indication that she'd been there recently, because the woman who now occupied the tent where we'd bought the necklace had racks and racks full of tie-dyed t-shirts and headbands, shorts, and flip-flops.

The disappointment was real.

"Sorry, *bébé*." He kissed the top of my head. "Maybe we could ask one of the people in the tents next to this one." He nodded to the one on my side. "Let's try."

Hope once again bubbled inside me, and this time I worked to push it down. I didn't want to be disappointed twice.

I walked into the tent—it was twice as big and far more crowded than it had been last time—but it was hard to tell who was in charge. People browsed from both sides of the tables because of how she had them set in a U-shape with an aisle on each side.

Nicky nudged me and pointed to a woman taking money from a customer. "There you go, *cher*."

The woman had short red hair cut into a bob and flipped forward toward her high cheekbones and pointed chin. Her eyes were green, and she looked like a soccer mom who'd taken up antiquing and matched her striped white and tan shirt to a pair of khaki shorts and those comfortable boat shoes all the kids were wearing.

I walked up and she smiled. "Hi. Can I help you find something?"

"I hope so." I smiled my most ingratiating Hollywood smile and pulled the box out of my purse. I held it though because I didn't want some wayward customer to mistake it as something being sold or anyone to try to walk out with it. "I bought this a few weeks ago from a woman who was in the tent next door. You don't happen to know her?"

"Of course." She examined the box but didn't touch it. "That looks like one of hers. I don't know her name though." Either this woman was truly regretful, or she should've been an actress. Her frown looked real. "Did she cheat you?" She got an eyeful of Nicky who'd come to stand behind me, and all the sudden her boobs were higher because she'd straightened her spine and pulled her shoulders back. Typical.

"No, not at all. I was just wondering if she knew the story behind this piece." I turned the box toward me and opened it then showed it to her.

She pulled a pair of glasses up from her chest where they rested on a chain. She didn't really look old enough for such a set-up—my elderly seventh-grade teacher had one like it—but she made use of it.

"Yeah. This box has a story." She lowered her glasses and leaned in like she was telling me a secret. "This box was made in the sixteen, seventeen hundreds. It was originally stolen—probably with the necklace inside—by a pirate from an English ship bound for Spain."

I didn't ask how she knew, but because I was holding the box, I trusted her. She was actually picturing said pirate's ship. "A pirate." I glanced at Nicky who smiled. There was a good story behind this thing.

"Yes. Captain Renfro Remington, also known as Renegade Remington." She reached for my little piece of treasure, and I snapped the lid closed like she was Julia Roberts, and I was Richard Gere from that scene in the hooker movie. Such a good movie. She drew back and squinted at me. "He lost his treasure over the side of his ship during a storm and then..." This was a woman who used her face to illustrate her words. She made her eyes wide and her mouth into a grimace. "They made him walk the plank."

"Because the treasure fell overboard?" Sounded harsh.

"Because they didn't *believe* it fell overboard. They thought the captain had thrown it overboard himself to keep them from it. They mutinied." If she didn't know the name of the woman next door, how did she know the story so well?

The thought wouldn't be pushed away. "How do you know?"

She smiled, pulled her phone from her pocket, and typed onto the screen. "I searched the internet after she mentioned Remington's name and found the whole story."

I looked at the cell for a moment. It was a Europedia page—one of those sites where the public contributed to the stories. I still wished the woman who sold the box would come back. Just because this looked like one of the boxes on the page certainly didn't mean it was.

"The woman pops up every once in a while. Never stays long, though." She leaned in and waved me and Nicky closer. "Especially since that insurance guy started coming around."

"Insurance guy?" What a tangled web.

The woman nodded and slipped her phone back into her pocket. "A while back, some treasure hunter claimed he found Renegade's treasure. A couple of necklaces, a golden chalice. Anyway, the New York Museum paid him a boatload of money to borrow it. It was insured to the nines." That meant a lot of money was on the line.

I was making mental notes as she spoke, but she wasn't finished.

"The New York Museum?" I was feeling a road trip. Nothing I liked better than Manhattan.

"Don't waste your time." She shook her head and snapped her gum. "The treasure was stolen from the museum. Now some hot-shot insurance investigator and some woman are searching the globe for the treasure."

I stopped liking her story when it came around that my necklace was stolen. I hugged my bag like she was threatening my necklace. For all I knew she was. I'd heard enough.

"There's also a rumor that the treasure might be cursed."

Nicky gasped. He was Cajun and believed in things like curses and voodoo and dark magic. "Cursed?" He cocked his head and looked at me, gave it a slight shake. "Oh, *cher*."

She'd pushed his magic freak-out button. He wouldn't even watch movies about curses.

The woman nodded. "Renegade's woman at his port of call, some island in the Caribbean, was a witch. I can't remember her name. I'm terrible with names. You could tell me yours, and I would forget it five minutes after you left."

Somehow she'd gone on a tangent, and I needed to redirect her. "A witch?"

Her mouth twisted to the side. "When she found out what happened to him, she cursed the treasure." She shrugged. "That was what I read anyway."

"Wow." That was quite a story. I wondered how much was true and what was legend, embellished over the years.

"There are a couple different versions online." She paused to take some money from one of her customers. "I would be careful looking it up though. Couple days after I did, the insurance guy showed up like he had a flag on the search."

Maybe he'd somehow tracked the woman who sold it. This woman had a point. If my necklace was part of the stolen goods, they could take it from me.

That wasn't happening. I only had this woman's word about my necklace. My curiosity, though, wasn't going to allow me to let this go.

I nodded, ready to get out of here, paranoid all of a sudden that someone might steal my necklace or force me to give it back. I hugged my bag closer. "Thank you for your help."

She gave me one of those appraising looks, then smiled. "Be careful. You never know who's watching or listening."

At least I wasn't the only one worried for my necklace.

Nicky and I walked out of the tent and into the open air and when we were almost back to his truck, I finally breathed a sigh of relief and slowed my steps from a speed-walk to an amble. "Pirate treasure?"

"Cursed, too, *cher*." He slid his arm around my shoulders. "You know, I have some vacation time and some savings." I didn't know exactly what he was saying but I liked that he was saying it. "Maybe we could find that island, get a couple of stamps in my passport."

I'd made him get one, and then we'd never used it. "You want to travel with me after the last time?"

"If you can find Renegade's island, I would like to see it." I loved what his accent did—softened—to the pirate's name.

I didn't know what I'd done in this life or another to deserve Nicky, but I was grateful to whatever entity had put him in my path.

"And," he continued. "This time there won't be any Shara Hewitt to cause trouble."

I didn't even know he knew her name. I liked that he'd blamed all of the incident in LA on her. He was certainly going all in for a *boyfriend of the year* prize.

We were at his truck now and instead of opening my door, he crowded me against it and gripped my hips in his hands. "Say yes, *cher*. Because now all I can think about is you in a bikini on the beach with me."

This guy gave sex on the beach all new meaning.

"Okay. Let's have an adventure."

He grinned, and as he lowered his head, he whispered, "You are my adventure, *cher*."

I didn't know what I'd done to deserve Nicky or what deity he'd pissed off to deserve me as his punishment, but I was going to be grateful until the day I died.

Chapter Ten

Delilah Bradbury Takes a Caribbean Vacation With Hunky Cajun

Delilah Bradbury was spotted at JFK catching a Caribbean flight with the hunky hottie who accompanied her in Hollywood last month when once again the banner of disgrace fell on her at the Association of Actors Awards. With Bradbury being yesterday's news, we can't help but wonder if this companion–a Louisiana native named Nicholas Pontchalac–is about to become husband number six or is this one of those breakup trips the likes of which Leo used to dump his flavors of the month. – Staff writer, From Your Lips Magazine

The box for the necklace was in my suitcase, but I was wearing the chain and the stone. I'd been trying the last few days to figure out how or if it was even possible to hone my focus so I could listen to a specific person's thoughts. Either it wasn't possible, or my brain couldn't handle the task. Either way, I gave up.

Now I was sitting on the plane in my aisle seat. I didn't like window seats, especially if I was flying over water. Nicky, who didn't fly often because he didn't like to travel much but had done so twice in two weeks for me, sat beside the window with the shade pulled down, sleeping like a baby.

I could hear everything. Someone wondered if the flight attendant wanted to join the Mile High Club. Someone else hoped her mother-in-law and seatmate would shut up about the books she was reading and just read it already. A man was praying for the flight's safety, and a woman was praying to meet her true love on the island.

Everyone on the plane had thoughts, and I could hear every single one, loudly. Over top of one another. I didn't have a choice.

I reached under my hair to unfasten my newly repaired clasp. Instead of holding it, I slipped it into the center pocket of my purse and put my purse between my feet. The voices quieted.

Before we left on this trip, I'd done some research on Renegade Remington, Pararey Island where the treasure was found, and the witch who was said to be his lover on the island.

There was an old grainy picture of her online. It was more a picture of a painting, but it was all I had to go on. She was tall and thin with black hair and a long braid. If she hadn't died a couple of hundred years ago, I might've believed that it was the woman from the flea market. The museum was definitely on my list of planned stops once we arrived on Pararey Island.

"Are you excited, *bébé*?"

I turned and found Nicky watching me, awake, and I smiled. That was just like him to be deeply asleep one minute and wide awake and in tune to me the next. He knew me, the smile on my face was probably a big hint. It had been a while since I'd had much to look forward to like this.

"Yeah, I think so, because I'm bringing the necklace home, in a way." It was exciting enough to have my blood racing through my veins. Bringing it home was good karma, I hoped. Who didn't want good karma?

He leaned in to kiss the top of my head. "Such a romantic heart, *cher*."

Nicky spent so much time looking for the best in me, and I didn't want to let him down. The truth was that I didn't know my honest motive for bringing the necklace back. It certainly wasn't to leave it there or give it back to some random insurance guy who would take it back to a museum and waste its gifts in a lighted display case.

That was not the plan. I didn't have a plan. I didn't even have a pl—. I just liked knowing I had something special that no one else had.

As far as I knew anyway.

Chapter Eleven

Delilah Bradbury's Unimpressive Arrival on Pararey Island

Long gone are the days when fans stood in line for hours to get just a glimpse of Delilah Bradbury. Bradbury arrived on Pararey Island by boat today to the deafening sound of silence. Only the rolling waves provided any sort of fanfare and could've equally been for the sand since Bradbury has been dubbed a has-been by former colleagues and the mainstream media. – Helen Hart, Channel 7, Entertainment Times, 6pm edition

When the plane touched down, after we collected our bags and while we waited for the ferry to take us to the island, my stomach was still clenched.

I wasn't afraid of flying at all compared to how I felt about boating. This wasn't boating. This was taking my life in my hands, oiling it with machine oil, and playing catch with it while I was blindfolded. It was insanity.

The so-called captain of our ferry, which was actually a four-seater fishing boat, was an older woman named Penelope who had a pot-belly pig as her first mate. She looked about like I pictured my mother would look if she'd lived through her cancer. A silvery-white bob, delicate gold glasses, and sharp blue eyes regarded me before she turned and nodded at the pig. "That's JL, but Arthur is so excited to meet you, Ms. Bradbury. He's talked about nothing else all week. It's been Delilah Bradbury this and Delilah Bradbury that."

I was doing everything I could to keep from throwing up over the side of the boat, so I couldn't answer. Wasn't even tempted to answer or even ask who the wonderful Arthur was. It didn't matter because Captain Penelope, of the white-haired, Gilligan's Island hat-wearing captains, didn't seem to care if anyone replied when she spoke.

But Nicky tried, bless him. "Is Arthur your...husband?"

She took her eyes off the water in front of her and turned to look at him, giving him a smile and a nod. The boat skipped over a wave and splashed heavily over it, and she let out a long, loud, "Yee-haw!" that would've made Bo Duke proud. This woman was at least in her seventies, riding the waves on our tiny ferry like a pro surfer.

If only I could make my stomach stop rolling long enough to enjoy the fact that I could see the island now, or rather the beach resort that stretched across the expanse of one entire side of the island.

When she pulled up to the dock, Nicky helped me out of the boat, then handed our luggage up to a waiting bellman who loaded them onto a cart and rolled them along the wooden planks that led from the dock over the sand to the hotel. My stomach immediately quietened. It wasn't back to normal, but it was a definite improvement.

"Bye," Captain Penelope called. "You go look for Arthur. He's the hotel manager and is meeting you at the desk."

We waved our thanks and turned to regard the hotel. There were no walls on the beach side of the hotel's lobby or the backside either. It was open all the way through and a cool breeze blew in off of the water.

Heaven.

I looked out at the ocean rolling onto the sand and sucked in the salty air for a moment, giving my stomach another minute to calm the frick down. Red and white umbrellas shaded the cushioned lounges on the hotel's portion of the beach. There were a few lifeguards on duty in big, tall, wooden chairs with floatation devices hanging on the sides. On the other side of the hotel, through the open air, a gated swimming pool with a slide and a diving board made me want to run and change into my swimsuit.

Fake palm trees sat in big, ceramic pots the color of the ocean at a seating area in the center of the room. The sofas were wicker or rattan with cushions the color of the pots and decorated with big, white flowers. A table also made of rattan or wicker sat between two sofas and was flanked on each end by a matching chair. This was a real island paradise. I could get used to this.

I was looking for a seventy-something man near the front desk, but the man there looked to be my age. Fifties at most. He was bouncing on his heels and looked like he wanted to launch himself at me if not for the stern-looking woman behind him who had a hold of his shirt. "Maybe her husband got called away," Nicky said. "Let's go let that man ask for an autograph."

I didn't have a ton of fans left in this world, but it happened once or twice a month. Nicky was used to it. He took it like a champ. Come to think of it, it'd been a while since I'd had one like this. It annoyed me a bit that she was tamping his enthusiasm. Partly because it had been a while since I was the cause of such enthusiasm, but also partly because...no. It was only that first thing.

His face lit up when I bypassed the other clerk to stand at his computer. "Hello, there."

"Miss Bradbury! I'm Arthur, the hotel manager."

This was Arthur? "Penelope's husband?" Nicky asked. I'd been thinking it.

"Yes, of course." He beamed and love spread across his face. "We just got married last week. I am such a fan. I've seen all your movies. Twice. Except Lost Highway. I saw that one seventeen times. Saw it at every single showing at the theater on the mainland." Lost Highway was the movie that had earned me my first Association Award. It was also the first love scene I'd ever filmed.

"I'm so glad to hear that, and I really appreciate that." How was he possibly Penelope's husband? It really was a stretch to say he might be fifty, and it was a stretch to say she might be seventy. At best, they were twenty years apart.

I pulled my bag up my arm and pressed it against my side. "You just got married?"

He sighed. "Penelope came to a wedding here at the island about two months ago and never left. We were friends at first, but it grew, very quickly, into something more."

Now for his inner thoughts. Yep. There they were.

Oh. Oh, no. He was picturing some extremely intimate things he did with Penelope last night.

"Ah!" I squealed and dropped my purse. "Uh, Nicky, um, uh, can you please hold this?"

I couldn't let that necklace close to me as long as Arthur was thinking about the hanky panky they'd done last night.

"I have you in our deluxe suite." Before he could hand over the key card, the pig ran through the lobby with Penelope chasing behind.

"JL! Dang you to heck! You're about to become the chef's breakfast special tomorrow morning!" Her shoes clacked against the tile floor as she gave chase around the seating arrangement and out toward the beach. For being so round, the pig was fast and for being older, so was Penelope.

I was turned back to Arthur. His face went soft as long as his gaze was on his wife. She ran out the back, chasing the piggy. He looked at me again and smiled. "You have a newlywed glow," I stammered. "Congratulations."

He ducked his head. "Thank you so much. I took the liberty of putting some pamphlets in your room of island amenities and also some vouchers for dinner." He spoke quickly, a few hundred words a minute. "If you want to go to the mainland during your stay, don't worry about the scheduled times. We have a two-seater available day and night. Penelope loves using it, too."

I smiled because it had been years since I'd received this kind of five-star treatment. "Well, thank you, Arthur."

"Please, Miss Bradbury. Call me Art. Or Artie. Or anything you'd like, honestly. If you need anything at all, I live at the resort in room 201. You can call my room from any hotel phone just by dialing star-201." He pushed the room key across the counter and Nicky took it.

If there was one thing I'd always done well, it was public relations. "Artie, I would love to take a selfie with the man who's been so great to me on my first trip to Pararey Island. Would you?" I pulled my purse close, then rooted around inside it while Nicky held onto it. "Thanks, babe."

As soon as I snapped the photo, I smiled at Nicky, but Art snapped his fingers at a passing bellman. "Roman, take Ms. Bradbury's bags to her room."

We followed Roman to the elevators and up to the fourth floor since a sign on the elevator door said the fifth was under construction.

Nicky managed the cool guy handshake-tip pass as Roman left and then he smiled, looked around our suite, and walked to the balcony doors to throw them open. "*Bébé*, look! Dolphins!"

Sure enough. Past where the rock cliffs shrouded one end of the beach and made a cove, dolphins played and jumped in the water. Nicky slid his arm around me and kissed the top of my head. After a few minutes, the dolphins moved on.

He released me and walked back into the room before he picked up a stack of pamphlets. "*Cher*, there are two tickets to the island playhouse performance of *Once a Pirate, Always a Renegade.*" I walked inside as he picked up the brochure for the playhouse. "They have a show every night at seven."

"Definitely putting that on the list." The island was proud of its association with Captain Renegade. There was a museum, a playhouse, an underwater dive to see what was left of his ship, and a treasure hunt, which was also a dive. I plopped down beside him on the bed and glanced at each pamphlet as he handed it to me.

"Says here that the actor who plays Renegade is a direct descendant of Captain Renfro Remington."

I smiled at Nicky. Sometimes, like now, I loved that he wasn't part of my Hollywood life. I loved that he saw the best in everyone and tried to find it. It was part of his charm.

"Sweetheart." I cupped his cheek with my hand. "We all lie on our resumes. For ten years, I listed horseback riding on mine, until I actually had to do it."

He laughed, and I loved the sound.

"I imagine there are a lot of folks on this island who claim to be direct descendants of old Renegade Remington." It wasn't like I could ask to verify with a copy of the family tree.

"Have they found any treasure in recent years?" he asked. He was so enthusiastic about all of this.

"Not that I remember reading about." I'd read plenty, probably enough that even if they had found some, I wouldn't remember. Mostly, the information available about his treasure had been about what was stolen from the museum. It was mentioned that there was thought to be a lot more than was brought up and that the witch cursed the jewels and anyone who found it.

"There's a treasure hunt that's also guided by divers. Do you want to do that, too?"

Of course, I did. I didn't travel all this way to enjoy the inside of our hotel room. Although, I did very much enjoy time with him inside that room. "Yes, please."

He nodded. "Good." He pulled me onto his lap. "Back in my day..." He spoke like he was about to be put out to pasture, but we were far from old. I wasn't even fifty yet, and he was thirty-seven.

I laughed. "Back in your day?"

He nodded. "You know, back when I was young and stupid and still thought hunting gators was fun, I used to dive all the time." His Cajun accent was an automatic sigh producer, and I did.

"With the gators?"

He laughed. "No, no, *cher*. I was bold, not reckless."

I grinned. There were, even after all these years together, still a lot of things we didn't know about each other. "What's the most reckless thing you've ever done?" We hadn't talked much about his life before me, although, and I only realized it right then, he knew everything about my life before him.

"I would say my most reckless thing was to fall in love with a girl whose car I was supposed to be picking up." He pressed his lips to mine. His kiss was soft, but it packed a punch. I came up for air on a sweet soft gasp and he smiled. "Best reckless thing ever."

It was a while before we made it downstairs for dinner.

Chapter Twelve

A(nother) Ring for Delilah Bradbury?

Has she finally found husband number six? After a day spent touring Pararey Island, perusing a flea market, then at dinner theater on the beautiful Caribbean island, Nicholas Pontchalac, traveling companion of Delilah Bradbury was spotted on the beach holding a suspiciously small velvet box. When seen later during a moonlit stroll on the beach, Bradbury's finger was conspicuously unadorned. – National Inquisitor

When we finally left the room the next morning, we took the island tour. The whole place was a postcard come to life. White sandy beaches stretched for miles and all the way around the island. There were cliffs to climb, acres of jungle vegetation, the resort, a museum, a playhouse, and a *coming soon* pier for families with a Ferris wheel, an arcade, food, drinks, and a small roller coaster being built. It was similar to the one on the mainland.

Right now, at the inner edge of that pier, there was a market set up with vendors at tables and under tents selling their wares. And, of course, there was a statue—a new addition to the island—of the man himself, Captain Renfro Renegade Remington. He wore a pirate hat with a feather poking out of the top, had a long coat, knee-high boots, and a telescope up to his eye. He'd had long hair that curled, and his face was set in a smile as if he'd just found land after months at sea.

The plaque at the bottom of the statue read: *Captain Remington born 2 March 1796, died 14 April 1827 at the hands of an ungrateful crew who made him walk the plank for crimes never committed. He roamed the Caribbean waters searching for riches until the day he died.*

I could see why Penelope had decided to stay on the island. It was rich with a magical history that had been romanticized to the point that piracy was celebrated. It was also quaint and beautiful, and oh, so peaceful.

Even after all that, it was the dinner theater that sold me on the whole place. Captain Remington, despite being a criminal—and not the Robin Hood kind who robbed from the rich and gave to the poor—was a local icon. A hero celebrated in every corner. It probably had more to do with the fact this island's rendition of Renegade depicted him as a handsome, gallant ladies' man of the Johnny Depp variety. True or not, it worked. The idea of adventure drew the tourists, the romance kept them.

It was a genius way to market, but total propaganda. He'd been a thief and probably a murderer. Who was I to judge?

After the show, it didn't take much to get invited backstage. Apparently, the news that I was a pariah hadn't yet reached Pararey Island, which was fine with me. Things were a lot nicer when people didn't know of my lunacy.

We walked backstage and a thousand memories made the experience brighter. There were racks of costumes, vanity tables with lights, and they were all lined up in a row. People, joyous people celebrating a fine night's work, were roaming around. They'd just performed an incredible show to a full house, and I remembered that feeling, but I was only here to see one actor, the one who claimed to be a direct descendant of Remington.

There he was, at the end of the line of vanities, using a wipe to remove the heavy stage makeup that kept him from washing out under the lights. One-half of his face was still unnaturally orange as he grabbed for another wipe.

The man was handsome in a classic, all-American way, but he was a blond who'd worn a curly black wig. I was well aware of the tricks of this trade, and he wasn't nearly as handsome as my mind and the script had made him.

We stood behind him silently for a moment as I assessed him. When he finally looked up, I smiled at him in the mirror.

"Hey."

Before I could get out, "Hi. I'm—" he recognized me, shoved his chair back so hard and fast it caught Nicky in his man jewels, knocked over a bottle on his table that started a domino effect of falling bottles and glass clattering against one another, then he held out his hand, grabbed mine when I didn't offer it, and shook until I was sure my arm might fall off.

"Oh, my gosh! Oh, my gosh! Oh, my gosh!" He ended on a next-level shriek like the victim in a slasher flick, covered his cheeks with his hands like he'd taken lessons in dramatics from Macauley Calkin, then spun and fell backward into his chair and fainted.

People on this island really loved me. The sensation was intoxicating. Now I regretted not wearing the necklace. I hadn't, because knowing other people's thoughts was exhausting, and I'd wanted a break. Maybe it was only exhausting in California where people hated me. I would have to check that out another time.

Right now, though, I had to deal with the passed-out man in front of me. I nudged him, and he slumped to one side, so I crouched in front of him, shook him again, and his head lolled. "Hey, buddy. Wake up." The activity around us continued as if everyone but me and Nicky were oblivious.

Nicky checked his pulse. "Oh, *cher*." He shook his head. "Help me get him onto the floor.

We moved him and one person stepped over him before anyone noticed Nicky doing chest compressions and me shouting, "Someone call for help. We have a man down over here!"

I crouched beside the guy on one side with Nicky on the other. I gave mouth-to-mouth while Nicky continued pumping the guy's chest with his hands. It took what felt like a thousand years for help to arrive and take over.

They yanked open his lace-up-the-front shirt and slapped some pads on his chest and his ribcage on the opposite side, then shocked him so that his body jerked as the electricity pumped through him.

"Did I kill him?" I looked up at Nicky as he pulled me close. My voice was barely more than a whisper because I couldn't stop picturing the actor falling into his chair, like his bones had liquified and couldn't sustain holding him up anymore.

"No, *cher*. I think you saved him." He ran his hand in small circles over my back as we watched them continue working on him. It was nice of Nicky to absolve me, but if not for me, that guy would've still been happily removing his makeup. Alive.

A paramedic shouted, "Clear!" again, and I moved back, covering my mouth with my hands. How many shocks could one person take? The paramedic listened to the actor's heart, then nodded. "We've got a pulse." The portable machine beeped a steady rhythm as they loaded the guy onto a backboard. I'd watched enough Grey's to know that the patient should never be moved without one.

"*They* saved him."

He nodded, smiled and when I moved away again, he held my hand and tugged me closer so that I was once again beside him. "When he wakes up, *cher*, he's going to remember that he met you, and it's going to make him very happy."

I hoped so, but more, I hoped he woke up. Even if it meant he blamed me for almost killing him.

Nicky put his hand on the guy's chest as he passed and whispered something in French—probably *good luck* or *don't die*, or maybe it was a prayer because that was the kind of guy Nicky was.

As soon as they wheeled him out, the others came for me, surrounded me like I was still the belle of Hollywood. Here, like nowhere else in the world, I was a celebrity. They fawned and gushed, asking me for tips and pointers. The woman who played the witch, Ariya, came to stand beside the chair where I was being worshiped.

"I read about Shara Hewitt." Maybe the bad press had followed me, after all. "She had *no* right."

I smiled. This place was my heaven. If it was up to me, I would never leave. “I think I got the better end of the deal.” I looked up at Nicky. He was definitely an upgrade from Mitch, and he’d outlasted all the other husbands combined. I shot him a smarmy wink, and he chuckled as he gazed at me with love in his eyes. Yeah. I definitely came out of that deal on the better end.

He'd been a good sport for long enough. I stood. “I should probably get going. It was a great show. I’m only sorry I didn’t get a chance to talk to the actor who played Renegade.” Geez. How selfish that sounded. “I’m sorry he collapsed.” I was definitely one of those people who needed someone to write my lines for me. “I would’ve liked to trace the Remington family tree back to Renegade with him.”

The fake Ariya wrinkled her brow. “You mean Dan? He isn’t related to Renegade. That was Remy.” Her fondness for this Remy was obvious in the dreamy look and soft tone when she said his name.

“Remy?”

“Ethan Remington.” Another soft smile and then her lip curled, and she sneered. “They called him Remy. He ran off with a woman.” She sighed. “You met Penelope at the resort?” When I nodded, she said, “He ran off with Penelope’s daughter.”

"The old lady with the pig?" I just wanted to be sure we were talking about the boat lady who kept a pig as her pet. "And the, ah, *robust* husband?"

Fake Ariya chuckled. "Yeah, they were a surprise that still has the island talking. But they genuinely seem to be in love, so I say more power to them."

"Right on." Nicky stepped forward. "Has this Remy come back?"

The woman shook her head. "No. Not as far as I know. They're out treasure hunting, I think."

I nodded. Didn't that figure? "Thank you so much for tonight. We had a great time." Geez. My freaking mouth. "Except for Dan collapsing. That wasn't great." I looked at Nicky for help, and he swooped me out of there. Thank goodness.

As we walked back to the resort, we took the beach path near the tide rolling in and under the stars and full moon.

"I hope Dan is okay." I couldn't afford to add a death to my laundry list of things that might've counted against me when I met St. Peter. Or Satan, if it happened to go the other way.

"We'll check on him in a little while." There was no hospital on the island, so he'd been taken to the mainland. Nicky kept his hand in mine. "*Cher*, I saw you tonight."

I thought there might be more coming, so I waited. When he didn't continue, I chuckled. "I saw you tonight, too."

He stopped walking and tugged me against his chest for a kiss that made my toes curl inside my shoes. "I mean, I really saw you and how happy you could be."

A red flag started blowing like it had been caught by a full-force gale. Like it knew he was looking for excuses to dump me, wanted to frame it so that he wasn't a bad guy, but rather a guy doing something for me. "Nicky, I *am* happy. With *you*. *Because* of you. What they think of me," I nodded toward the path we'd just taken to the playhouse, "doesn't matter. Only you matter."

I said the words slowly, like they were the most important in the world, because in that moment, in that exact order, they were. I needed him to know the depths of my feelings.

He smiled down at me and after another quick kiss, we started walking toward the resort again. "How come you never had babies, *cher*?"

This question was one of those out-of-left-field scenarios that I'd known would happen someday. Usually, I was the kind of woman who had an answer at the ready. This wasn't the way I'd imagined the conversation happening. I should've known, though. He'd said something about it not too long ago. I'd hoped we'd nipped that in the bud, though.

"Well..." The guy who'd said *and the truth shall set you free* was a jerk off. This wasn't a truth that I liked to share, but I didn't have anything else to give him. "I never stayed married long enough. If I couldn't keep a marriage together, how was I going to keep a kid together?"

"Oh, *cher*. You would've been a beautiful mother." He used beautiful in a lot of places it didn't usually work, and the way he said it always made it sound like it worked.

I walked off of the path toward the beach and sat on the sand. He followed and settled beside me.

"My career always came first." That had been why marriage number one hit the skids. He'd been insecure about my job. He'd wanted kids. I'd been trying to make my way in Hollywood and had been very young to think about children. I'd worked crappy jobs just to stay in the game, constantly busy. "I wanted to be someone before. I gave up the possibility of children to have my career."

In Hollywood, once a woman started breastfeeding and being a mom on set, she didn't get the leading lady roles anymore, the ones that made people remember her name. In this case, my name. Sure, a few women managed to do it, but it wasn't the norm. There was always someone younger, more willing to shoot scenes at two in the morning who didn't need four hours in a makeup chair to cover the bags and the stress lines. I'd seen it happen. I didn't talk about it.

"Oh."

"Now, it's too late." Not the best idea to point that out, I supposed. "Is your biological clock ticking, Nicky?" I said it lightly, but the weight on my heart as I waited for his answer was heavy.

He leaned back in the sand on his elbows and stretched his legs out in front of him. He was oblivious to the panic attack brewing inside of me as it occurred to me that I was depriving Nicky of having kids, a family. Oh, no. I was that cliché of a woman. Aging. Selfish. Meanwhile, he was being cheated, by me, of something he really wanted.

I was going to lose him.

Damn it. Promise or not, I wished I had the necklace right now.

I couldn't deny Nicky kids. For the first time in my life, I cared more about someone else than I did about myself. Hell of a time for it, too. Probably the worst time ever, but he deserved the life he wanted. I turned to Nicky, and he turned to me.

At the same time the panic bubbled out of me in words that said, "I think we should break up," he turned so he was mostly on his side and said, "Marry me, *cher*."

I said, "What?"

He said, "What?"

We did it all again in exactly the same order at exactly the same time.

This time when he finished, I said, "Marry you?" and he said, "Break up?"

That's when it all went straight to hell.

Chapter Thirteen

Bradbury blows it—Again

Delilah Bradbury is as well-known for her failed marriages as she is for her acting career, and it looks as if the mystery Cajun who's been seen parading her around Pararey Island has narrowly avoided becoming Mr. Bradbury #6 as he stormed off the beach, leaving Delilah to wallow in her own inadequacies. – National Inquisitor

In hindsight, suggesting a break-up at the same time Nicky was proposing and then doing it *twice*, was not a bright, shiny moment in my forty-seven-year history. Probably wouldn't have been a shining moment in anybody's history ever.

"*Cher?*"

For a second, all I could think of was a commercial I'd done way back at the beginning of my career. It had been my first job in Hollywood. The pay had been three thousand, which had felt like three million at the time. It'd been for a flavored coffee whose slogan was celebrate the moments of your life. This was not a flavored coffee moment. Not a moment to celebrate, yet the slogan from that commercial repeated through my head like an earworm.

"You want to get married?"

He nodded but sighed and ran his fingers through his hair, flipped the top to the side and had this moment not been so fraught with my idiocy, I might've swooned. Heck, I probably should've just so we weren't concentrating on all the things we were each thinking.

This vacation wasn't supposed to be about breaking up or changing anything about us or our relationship. I liked things as they were.

"Not if you want to break up." He didn't sound angry. He was hurt, and that was loud and clear, and it made my stomach ache. My head pounded. My hands wobbled.

There were a thousand reasons to throw myself against him and beg him to forget that I'd said anything at all. Beg him to remember how much I loved him when my head wasn't shoved firmly up my own rear. I loved him so much this was killing me. All the realizations were unfair. He was the best person I knew, and he deserved better. He deserved the opportunity for children. I loved him too much to be the reason he didn't have kids and he loved me too much to tell me it bothered him.

He stared at the water. "You want to break up." This time he said it with a slight shake of his head, a scoff, and a tone. It was the tone that said he couldn't believe it.

"Nicky, I want you to be able to have a family. I can't give that to you with my old lady eggs." It was breaking pieces of me into splinters to say it.

"You are my family, *cher*."

"Nicky—"

"Why do you get to decide?" He shook his head. "I followed you across the country because I knew even then that I didn't want to ever live without you. I don't want to now, either." He took a long, slow breath. "I don't want children if they aren't with you." He looked away, mumbled a few words in French, then turned back to me. "Don't do this, *cher*. Please."

I sighed. It wasn't like my mind was made up or that I'd even thought this through before the words came tumbling out of my mouth.

Yet, they continued tumbling. "Nicky, you have so much love inside of you." It was a shame to waste it on me. "You would make a great father, and you would have such beautiful babies."

"I don't want babies unless they're *our* babies." He shrugged. "We could adopt if you want, or we don't have to have babies at all." He took my hand in his and gave it a squeeze. "You are the most important person in the world to me."

The sincerity in his voice made the ache in my chest worse. "Why did you ask me about the kids I haven't had?" Maybe if he could explain, I could work through it. "You also mentioned it not too long ago."

"I just wondered if you regretted not having children." He reached for me. "*Cher.*"

I couldn't touch him and still do what I knew I should do. "You're still young, Nicky. You should have kids." I was trying to be a grown-up about it all, but in truth, I didn't want to be mature and reasonable. I wanted to throw a tantrum because I wasn't enough. I wanted him to want me in spite of it.

Despite that, I had to do the right thing. I couldn't let him regret this later.

"I'm not that much younger than you, so stop with that, *cher.*" It was like his mind was telling him to be extra angry at me. "I don't need you to tell me what I should have, Delilah. Why do you get to decide what is best for me?" He hardly ever called me by my name. So seldom, in fact, that it startled me when he did it now. The last thing in the world I wanted was to hurt him. Well, the second to last thing. The last thing I wanted to do was lose him.

"I just don't want you to be cheated out of the life you want." I was trying to be noble, trying to release him from whatever obligation he might've felt for me.

"Did you ever stop to think that the reason you've been married so many times is that when things are going well you sabotage it?" Without waiting for me to attempt to defend myself, he turned and walked toward the hotel. I should've chased him, should've caught up and begged him to ignore me, chalked it all up to the trauma of almost killing a guy tonight. I should've told him that maybe he was right. Things were so perfect and now I did this.

Coulda, shoulda, woulda. I didn't move. Instead, I sat in the sand, watching the waves roll in and out until it hypnotized me enough that I could almost forget that I'd just lost the best thing that had ever happened to me.

A pig ran past me on the beach. For a second, it was surreal as he frolicked in the surf. Then I remembered Penelope, the woman who'd driven the little ferry. She walked up as the piggy got out of the water and shook it off, flinging droplets in about ten directions before he hurried toward me. He was large and round with short legs and the sand didn't make it easy for him to run, but he was giving it a going-to-market kind of try.

"Hello. I didn't see you there." Penelope smiled, and I tried to smile back, but the tears were just waiting to fall. "It was time for JL's nightly dip in the ocean. He can't sleep without it."

She moved closer and looked at me again. "Honey, are you okay?"

I could've said I was fine and just wanted to be alone, but that wasn't true on either count. I wanted someone to tell me that if I had to lose him, I'd done the right thing, at least. Of course, I wasn't sure I wanted to confide in a woman who walked a pig on a leash. It was either her or tell my troubles to the little mermaid and hope she was real.

"Man trouble." She smiled and twisted down to sit on the sand beside me. She dusted her hands against each other and crossed her ankles in front of her. "It's always man trouble." She put her hand on my arm. "Don't tell me that Cajun dreamboat is the one causing you such grief." When I nodded, she shook her head. "It's always the pretty ones."

"Yeah. Younger and prettier." He was my weakness. My blind spot. My... everything.

"Honey. I've never met a number that mattered." That was true, coming from her. "What's wrong with him? He got a wandering eye?"

"No. He never looks at anyone but me." Not even on a beach full of bikinied hard bodies. That was the truth. A man like Nicky in California, hell anywhere, could've had any woman he wanted. They all looked. Once, a woman saw him holding my hand across a table at a restaurant, and she waited until I went to the bathroom then came over, drank my glass of wine, and gave him her number. He'd told her off before he'd known I was walking back toward him.

When we were together, he always made me feel like the only girl in the world.

"He drink? Get mean?" She cocked her head like she was trying to pop the joints. "I could tell Arthur. He could use his golf clubs to have a little chat with your man."

"No, it's nothing like that." For the life of me, I could hardly remember what the problem was.

"Is he bad in bed?"

"No." God, no. He was quite masterful in that particular arena.

"Are you?"

"I don't think so?" If I was, would he always be in the mood? Wouldn't he have mentioned it? Tried to make things more to his liking?

"What's the problem? Money?" I shook my head. I hadn't had money in so long I didn't care much about it anymore. "Well, if it isn't sex and his eye doesn't wander, there's no money problems, and he isn't mean when he drinks, what the world is it?" I couldn't tell if she was really frustrated or acting so for my benefit because she thought I should change my mind.

"I'm too old to have kids." There they were—the most bitter and worst-tasting words in the English language.

"Did he ask you to have kids?" That wasn't really the point because Nicky didn't ask for things. He didn't demand them either. He just accepted. This wasn't something he should've had to accept. He had so much love inside him it seemed selfish to deny him or the child I couldn't give him.

"Not in so many words." She cocked a brow, so I explained. "He asked why I don't have any already." I didn't want to tell her or him that I'd called myself career-oriented as a younger woman, but in truth, I'd been selfish. To my husbands. To myself. I just stopped talking.

She shook her head. "You young people. Always making problems where there aren't any." When she chuckled, I frowned. I didn't care at all about being laughed at. "Do you love him?"

Of course I did. I loved him the way poets described love and singers sang about it. Wholly and completely and so much it caused an ache in me to even think about losing him. "Yes, and it's killing me."

"Don't let a problem that can be solved be the thing that breaks you apart." She was a wise, wise woman. Even if I hadn't just seen and heard proof of it, I would believe it, because she had years of wisdom in her eyes. "My daughter just met the man she's been waiting for all her life on this island." She looked out at the water. "She was married before to a man with an eye for the ladies. A hockey player did a lot of traveling."

"That's rough. My second husband was a rock star." He'd been a good singer, fabulous guitar player, and a terrible husband. He'd apparently had a thing for actresses, as well as a secretary I'd discovered when she showed up on set and he'd sent her flowers with a lewd and explicit card. He'd been chapter seven in the tell-all.

She nodded like she understood. "When she got here for her daughter's wedding, she thought she'd turned him into a pig." She nodded to her porky friend who was currently digging himself a bed in the sand.

"Did she have a wand? Some Harry Potter magic?" There I was taking advice from a woman who thought her daughter had magical powers. Frick.

Penelope laughed. "Goodness, no. She wished it."

That was better. Although, my cynic days were fewer now, especially since I'd gained the ability to read minds. I believed in live and let live. I had real problems not of the I-turned-my-husband-into-a-pig variety. Still, I didn't want to be alone. "Wished it?"

"Yes. It's such a perfect story." She held up a handful of sand and let it filter through her fingers. "She bought herself a necklace at the market on the pier." A market? A necklace? It sounded familiar. I shoved a bit more cynicism away. "The woman who sold it to her, told her a story and said that there were three magic stones cursed by a witch. Every time Camille made a wish, something happened."

"Really?" Holy freaking crap. That sounded awfully familiar.

"Of course, everything could be explained, or rationalized away, but the necklace was part of Renegade's treasure. That much was certain." She shrugged. "The witch was his mistress. The story goes that while he was at sea, he sent three stones to Ariya. He never made it back to her. His crew killed him." This hadn't been in the theater production. The mutiny had been featured in act three, but no one had mentioned three stones.

"I don't remember that in the play."

She smiled serenely. "The witch's diary was only recently found." She shrugged. "After Renegade was killed, Ariya cast a spell on the first stone. It was a yellow color. Citrine. It was the wishing stone. She tried to wish Renegade back to life."

I wasn't judging. I was only on this island because I thought my necklace let me hear the thoughts of others. "Did it work?"

She nodded, eyes wide. "But he wasn't right, if you catch my drift, and she thought she was dreaming."

"Yeah. Right or not, lovers returning from the dead is kind of unbelievable." So many things in my life were as of late, so I was in no position to comment. "What happened?"

"Renegade convinced her that they needed to know what everyone around them was thinking because he was sure they were all after him to kill him." She shrugged. "The mutiny got to him, I think."

Well, he had just been killed by his crew. A little paranoia fit the situation. It didn't, however, quite fit the fairytale, happy-ending criteria. "That's terrible."

"Yes, because the last thing a pirate who pillaged from port to port, supposedly died at the hands of his men then showed up again after they thought he robbed them and faked perishing at sea needed to know was what people thought of him." Penelope shook her head. "But Ariya loved Renegade. She would've walked through fire if he'd asked it. She would've died without him. She spelled a second stone."

This was quite the story. I wanted to remember all of it to tell Nicky. "Do you know the color of the second stone?" I did, but a part of me wanted to make sure.

She nodded. "I know about all the stones. Her diary even has drawings of them. Quite accurate if the citrine stone is one to go by." There were so many things in this life that sounded unbelievable but were true. This might've been one of them. "All three of the stones were found and put in a museum in New York, but—"

This part I knew. "They were stolen."

"Yes. All of them. Yellow, blue."

"The third stone?" I was dying to hear it all.

"Black, I think. An onyx. I'd have to go back and read the story or ask Remy."

"Remy? Would that be the descendant of the pirate who was acting at the playhouse?" The pieces were coming together and the random information I'd been collecting made a lot more sense. It was all jumbled, a mixture of what I'd read and what I'd overheard in people's minds.

"Yes, that's him. A real looker, that one. No wonder he was able to turn my Camille's head after all those years alone." She shrugged. "I imagine he turns a lot of heads, like your Cajun Frenchman. It's such a beautiful language when spoken by a man who looks like him."

"Language, yeah." I could only parrot her words because now my Cajun Frenchman was probably up in our room, packing and wishing he'd never met me. It probably wasn't the first time he'd had such thoughts. "Yes, it's perfect."

"My dear. This too shall pass." She patted my shoulder, then stood and brushed the sand from her clothes. "Come on, JL. We should get a move on. It's past your bedtime."

"That's the pig your daughter thought was her husband?"

She nodded. "Funny, right? I believed it too. We both spent three days calling him Jean-Luc after her ex-husband."

"Where was he?"

"Oh." She shook her head. "Turned out he was afflicted with the realities of his mid-life, and a very young, very pregnant girlfriend. A recipe that led an already weak man off to a three-day bender."

"I wish I knew a witch. I could use a spell right now that would make me young and save my relationship." The thought of losing Nicky was a heartbreak more than my old heart could handle. A bender didn't sound so bad to me.

"It's going to be okay. You don't need a spell. That boy loves you. Even the satellites in the sky above can see that." I hoped so. I feared it was going to take more than love. Yet, she continued to smile at me, and patted my shoulder one more time. "Sleep on it. Everything looks better in the sunlight." She smiled and turned to walk away.

I still had a question. "Penelope?" When she turned, I stood. "What did the third stone do?"

She came back to stand in front of me. "When Remington started to fade, his body was already dead and he was headed back to the great beyond, she spelled it to stop time, so she could have a few more minutes with him."

"Did it work?"

Penelope shrugged. "He walked out to sea one night and never returned. They never found his body, either. The heart-broken witch went away and was never heard from again." I nodded and her face softened. "Go talk to him. You don't have to be youthful. You only have to be you. He's already there."

It wasn't like I had a lot of other choices. She was right. "Thank you." I headed straight for our suite. When I got there, I found his luggage still unpacked, his shaving kit still in the bathroom and his wet towel hanging on the shower door. What I didn't find was Nicky.

Chapter Fourteen

Delilah's Drunken Beach Day

Delilah Bradbury spent the day at a cabana bar on the white sandy beach of Pararey Island, looking somber and throwing back tequila shooters during a heated argument with her companion. —National Inquisitor

I searched the hotel and the beach. I checked the restaurant, watched the buffet line for a minute, then walked down the path away from the hotel and toward the cliffs at the far edge of the beach. I finally found him at a bar near the water where the path wound closer to the cove made by the rock formations. The bar was one of those tiki-designed places with bamboo accents and a thatched roof.

He was on a stool with a glass of bourbon in front of him.

“Nicky?”

He turned and looked at me, then looked away again. I walked to the stool beside him. “Do you mind?” Even if he did, chances were I was going to sit there even though there were five other stools I could’ve chosen. I was determined.

He did that cool guy wave at the bartender who must’ve been wearing a piece of cursed jewelry of his own, because he put a drink in front of each of us.

“*Cher*, I don’t feel like fighting.”

We never fought. “Are we going to fight?”

He swiveled toward me. “Are you planning to tell me what I need? What I *should* have?”

Wow. He’d never taken that sort of tone with me. “No.” That was a talk for another day. “I love you, Nicky.” When all else failed, when all the other words were between us, that was true and could never hurt to tell him.

It was the kind of thing I was happy to tell him. Happier to know it, to feel it.

He looked at me and nodded but didn’t say it back. Not because he was pouting, but because he was probably knee-deep in doubt, or maybe he was trying to figure out how or why he’d let himself get mixed up with a nut job like me.

"Nicky, I would love to marry you. I'll do it *today* if you still want to, but only if you can *promise* me you don't care about having your own kid." I stared and waited.

He threw back another drink and then pushed away from the bar. "It didn't matter to me until you made it matter." He leaned down. "I was never happier than when you called me Repo Ron."

I missed those days, too. "Don't walk away, Nicky." I couldn't help the waver in my voice or my tears.

He sighed, and it was long and loud, an angsty teenage girl sigh, but he didn't move. He stayed, and that had to mean something. "Let's just get through this vacation, and we can figure out what to do once we get back home."

That didn't sound good, but it gave me a few more days to figure it out.

I nodded, and he used his thumb to brush away the tear that slipped down my cheek. "Come on, *cher*." He held out his hand and when he took mine, he didn't bring it to his lips like he usually did, so I kissed his instead and held it over my heart.

"Nicky..."

"We're okay, *cher*."

"For now?" It was only smart to clarify so I could prepare myself.

"We're okay." Repeating the same thing told me absolutely nothing, but I didn't want to nitpick and start another fight. Of all the things Nicky and I had ever argued about, this one wasn't something I'd ever thought would be an issue. What kind of crazy person said no to marrying someone she loved more than life itself?

He held my hand but didn't smile or look at me or anything else. I might as well have been holding a piece of driftwood.

We were definitely not okay, and I had no one to blame but myself.

By the time we got back to the hotel, there was no sign of Caribbean breezes, but even without them, it was downright chilly.

I waited until we were in the room, until he was in the shower before I let the thought I'd been having take root. It was wrong on ten levels. I shouldn't have even been considering it. Shamefully though, I did consider it. Worse, I pulled the necklace out of my bag, snuck into the bathroom, and listened.

She doesn't love me enough, and I'm tired of all this crazy. I wouldn't have time for a baby because I have my hands full of her. She's like a gator fighting the hook.

I pulled the necklace off and put it on the dresser, but that was too close. Snatching it up, I rushed into the living room and set it on the coffee table, then slapped a magazine over it.

When he came out of the shower, I was in bed facing away and pretending to sleep as tears slipped down my cheeks.

There were a few conversations I wasn't prepared to have. I needed a few minutes, tonight at least.

Chapter Fifteen

Delilah Nearly Dies During Dive With Award Show Mystery Man

During a guided dive off the coast of Pararey Island, former actress Delilah Bradbury had to be rescued by her dive companion. No injuries were reported, and Bradbury declined medical treatment. — staff writer, For Your Lips magazine

By morning, I'd had no sleep, no reprieve from the thoughts that wouldn't release their hold on me. One more night had done absolutely no good.

"*Cher*, I signed us up for a dive to see the ship." There were remnants of the captain's ship under the water at the edge of the cove.

Rolling over, I blinked up at Nicky. “The ship?” I tried for an excited smile, but I didn’t want to be too crazy. “Yeah?”

“Yeah.” He walked toward me, but I went into the bathroom and shut the door, pretending I hadn’t noticed. My heart was still broken. He was tired of me, tired of all my crazy and that hurt. Made my stomach hurt.

When I came out to get my shampoo from my bag, he was on the balcony, looking out. I wanted to hug him from behind, to apologize and pull him into a squishy kind of bear hug, but I did neither.

“I’ll just be a few minutes.” I was going to have to get used to being without him, so hugging him now would only make it harder in the long run. I had to build up some immunity.

I’d barely stepped into the shower when the door opened, and he stared. “I don’t want to have kids, *cher*. I’ve never wanted kids. That’s why I asked why you didn’t have any because if you still want them, I’ll work around it. I want you, *cher*. I want us.”

It took a couple of seconds for the words to sink in, and that was a hundred percent his fault. He was standing there wearing a “want me” look, and it was hard to think. Instead, I stepped in and squirted shampoo into my hand.

“What if you change your mind?” Mid-lather was as good a time as any to ask.

He smiled and yanked his shirt over his head. "I'll dump you, of course."

"Of course." I couldn't help but smile back, knowing he was kidding about dumping me. At least I hoped he was.

It ended up being one of those showers where we came out dirtier than we went in, and it was perfect. Nicky Pontchalac was one of the best men I'd ever met, and he was quite skilled at making up.

"You know," I said when we were both dressed and walking toward the guy who was going to take us on the boat to scuba dive. We were both experienced but were going to take the class anyway. "We—"

I turned my head toward the market and my words died in my mouth when I saw her walking. "Holy freaking crap." It was her. The woman who'd sold me the necklace. I didn't have time to explain to Nicky why I was running toward her and away from him at full speed. I raced across the sand as it shifted and slid under my feet. She was coming from the hotel. She had the same black braid, the same long skirt. When I caught up, I spun her around by the shoulder. "Hey!"

Crap. Dang it! It wasn't her.

"I'm so sorry, I thought you were someone else." I held up my hands in the *if you want to punch me, go ahead* sign of surrender.

She only shrugged. “It’s no problem. It happens to me a lot these days.” With a laugh and wave, she walked away.

The heat of how ridiculous I felt rolled across my face as I walked back to Nicky and shrugged. “I thought it was her.”

He didn’t comment more than to kiss the top of my head, his signature move, but his thoughts from that morning floated through my head. He was tired of all my crazy, and I knew it, but still, I’d chased a stranger across the beach. It wasn’t like I had a plan for when I found her, so chasing her wasn’t so crazy.

We were on the beach in front of the scuba place and while he signed all of our forms, I looked out at the horizon. The beauty of this place wasn’t lost on me. The water was mostly clear, and the beach had fine white sand. I’d never been anywhere so lovely, and I’d lived in Paris for a time during my third marriage.

I glanced at Nicky. He was still talking to the guy about our equipment, so I continued to watch the horizon. In the glare of the sun, I saw it. A ship with at least four white sails, a dragon carving on the prow, and cannons sticking out of gunports.

When I blinked it was still there, so I took a chance and looked away. “Nicky, hurry! Look!” I pointed to where the boat had been sailing outside the cove, but now it was gone.

"What?" He came to stand beside me. "Did you see the dolphins again?"

As if dolphins could make my tail wag quite the way a pirate ship—a ghost ship—had.

There was a certain amount of disappointment when I shaded my eyes, searching, and the only thing I saw was water. Miles and miles of it. Nary a sail in sight.

I nodded at Nicky. "Yeah. Mm-hmm. Dolphins."

There was no way I was telling him what I'd seen. He was tired of my crazy.

Instead, I walked back to the scuba instructor's boat so we could take off. Once onboard, I changed into a wetsuit in the cabin below and smiled. In the cabin hung a picture of Captain Renegade Renfro. It was obviously some sort of photographic reproduction, but the photo bore a distinct resemblance to the captain of this boat. Odd.

I wanted to mention it to Nicky, but there wasn't time. By the time I climbed the steps to the deck again, we were already at the dive site. He grinned when he saw me. "Oh, *cher*." He pulled me in for a hug, his breath hot against my ear. "I have a very distinct fantasy for this outfit of yours and it's very inappropriate."

My skin flushed with heat. I couldn't lose this guy. No one had ever made me this giddy. That was the word. I was *giddy* for him. All I could do was hope he asked me to marry him again someday.

Below the water, things were quiet and beautiful as Nicky, and I dove deeper until we spotted the outline of the ship at the bottom of the ocean.

Nothing compared to what we found when we got closer. The ship was mostly intact, so we explored the interior. There was a cabin below deck with bunk beds. The mattresses were gone, if they'd ever existed, but the frames were there. Barnacles had attached themselves to the pillars and beams that held the deck over the cabin. There was a candlestick holder on the floor of the cabin, but it wasn't the least bit tarnished. It was like it had just been put there for us to find.

I looked at Nicky, pointed, nodded, moved toward it, and picked it up. I had a feeling the dive company probably planted artifacts for their divers to find, but Nicky was happy. I continued moving through the cabin and back toward the deck. As I was almost up the steps, something or someone grabbed hold of my shoulder, and I couldn't move. My mask filled with water and my air regulator wasn't regulating.

I was eighty feet below the surface and couldn't breathe or move. Naturally, I did the one thing that a scuba diver shouldn't ever do. I panicked.

I tried to twist. Couldn't.

Tried to move. Couldn't.

Tried to see what I was caught on that had disengaged the hose to my valve. My lungs were burning, and I was about to drown. "I want my stones back," a voice said, and I twisted to look. Without warning, I was able to move, free of whatever had been holding me and the hose that was supposed to be over my shoulder was floating free now, only attached to my regulator.

A hand clamped my shoulder again and Nicky moved behind me. He shoved his regulator at me, and I took it, sucking in a deep breath while he checked my valve. After a minute, he rustled the hose and tank on my back, then nodded at me. I gave his regulator back and cleared my mask as I filled my lungs again with my own regulator.

We had to surface slowly, and by the time I saw the sunlight through the water, I was convinced I'd imagined the voice and that I'd probably snagged my wetsuit on a piece of wood or a nail in the ship and that my hose had come unhinged when I'd tried to break away.

What my mind told me had happened wasn't possible, and I wasn't about to spread my crazy around.

When we finally got back on the boat, Nicky hugged me hard and tight. "What happened down there, *cher*?" He pushed my hood down and kissed my head, my forehead, my eyelids, my cheeks and finally, my mouth. "When I came up from below deck, your hose was unhooked, and you weren't moving."

I wasn't moving? "I tried to move." My voice was weak and raspy. I glanced at the boat captain. He was fiddling with some paperwork at the helm. He looked over at us and smiled, then winked, and my red flag alert went off.

"Let's get you back to the hotel. I want to have a doctor look you over." Nicky ran his hand over my back. "Scared me to death, *bébé*." He pulled me close and kissed me again. "I can't live without you."

I knew the feeling. Knew it way too well.

Chapter Sixteen

Delilah's Deep Dive Fail #almostdrowned

QUICK! Somebody call Aquaman! Delilah #almostdrowned #saveheratallcosts— Twitter user @delilahwatcher

There was a scheduled treasure dive for the next day, but no way in hell, not even if Captain Renegade came back and invited me himself, that I would ever consider going that deep underwater again. We'd been back on land for over an hour and still, I wasn't solid yet. I was a quivering mess.

I hadn't spoken to Nicky about what happened. I had no idea what he believed had happened. I only knew what I *thought* had happened, and I was having a bit of trouble accepting it.

Supposedly, when right at death, your life flashes in front of you. That's mostly correct. I'd been on the verge of death, I was sure of it. I'd seen pictures of my life. Me at ten with my best friend Melanie, me at fifteen with my first real boyfriend, Joey, each one of my weddings, Nicky. It'd all gone through my mind.

Nicky led me back to the hotel, stopping every few minutes to hug me as he murmured things like, "*Cher*, are you okay? *Cher*, I love you so much. I can't lose you, *cher*."

It had certainly been a good day, for the most part, one for the books and not one I would ever forget. I had no idea what had happened on that ship below the deck, but it had certainly felt like fingers curled into my shoulder. I'd heard the voice. It'd been deep and raspy. British. A man who wanted his jewels back.

No way should that hose have come off the tank like that. The sensation had been frightening on about ten levels, and I couldn't shake it, although I'd quite mastered the art of shaking.

When we were in our room, he led me to the bathroom with his hand at the small of my back. "Let's get you into a hot bath, bébé."

I shook my head. "Nope. More water is not what I need."

"A shower then, so we can wash the ocean off you." He helped me undress, then stopped. "*Cher*, you're bruised."

He touched my shoulder, and I hissed in pain but turned my gaze to the mirror. Those were definitely fingertip prints on my skin. He turned me, kissed every spot and discoloration. "All better?" he asked when he was finished.

I nodded. Not because it was all better but because he was right. Those were fingerprints, and I couldn't look away from them. "It wasn't you, right?"

"No, *cher*. I would never." He kissed my shoulder again. "What happened on that boat?"

"He wants his jewels back." Oh, damn. My crazy came out. It'd just slipped out accidentally.

"*He*?" Nicky had his spooky Cajun look on: wide eyes, flared nostrils, lips parted just the tiniest amount. He'd been wearing it when I'd taken his horror movie v-card, too.

I shook my head and shrugged. In for a penny. "Captain Renegade. He was down there with us, and he wants his jewelry back." Even to me it sounded ridiculous. Two-hundred-year-old pirates didn't come back from the dead to talk to divers intruding on his final resting places. If not *final* resting place, definitely a place he'd called his own in life.

"His jewelry back?" Nicky's brow creased in the mirror.

"The necklace. My necklace and the one Penelope told me about."

"There's a second necklace?" Those lines in his face deepened.

It was a little like we were playing a game. "Yes, it apparently grants wishes." I could have used some of that right in this moment. I had some wishes I needed handled.

Nicky looked at me like he was sure I was losing whatever was left of my marbles, despite seeing the bruises with his own eyes.

"I'm not crazy, Nicky." I wished he would stop staring at me like I was. I didn't like it. Not one bit. I could still hear his words running through my mind. *I'm tired of all this crazy. I'm tired of all this crazy. I'm tired of all this crazy.*

"I know." The look didn't waver. I didn't have an answer for the question in his eyes. He turned on the shower, and I stepped inside. It wasn't like the boat where the water had pressed on my chest and made me feel like I couldn't escape. I could breathe just fine.

It was better when Nicky climbed in behind me and turned me so he could wash the saltwater from my hair. He lathered with gentle hands, then turned me again and tilted my head up so he could wash the shampoo out.

"It's okay, *cher*. I've got you." I was still shaking. He held me close to him as he slid the loofah over my skin. This wasn't one of those sexual showers, one that he was using as a prelude to sex. This was Nicky taking care of me. This was him holding me while I worked out a fear that had a death grip on me. Well, not death grip. That was a poor choice of wording. The idea was the same.

By the time I climbed out of the shower, the trembling had stopped, and I could stand without my knees knocking together, so Nicky was less worried. Although he didn't go much farther than a couple of inches away from me.

"Nicky..." I wanted to talk it out, wanted to make it make sense, and find a reason for the fact I was losing my mind. Because if I wasn't losing my mind, that meant something outside of reality was at play here, and how the hell was I supposed to deal with that? It wasn't like someone had written a script or there was a director who could tell me how to handle it.

Nicky smiled at me. "I ordered room service."

I hadn't even heard him make a call. "Thanks." I wasn't hungry. Not really. I was too wrapped up in myself, in the weirdness of my day, the bruises on my shoulder, and especially how they got there, to care much about food. Nicky was the kind of guy who thought food could solve a lot of the world's problems.

Still, I had more to worry about than whether or not he ordered a shake and fries with the burgers. Now that I knew they were there, I couldn't stop feeling them. It was a dull ache, but an ache, nonetheless.

It was an ache that lasted even when room service knocked on the door, and I went to answer. When I yanked the door open, a man and woman stood on the other side with nary a tray of food to be seen.

“Miss Bradbury?” The man was handsome in a *probably a pirate in a former life* kind of way. Around my age with dark hair and eyes like little dark orbs. The woman was pretty, came from money—I could sniff out a professional facial at eighty paces even though I hadn’t enjoyed one in years.

“Yes?”

He nodded and whipped out a badge wallet, flipped it open like he was auditioning for the part of Maxwell Smart, then walked past me. “I’m Ethan Remington.”

“The actor?” The one who was the direct descendant of Renfro Renegade Remington? What a coincidence.

“The insurance investigator.” He clarified with such authority that I didn’t dare question. I shut the door after the woman and walked toward Nicky.

Nicky held out his arm to me, silently beckoning me closer, and I didn’t hesitate. I’d already had a really weird day and now this. “What can we do for you, Mr. Remington?”

“Remy, please. You were at the Association of Actors awards a week or so ago?” Everybody in that room knew I’d been on that show. I nodded because there was no point in denying it. “You were wearing a necklace.”

I nodded. “Yes.”

The woman nodded. “Yes with a heavy stone? Beautiful blue. Was it a sapphire?”

I nodded. "I think so." They were here for my necklace, which I had no intention of giving up, so I just shrugged. "I really don't remember. It was borrowed."

"Borrowed?" Remington shook his head. "You didn't purchase it?" He pulled a photo out of his pocket. "From this woman?"

It was definitely the woman from the flea market, but I shook my head. No way was I admitting knowing her. They couldn't have my necklace. I loved my necklace. Besides, the pirate wanted it back. It should definitely have gone to him first before I even considered giving it to this insurance inspector.

Remy cocked his head and considered me as though he knew I was lying, which of course I was. He pulled the photo back and returned it to his pocket.

"Who is she?"

He sighed. "Her name is Ariya Thornbridge. She's the granddaughter of a witch who lived on the island." He motioned to the settee. "May we?"

I nodded, but all I wanted was for them to leave. For them to leave me and my necklace alone. I forced myself not to look at the coffee table *right* in front of them. I'd left the necklace on it. There was only one magazine separating them from the box that was clearly the one they were after. "It's a coincidence, I guess, that Ariya is also the name of Renegade's witch."

"You know who Ariya is?" the woman asked, then she exchanged a glance with Remy.

Crap.

She turned back to me. "Did you experience anything strange when you put the necklace on?"

Crap-crap. They knew. "Strange?" The power of the necklace was *my* secret. I wished I was wearing it right now. If I had the citrine necklace I could wish to be wearing the sapphire necklace. Then I could hear what they were thinking. But that was too much to ask.

Remy nodded. "Yes, strange. There are legends about Renegade's treasure. Powers imbued into three specific jewels."

I'd heard this before. "Penelope mentioned the story about the witch who used the stones to bring the captain back." I nodded because I liked the romance of the story. That she'd done it all for love. I understood the sentiment.

Romance or not, they weren't getting my necklace. It was mine. *Mine.* "You think my necklace"—dammit—"I-I mean, the one I wore for the award show is one of Captain Renegade's stones?" They knew I thought it, too. Otherwise, I wouldn't have been on the island. I would've been licking my wounds in Massachusetts, hiding from paparazzi, ignoring requests for interviews like I was some kind of diva with a choice. Sometimes, I missed those days. Not so much right now. Now I had to deal with this guy wanting my necklace. *Mine.*

"We know it is." He pulled a folder out of his jacket, and I wondered what kind of pockets were in the thing. He opened the folder and set three photos on the table in front of the small sofa. They were obviously from the museum, but instead of necklaces, the stones were on small pedestals under glass display boxes.

He pulled out a close-up of me on the stage before hell broke loose at the Dolby. A blind man would've been able to tell that the stones were the same. Color, cut, size, all the same.

"How did you happen to find me?" I hadn't told anyone where I was going.

Like she was a magician, the woman with him opened her hand and a yellow stone slid down a long chain to dangle between us. "I wished for it."

She had the wishing necklace. That definitely made her Cami Danes-Lacroix. "You're Penelope's daughter."

That must've meant Penelope had called her and told her where to find me. Or maybe someone on the island recognized me and gave her a head's up. Certainly, Arthur knew who I was. He could've made a call. Even knowing what I knew about my stone, I couldn't quite believe that hers worked the way she said.

Ethan looked at me. "When the necklaces were stolen from the museum, there was no video footage of the thief. Somehow, she managed to avoid seven cameras that were all aimed directly at the jewels and another three door cameras and a laser sensor."

"Why would she steal the jewels just to sell them, and for so cheap?" It'd been a bit expensive for me, sure, but I was brokeish. She could've gotten millions out of these things. If she'd wanted to bring them back here, she could've done it herself.

He smiled. "I'll ask her when I see her." This was a guy who knew exactly how handsome he was and that his smile could get him just about anything in the world he wanted.

Except my dang necklace.

Cami leaned in, and even though we hadn't been introduced, she said, "Delilah. Ms. Bradbury. We both know that the necklaces are powerful. The legend is that the second is more powerful than the first."

Legend shmegend. They weren't getting mine.

Remy leaned back and crossed his legs. "A former concierge at the hotel told us that he was hired to steal the first necklace."

"She sells the necklaces to steal them back and what, resell them?" I assumed that he meant the same woman who'd stolen them from the museum hired this concierge to steal them back once she sold them.

"I don't know. I only know that the necklaces have been stolen. Sold to you and to Cami. Now there are two necklaces in the same place." Hers seemed to be glowing, and I wondered if mine was as well. Then, like it was tattling, Cami's necklace pulsed a yellow hue beaming rays like the sun onto the table in front of me.

Oh, come on.

I tilted my head, prepared to carry this lie as far as it would let me, which currently seemed not far at all.

Remy looked at me, assessing whether or not he could trust me. I wanted to be someone who could be trusted, but at the same time I was fully prepared to use whatever weapon I had in close reach so that he or his woman couldn't take what was mine. There was no mistake that the necklace was *mine.* The woman leaned in. "I know the power, the need to hold onto it." She huffed out a breath, shook her head then turned it into a nod. "I really know."

She was trying to establish a rapport, but we weren't sisters in this. My necklace was mine and she was working for the wrong side, the side that wanted to take what was *mine.* I wasn't having it. The yellow one could shine a mystical ray of light on the magazine over the box as much as it wanted to.

Cami leaned forward and picked up the magazine, exposing the intricately carved box. Oh, cheese and rice. I snatched the box off of the table before they could get their grubby hands on it then glared at them.

Remy was handsome. Noticeably. Actually, the kind of handsome that could stop a woman, make her look twice. He was almost Nicky-handsome. Not quite. Not handsome enough to stop me from shaking my head. "Can you prove that this necklace is *the* necklace, that it's *his* necklace?"

It was going to have to be conclusive. Or they were going to have to pry the damned thing from my cold dead hands. The strength of my convictions and the need to keep my necklace were that strong.

"Remy?"

He pressed his lips together and shook his head.

"The barcode..." Cami's face pinched as she looked at him.

"Barcode?" I wanted the answer without the risk. I held my necklace tighter.

"The museum etched barcodes into the stones and the various pieces of treasure. It's a safety measure that helps in the case of theft. It's small. Too small for the naked eye." He shrugged like the revelation of a barcode wasn't the very thing she was talking about. "I would simply have to take it to the jeweler on the mainland."

The chances that this was Remington's necklace were a little bit too high for me to trust it. No way was I letting him have it or take it out of my sight.

"I can't force you to turn the necklace over." He cocked an eyebrow at me, and I waited, trying so hard to keep my face expressionless as I listened to his thoughts. "I'm not a police officer."

I'm such a liar. I could've brought the police with me to recover the stolen property. If I take this necklace, I have to take Cami's.

That was when I knew I had them. "Obviously, you both know who I am. It would be impossible for me to hide anywhere in the world right now." Since the smackdown on TV and reports of my arrest, the subsequent social media bashing and support, Shara's regretful statement afterward and the pictures of me online and in print with my mouth in a grimace as Shara dragged me around the stage by my updo, there wasn't a lot of hiding I could do. "Decide what you want to do about the necklaces, and then maybe we can figure something out."

I could be accommodating so long as he didn't try to take the necklace from me. This was my way of reacting to his way of stalling. Plus, he didn't want to take her necklace any more than I wanted to give him mine.

"Okay." Remy nodded and stood, held out his hand to me first, then to Nicky. When the handshaking was done, and they were out the door, I looked at Nicky. He was about to tell me that I should give them the necklace. I held up one finger, shook my head, and walked past him to the bathroom.

There was angry hair brushing to be done. If he wasn't careful, it was going to be his hair.

Chapter Seventeen

Delilah Bradbury Rushed to Hospital With Head Injury

After an unspecified incident in her hotel room, Delilah Bradbury was rushed from the hotel resort on Pararey Island to a mainland hospital where she walked out under her own power. A hospital spokeswoman said they could give no comment. — Staff Writer, From Your Lips Magazine

"*Cher*, this is one of my better ideas."

"Yeah," I said with a sigh. There wasn't a whole lot better in this world than getting skin-to-skin with Nicky in a bubble bath. It was heaven.

As much as I liked it, my mind continued replaying the day. The highlight reel of it anyway. I knew what had happened to me during that dive. I saw, felt, Renegade. He'd left evidence.

I wasn't a big believer in ghosts. I'd never watched those shows where they took their equipment into old asylums and hunted for spirits of the past. I watched the occasional scary movie, and if it was a ghost story, I didn't turn the channel. On the whole, I was a 'what I could see was what I believed' kind of gal. I'd seen—at least felt—a dead pirate's hand on my shoulder, and his voice in my ear.

Nicky leaned his head down and kissed the bruise where Renegade's hand had touched me. "I don't know what happened, *cher*, but if anyone ever hurts you like this again, they're going to have to deal with me."

I smiled. Ten years ago, I never would've guessed that I would be able to be happy again. Here I was. Happier than I'd ever been with a man better than I deserved on an island I could easily convince myself never to leave. This was not my dream. This was *better*.

"Maybe I imagined it. Maybe I hit my shoulder on the… boat?" It was as likely a possibility as any other. It probably made a whole lot more sense than dead pirates and cursed stones. I wondered why the stones were called cursed when all mine had done was let me know what others were thinking. Once the thought took hold, I couldn't shake it. About the time Nicky started kissing the side of my neck, I stood and stepped out of the tub. My foot slipped on the tile. Once again, my life flashed before my eyes as I fell, sank like a stone, and smacked my head on the side of the tub with a loud clunk.

It was cast iron and claw foot and the battle between my skull and said tub was not won by the skull or the soft tissue over it. My head split open and bled so profusely that when the paramedics arrived, I looked like Carrie at the prom, except in a fluffy robe instead of a prom dress.

Spots floated in front of my eyes. They raced around until they formed into what looked like a certain pirate. He had a bandana tied over the crown of his head and wore a long coat. He had a messy goatee, black curly hair that looked impressively soft for a dead guy who'd lived about two hundred years before the invention of leave-in conditioner and curl-defining mousse.

He stood behind the EMT with his hands in the air as he mimicked the guy shining his flashlight in my eyes. He was singing.

There once was a man who sailed a sea,

He lost his love for piracy,

He met a witch and fell in love,

She let him down.

She let him die,

And then she did his treasure hide

Now whoever has the stones

Suffering they will know.

I turned to glance at Nicky who was staring at me rather than the dancing pirate shivering his timbers behind the guy who was about to get a penlight shoved up his left nostril and pulled back out the right.

The fear on his face, the worry should've stopped me, should've kept me quiet. But oh, no. Not me. I couldn't be normal. Instead, I busted out the lyrics of the pirate's song. The room fell dead silent except for my sea ditty.

All eyes were on me. They'd bandaged my head, so the bleeding was minimal, but I was bouncing up and down like disco Dolly in time to the invisible pirate in my room.

"*Cher*?" Nicky stood and came toward me. When I danced away, he looked at the EMT. "Is she okay? Maybe she hit her head harder than we thought?"

Maybe. Or maybe I was dancing with the ghost of a dead pirate. At this point, it didn't matter.

I smiled at him. "I'm fine, Nicky. Just fine."

When I looked back at the spot where Renegade had been getting jiggy to his not-so-rhymey shanty, he was gone.

I didn't feel the loss until I looked back at Nicky. He wore such a look of concern, had I not been aching with sadness, I wouldn't have stopped singing and looked away and maybe Renegade would still be there. I couldn't be sure.

"Do you know the first time I saw you, *cher*?" I didn't, nor did I know why it mattered, but his voice was soft and brought me back to the stark silence of the room. His voice always cured my ails, or at least, it made me not think of them.

I shook my head and closed my eyes to savor the sweet tones when he spoke.

"There was a tip that came in on a high-dollar repo. They said the car was at the beach." He moved closer to me. Over the years, he'd told me a hundred thousand different stories, but never this one. It was the beginning of our story, though, so I knew it. This was the day we'd met, the same day he hadn't taken my car.

"Somerset Beach," I whispered. A private stretch of land where I'd sat, staring at the waves for hours, contemplating death and how easy it would be to end it all, but also how it would've destroyed my mom and she would've cried for all of eternity. I couldn't do it.

"I saw you lying in the sand at the edge of the water. Your arms were straight out, your hair was wet, and the water slid onto the beach around your body." He made it sound so romantic, but it wasn't. I'd been pathetic. Thought I wouldn't ever find my way back to happiness. "I'd never seen anyone so beautiful."

"Nicky." I couldn't do more than whisper his name around the lump of emotion in my throat. He said all the best words. Always.

Now he had his arms around me, his chest under my cheek so I could hear the steady beat of his heart. "I fell in love with you that day."

"You didn't even know me." I wanted to believe him. How I wanted that to be my story, the one I would tell the author I planned to hire to write it.

"I know. I knew I loved you." He kissed my forehead.

I looked up at him, into those eyes that made my heart beat, that made my stomach flutter. He was real. Not an illusion like the pirate I'd been singing with.

"I couldn't live without you then and I can't live without you now. Let them take you to the hospital."

I nodded, even though it included a boat ride to the mainland and a bill I probably wouldn't be able to pay. As a reward for my agreeing, he kissed me softly on the mouth this time.

I didn't see Renegade again that night, not at the hospital where they stitched me up or on the boat coming back to the island. Not at the hotel or even in my dreams. By morning, I had convinced myself that seeing Renegade had simply been a result of hitting my head.

Instead of concentrating on such crazy notions, I decided to take the island tour with Nicky. I wasn't looking so much this time at the landscape, but more at the rich history, at the potential, imagining how the love story between Renegade and Ariya unfolded and how I could spin it so it sold, how I could make it great.

"*Cher*?"

I'd never considered myself the brains behind the story before, the creator, and I probably couldn't do it now since the story was already written and performed nightly at the island theater, plus it wasn't fiction, but I was a woman with a thought and the thought evolved as I followed the pack.

These people—the ones on the tour—hadn't come to Pararey Island for fresh island margaritas and scenic tropical sunsets. They could get those at any one of the more luxurious resorts. These people, like me, had all come here for Renegade, for his story and to be a part of his legacy, the same legacy that the island had been capitalizing on for decades.

I didn't know the legalities, if it could be done without a multi-gazillion dollar lawsuit, or if I could accomplish it at all, but I was one hundred percent going to try. The rest were worries for later.

"Nicky?" I held him back as the rest of the tour moved forward.

"Yes, *cher*?" He spoke with such patience, as if he was truly dealing with someone he thought was crazy.

Once more I marveled at my good luck in finding him. "I have an idea."

For the moment, there was no witch's curse, no pirate's promise of suffering to scare me.

Chapter Eighteen

Bradbury BF Has Sordid Past!

THE TRAVELING companion and presumed boyfriend Delilah Bradbury has been squiring around her Caribbean island holiday is a man with a mug shot. In an Inquisitor exclusive, a former friend of Nicholas Pontchalac said Pontchalac spent six years in a Louisiana jail after robbing treasure hunter Myron Brickner.

When we returned from the island's library after the tour and a long, dedicated research session, the insurance guy was back, waiting outside our room. He was dressed like a pirate, complete with a giant feathered hat and a very convincing sword hanging from his belt.

I sighed. "Ahoy, matey." I nodded at him as Nicky chuckled and slid the keycard into its slot and pushed the door open when the little light turned green.

"Ms. Bradbury." He smiled, and I imagined women all over the world would probably swoon from that smile alone. "I'm filling in while Dan recuperates."

Oh, we were back to last names. "Mr. Remington." I wasn't fooled. I was already the proud girlfriend of a guy who had a smile like sunshine. This one wasn't nearly as good.

When I got past him, I turned and stood in the doorway, one arm on each side of the frame, doing my best to block him from entering. Not that he couldn't have physically moved me, but he just didn't seem the type. "Can we help you with something?"

"Your necklace is the second necklace."

I nodded because there wasn't much point to denying it anymore. "Yeah."

"May I?" He nodded to the inside of my suite, and I wanted to say no, wanted to tell him to go away, but there was a story to finish, and it was mine now. Maybe that was how I could spin it all. I could tell the tale of Renegade and Ariya inside the story of the modern-day necklaces. To tell it, I had to know it, so I stepped back and let him walk past, then shut the door and followed him into the room. When he sat on the sofa, I sat in a chair opposite the couch's left arm.

"So, back to acting." I cocked a brow at the waistcoat and sword that was sticking straight out now, alongside his thigh and extending past his knee, the feathered hat that hid the slight curl to his hair, and the thick black belt. "Or are you planning on heading out to the high seas?"

He had a different smile now. Kind of bashful. Still adorable. Not enough of a reason to fork over the necklace though. If it came to it, I supposed we could let the law decide who the necklace belonged to. I hoped it didn't come to it though. Might've even said a little prayer as such.

"Mr. Remington." I was going to tell him that there was no way I was turning over the necklace, but he shook his head.

"I need to speak with you in private. About your friend." He nodded to the bedroom area where the door was shut.

"Mr. Remington?" I didn't know what he wanted to tell me, but I knew everything about Nicky I needed to know. Nothing he could say would make a difference.

He glanced at me and leaned in. "It just so happens that your boyfriend has a police record for theft." A lot of things happened, but this one wasn't true. Nicky would have told me. I sighed, fully prepared to tell him exactly what he could do with his theories and lies about Nicky. Before I could, he continued. "Nicholas Pontchalac. Six years for residential theft." He leaned in. "He was part of a team."

"Residential is a house. Not a museum." I shook my head. "Nicky didn't rob a museum. Your report says he didn't." He couldn't.

"Not that he got caught doing. Six years in prison is plenty of time to plan better. To figure out how not to get caught. You're in possession of stolen goods."

"I bought that necklace at a flea market." I glared at him and set my jaw.

"From a woman who no one can find." He glared right back.

"Same woman your girlfriend saw." It seemed only reasonable to remind him that the holes in his story were big enough for someone to drive a tractor-trailer through.

"Your boyfriend robbed a treasure hunter in New Orleans. You know what he stole?" I didn't have to guess. He flashed a picture at me. Three stones. One yellow, one blue, one black. "I can show you the report." He raised his eyebrows as if he was waiting for me to answer, as if it was a serious suggestion.

No freaking way. He had done no such thing. "Anybody can type a report. These are the days of Microsoft Office and Photoshop. Why would I believe you or what some report says?" I shook my head. There was no way this was true. Honestly, I didn't know much about Nicky's past. About who he was before I met him. I only knew that Repo Ron was a cousin or some family member. Softer, and with less conviction than only a moment earlier, I said, "Nicky would've told me."

"Or he would've used you to get the jewels back?" This guy was barking up the wrong Cajun tree. As the door to the bathroom opened and Nicky walked out, Remy stood. "I'll leave you to it."

While I didn't know what he was leaving me to, I knew what I didn't want to bring up. Because if it was true, I would be hurt and if it wasn't, Nicky would.

"Did he come back for the necklace?" Nicky was framed by the bedroom doorway. Past him, over his right shoulder, the dead pirate captain waved at me, a three-fingered sarcastic kind of wave like he was aware he shouldn't have been in my room. Or in my imagination. I couldn't tell.

I walked toward Nicky, then past him and into the bedroom, but before I made it to the bed, Renegade was gone.

Nicky laughed and followed me in. "Right on, *bébé*." He caught me by the waist, and it was a good hour before we talked again.

Chapter Nineteen

Delilah's Darling Brings Her to the Scene of the Crime

A SOURCE CLOSE to the couple says that the treasure of a pirate captain from the 19th century is the reason Delilah and her mystery man are on Pararey Island. –National Inquisitor

AFTER WE WERE FINISHED, while he showered and I waited for him to come back, I slipped on one of the hotel robes and went to the dresser, pulled out the necklace, and dropped it into the pocket of my robe.

I had to know. Some part of me had talked the rest of me into thinking this was the right thing to do. That I could use the necklace without it being a complete violation of my relationship. That part of me didn't consider anything else than my need to know the truth. A truth I should've known in my heart.

Fortunately, the good person in me came to the stark realization that I shouldn't listen to myself. Not trusting Nicky was wrong. I was doubting the man who'd saved me from myself. The man who'd brought me through the worst days of my life.

I put the necklace back in the dresser and walked out of the bedroom to the other room and pulled a tiny bottle of vodka and a bigger bottle of orange juice from the mini fridge. I needed a drink while I waited for Nicky.

Nicky looked at me, and his smile faded. "*Cher*?"

When I didn't answer, he sighed and sat on the now vacant sofa. I didn't speak, because to give voice to Remington's accusation put a value on it, like I might believe it. I didn't.

Nicky held out his hand, and I took it, then let him pull me onto his lap. When he took a drink of my orange juice he chuckled. "I thought you quit that, *cher*." It wasn't judgment because Nicky didn't judge. It was only an observation. I had quit drinking. Or said so anyway.

I set the glass on the table. This was ridiculous. All I cared about was the man holding me. His past didn't mean anything. Not even when Remington, the ghost, appeared again and started singing.

A thief is a thief, he'll take from you

All the lies he'll say to you.

When's too long to go away

A liar he will stay.

He-he-he stole my jewels

Now give them back!

Don't be a fool!

Pirates lie and cheat and steal

Take this threat as real.

"Shut up." I stared at Renegade, but he continued humming in tune and dancing his jig.

Nicky looked back over his shoulder. "*Cher*?"

"I can see the ghost of Renegade behind you, dancing and singing, mocking me." I stared at the space behind him still even when the pirate moved closer to me now. I probably could've reached out and tried to touch him, but I was too scared. What if I touched him and he was solid, which meant he could hurt me, or if he wasn't, which meant I was definitely crazy?

Nicky chuckled. "That bastard."

I was beyond being surprised or scared. I had a necklace that could read minds, or rather that allowed me to read minds. I'd lived in Hollywood for a really long time, did movies, saw, and heard my share of dead people stories, at least. I'd suspended my disbelief years ago.

"He's singing that you stole his treasure." I actually wished he could see how the pirate dancing in our room was, bouncing from one foot to the other. If I could believe the necklace let me read minds, seeing a pirate wasn't completely unhinged. I told myself so anyway.

Nicky buried his face in my hair. "Oh, *cher*."

I nodded and wrapped my arms around him. "I know. It's ridiculous."

Certainly, there was no pirate dancing in my room, and my boyfriend of so many years wasn't a secret thief. Hell, at this point, I couldn't even be sure I was actually on Pararey Island.

When he lifted his head, his expression—serious without any hint of his usual smile—contradicted all the things I thought I knew about him.

The pirate started in again.

He's a liar and a thief

Six years in jail he did receive

He was young then now he's old

So many lies he told.

He-he's a man of con, and now he drives for Repo Ron.

My stones they must come home

Or pain you will all know.

"*Cher.*"

"He says you stole the stones."

Nicky shook his head. "I didn't steal the stones." He watched me watch him, but his gaze didn't waver.

"I knew it." Ha! I shot a glare at the pirate who was moving closer to Nicky.

"I drove the getaway car." He said it softly, etched the words with regret that danced through the air to my ears accompanied by a stab straight to my heart.

I didn't have words, so I scooted off of his lap and sat silently. I drew my arms from around him and held them in my lap.

"I went to jail."

I nodded. "Six years?"

"The guy who 'donated'"—he used air quotes—"the treasure to the museum, is the guy I drove the getaway car for. We stole the jewels from a treasure hunter who was on a plane with us after we did a different job, and he'd just come from the island with the stones. He bragged to the guy I worked with about the treasure he was smuggling back."

Remy had been telling the truth. I stood and walked to the window and looked out. I needed a second to get my head together.

He didn't move toward me. "I went to jail, and he kept the stones, but he swears they're haunted. That was why they ended up in the museum."

"Who stole them from the museum?" I turned to face him because I had to know the truth. I somehow thought I would be able to tell if he was lying. It didn't occur to me at that moment that I hadn't been able to tell in all the time we'd been together, and he'd been a big fat liar the whole time.

"I don't know. The woman maybe?" He shrugged, and I wanted to believe him, I wanted it so bad, but this was the moment that the realization of the years of lies came crashing through. They were heavy enough that I almost buckled underneath them. He cupped my cheek and turned me back to look at him again.

"Nicky." I didn't know what else to say. I couldn't think beyond the crush of disappointment. My illusion of the perfect man shattered.

"Cher, I didn't want anything to do with those stones once I got out of prison. I got a job. Fell in love with a woman." He smiled softly. It was the smile I loved most of the thousand kinds he had. I could see the emotion in this one–the love, the happiness, the contentment. "I was only seventeen, *cher*. I made a mistake. I didn't even know that he got rid of the stones, and they weren't on the police report of what was stolen."

"It was your idea to come here." That certainly couldn't have been a coincidence. On the other hand, he would've had to have known years ago that I was going to be asked to hand an award to Shara, that he would find the stone at a flea market, that it would match my dress, and that I would care about the story enough to want to come here.

"Yes. I saw the stone. I had a dream about the pirate. Once I got the idea, I couldn't talk myself out of it. I tried. I knew something would happen if we came back, and I argued with myself against all of it. Against lying to you and coming here, but I couldn't change my own mind. I went back to the flea market. Asked for the woman, and she was gone. I told the other woman the story. I knew you'd go there. I needed you to want to come here." Obviously, he knew that once I got an idea into my head, it stayed. I was like a dog with a bone. And he'd manipulated me into this.

"It isn't true? The story?" That couldn't be right. I'd found information online.

"It's true. I looked it up when I was in prison. I needed you to know it, to believe it."

"Why?"

"Because I did wrong. I wanted to bring the stones back to their home, to try to fix what I'd stolen."

To their home? "*What*?"

"I had a dream, *cher*. Many of the same dreams. The stones belong here." He'd never told me about a dream, and I didn't care at this point. A bigger truth had come to light.

He was a liar and a manipulator. Also, he was the only person in the world who loved me. I was conflicted enough that my stomach ached almost as much as my heart. I laid a shaky hand over it. This couldn't be right. This was Nicky. He didn't lie. Or steal. Or apparently, tell the truth.

"Why couldn't you just tell me? If you wanted to come here, I would've come with you. It's a tropical island, for goodness' sake." Who would say no to that? There were tears. Mine. Not his. "You lied to me, Nicky."

He nodded. Wasn't going to bother denying it because there wouldn't have been a point. We both knew the truth. I needed to know the rest of it. "Was it all a lie? Us?"

The trust had been broken. The foundation of our relationship was crumbling, about to sink. I shook my head and my heart ached and broke like it hadn't ever been and would never again be whole.

"No, *cher*. You're everything to me. Everything I have ever wanted in my life." I couldn't think of a reason why he would lie about that. He was younger. More beautiful. Could've had anyone he wanted. Plus, he knew I had almost nothing to my name when we met. I wasn't exactly a big prize. Not then and not now.

Maybe I didn't want to think about it, but I owed it to myself. "I need some time, Nicky. To think. To process." To not feel like such a stupid old fool.

He nodded. "All right, *cher*." He turned and walked to the door. "While you're thinking and processing, will you do me one kindness?"

I nodded because I loved him, and he'd saved me when I needed to be saved. Liar or not. "Yes."

He didn't look at me but looked down at his hands and then ran them down the side of his legs. "Will you remember I love you more than anything in the world and I would die before I hurt you on purpose? Would you remember that for me?"

Again, I nodded at him, and he half smiled, turned to the door, and walked out.

For a second, I couldn't breathe. I hadn't been without Nicky in a very long time and to know that I was facing a future without him took the air from my lungs.

I wanted to call him back, wanted to ask his forgiveness for not being a big enough person to look past this, to forgive him for the one lie he'd told, despite that it was one whopper of a lie.

Instead, I curled my fingers into my palm and hoped that he hadn't just shut the door on our future.

Chapter Twenty

Delilah Bradbury Having Trouble in Paradise?

DELILAH BRADBURY's mystery boy toy was spotted hitching a ride by boat back to the mainland sans his leading lady. While there have been no public squabbles since the scene at the tiki bar a couple of days ago, Delilah didn't accompany her new squeeze on his late-night boat ride, and he didn't return to the island with the resort's water taxi. –National Inquisitor

I spent the better part of that night wishing Nicky was beside me, wishing that the past didn't matter, but I was on this island simply because the past had come to matter so much. Renegade's story was now more important to me than ever.

Pulling out my laptop, I started typing. Words poured from inside me. Page after page, detail after detail. The legend. The man. The romance. It was all there. When I read back over it, I fell a little bit in love with Renegade.

By morning, I was exhausted. After I read the screenplay–and loved it a second time–I thought of Nicky. Went over every minute of my life with him in my mind. The good ones. The ones where we were just a little bit off. The bickering, though we didn't do it often. The loving. This guy was my *everything*. That I even considered a history he had before he met me as a reason to end things cheapened our relationship in a way that made me ashamed.

There was nothing unsavory about Nicky. He'd gone off the path as a kid. *I'd* been an adult when I lost my way–or maybe I'd never been on a path at all but was wandering–and I had a trail of ex-husbands to prove it. I'd gone over the edge on national television. I was no prize and yet, he spent every day treating me like I was a queen. Every day wasn't an exaggeration, either.

That was all before the stone came into our lives.

Dawn came in like a lion of light in my room, making everything brighter, and I didn't like it one bit. Although, it didn't wake me. I'd already been awake wondering where Nicky had gone, if he was ever going to come back to me, if I had lost the one guy who loved me, no questions asked.

It was around five, after I'd tried for an hour and been unable to sleep, that I couldn't take it anymore. I had things I had to do in order to put my life back together and lolling about in bed pretending like I could sleep without him wasn't going to accomplish anything.

I had connections here. Well, I had Arthur. A fan. He would tell me where Nicky was, if he knew. If Nicky had gotten a different room in the hotel, anyway. He would also let me connect to the hotel's Wi-Fi so I could send the script to an agent.

When I opened the door, the more generic version of Scully and Mulder stood on the other side. "You have the psychic rock after all?" Remy asked, one eyebrow cocked like the rock should've told me they were on the other side waiting to come in.

"No. I was just on my way out." Instead of inviting them in, I joined them in the hall and pulled the door shut behind me. "A little early for a social call, don't you think?"

"We need to talk to you." Cami looked at me and Remy's smile faded from his face. It didn't stop him from being handsome, but I couldn't have cared less what he looked like. I just wanted them to go away. I had my own problems to deal with and the necklace wasn't it, right then.

I sighed. "Look, I didn't sleep very well, and I'm not in the mood for your Scarecrow and Mrs. King act."

"Who?" Cami scrunched her nose.

"Kate Smith and Bruce Boxleitner in the eighties?" I shook my head. TV was wasted on our generation. "What do you want?"

"Have you spoken to your boyfriend?"

"That's really none of your business." I turned and walked toward the elevator. They followed because my room was at the end of the hall, and unless they wanted to jump from a window, there was nowhere else for them to go. The unkind part of me, the part I had been trying to whip into shape for years now, kind of hoped they chose the window. That part was also busy blaming them for the mess I was in with Nicky. I'd been living in ignorant bliss all these years. There wasn't a reason to change that. They didn't have any business telling me things that were none of my business.

I just wanted to find Nicky.

We both had pasts. Neither of us were proud of them, but those same pasts shaped us into who we were at that moment, in that placc, in that spacc of time. It had been me, after all, who had insisted we do that stupid pact about not talking about our pasts. If I hadn't done that, he might've told me about his jail time.

If the tattoo on his shoulder was one of those prison jobs, then I was okay with that. Really okay. That was one fine tattoo. Even if it wasn't, I couldn't judge. I'd been sketchy before. Done things I wasn't proud of in life.

I was almost tempted to take the stairs, but as soon as I walked up, the elevator doors slid open, and I stepped into the car because I was a grown woman who could ride in an elevator with them without falling apart and telling them about Nicky. It wasn't my story to tell. Although neither was Renegade's, and that wasn't stopping me.

Remy and Cami walked in behind me. I pulled out my phone, but it had been weeks since anyone besides Nicky had called or sent me a text, and the service on the island wasn't exactly top-notch, so I stood pretending to look at new messages which were actually old messages.

Instead of rereading the news articles about me that Shara had shared and reshared like she had them scheduled or on reminders, I opened my messaging app and sent a quick text to Nicky.

Just wanted to say I love you and we can work this out.

There wasn't much I wouldn't say to get him to come back to me. If he wanted me to promise everything I owned, I would. Gladly. Just to know I wouldn't have to live another minute without him. Not knowing was making me sad.

As soon as the elevator doors slid open, I stepped out and fast-walked to the counter. Art was indeed at the desk, and he smiled, skin flushed, when I walked up to his partitioned piece of the counter.

"Good morning, Miss Bradbury. How can I help you today?"

As he asked, the pig went for a trot through the lobby–for all I knew it was his morning jog. I was from California. My association with pork began and ended at the breakfast buffet, so to see the *not-yet-ready-to-be-cooked* version running through my hotel took some getting used to. Yeah, I was well aware of the irony of such a statement coming from someone who thought she was seeing ghosts, but it was the truth of it.

"Have you seen my handsome Cajun friend?" I asked quietly because I didn't want Sherlock Remy to hear that I didn't know where Nicky had gone.

Art looked around like he was about to tell me state secrets, then waved me closer and whispered, "He went to the mainland last night." This was a guy who was completely on my side. I really liked that about him. I could've used better news though.

I smiled and nodded because I didn't even want Arthur to know that I was dying inside. Without moving my mouth, I asked–softly, "Did he mention a return trip?"

Art shook his head almost so imperceptibly that had I not been watching I would've missed it.

He looked at me, or more gave me a look that said he had my back. I appreciated it because, over the years, I'd lost all the people who'd looked at me like that once upon a time. I'd either driven them away with my diva behavior or they'd left to find the greener pastures that happened without me.

Normally that was all okay because I had Nicky. Now, I didn't know if I did. I was as sad about that as I'd known I would be.

He nodded to Penelope Danes. "She might be able to tell you more since she's the one who drives the boat back and forth to the mainland."

I clasped his hand and gave him a squeeze. "Thanks, Arthur." If I ever made it back to Hollywood, I was going to dedicate my first five projects to him.

I approached Penelope slowly because she was holding the leash of the pig in one hand and a cup from the resort's coffee shop in the other. "Penelope?"

She stopped walking and smiled at me as the pig sniffed the furniture like he was a puppy looking for a place to take a leak. If he was, that was all his business. Not my furniture, not my business. He stared at me for a quick second then moved on to more interesting pastures, so to speak.

"Yes, dear?" She had her hair all pulled back in a neat bun at the nape of her neck, and her dress was a flowery print with a lacy collar. "What can I do for you?"

"You took my handsome Cajun to the mainland. Do you know if he plans to come back?" I stood silently, but I was an internal mess, probably in need of medical help–racing heart, sweaty in places women weren't meant to sweat unless they were exercising, lung burning from the lack of oxygen being pulled in because I was holding my breath.

She nods. "Yes, dear. He just needs a minute to get himself together and gather his courage."

I didn't like the sound of that. There were about a thousand too many reasons a man in this situation might need to gather his courage. I picked the most obvious. "His courage to break up with me?"

She shook her head and chuckled. "You young girls. How you worry about nonsense." She patted my arm, but it told me nothing. "I'm supposed to get him this morning."

I nodded, thanked heaven for my good luck, made a couple of promises never to misbehave again, promises me and the good Lord both knew were probably hooey since I was the same girl I'd always been and that girl was prone to misbehavior, then smiled through a mask of tears. "If you could tell him that I love him." My heart ached with exactly how much. "Plant the seed for me so that he knows I don't mean to act up."

She smiled again, like the mother of consolation. "He knows." She shook her head, and I had the feeling there was going to be some advice forthcoming. Though I'd never been a mother, I knew that kind of motherly look because I'd played a mother in a made-for-TV movie. "Sometimes, a man just needs a good minute. That boy loves you. You being foolish isn't going to change that."

"Did he say I was foolish?" My heart lurched to a halt, then started again almost immediately. Even if he did say it, it wasn't like I'd given him much proof to the contrary. "Of course, I was foolish. I usually am."

"Beautiful men bring that out in the best of us." She grinned. "I'll bring him back to you and everything is going to be just fine. You'll see." I could learn to love a woman who spoke with such confidence that she was right.

Penelope wouldn't be going to the mainland for another hour, so I had time to send the screenplay to Christian Whitworth, an agent I was well acquainted with. I would've sent it to more than only him, but his was the only email I knew by heart, and I didn't trust just anyone with such a poignant story so dear to my heart.

I walked back toward Art after I made sure Sherlock and Watson were gone. I needed the Wi-Fi password and a few minutes of uninterrupted email time.

Chapter Twenty-One

Bradbury Boy Toy Returns to Island For Romantic Reunion

Nicholas Pontchalac returned to Pararey Island today and to Delilah Bradbury where the couple was seen in a passionate embrace before they escaped on the elevator. – National Inquisitor

I stayed in the lobby and the surrounding area for a while, but hovering did nothing for my self-esteem. So, I went out by the pool. From there I couldn't see the lobby. Not all the way through anyway, and I needed to know when Nicky arrived. We needed to talk about things and the sooner we started, the better.

I sat out by the pool, not so mindful of the Caribbean sun and the effect on my pale skin that hadn't really been exposed to anything stronger than set lights since I was twelve. My mom had always said that my skin would turn to leather under the harsh rays. The Caribbean sun was not to be underestimated. It took less than half an hour before I was red. Another half hour and I could've given a tomato a run for its money, but that was when Nicky returned.

The boat floated into the docking area, bumping the wooden piling as Penelope pulled in closer, and I finally laid eyes on Nicky–hair windblown, sunglasses protecting his eyes from the sun and hiding them from me. Next to Nicky was a woman. She was younger, blonder, thinner, and he helped her out of the boat and then leaned down–she was a foot shorter–to say something to her that made her smile. He waited for Penelope and the pig to climb onto the dock then they walked in a group, but Nicky stayed beside the blond.

My fingers curled into my palm. He'd been away one night and had found himself an island honey. Technically, she would be a mainland honey, but I wasn't in the mood for technicalities. Suddenly, I was in the mood to claw out some eyes. Instead, I stood and waited for him. When he came toward me, even as unnerved as I was, I couldn't take my eyes off of him. He was all lean muscle and easy stride, the kind of stride a woman should watch, could watch for hours. Especially if I was said woman.

He stopped in front of me and pulled me in for a kiss that almost made me forget he'd reappeared with someone else. As he leaned back and smiled down at me, the woman who'd seemed too well acquainted with him went inside with Penelope and her pig. "I missed you, *cher*."

I looked at him. "You make a new friend?" I wasn't saying anything else until I had an answer. One I believed.

"Yeah." His brow creased, and he shook his head. "Wait, no. Not a friend." The head shaking became more intense. "No. No. No." He took my hands and widened his eyes. "No, *cher*." One last time, he added, "No. She's a woman with information. She's a psychic."

"Information?" My tone was clipped and short. I couldn't hide the jealousy even though he'd never given me a reason to be jealous, and he was holding my hands in his right now.

"Yes, information." He nodded. "She knows about your stones."

That was fine as long as she didn't know about *his* stones. "What about them?"

"She can explain better, but she said the stones lure you in, then turn on you." I didn't know what that meant, but it didn't matter because then he smiled softly and pulled me against him. "Turns the wishes backward, lets you hear voices that aren't there. Will speed up time when the third stone turns." He paused and switched gears. "*Cher*, if you hate me, I understand. I lied. I was wrong. I should've told you who I was and what I did."

I nodded. "You should have, but I could never hate you. If I hadn't made that rule, you might have. I'm actually not mad about anything before the market. Once we saw the stones at the market, that's when you should've told me about them." I loved him way too much and hate took too much energy. I smiled because he was Nicky. *My* Nicky.

"You may not hate me, but you can't have forgiven me. What I did was a betrayal."

This felt like one of those moments that needed some truth and some sentiment. "It was. But it's not of the deal-breaking variety. Nicky, when you found me"—literally, he'd been hunting for the car– "I was lost, a train wreck of a human being. I was sad and lonely. Not to mention disgraced and broke. Every single day, you take me as I am. Whether it's a good day or a bad one, you're always beside me." I pulled him down for a soft kiss and laid my head over his heart. "I don't care about anything but you." I would give my stone back and hunt down the others if it meant Nicky and I could live in peace and happiness. We'd work through this, the trust would return.

At least I hoped so.

He glanced at me, eyes clear and wide. I could see forever in them. "Maybe we should help Remington and Cami find the other stone. Make right what I did wrong."

It was an idea. "Do you believe the stones are cursed?"

He nodded. "With every fiber of who I am." He spoke softly but with conviction. "A strong curse."

I wanted to... believe him or disprove him. I couldn't tell which. Maybe I just wanted to protect my stone but in my gut, I felt the truth.

"I need to see if it's true." It was fast becoming stronger than a need inside of me. It was almost a compulsion.

He glanced down at me and then away as he pulled me close again. "I can't lose you, *cher*."

I would give everything I had to keep him. "You won't."

Chapter Twenty-Two

Former Bradbury Manager Shopping Screenplay

Christian Brickner, the former manager of Delilah Bradbury and current manager of several A-list superstars, including Shara Hewitt, is reportedly shopping a screenplay written by the former starlet herself. He's in talks for the top-secret project with Achilles Entertainment, Allegiant Productions, Ignite and the brand new Myst Creations. – Staff Writer, Encore Magazine

I sat beside Nicky, and the woman across from us–his companion from the mainland–studied me. Only me. She was probably in her early thirties, with shoulder-length brown hair that reminded me of the way light filters through honey. She sat with a ramrod-straight spine and didn't look at Nicky.

"What's your name, darling?" If she was truly a psychic, shouldn't she have known already?

I tried not to be offended that she hadn't heard of me. "Delilah Bradbury."

She nodded as if she agreed. "Yes, Miss Bradbury. I know you." She paused and started. "I've seen you."

"My movies?" I asked because something about her said she wasn't a fan of my career.

"No. I saw a vision of you." Her voice was like lead, heavy and dark. "You wear the mark of the pirate's hand on your shoulder." She wasn't exactly asking, and no way in hell was I confirming. That she knew about the bruise sent shivers of apprehension dancing over my skin. I glanced at Nicky, and he shook his head almost imperceptibly. He hadn't told her.

"Twenty-two years ago, a man named Myron Klinger came to Pararey Island. He was a well-known treasure hunter."

He must've been the guy Nicky and his friend robbed. "He's the man who found the stones?"

She nodded. I held Nicky's hand under the table. He was understandably pale even beneath the island glow of his skin. I gave his hand a squeeze and was just about to give another when he squeezed back.

"He brought his treasure home to the states where it was stolen and later turned up in a museum in New York." She didn't elaborate, and I was glad since I thought the details might upset Nicky, and he already wasn't faring too well. His usual smile was missing, and his face was drawn.

When I looked at him, Nicky nodded almost imperceptibly, but I saw it. Or maybe more, I felt it. It didn't matter. It didn't stop the woman from talking.

"The man who stole the stones from Myron turned himself in for the theft." She spoke with familiarity, and I wondered how she knew him. I didn't ask because I didn't want to interrupt this train of thought.

Nicky nodded instead and added, "He turned in everyone involved." That included Nicky.

"Yes. The curious part is that when the police asked why he'd turned himself in, he told them that a pirate had told him that it was the only way he would ever know peace again."

To anyone walking by or to anyone who didn't know the gist of the story, it would've sounded ridiculous. The ability to suspend disbelief and take odd facts at their face value wasn't one that all people could master. This accounted for pessimism and skepticism, all the bad *isms*.

I was glued to her every word. She cocked her head at me. "Do you know the curse of the stones?"

I knew it well enough that I wrote a screenplay about it, though I didn't mention that to her. "Yes."

"You know that Ariya is trapped in time? That until the stones are brought together and returned to the sea, the spell cannot be broken and Ariya cannot be reunited with Renegade."

Actually, no. I hadn't known any of that. I kept my lack of knowledge to myself. "What happens if the stones aren't returned to the sea?"

"The curse will linger until Renegade's jewels are returned." She spoke with such finality and authority I didn't dare doubt her.

"Who stole the treasure from the museum?" Nicky lifted his gaze to meet that of the woman.

She shrugged. "A common thief who tried to increase her fortunes by claiming to be Ariya Thornbridge. She's a pretender." Her tone was dry, and her opinion of the pretender wasn't hard to infer.

"Is she haunted, too?" I asked. Beside me, Nicky was still quiet, and I gave his hand another squeeze.

"The curse affects those who hold the stones." I was currently holding one and Cami had the other, wherever she was. "Until the stones are brought back together and returned to the sea, the curse will remain."

"How do we return them? Just toss them into the water?" It seemed a bit too anticlimactic. All my years in Hollywood had taught me to expect an ending with flair.

The woman shook her head. "The curse must be removed at midnight on the first night of the new moon." It sounded like some Harry Potter hooey to me, but I wasn't judging. If she knew how to do it, great.

That still told me nothing about the process, but I had time to research. We still didn't know whether or not we could find the third stone. Although Sherlock and Watson had found me. Of course, I'd been wearing the gem on television and made headlines for my night in the slammer. I probably wasn't so hard to find.

As Nicky and I walked back to our room, Captain Renegade's ghost danced down the hall in front of us, and Nicky remained blissfully unaware. While the pirate hadn't threatened me, and I wasn't especially afraid of him, I couldn't wait until he was gone. Even if it meant giving my necklace back to the sea.

Chapter Twenty-Three

Achilles Entertainment Makes a Big Buck Movie Deal with Delilah Bradbury

A SCREENPLAY WRITTEN by former A-list actress, Delilah Bradbury, has reportedly sold for an undisclosed eight-figure amount. While the project has been kept under wraps, the studio is looking for actors for what they are calling a new franchise to add to their catalog of established projects. Bradbury will be named executive producer on the project. –Staff writer, Encore Magazine

By morning, I was renewed, refreshed, and had a very naked Nicky lying beside me in bed. There was no better way to wake up than with that man's *good morning* nestled against mine.

I could've done without the phone ringing on the bedside table. I considered ignoring it for the foreseeable future, but it was a California area code. It was Christian Whitworth. "Hello?" If I sounded timid, it was because I was.

"Delilah!" I held the phone away from my ear because Christian had a screech of impressive volume, and it was painful to listen to. "Are you sitting down?"

I glanced at Nicky and smiled. "Kind of."

His voice went higher and sharper. "Warner wants your screenplay." That really had been a screech.

"Do they now?" A bubble of excitement formed in my belly, but I didn't want to get my hopes up. For all I knew, this was some sort of epic prank.

"They do! Seven zeroes, Delilah. Seven zeroes behind a one, but it's *seven* zeroes." Ten million dollars? I gasped. Holy crow. Ten million dollars.

I sat up. "Ten million dollars?" I had to have heard it wrong. Repeated it wrong. Said it wrong again. "Ten million dollars?" Then I dropped the phone because I fainted.

When I came to, Nicky was holding a washcloth to my face.

I hadn't even told him about the screenplay yet. "Ask me to marry you, Nicky."

The washcloth was red with my blood and my head was tipped back but I could see his face, his eyes. I could see myself, my forever in them. "*Cher,* I love you. Will you marry me?"

"Yes." I smiled. "I'm going to take care of you forever." Then, I told him everything. About seeing the pirate, although I'd already told him that, but this had a tie-in to the screenplay and how the words had poured out of me onto the page, how I didn't even remember writing some of it, but also how when I read it, I fell more in love with this place and their story. I told him how it was a mixture of the old and the new. How it was worth ten million dollars.

"I would marry you if you had nothing." When he said it with such sincerity in his voice and those eyes that could see straight to my soul, I believed him. He could've told me he was a purple people eater, and I would've bought it.

I nodded. "I know. We need to get married now before anyone knows about the deal." I could just hear the headlines in my head. "Bradbury pays younger boyfriend to marry her," "Bradbury Buys Hunky Husband," and maybe even "Bradbury boy toy marries for money." The tabloid reporters were really clever when they had new material to work with.

"Today? You want to get married *today*?" His eyes were wide, but his lips tilted into a smile. "Today." He nodded. "Today."

Why not? We'd been together long enough to know everything about each other. Now at least there was nothing that scared me about the idea of spending the rest of my life with him. I certainly wanted to walk down the aisle with him *today* before he had a chance to change his mind.

An hour later, we were dressed in the fanciest clothes to be found at the boutique in the lobby of the hotel, and I had Penelope on one side of me while her pig roamed the beach and Arthur stood beside Nicky. Cami and Remy were our only other guests. We hadn't told them yet about the woman from the mainland, or what she'd said, or about the screenplay, only that we wanted to get married.

That was all we'd had to say to Penelope. She'd arranged everything from the flowers I was holding, and Nicky was wearing, to the wooden arbor we were standing under. It was a beautiful sunny day, a perfect island day according to Penelope, and when Penelope said something was perfect, there was no doubt about it.

The man in front of us was dressed in a traditional black priest's robe and a funny-shaped black hat with a ball on top. He held a book with the word matrimony on the front. I'd done this so many times, I probably knew the ceremony better than he did, but I stood waiting for him to speak.

"Marriage is a lifelong commitment between two people." Penelope cleared her throat and shook her head at him. He cocked a brow but turned back to me and Nicky. "Marriage is a promise not to be taken lightly." This time Penelope sucked in a loud breath through the side of her mouth so that it made a soft winter wind against the window sound. "Okay. Maybe we should start the vows."

Nicky smiled like we were the only two people in the world and when he started talking, I believed it. "*Cher*, I knew as soon as I met you, when I saw this smile and these eyes," he ran his thumb over my eyebrow and down to my lips then took my hand again, "that I never wanted to let you go. You're the center of my world, the love of my life, and my best friend. I'm going to love you until I die and then beyond, no matter what happens."

Words like that were enough to make a girl swoon. When he put that together with those eyes, that body, the linen shirttail flapping in the breeze just enough to show me the abs he had under it, I was having trouble breathing. For Pete's sake, I even found his bare feet in the sand sexy.

Now it was my turn. "I've done this before." He smiled and gave my hands a squeeze then a shake. "I never walked into it knowing that the person I was marrying was exactly the person I wanted to grow old with. Nicky, you're the man I dreamed of when I was searching for my person. I want to spend the rest of my life showing you that I'm worthy of you, of being the one you love and the one who loves you back without condition or judgment or complaint." I couldn't imagine having anything to complain about. "I'm so lucky to be the one you picked to spend your life with, and I'm going to make sure every day that you know that I know how lucky I am."

He smiled and reached into his pocket and pulled out a ring that took my breath away. It was an oval diamond on a pedestal with a tiny halo of little diamonds holding it onto the rose gold band. It was *gorgeous*. I held out my left hand because that ring was going on it if I had to use a shoehorn or a teeny-tiny little pry bar. With my other hand, I covered my mouth as he slid it on. It fit like he'd known my size.

Then Penelope handed me his ring. It, too, was gold. A plain band with a tiny little diamond. I slid it on his finger, and he smiled. The guy in the robes asked if we promised to love, honor, and cherish, we said our *I dos*, and then Nicky kissed me. There was the formality of paper signing, and then Penelope popped the champagne and Arthur promised that if Nicky ever hurt me, he would be meeting the business end of Arthur's boot. Some words about a baseball bat were also thrown around.

At dinner, I told Cami and Remy about sending the stones back to the sea and how we had to do it soon before the bad luck started, and we made a plan. Starting tomorrow, we were starting the hunt for the third stone, but we also had to figure out what kind of process was needed to lift the curse.

Starting tomorrow, we were going on an adventure. And then I would be making a movie.

Onyx Interruptions

Chapter One

It's Not Easy Being A Mom. If It Were, Dads Would Do It.

IT HAD to be the excruciating and exorbitant amount of pain that had my mother thinking this was a good idea. Or maybe it was the morphine drip that was finally cutting through her pain. What it wasn't, either way, was good sense. Not that it mattered since it wasn't going to happen.

"Mom, I cannot just drop everything and run off to some Caribbean island to drop off a necklace. What I can do is package it, address it to wherever you want to send it, and take it to the post office. I'll pay the insurance for it. I'll pay for express shipping. I'll wrap that bad boy in bubble wrap and a combination lock, then call the..." I didn't even know who the hell she wanted it sent to. "Person and tell them the combination, and wait on the phone while they unlock it. What I will not do is get on a plane to a place I have no desire to visit to hand-deliver a necklace that is most definitely not cursed."

Curses don't exist unless they are of the four-letter variety, and that was where my mother and I differed in opinion.

She believed that falling and breaking one's hip at the tender age of 71 was a sign from whichever deity she was currently praying to. A sign that the necklace she'd been hanging onto most of her life was ready to go back where it came from, and until then, it would have no mercy on whomever owned it. I didn't buy it. I'd never bought the line of crap Mom believed in.

She'd always been quirky, but in the last few months, she'd gone so far around the bend, I didn't think I was going to be able to bring her back. I still hoped I could though. As I gazed down at her, noticing that she seemed to have lost some weight in recent years, my heart ached. When my mom was young, she had blonde hair, the same shade as my own, and bright blue eyes that more than a few fellas seemed to notice. Those days had faded away, and while my mom was still a beautiful woman, her blonde hair had faded to white, and more than a few wrinkles surrounded her blue eyes. Eyes that were now hidden behind glasses.

I guess none of us can escape time. Not me, a woman in my forties, nor my mom, a woman in her seventies. Yes, we were in different places in our lives, but I'd never seen her as... old. If anything, she sometimes seemed more youthful than me. Now, staring down at her thin body draped by a white sheet, it was impossible to ignore the fact that she wasn't as young as she once was.

"Em, I would go, but there's a reason the ghost of Renegade wants you there." Oh, sweet Jesus. Now she was saying a ghost—the family ghost apparently—was the reason she had fallen over her mostly evil cat, Rufus, and broken her hip so now she was lying in a bed at Mass Gen waiting for a surgery that she wouldn't agree to. Probably a little bit druggy from the pain meds she *had* finally agreed to, so I could forgive this lunacy... this time.

To be fair, it wasn't necessarily all her fault. All of her life, she'd been told we'd come from a long line of witches—the Thornbridge line. She was convinced she had magical power and that she could cast spells. I didn't doubt that *she* believed she had skills. Her "spells" seldom worked and her "potions" gave the neighbors hives. If witches existed, and she was one of them, she was a really poor witch.

As much as I loved her, she wasn't psychic either, or she would've known that I couldn't leave my job to go running around the globe, even though I knew how much it meant to her. "Ember, what are the chances that on the day I was supposed to fly to Pararey Island, I would fall and break my hip?"

With *that* cat, who seemed possessed by a disagreeable, cantankerous, angry spirit. The chances of a broken hip increased exponentially by the day.

I sighed. She sighed. A moment later, it seemed like the entire room sighed. Suddenly, the vinyl privacy curtain rustled behind me, startling the daylights out of me. It took a second before I realized the AC was running and had caused the curtain to move. My heart raced and my brain went into overdrive. I took a breath and reminded myself it was just the HVAC system, that was all, nothing more. This resulted from years of living with a woman who said everything I touched came alive around me. It was the power of being a *Thornbridge*. That was her explanation anyway.

"Ember, you're wasting your skills here." If she'd said this once, she'd said some version of it a thousand times. I didn't believe it any more now than I did then.

"My medical skills?" I probably should've kept my mouth snapped shut, or maybe tried agreeing with her, but nope. I was at the breaking point. The point of no return. The point where reason was gone.

She grimaced, and turned her head away from me, because, as she'd also said before, she didn't appreciate me mocking or demeaning her belief system because I didn't share it (although she said I should've). Maybe I was, but I'd grown up on the wrong side of my mother being a witch.

"You know very well the skills I'm speaking of Ember." She'd taken *that* tone—the one that meant I'd disappointed her.

As often as I could when dealing with my mother, I refrained from rolling my eyes. This time I couldn't help it.

She huffed and puffed like a method actor rehearsing for the big bad wolf. I softened my voice. "Mom, I'm not going to the Caribbean." Maybe trying a different approach would appease her. "You're hurt. What kind of daughter would I be to run off on vacation"—I hadn't accrued enough PTO, anyway—"when you're going to be fresh out of surgery?"

She certainly wouldn't want to go to a rehab center for recovery, just because she'd shipped me off to an island that she swore was calling the necklace she was holding home.

She shook her head. "I'll have one of the girls"—her coven—"come to stay with me. This *bad luck*..." She threw up the air quotes. "Certainly, isn't going to end until that stone is on its way back to Renegade."

"Renegade?" If someone had been listening in to our conversation, it would have sounded like Mom had herself some big, bad, biker, sugar baby and she was sending me to return his jewelry, but I'd heard the name before, and he wasn't a biker. Sadly, I almost wished he was. I would've known how to deal with a guy like that. No, this was Renegade, a name I'd heard as far back as I could remember. She hadn't brought him up in a long time, I thought she might've realized I'd grown out of my Dread Pirate Roberts phase and forgotten. Now, the red flags waving in my mind were blowing in the breeze. "Not this bull… crap again." She liked spells and potions. Hated curse words. I tried to be respectful.

Her face tightened into an expression of stern indignation. "Do you ever listen when I talk? Or read the family newsletter?" She shook her head, and sighed, her regular exasperation at me on full display now. "Renegade was a pirate and the first true love of Ariya, the first known witch in the Thornbridge line." Her glare deepened because I might or might not have been pretending not to know what she was talking about. "This is your heritage, Ember. Your history. Shame on you."

Now she was on the high road.

I'd dropped the *bridge* from *Thornbridge* right around the time she'd started her magic shop and put an ad in the paper for like-minded women to join her coven. It had been sometime around my second year in college. I didn't want to be associated with the family history of witches or the craziness that went along with them. "I don't do family history." Mostly because it was full of ridiculous tales of a dead pirate, his witchy women, and the women who cult-worshiped them. My mother included.

Despite all my accomplishments, my mother was disappointed in the fact I wasn't practicing witchcraft. I had worked hard to become a Doctor, a respected physician. It was because of this medical training that I was legitimately worried about her. Maybe she had done more than break her hip and had a concussion or a bleed.

"Sweetheart, the stone is cursed. If I don't get it back to Renegade, things are going to get worse." She spoke with such certainty that I refrained from rolling my eyes at her, more sad for her than annoyed. It wasn't her fault. She'd been taught these things since she was young. I'd been taught these things, too, but I'd realized they were nothing but stories a long time ago.

"Who tells you this stuff?" I was beyond frustrated—dry-eyed but my voice had climbed an entire octave.

She waved me in closer, as if she was going to tell me a secret, and there was nothing I could do but comply, so I leaned in. "Renegade. He's the one who told me."

"The ghost of a dead pirate."

"He wouldn't be a ghost if he was alive."

I couldn't argue with her logic on that statement, but it didn't make it right. Now, I was beyond disbelief, "Mom."

She held up her hand. "I know what it sounds like, Ember." She shook her head and I stood straight. I needed to check her pupils to make sure she didn't have a concussion. Her voice was strong. "He came to me in a dream."

"Mom, when you fell, did you hit your head?"

I used my fingers to palpate her scalp, but I didn't feel any bumps or lumps. She slapped me away. "No." She stilled, then frowned. "I don't know, actually."

My mother had always been eccentric, but now she was "talking" to a ghost in her dreams. This wasn't going well. "I don't feel anything." Although, on some rare occasions, there wouldn't be any external or visible contusions. "Maybe I should have them order a CT scan."

"Ember." She was using her stern voice. I stopped moving and looked at her. Finally, she sighed. "He came to me in a dream, but he's been with me ever since."

I glanced around the room. Now she was seeing and talking to dead people? Family history or not, I wasn't buying it. I humored her. "Is he here now?"

She cocked an eyebrow. "No. I haven't seen him since I woke up." I loved my mother. She'd supported me through all my ups and downs, through broken hearts where she'd given me potions to handle the situation, and when I needed help studying, she'd stayed up late helping me learn the names for every muscle, bone, tendon, and piece of named tissue in the human body. This was getting out of hand.

"Mom..." I didn't know what to say that wouldn't sound harsh and ugly.

"The other stones are already on the island." She tried to sit up, winced, and relaxed back against the pillow. I hated seeing her in pain. Hated it, but she'd only agreed to a very low dose of morphine and nothing else, including refusing to do surgery.

"Rest of the stones?" I asked her. "Ariya and Renegade fell in love."

With frustration came impatience. "Mom, I've heard the story before. We don't have time for a retelling of their fairytale love story."

"It's not a fairytale. It happened."

Of course it did. "Ariya loved Renegade. Renegade was a pirate. Piracy is a dangerous job."

"It was a mutiny." She was exasperated, and it made her voice shrill and loud.

"His crew thought he was a thief. Let's face it, he probably was." He was a pirate. That, by definition, made him a thief. "For heaven's sake, Mom. Have the surgery. Maybe he can come to you again while you're under anesthesia."

She cocked her head for a moment, as if considering it, then shook her head. Dammit. "I'm not going to consent to surgery until I tell the story." This wasn't her first attempt at bribing me with this surgery.

"Do you promise? If I sit and listen again, you'll sign for the surgery?" It would help her. The pain would be manageable. That was all I wanted for her. We had about twenty minutes before she would lose her spot in the OR and have to wait until later. When she nodded, I sighed. "Fine. Tell the story."

What other choice did I have? On any other normal day, I didn't mind the story. In fact, when I was young, I loved it. Now though, I was an adult, I was over fairy tales, and I was so over her craziness.

I realized that letting her bribe me with surgery set a bad precedent in our relationship, but I doubted I would be in this situation with her again. I sincerely hoped not, anyway.

"When Renegade died, Ariya was devastated, and she tried to bring him back. She infused the stones with magic." She spoke with passion, and for all the time I'd heard this story, I didn't remember this part.

"Stones?"

Mom nodded. "Yeah. Three stones. Citrine. Sapphire. Onyx." She lifted a finger for each one.

"How did you end up with one?" I wanted to hear the rest now.

"That isn't your concern." Uh-oh. "The point, sweet"—her pet name for me—"isn't how I got it. The point is that it needs to get back to the island. You have to take it." She smiled. We'd now reached the portion of our conversation where the precedent I'd only just set by indulging her was back to bite my ass. "I'm not having surgery unless you promise you will take the stone back to Pararey Island." Had she looked even a little bit smug, I might not have told a lie. She needed this surgery. This meant a lot to her, so I nodded. "Fine. I promise." She would never have to know one way or the other.

That was the lie that started it all.

Chapter Two

The Doctor Is In...competent

My mother was in surgery, and I was holding the necklace with the large black stone, an onyx, I'd retrieved from her purse. It was smooth on one side, like someone had once used it as a worry stone, something I knew my mom sold in her shop. A necklace that didn't look the least bit dangerous, even though some small part of me hoped by holding this stone I'd see what my mom saw. That there was something special about it.

Unfortunately, there wasn't. Whether my mom was losing her mind, or so caught up in her old beliefs that she felt it was important, I had to admit that this onyx-whatever was nothing unique or important. It was just an old rock made into a necklace.

I'd lied to my mother. I wasn't going to the Caribbean. I didn't believe the tragedies of life were more than that. Mom had broken her hip. It had nothing to do with a dead pirate or his woman's curse on this particular stone. If it even was the stone. I doubted it. I dropped the jewel back into the velvet bag and put the bag into the box.

I stowed her bag in my locker. While she was in surgery—which would take a couple of hours—I worked. Hospital staffing hadn't been courteous enough to account for my mother's broken hip, so I still had patients to see and orders to write.

There was always a patient who needed something and having a doctor ease their minds was often more comforting than a nurse, even though there isn't a doctor in the place who doesn't know that nurses run the world. Even if we rarely admit it.

I walked the post-op recovery hallway. These were patients whose pain was numbed by medication, so there wasn't any talking or moving about, just silence. For a couple of minutes, there was peace, a gentle quiet I desperately needed, while trying my hardest not to think about my mother.

I saw a familiar woman heading toward me and tried to hide my worry with a smile. "Good morning, Deb." She was the floor nurse, in charge of all the nurses in this hallway. I didn't generally work up here, but today I wanted to be close to my mom, so I'd asked to be assigned here.

"Dr. Thorn." She smiled and handed me an iPad. We didn't do much on paper anymore. This was faster, more sanitary, and way more efficient and all the records went straight to billing, so there was that, too.

The only other sound was my steps on the tiled floors and there wasn't a lot of that, because I was wearing Crocs.

"Quiet this morning."

As soon as the words were out, Deb jerked her head toward me. "Oh, no, you didn't."

Of course I did. Before I'd even realized that I'd jinxed us all, alarms beeped, and call buttons were pressed. The ward erupted in light and sound. In a way that made me feel like I was on some kind of hidden camera show, where someone behind a camera was waiting to jump out and scream, "Gotcha. All your patients are fine." Because normally, saying it was quiet was asking for trouble, but not like this, never like this.

I scurried, hurried, and rushed from room to room. When the commotion calmed, and there was a second to take a break, I stepped to the nurse's station with the iPad. "209 needs..." She rattled off the names of the meds. "221 TOD"—time of death—"was 1141."

I filled in the med order and my portion of the death certificate then sent a message to the transport team. When I finished, I handed the iPad to Deb, because my shift had ended a while ago. Now, I could finally focus on Mom instead of popping in and out of her room when I could.

The entire episode had only taken almost two hours, but by the time I made it back to recovery to check on Mom, I was exhausted. Thankfully, she hadn't arrived yet, so I sat in the chair in her room, alone with my thoughts for just a moment. I sat in the quiet room preparing myself to see my mom after her surgery and shake off the bad luck I'd just experienced.

When she finally made it back, I sat beside her bed and held her hand.

Quirky or not, she was still my mom. Even though our belief systems were very different, I would be lost without her. No one would be there to text and remind me to eat or to stop by my place and restock my groceries. Countless times over the years, I'd gotten home after a long week, hoping to open my fridge and find a forgotten hotdog in some back corner, and instead found a packed fridge, along with a few home-cooked meals. Other times, she'd leave her darn crystals and powders around my house, as "protection." Once I even found tiny mirrors she'd hidden in the corners of my house. Why? No idea, but I knew she'd done it to help me in some way.

That was my mom. A little crazy, but so full of love. Now she was hurt.

I fell asleep sitting next to her, tears sliding down my cheeks, and only woke when someone touched my shoulder. My first thought was of my mother, of tragedy. Probably because I saw so much, and I'd lost the patient in 221 today. When I looked, she was awake, sipping from a cup of water.

"Doctor Thorn? Dr. Warren needs to see you." I looked out the window. Mom's room was on the west side of the fifth floor, and she had a beautiful view of the Charles River, then back at my mom before realizing the person who'd spoken was a nurse who was standing beside me.

I didn't mean to be rude, but she wasn't my priority right now.

"Mom, are you okay?" I was groggy and probably sounded stupid.

Her eyes were glassy, but she nodded. "Safe and sound," but the words came out raspy.

I turned to look at the nurse who'd woken me from what I'd thought was a short nap, but then I glanced at the clock and shook my head. I slept for at least three hours. It was almost four. I nodded at the nurse. "Thanks, Erin."

"He said it's urgent."

I nodded, stood, and stretched because I didn't care what anyone said. Hospital chairs were not meant for sleeping, even the ones that reclined. "Mom, will you be okay if I take care of this quickly?"

She smiled, but it didn't quite reach her eyes. "Go."

I turned, fully intending on making whatever errand this was go fast, so I could be back at my mother's side. There were any number of reasons Dr. Warren, the Chief of Staff, may have wanted to see me. I didn't speculate. He was no-nonsense, but so was I. We worked well together.

That didn't mean I wanted to walk into his office looking like Rip Van Winkle, who'd only come awake from my long winter nap. I made a detour to the locker room to change into my street clothes.

My shift ended hours ago, long before I went to help on the post-op floor, but as I'd had to be at the hospital for mom, anyway, pitching in made sense.

It was only about thirty minutes from the time I woke until I walked into his office, but his annoyance was like a third person in the room.

My spine stiffened, and I stood straighter. "Doctor Thorn." His voice was like steel, but with the bite of an angry viper. Even at his worst, he wasn't generally so... angry.

"Dr. Warren." I nodded and took the chair in front of his desk. I was a no-fear kind of gal.

He opened a file folder and pulled a sheet off the top of the stack of pages inside. He'd apparently reviewed it before I arrived.

"Dr. Thorn, is that your signature on this order?"

I looked at the page. It was my name in my handwriting, very clearly on the order which transferred responsibility for the patient in 209, a JD Remington, to the transport team for transport to the morgue. The transport team was made up of two orderlies who worked the entire hospital. I didn't personally know them or how they were chosen for such a job, but I regularly assigned patients to them.

He nodded and slid the paper back into his folder. His face was the color of a garden tomato, and I could almost see the steam rolling off him.

"Dr. Warren, I personally performed CPR on the patient for eleven minutes. He was given..." I rolled out the information as best I remembered. "He was pronounced dead at 1141 this morning."

"JD Remington had surgery to remove kidney stones." He was irate as he opened his file and pulled out another paper. "You ordered Ciprofloxacin for Everett Mulcahey, who indeed passed at 1141. Thirty-three minutes before you ordered the course of IV antibiotics." His voice was very controlled now. His stare would've melted iron.

"What?" Things had been chaotic. Crazy. I'd not signed the orders until everything calmed. I tried to remember what Deb had said. Murmured the words as I recalled them. "209 needs Cipro and a morphine drip and monitored intake and output. 221 TOD 1141." I must've messed up the orders and the room numbers.

"You sent JD Remington, a clearly live patient, to the morgue. He was asleep and woke up in one of the refrigerators."

Oh, shit. I said, "Oh," because I was ever eloquent when surprised. "I'm guessing Mulcahey doesn't need a morphine drip." I probably shouldn't have been so lame as to try for levity in the face of such consternation and anger. I didn't make mistakes like this. Ever.

He shot me a glare I more than deserved. "Dr. Thorn."

I sucked in a breath. I didn't make mistakes like this. Avoidable. I should've slowed down, paid attention. Checked the numbers and the information I entered into the system. This was my mistake and because I hadn't checked, I couldn't say otherwise.

A sheen of sweat broke out on my forehead.

"JD Remington is a personal friend." Every word sank my "personal" ship. I was going to be lucky to walk out of this office with a job. Pride was a pipedream, and I was ready and willing to surrender it. "I will apologize."

He nodded. "Yes, you will. His son wants you fired."

I was waiting for that—hands folded in my lap, tears at the ready, kind of waiting to fall.

He twisted his mouth to the side. "I don't think that's appropriate."

"Oh, thank God." The breath of a thousand half-shattered dreams and a couple of hundred grand in student loans whooshed out of me.

"I'm going to give you some time off to consider your position and to let Remington's son cool off." He shook his head and folded his hand on the desk. "We deal with lives and some we save, some we don't. We make mistakes and it costs lives. You're very lucky no one was hurt." He didn't specify the amount of time he was giving me to think, now probably wasn't the time to ask. The gist of it was I still had a job. Dr. Warren continued, "there will be a permanent mark in your file."

That was fine, too. I planned on working at Mass Gen until I died there. The note in my file guaranteed it. I nodded. "Yes, sir."

"You'll need to write a formal letter to the Remingtons. An apology dripping with sincerity." He cocked an eyebrow.

"Yes, sir. It will be soggy and smeared with my tears of regret." I cleared my throat because I wasn't sure it was the best idea. "Won't that put the hospital at risk in case of a lawsuit?"

On an ordinary day, I would have shut my mouth and walked out with what was nothing more than a slap on the wrist. Nothing about this day was ordinary.

Dr. Warren shook his head and blew a whistling breath from his nose. "As I said, JD Remington is a friend. He won't sue the hospital."

There was nothing implied in that statement. If JD Remington sued anyone, it would be me and the letter was to be my releasing the hospital from any responsibility or liability, and there was no way around it.

Before I left the hospital to begin my formal suspension, I stopped in to check on Mom. Through tears, I told her the whole story, and she smiled as if she'd just won the lottery. "Now you don't have any reason holding you here. You can go to the island." She spoke of it with such familiarity for a place she'd never been to before.

"Mother." I didn't care if that damned necklace never made it back to Pirate Island or whatever it was called. "I have plenty of reasons, Mom. I have a boyfriend." Although, if I was honest, I couldn't remember the last time I'd seen him for more than a quickie or talked to him about anything more than when I was free to have a quickie.

"Cliff won't care if you take a vacation."

I wondered if she got his name wrong just to piss me off or if she really couldn't remember. "His name is Clay."

She rolled her eyes. "Seems apt." She sighed. "He's not a keeper, Ember. He isn't the one you can't stop thinking about."

When she was right, she was right. I didn't have to like it. I couldn't remember the last time I'd had a conscious thought about Clay before today. To be honest, I couldn't even say for certain that he was still my boyfriend.

That wasn't a fact I planned to share with my mother. "Mom..." I decided not to argue, I could let her live her life with delusions about the necklace being cursed. Right now, I had more pressing matters than a pirate's witch's curse. "I'm going to go home and change. I'll be back later. Do you want me to bring you anything?"

She shook her head. She never asked for much from me. Except for sudden trips to an island I had no desire to visit, it was like she was having a midlife crisis on my behalf. "Honey, I know you think this trip is a bad idea, but maybe it's come along at a time you need it." She took my hand. "Maybe Ariya knew you would need to go, and she chose you."

Now she wanted me to believe that the stone began calling for its island home at the exact time I made a mistake that would get me suspended. *Of course*, the stone knew my mother would fall and break her hip, so I would be the one who would have to go to the island for her. That was a stone with one hell of a mind for planning.

Chapter Three

When Everything Goes Wrong...Go to Bed

When I walked into my building, there was a... scent. It smelled—strongly—as if someone had died and began decaying or worse as though someone had crapped out a decaying corpse. I hurried to get my mail from the little wall of boxes in the lobby so I could get the hell out of there and light a candle or something.

I covered my mouth and nose with my hand, and since I was in a first-floor apartment, I sprinted down the hallway to 1C. The building was two floors of apartments that made a U around a beautifully landscaped courtyard. I had two bedrooms, a kitchen with a separate dining area, a living room with a fireplace, and a bathroom with a walk-in shower and clawfoot tub. I loved my place.

As I made my way to my apartment, the smell seemed to get worse, more pungent. I tried not to breathe, but also tried to ignore the bad feeling in the pit of my stomach. I hadn't been home in a few days since I'd worked a twenty-four-hour shift, so I'd spent the night at the hospital, worked another twenty-four-hour shift after sleeping for eight, and then Mom was injured so it had been about three days since I was home, but this smell was the kind of thing I would've remembered had it been around before I left.

Finally, I was at my door, fumbling for my keys, about to pass out from holding my breath. I slid the key into the lock and twisted the handle, opened the door, took a short breath, then closed the door again.

There was no denying that the stench was coming from my place. Oh, God, it was so bad.

At just the moment I was going to run screaming from the building, the rental manager—a forty-something stoner with a comb-over and slight build—walked out of my neighbor's apartment.

"Oh, good. You're here."

I begged to differ. There was nothing good about being here. He was wearing an N-95 mask, so he had some blockage of the odor. I didn't speak. I was busy trying to inhale the laundry scent of my shirt through the sleeve I had pressed over my face.

"2C had a broken drainpipe." Oh, this was starting so badly. "Apparently, 2C also had a case of explosive..." I held up my hand because I didn't need all the details. Explosive pretty much said everything I needed to know. He frowned. Neil Sheridan didn't leave sentences unfinished. "Stomach flu."

What happened next was my own fault. "Explosive stomach flu?" I shouldn't have asked. I knew as soon as the words were out of my mouth.

He turned, so he was ass facing me, made the sound of a bomb exploding then opened and closed his hands in unison, extending from his hind quarters outward. As if I couldn't have visualized an explosion without his acting it out for me.

"Anyway?" The smell was intense, and I wanted to get out of here as quickly as I could. I didn't need the play-by-play.

"Anyway, the weight of the sewage in your ceiling was too much, and the drywall collapsed."

"Collapsed?" Oh, the mess. My bathroom was beside my bedroom. Next to my closet. My heart sank in mourning for the clothes I was never ever going to wear again.

He nodded. "Do you have renter's insurance?"

I was a responsible doctor who owned my own car, paid my student loan payments on time every month, and I had my own place. Of course, I had rental insurance.

I hoped.

The building's insurance should've covered—

"No worries. I have the owner on speed dial. I'll get you handled." He smiled and looked me up and down like this was the first time he was seeing me. "You have a place you can stay until I get this cleaned up?"

I could stay at Mom's. She was going to be in rehab for a bit and I would have the place to myself. "Yeah. I should be fine."

He lowered his head. "Well, if that falls through and you end up needing a nice warm bed to cozy into, mine's king size and I don't mind sharing." He wagged his eyebrows.

There was nothing significantly wrong with Neil, but he was at least half a foot shorter than I was and he looked a bit malnourished. He could've been thirty or he could've been sixty. I had no way of knowing because he'd never said, and I wasn't getting close enough to ask. I just wanted to get the hell out of there before I was only ever able to smell this stench again.

"I'll keep that in mind." I turned back to the door as if I was going to go in.

He moved to stand between me and the knob. "Oh, Doc, I wouldn't go in there." He only ever called me Doc, even when I corrected him with my name.

Right now, I didn't care what he called me. I just wanted to survey the damage, get some fresh clothes if I had any, and get the hell out of here. "I'll be fine."

"Your place took the worst of it." He shrugged one shoulder and held the pose.

Of course, my place took the worst of it. My mother was cursed.

I rolled my eyes at my own thoughts. "I have to go in. My things are in there."

"It's a biohazard. You're going to want to buy new things."

He was right, and I couldn't stand the smell anymore. I turned to go to my mother's because what else could I do?

In the month I'd been suspended from work, the level of insanity in my life had climbed to epic heights.

I'd had to move in with my mother because of the three inches of water and excrement in my apartment. This meant I had to leave my car parked on the street out front because Mom didn't have a garage. Technically, she did, but it had long ago—right around the time she'd sold her car—been converted to a she-shed. Her lawnmower now lived on the porch and her snow-shovel hung on a hook in the kitchen by the back door. Her weedwhacker sat beside the sofa. They were remnants of my dad's life, they didn't get used, not since before Dad died, but were "sentimental" to Mom.

She was up and walking, using her walker, and generally doing well, but since she'd come home after her stint in rehab, all she wanted to talk about was that damned stone. Today was yet another battle and I didn't have time.

"You said you would take it to the island for me, Ember." I closed my eyes. This was her new mantra.

Yes, I'd said it. No, it hadn't been true. "Mom, right now, I'm going to the hospital to try to get my job back." I'd gotten up early and driven to the bakery to get a box of Dr. Warren's favorite donuts, and I'd booked an appointment to speak to him. An appointment I was going to be late for because I'd put down the convertible top on my car, but my hair had been blown apart on my trip to get the donuts.

I was standing in front of the mirror in the bathroom, trying to put myself back together again. I couldn't go in disheveled, like I didn't care. I cared. Much.

"Honey, all these things, all this bad luck you've been having, is the necklace." Along with her new mantra, she had a new song, too. This was it. The necklace was working out its curse on me because I'd transferred the bad luck onto myself when I agreed, then reneged on taking the necklace "home."

"I told you before, Mom. It was a broken pipe. It didn't have anything to do with luck." My suspension from the hospital was due to my fatigue. The broken toe on my left foot was a midnight trip to the bathroom and a metal bed frame. The flat tire yesterday on the highway was because of a nail. Everything had an explanation that had nothing to do with her necklace or luck.

She moved to stand in the doorway to my old bedroom. There was still a poster of Bon Jovi on one wall and Delilah Bradbury on the other. He'd been my fantasy of an older dream man and she'd been my hero.

Now their smiles, the ones that had looked so good to me when I was killing it in college, seemed more like smirks and I wanted to tear them down, but I didn't have time thanks to a long line at Barker's Bakery.

So far, Dr. Warren had been resistant to the idea of bringing me back. It had been a mistake to send Mr. Remington to the morgue. I'd apologized. Repeatedly. Sent a florist's worth of flowers to the family. They'd filed suit against me and the hospital, anyway. I was hopeful that given this extra time, Warren had cooled off and we could talk.

I was almost finished curling my hair—I was using the high heat this time—when my phone pinged with a text. Clay's photo flashed onto the screen. I'd been trying to get a hold of him for a week, but he'd seemed to be ignoring my calls and my texts. I had half a mind to ignore it, but the other half couldn't resist a quick look.

CLAY: **This isn't working. I'm seeing someone else. Please stop calling.**

I'd been dumped by text message.

For a couple of seconds, I stared at the screen. I reread the message a few times. It was unfortunate that at the same time I was reading and rereading the text, holding the phone in one hand, I was holding the curling iron in the other. I had a large section of my hair wrapped around a four hundred degree burning stick.

When I finally smelled the burning hair, I yanked the wand away and the entire portion of my hair went with it.

I said a couple of swear words, and my mother stared at me. She opened her mouth to speak, and I held up a hand. “Do not. This has nothing to do with a dead pirate or his mutiny booty.”

There was no hiding the missing hair, and I didn’t have time for a salon appointment. I stormed past my mother toward the living room. “Where are you going?” She barely got the words out before I made it to the front door.

This absolutely couldn’t be happening. I shrieked and ran outside.

There were about eighty birds attacking my car because I’d left the top down and a box of fresh donuts on the front seat.

I ran out of the house, arms spread, flapping, while I squealed loud enough to draw attention. Mom’s across the street neighbor, John Dole, stared and probably locked his car when he went inside.

My car was trashed. I was missing a very noticeable chunk of hair. I had three pairs of jeans and four shirts to my name. My apartment still smelled like a sewage plant before the treatment began. I was tired of it all. Not to mention my mother was standing at the front door watching me humiliate myself for the entire street to see, and the incident would probably be posted later on YouTube.

Each thing that happened to me recently had a perfectly reasonable explanation, individually. All together? This number of bad happenings was something illogical.

When I stomped up the steps, she pushed the storm door open, ready again to remind me of the curse. I shook my head before she could. "Just book me a flight."

What other choice did I have?

Chapter Four

Isn't It Ironic. Don'tcha Think?

His face was perfection. Eyes decadent like Swiss chocolate. Hair like satin. I was just a woman on a plane trying to resist the urge to breathe him in. Making matters worse, while he looked like a model, he smelled like heaven. I was tempted, recently dumped, going through hell, and unable to take my eyes off this younger man.

The word cougar came to me, and I dismissed it for no other reason than I didn't like the implication. That, however, didn't make it untrue. Because I was knee deep in thoughts. Inappropriate thoughts unless I wanted to re-up my mile-high membership. Again tempted, but I looked away. Out the window at the tarmac. There was one of those luggage cart trains below, driving back toward the terminal, and I watched for a few seconds.

"Hello." Even his voice was pleasant. Smooth. Syrupy.

When I looked toward him again, he smiled and I, smooth as I am with men and always eloquent, said, "Woah." It wasn't like I would've said it to a horse if I was Brad Pitt in Legends of the Fall. It was more like a moan, low and deep, part whisper, part gasp, part prayer. I could embarrass myself in 3-part harmony.

His smile didn't waver because he was so hot that he probably merited a lot of looks and a lot of this kind of reaction. Certainly, he was used to it.

I stared for a second longer than was socially acceptable, and he didn't mention it. I smiled. "Hi. I'm Ember."

For a second he stared at me as if he'd never had anyone introduce herself to him before—I didn't believe that for a second —and then he cocked his head. "That's a very unique name." I would've commented and said I was a unique kind of girl, but it sounded cheesy, so I just smiled. "Are you by chance a doctor? Doctor Ember Thorn?"

That was weird. Although maybe I'd treated someone he knew or a family member. I pasted on my brightest smile because my pride kicked into a higher gear. "As a matter of fact..."

His nostril flared—just the one—his eyes narrowed. It didn't make him less attractive—not in any way I could see—but the stare was unnerving. "You're Dr. Ember Thorn?"

I nodded again. "Yes. Is that a problem?"

He scoffed. "A problem?" Shook his head. "A problem?" His voice climbed an octave. "Yes, Dr. Thorn." I'd never heard my name spoken as a curse word before. "There is a problem."

I hadn't worked in more than a month, so it couldn't have been a patient I'd lost. "Do I know you?"

He shook his head, but not in the no-you-don't-know-me kind of way. He was shaking his head in the I-can't-believe-you-don't-know-how-I-know-you kind of way. "My father is JD Remington, the very much alive man you sent to the morgue."

Oh crap. This was going to be seven long hours.

I looked for the flight attendant. Maybe it wasn't too late to switch to a later flight. Although I could feel this one moving so it probably would cause a bit of a problem to deplane right now. Maybe I could get a different seat. I didn't care if I had to sit on the pilot's lap. Anywhere was better than in this seat next to this guy.

The flight attendant was otherwise engaged, and I sighed. There was nothing for me to do but grin and bear it. I looked at him, sucked in a breath, and held it. I certainly hadn't intended to send his father to the morgue. I also wished it hadn't happened. More than anything, I wished I could go back and undo it. In lieu of that, I chewed my lower lip. "I'm... embarrassed and so, so sorry." I could've given him the usual excuses for mistakes—fatigue, long shifts, under-staffing. Those were excuses I gave my boss. This guy, this whole family, deserved better.

"As you said in your letter."

The apology I'd been forced to pen for "the family."

His cocked eyebrow and still flared nostril with a now added lip curl said he was unimpressed by it.

I didn't know what else to say. I'd apologized. Sincerely.

Instead of speaking, I sat quietly, but his disapproval and anger were like entities in our seating aisle. I took another look for the attendant, but she was busy with the drink cart.

"Your father's breathing and heart rate were slowed by the herbal supplement he was taking for his... dysfunction." Herbal Viagra wasn't safe. I didn't care what people said.

"My father wasn't taking a supplement." His voice was low, heated, and incredibly sexy. I didn't want to stop hearing it.

"He was." It was why he'd been with us in the first place. I'd read and reread that case file about a thousand times since I'd been suspended. Especially since the lawsuit had sprung up. I could recite every detail now. "It was a mistake anyone could make." I hated that it was me who'd made it.

"Any incompetent someone."

I sighed. There was nothing I could say that would undo what had happened to his father. Not that I wasn't willing to try. "It was an accident."

He rolled his eyes. He looked away because the flight attendant had made it to our seats. "Would it be possible to switch seats?" He asked brusquely.

Our flight attendant's name was Ross. "The flight is full, sir." He smiled patiently, like he'd been asked this question before. "Can I get you a drink?"

He ordered a double shot of whiskey on the rocks and sighed. We were stuck and there was nothing either of us could do about it. I sighed. This seven-hour flight was going to take eleven years. Or it would feel like it. It made sense to sit back and try to sleep, read, do anything but try to fix an unfixable situation.

Instead, I whipped out my credit card and paid for his drink and ordered a drink of my own. "Double Patron." If we were going to drink, I was going to drink to get drunk.

He scowled, and I saw the disapproval. "Big drinker, are you?"

It occurred to me after I drank my double shot that I probably shouldn't have been drinking anything but water while I was sitting next to the guy who was suing me, but he was already suing me. Not many ways he could make it worse. Unless he married me and made me miserable every day of my life.

I laughed out loud at the thought.

"You find this funny?"

My lips twitched because I did truly find it amusing and I probably shouldn't have. Tequila pushed my giggle button. I covered my mouth and looked at him. "Not at all." Another giggle busted free. I lifted one leg and slapped my knee like I found myself the funniest woman in all the land.

The box on my lap shifted and slid toward him. He caught it and a part of my leg, too. Now I was tingling.

"What is this?" He turned the intricately carved box over in his hands.

The box was actually the valuable part. The stone itself was worth about thirty bucks. The jeweler had been salivating over the box when I brought it in to be appraised. Turned out he wasn't only a jeweler but a collector of rare artifacts and there were only a few of these boxes in the world, apparently.

"It's a black onyx apparently cursed by the witchy lover of some dead pirate. Now I'm cursed until I deliver it back to the dead pirate on some tropical island." I couldn't believe I'd just said all of that out loud. No wonder he thought I was incompetent. I sounded insane.

"You're going to Pararey Island?" He shook his head.

"Look, all I want to do is bring the damned stone back and shut my mother up." If it rid me of the curse recently plaguing me, all the better.

"Jesus." It was safe to say he wasn't praying. "You too?"

"Me, too, what?" I wasn't sure I cared.

"I'm going to the island to stop some big-time Hollywood has-been from exploiting my family's history for her great comeback." He pulled a folded packet of papers from the inside pocket of his jacket. "I have an injunction."

I wasn't certain of the laws these days. "Is an American injunction valid on a Caribbean island?" I wasn't being sarcastic. I was legitimately curious.

He shrugged. It was the most human thing I'd seen him do so far. "I'm going to find out, I suppose." Even his uncertainty was adorable. "This is my family legacy they're messing with."

"Are you sure they're messing with it? Have you read the script?" Maybe it was the tequila talking, but I wasn't baiting him on purpose.

"I was an actor, and this is not how you do things."

"An actor?" I was curious. Again.

"In high school, I played the best damned Danny Zuko since Travolta." He cocked his head like he was daring me to contradict him. Although based on what—I hadn't seen him in the play—I had no idea, also no idea why he thought I would call him on it. I also didn't tell him that a high school production of a stage play was a whole world away from a movie set.

I also didn't tell him that I'd played Sandy in high school. Opposite sides of history, sharing an aisle on a plane to the island where we were each heading to handle our bits of that history was coincidence enough for me for one day. My Sandy to his Danny. It was one of those historical nuggets that could go without saying.

We slipped back into some tense silence. I hated it. I had a pathological urge to make things better. I hated when people hated me.

"What do you do for a living?" I heard myself ask before I ever meant to or even considered doing it.

He looked at me. "We're doing this now?"

I shrugged. "Why not? It's a long flight."

Maybe the whiskey kicked in because he didn't sigh or scowl or grimace. Maybe it was a good sign.

"I'm a contractor." When I didn't move or light up or respond, he said, "I build things."

I was staring because his job explained a lot. His body, for example. The arms. The Biceps, flexors, extensors. Oh God, the flexors. "Wow."

I hadn't meant to say it out loud. I rolled my eyes at myself. Also didn't mean to twist my hair around my finger while I looked at him. Or lick my lips. Or push my boobs out. Or shoulder shimmy. I did all of those things. Patron brought out the big ol' ho in me. Apparently.

I would hate myself for it another day. Right now, I wanted to cop a feel, lick his lips, lick his biceps. Hell, I would've licked his feet if he kicked his shoes off and asked. Okay, maybe not, even hot guys have sweaty feet, but the rest I was up for.

I should've known better than to indulge in tequila.

He was watching me now—probably thanks to the shoulder shimmy—and he smiled. I wished he was my type because my mind was all about the fantasy of him—the body, the smile, those freaking arms—and I wanted... what I wanted.

I hadn't flirted in a while. Hadn't done much of anything in a while. I'd met Clay at the hospital, had actually dumped a drink on him. This was my first foray into the enticement of a man on a plane. This one was yummy. Too yummy to be my type. Out of my weight class, yummy. Oh, and his family was suing me, so he was basically my enemy, so definitely a guy who was off-limits.

Dammit.

Chapter Five

I Wanted to Drown My Troubles, Not Myself!

We arrived at the island without too many more incidents. I didn't spill a drink on him that required him to take off his shirt. I didn't "accidentally" drop my hand in his lap or brush a boob against his arm. All of our body parts stayed in our respective seats, although we did manage to drink until I saw double the yummy.

He smiled more. I really liked that.

Too soon, we landed and when it was time to deplane, he stepped back to let me go in front of him even though everyone else had remained seated, onto the next destination. I might've staggered a couple times. The first time was strictly unplanned, and his reaching to help steady me after the first stagger might've been responsible for the second stumble, but I wasn't certain. I wasn't going to start throwing blame around when we'd just become... drinking buddies?

We waited at baggage claim for the spinner to start spinning and I watched that thing spin about forty times before it occurred to me that my luggage wasn't coming around.

"What's wrong?" Will Remington—wasn't that just the best name?—laid his hand on the small of my back when I didn't move. I probably looked as though I was mesmerized by the silver panels spinning in front of me.

"My luggage isn't here." Like a crazy person, I laughed. Cackled even. People stared and I couldn't stop. At least I still had the little box of death. I had a grip on it that—had the box been lesser made—could've crumbled the wood.

The captain's curse or whatever we were calling it had affected my luggage on the day I was on my way to return the jewel. A good daughter would've called her mother and told her, but the last thing I needed—especially while I wasn't quite sober—was another "I told you so" from the home front.

Instead, I stared at the luggage spinner as though it wasn't empty before Will led me to the service desk. The airport was literally two desks, the aforementioned luggage spinner, a juice bar, and a metal detector. There were three people inside the building wearing airline uniforms, one working the juice bar and a guy in coveralls who'd been the same guy throwing the luggage from the plane's cargo hold to the conveyor belt that moved it inside to the spinner.

I let Will lead me to the counter where one of the employees stood. "Hello. My name is Ember Thorn. My luggage didn't come off the plane." I turned to point out the window. The plane was now backing from the terminal. My suitcase was probably stuffed in some dark corner of the cargo hold and driving away because I was cursed by a dead pirate's woman.

"You'll have to go to the service desk and take a number. Have a seat and when your number is called, someone will take your claim." She spoke perfect English, and I was glad. If there was one thing I knew, it was procedure. I could follow procedure. I was quite the master at it, even. I nodded once, solemn, and serious.

I walked to the desk and took a number from the pull-tab machine. Number 178. I looked around, caught the eye of the woman at the desk, and she nodded to the seating area a few yards from the desk. Will guided me to the seating area. I showed him my number, and he smirked, obviously amused by my trauma.

After a few minutes, I caught her eye again. "Do you know how long it will be before...?"

She shrugged and went back to typing on her computer. I sat back with Will beside me. He smiled. "Don't worry. We have time before the ferry."

I nodded because it was nice to have someone to wait with. The rest of the passengers from our flight were heading out on the plane that was now headed toward the runway, likely with my luggage. “You have to stop that plane.” I jerked a finger toward the window. The woman didn’t even lift her head as the plane and my luggage went coasting toward the clouds.

It was only a few seconds later—too late to save my clothing from flying away—that the woman who’d been at the counter moved to the desk marked service. She twisted the machine toward her, looked at the pull tab still hanging out—presumably number 179—and called out, “178.”

I looked around, even though it was my number. We were the only people in the waiting area. The only customers in the whole damned place.

Will chuckled then glanced at me and stood, held out his hand. “I think she’s ready. Better hurry before she moves onto the next customer.” He was right.

I walked to the desk, almost wholly steady, and sat in the chair across from her. “My luggage is missing.”

She nodded. “Did you check luggage onto the plane?”

Of course, I did, or I wouldn’t have been at the desk taking up her time. I nodded slowly. Tequila-soaked anger was the last thing any of us needed. “Yes.” The word was calm and measured.

"Are you certain someone else didn't mistakenly take your bag off the carousel?" I'd never been able to manage to smile while speaking, but this woman had mastered the skill. She nodded to the baggage spinner.

"We were the only people who deplaned." The words hardly slurred at all, and I was proud.

She cocked an eyebrow at Will, and her smile broadened. "On your way to Pararey?" When he nodded, she grinned. "To the resort?"

I cleared my throat. She could flirt on her own time. Plus, I'd seen him first. We had history. Of course, he was suing me, so she might've had the upper hand, but...

"Her luggage?"

Her face cleared, and she shot me a glare. "You'll have to go to the airline's website and fill out a form." She smirked. Everyone in that airport knew I wasn't getting my stuff back.

At least, I still had my purse with my money and my credit cards and the damned jewelry box with the cursed stone.

Of course, I still had the stone. I couldn't wait to send it back to the ocean. Although my mother had cautioned me that I couldn't just toss it and head out. It had to be done at a specific time in a specific way. There was something about a full moon or a new moon. Honestly, I hadn't listened.

"Fine." I pulled out my cell phone. I would fill it out right now. The sooner the better.

Except I didn't have service. She cocked an eyebrow and I wanted to smack the smug satisfaction off her face. "No cell towers in this part of the world."

"I'll wait until I get to the island."

This time, she laughed. "Oh, there's definitely no cell service there."

"How am I supposed to get my luggage back?" This was ridiculous, and she was about one smirk from me showing her that thanks to Anatomy 101, I knew all the best places to punch. She wasn't going to like any of them. Tequila did that to me.

"You have to fill out the form on the website." She shook her head. "If you can prove you checked bags, you'll be reimbursed in the amount of $100."

"A hundred dollars?" I stood and leaned across her desk. "My jeans cost more than a hundred dollars."

"Come on, Ember. The ferry is going to be here soon." He pulled me away, and I let him because Airline Barbie wasn't going to help me. My luggage was headed to destination unknown.

My mother would have chalked it all up to the curse, but this was shoddy business. Nothing more. Even half-tipsy, I knew this didn't have anything to do with curses or witches or irate dead pirates.

I sighed and went along with Will. The airport on the mainland was on the water, and we walked outside to wait for the ferry from the resort to return to take us on to Pararey Island. There were two long wooden benches, and we sat fairly close together on one.

It wasn't quite close enough for me to be happy but was probably too close for him.

We didn't really look at each other—unless semi-covert glances counted—although we were the only people waiting, and aside from the water, there weren't many other places to look.

He was probably busy remembering that I was the person who'd sent his very much alive father to the morgue. I certainly was, and the shame was real, even though I'd apologized repeatedly.

When the boat arrived, it occurred to me through my slightly tipsy haze that this was no fairy tale and there was no such thing as love at first sight, so fawning over him was ridiculous. I walked past him to the boat dock.

The ferry was nothing more than a speedboat with peeling paint and an old lady at the helm. She held out her hand to me, and Will steadied me at the waist as I climbed down.

Slowly. Partly because I still hadn't found my balance and partly because I liked the way his hands felt.

When I moved into the boat, a pig snorted. It was a boar. Or I thought so anyway, but my knowledge of farm animals and wildlife was almost non-existent. All I knew was, pigs didn't belong in boats on water. Every time he moved or lifted his head or oinked, the boat shifted.

Will handed his luggage to the woman, and she took it—spry for an older woman with a bouffant hairdo and long mu-mu sort of dress—and set it off to the side of her steering wheel.

She gave the pig a good pat on his head, then turned back to the wheel. She took off. Fast. I tried to hang on, but the speed, combined with the pig moving now, and I stumbled back. Possibly I was pulled down by the back of my shirt.

My ass hit the side of the boat, and I went over backward. Flailing. Sinking. Water in my eyes and nose and mouth before it occurred to me to close my yap.

I sank faster than it ever showed on TV, and then, right about the time my lungs started burning from lack of oxygen, I remembered I couldn't swim. I fought though. Kicked. Did things I thought I remembered to do in case of drowning, but I continued sinking. Dying probably.

I stopped fighting. I let the water carry me down. Before my body reached the seabed, a hand touched my ass. What fresh hell was happening now? I was being pushed up. "Go." I opened my eyes, the salt stinging, making it difficult to focus on the voice. "You don't belong here." I saw him. He was exactly the way my mom had described him. He had a bandana around his forehead, black curly hair, taken by the water and swirled into wavy curls, eyes as blue as a summer sky. Sword at his hip. "Go get my stones back."

I was being pushed to the surface by a pirate. *My* pirate. Was how I thought of him at that moment, anyway.

Or maybe I blacked out. I came to when Will yanked me by the hand up toward the surface, when the blood stopped going to my brain. I felt his arms around me—the pirate's or maybe Will's—and I could feel myself rising, coming up to the surface and into the light.

I was on the boat, lying flat as someone put his mouth on mine—his perfectly soft, delicious mouth—as someone else pushed on my chest. I coughed and spat. Hard.

I knew exactly what I saw and exactly what I felt, also what I'd heard. As realistic a person as I'd always been, as certain my mother's compass didn't point north, as positive as I was that no curse existed, I'd heard a man's voice. A pirate's voice. I was sure that I'd heard the voice of Captain Renegade and he wanted his jewels back and he didn't seem to be in the mood to wait much longer.

Chapter Six

Warning! Fangirl Alert! Approach With Caution

THE ISLAND WAS STILL twenty or thirty minutes by boat, even at the speed of sound which the old woman navigating our boat seemed to be intent on driving.

By the time we reached the island and the dock at the resort—which as far as I could see was the only thing that occupied the island except some jungle behind it—my hair was dry. There was seaweed intertwined with the strands. I smelled like a swamp, which was what I'd always thought any body of water, standing, or moving smelled like.

It was better than the smell of my apartment. That had followed me after I'd made a visit to retrieve anything I could save from my house to take to my mothers. Turned out nothing had been salvageable, and the stench had stayed with me. Until now.

When we arrived at the resort, it took a couple seconds before I got my land legs back and I staggered and swayed. The old woman pushed Will out of the way and supported me herself. "Now, now, dear."

She walked between me and the water on one side and kept a tight arm around me while the pig trotted beside me on the other side. When I stumbled over a warped board that was sticking up at one corner where it was screwed to another, she tightened her hold. "Can't have you diving off the dock the way you did the boat."

I hadn't dived off the boat, but I didn't correct her. All I wanted out of life was a shower and some clean clothes. I hitched my bag onto my shoulder—it was going to take an army to get this, this, thing away from me. Not that it had clothes in it or much I could use to repair the damage done by my impromptu swim with the pirates, but it was all I had that was mine.

The woman and her pig led me to the counter and towards a man whose name tag read Art. She walked through an opening and stood beside him, kissed him on the cheek. "Darling, Miss Thorn's been the victim of a rather unfortunate accident."

"An accident?" He cocked a brow, as if this wasn't their first foray into passengers going "accidentally" overboard. He crossed his arms and waited, lips pursed, foot tapping loudly against the brown tiled floor.

She explained. Blaming it on her pig. Blaming it on the wind. Blaming it on the rough, choppy waves. Art looked at me. "My name is Arthur, Miss Thorn, and I am at your service." He stepped forward and began typing and staring at his computer screen. He shot a one-brow cocked, lips tight, nostrils flared look at the old woman. "Since Miss Penelope dumped you in the drink"—he leaned in. "That's what we sailors call the water around the island." He straightened and winked as if the secret was for my ears only. "I'm going to comp your stay and your meals and drinks for the time you're here." He grinned. "It's slow season and we're charging plenty to the film crew."

"Film crew?" Beside me, Will stiffened, and I glanced at him. "Oh right. The film crew that's making the movie about the Remington pirate." I knew his name but didn't say it because I didn't want to seem overly familiar with the story. Although I had no reason why. Maybe because I'd spent so much of my life hiding from anything less than realistic.

The older woman, Penelope nodded. "Yes. It's so exciting."

I looked at Arthur. "Is there a gift shop where I can buy some clothes? Mine were lost by the airline." The irritation burned through me.

He nodded to a small shop just off the lobby. "We have island t-shirts, some boutique items." He clapped his hands together. "It's new. You'll be our first customer." He rooted around on his counter and finally handed me a slip of paper. "Take this voucher. It entitles the bearer"—his cheeks went ruddy—" to a free Captain Renegade's Booty shirt."

"Thanks." I took the voucher and put it in my handbag with the room key and the island map he'd handed me. At least I still had my bag and the necklace.

"You're in room 221. Right now, the hotel is overrun with movie crew, and we've had some staffing issues, but if you want to get a drink in the bar, I can let you know when your room is ready." He leaned in again. "They start filming tomorrow and we're all so excited." I believed him. People who weren't excited didn't squeal in such a shrill tone. "The publicity has been..." He gushed with a full shoulder shimmy. Everything changed as a man walked through the lobby in a hotel uniform, Art's easy smile and open-eyed gaze turned to a glare at the passing staff member. "Unfortunately, not all of my staff think it's important to arrive on time for his shift." Louder he added, "Yeah, I'm looking at you, Ronald." Ronald turned and glared. "That's right." He did the weird V-finger thing and flicked them from just a few inches from his face out into the air toward Ronald in the well-known, watching you motion. He held his glare for a moment, then turned back to me and smiled.

"Thank you." I didn't want to walk away while Will registered because I wanted to hear him tell these "very excited" hotel people that he was here to put an immediate halt to the production of their movie, but the potential for procuring clean clothes that didn't smell like they'd been freshly pulled from "the drink" was of upper-level importance in this moment. More so than watching the spectacle Will was sure to make.

After I purchased a shirt that said, "Pirates have good booty" with the picture of a pair of butt cheeks on it, and a pair of Captain Renegade pajama pants that were designed to look like they had a button flap in the front, I walked back into the lobby and Art pointed me toward the restaurant.

He certainly hadn't exaggerated about how crowded the place was. Every table was full, so I had no choice but to sit at the bar. I set my bag on the bar and turned to look around. Oh, my goodness. It was a who's who of the tabloids. Many familiar faces.

Oh, dear God. It was... and she really did wear Prada. Was that... after his divorce, which had gone on for years now, it was no wonder he was hanging out in the Caribbean.

I saw her. The her-est her of all the hers. Delilah Bradbury. Regal and tall. A blonde this week wearing a pair of artfully distressed jeans with a crisscross waistband top that dipped low at the collar. I couldn't believe it. I was in the same restaurant as Delilah freaking Bradbury. Maybe the tides were changing.

I went full forty-year-old fangirl. My heart was hammering, and my hands were clammy. I truly knew what it was to be all aflutter. She walked over to Art and smiled. I couldn't hear what she was saying, but it didn't matter. Whatever she said was probably brilliant and profound and worthy to be taken down by whoever documented such things. She was Delilah Bradbury. Movie star. Oscar winner. Woman who spoke her mind. Suffered for it, then came back stronger and better than ever.

"What can I get you, sweet... heart?" The bartender's voice lowered, and he pulled his head back as if the very sight of me had scared him.

I didn't go with the obvious reply of a shower, and instead flashed him a smile. I was in the same room as Delilah Bradbury. There wasn't anything he could do to zap my euphoria.

He gestured to the bottles behind him with a jerk of his thumb, as if I was unfamiliar with the concept of alcohol. "Tequila. A double."

I'd been suspended for a month. I knew alcohol. Safe to say we had become intimate acquaintances, and since I'd started the day with tequila shooters, I figured I'd just as well end it that way. Hopefully, by the time I had a couple drinks, my room would be ready, and I could shower and sleep.

I tried not to stare at Delilah Bradbury and the man beside her. I'd seen him before—I ate up all the entertainment news when it was about her—in photos and on TV at the award show when Shara Hewitt had attacked her and they'd both ended up in jail. He was certainly handsome.

The bartender set my drink in front of me and smiled. "You need a menu?"

I looked at the dining room. "I'll wait for a table."

I was on my second double tequila—this one in a margarita with lime and salt—when he led me to my table.

Right.

Next.

To.

Delilah Bradbury.

My fangirl heart was pounding. I was close enough to see the freckles on the bridge of her nose. Probably from the island sun. I could've squealed in delight. I didn't.

Instead, I held up my menu as if I wasn't watching her, then looked around it because I absolutely was. I was listening because if Delilah Bradbury said it, I wanted to hear it.

"Did you ever just have one of those days, Nicky?" Even her frustration sounded elegant.

His chuckle was pure music. "What day, my love?"

"You know what day." She smiled at him. How the man didn't drop into a swoon, I didn't know. "I got a message from Dr. Hilburton."

"I'm going to need more, Dee."

She sighed. I wasn't just eavesdropping. I was mentally recording every motion and gesture, every expression and tone. "The on-set doctor I hired because the island's mayor or chancellor or... governor,"—she waved a well-manicured hand through the air as if the title didn't matter—"wouldn't sign the permits until I agreed to all his stipulations. Anyway, Hilburton left a message for me at the desk and said he quit. No reason. No warning. Just quit."

"We'll find a new doctor."

My hand shot into the air, just as quickly, I jerked it back down because while I was very clearly listening in, I didn't want to look like I was listening in.

Besides, she wasn't finished. "The actor I hired to play Remington won't come out of his trailer because the assistant he hired let the fruit and cheese touch on the fruit and cheese tray he ordered, and she wouldn't order him a new one. She called him a spoiled brat."

"Why didn't she just order another one?" It was a reasonable question. Although I wished I hadn't asked it aloud.

When she answered, I wasn't so worried. "She said being his assistant was ten times harder than being his mother and walked out. Demanded they ferry her back to the mainland and flew home."

Oh wow. It really was one of *those* days.

She wasn't through. "Some American judge"—she said American as if it was a swear word—"issued an injunction to some irate Remington who claims he's related to Renegade. This Yahoo"—she pronounced it YAY-hoo—"has the balls to come to the island and try to stop me from filming, as if Pararey Island belongs to the US." She rolled her eyes. This woman even had perfect lashes, each one long and curled and individual. I stopped obsessing over her eyelashes as a thought occurred to me. I had an opening.

I lowered my menu. "Miss Bradbury, I couldn't help but overhear." I could have, but that was my secret. "I can solve a couple of the problems you're having." Oh yes I could. I was almost too excited to speak, which might've been why I sounded like I was auditioning for the voice of Minnie Mouse. "First, my name is Doctor Ember Thorn—used to be Thornbridge like the witch in your story, so quite a coincidence, right?" I widened my eyes. "You don't even know the half." I couldn't quite remember the half well enough to make it make sense either and, judging by the depth and sound of her sigh, I seemed to be losing my audience.

I rushed on. "Um, but I am a doctor and I'm currently staying at the resort." Problem one solved. "I can be your doctor. Your movie doctor." I was swaying like I was caught in a tornado wind, but my medical license was still in good standing. When she cocked an eyebrow, I held up my hand. "I know what it looks like. I'm having a day myself. Lost my luggage, fell off a boat, got almost blown away by Grandma Claus, the boater." I nodded toward the hotel lobby where I presumed the old woman, and her pig were still working. "On the plane coming here, I sat beside a guy who hates me deeply. Which brings me around to problems number two and three."

She cocked a brow. "Are we finished with problem one?"

I nodded. "As soon as you hire me." When she made no move to do so, I cleared my throat. "Problem two isn't as cut and dried as problem three, but they are definitely connected. The man who is holding the injunction is the man who was on the plane with me. My idea is... if he happens to be the actor who plays Renegade in your movie, he would be less inclined to enforce the injunction. It would solve problem two and three." I swiped my hands together as though I was washing the dust from them. "Ember Thorn, problem solver." In case the doctor thing didn't work out.

She shook her head. "I can't just hire some random man off the street to be the star of the single most important project of my life. I don't know if he can act, or if—"

"He can. He can act." I nodded enthusiastically, and the world bobbed for a couple seconds after I held my head still.

"He was the best darned Danny Zuko in some high school. Somewhere." I cleared my throat again. "I could ask him."

She looked at her guy and tilted her head. He shrugged.

"If you need a female actress." I grinned. "I played a very convincing Sandy." I flashed what I hoped was a winning smile.

She gave me a once-over and there was no question, she wasn't buying it.

"Whether you believe me or not, I am a board-certified physician. I took the Hippocratic oath and everything." I held up the Girl Scout honor pledge. "I was a Girl Scout, too." When she didn't do much more than quirk a brow, I put my hand down.

Her man leaned in and whispered something to her, and she nodded. She looked up at me and I could see how the world had fallen in love with her. A thousand times over. This was a woman with expressive eyes.

"Where is he? This Remington descendant?" She lifted her glass of wine and finished her drink, then looked up at me. "Does he have the look?"

"Oh yeah." Will Remington had a look, all right. Even if it wasn't the one she was referring to, he was definitely a man with a look.

I glanced around the room. There he was. More gorgeous than my memory had given him credit for being. I pointed. "He smells good, too." I smiled. "We have history. Let me talk to him."

A woman walked over and stood next to Delilah's chair. "Miss Thorn." I was not going to correct Delilah Bradbury to call me Doctor. "This is Cami Danes-LaCroix soon-to-be Remington."

Another Remington. Interesting.

"Have you guys seen the captain? The real Remington?" When no one answered, I rocked back and forth from heel to the balls of my feet. "I did. Him and baby Remington over there,"—I pointed to Will again—"saved my life." Cami, Delilah, and Nicky stared at me. "When I fell out of the boat."

"Captain Renegade saved you?"

I shrugged, only half-sure now of what I'd seen. "I think so." It was my story. I could tell it the way I wanted. "Anyway... Will..." I motioned to him again. "There's your Remington."

All I had to do was convince him.

Chapter Seven

Strangers Have the Best Candy

I SEXY WALKED TOWARD HIM. At least I thought I did. I hoped there was more sway and less stumble in the walk. He chuckled and shook his head. "Did you come to buy me a 'thanks for saving my life' drink?"

"You bet." A little good will never hurt.

It had been more than an hour since I'd been this close to him, and I regretted every second of that hour. Wasted time.

"What?"

I must've said it outside of my thoughts. "Nothing." I laughed too loud, then stopped and pulled my lower lip between my teeth. I had to pull it together. Delilah Bradbury was counting on me. I wasn't going to let her down.

When the bartender handed us our drinks, we clinked glasses and chugged. Or maybe I chugged, and he sipped, I couldn't be sure. "They might have to shut the movie down."

"Good." He grinned. "You somehow do that?" He motioned to the bartender. "Two more."

Oh God no. I couldn't drink another drop. I dropped my head, hoping the world would calm itself, and held up one hand in the international signal for hang on, there's a possibility of vomit. When I lifted my head again, he smiled. "Will... is that short for William?" He nodded. "Aha." It wasn't a huge discovery, but I even poked a finger into the air as if I was Ben Franklin and had just discovered electricity.

"Aha?"

"I think I meant, 'ah.'" I shrugged. "Who knows, really?" I'd come over with a point to make.

"You were saying?" Now we both wondered what it was that I'd wanted. This wasn't going so well.

I glanced into the dining room and saw Delilah and her friends watching us. It came back to me. "Right." I blew out a shallow breath. "Okay. They might have to shut the movie down."

"I said, 'good,' and now we're back to where we were before you got sidetracked." His grin, even though I was fairly certain he was making fun of me, was adorable.

"Yes, well, as I was saying, they might have to shut down the movie because they lost their Remington." He faked a pouty face, which might have even been aimed at Delilah, but I couldn't be sure. "Anyway, you,"—I ran my finger down his chest—"are a Remington." He cocked an eyebrow. He wasn't getting where I was going with this. "They need a Remington, and you are a Remington. Best Danny Remington in the history of Greasy Pirates." I paused because I was sure that wasn't right. "Or something like that."

He chuckled. "There's logic in there somewhere."

"It's an opportunity. To tell your family's story. To be the guy..." Oh, he was the guy. I shook off the lust. "This is your chance to help shape the story." I took his hand and led him to my table. "Sit. Tell me the story."

He could've told me the history of the phonebook right about then and I would've sat mesmerized, hanging on every word and digit. Instead, we were at a table very near Delilah Bradbury and he was going to tell me the tale of his ancestors. Not that I hadn't heard it from my mother—repeatedly—only hers was from the side of my ancestors. History was always skewed toward the teller. It would be interesting to compare and contrast.

He straightened his fork and spoon, so they were perfectly perpendicular to his plate and the knife on the opposite side. "I haven't heard the story in years…" I didn't interrupt with more than a smile. "My great-great-great-great grandpa, or something like that, was a pirate named Renfro Remington. They called him Renegade."

I clicked my tongue against my teeth. "I could've heard this much from Art, the lobby clerk."

Will grinned. "Tough audience."

"Not so tough." I was practically dripping with attraction. "Completely open… to listening."

"Promise?" he said, followed by another grin.

I nodded, trying to look as innocent as possible.

"Great grandpa times four or six or whatever"—his smile was potent, swoon worthy—"fell in love with a witch. He went off to sea, and she cast a love spell to bring him home." I could've listened to him talk about love spells all night long, but he moved on. "When he didn't come home with his crew, and she heard word of the mutiny…" He shook his head, solemn now when before I hadn't even been sure he believed any of it.

None of the story mattered at this moment. All that mattered was that Delilah Bradbury needed an actor, and he was perfect.

"Perfect?" I wasn't sure how much I'd said aloud. This was a new affliction—speaking without having realized it—and I wasn't a fan. Also, I didn't know how to stop it.

"For the part. You're perfect for the part."

He shook his head and looked away. "No."

"Will." I reached across the table and gave his fingers a squeeze. "They need an actor and you're here. Best damned Danny Zuko since Travolta." I wasn't above using his own words to convince him. "It's your history, your family. No one's going to care for it the way you do. No one's going to love it or help shape it. No one else can tell it. It's your family. Your story." I couldn't tell if he was buying it or not.

He kept a blank stare, an unwavering expression. "I don't know."

I nodded like I understood, but I really didn't. This was his chance to make sure the story got told with care and concern. Turning it down was not in his best interest or that of the movie.

"Meet Delilah. Read the script." I lowered my voice because like I'd overheard Delilah, we were close enough she could hear me. "The movie is going to be made, with you or without. Isn't *with* better?"

He sighed because I was right, and we both knew it.

I had him. I turned to Delilah and was once again struck by all the beautiful people on the island, but she was the shining star. "Delilah." Too familiar. "Miss Bradbury, this is Will Remington."

"There's definitely a resemblance." Her friend Cami looked Will up and down, something around her neck blurring with the movement. "He could be Remy's younger brother."

Delilah flipped through a binder and pulled out a photocopy of a picture of a tintype. The man in the blurred, somewhat foggy Xerox could've been Will. I would've guessed it was.

Even Will blinked a couple of times.

As I stood staring at them, what I had seen moments ago on Cami's neck—hives, I'd thought—were growing. "Uh, Cami?"

I motioned to my throat, and she grabbed hers. "The pox." She picked up her spoon and turned it this way and that, left and right, as she twisted her head to see the spots darkening on her throat. "It's the pox. Remy is never going to marry me now." Her nostrils flared. "It's that damned curse, Delilah. Even you can't deny it anymore."

Curse? Could this possibly be a coincidence? Exactly how many curses were on this pirate island?

Delilah looked at the spots and when Cami glanced at her, Delilah wiped her grimace away. "Remy is going to be on the mainland for a couple more days. We can get you some calamine. I'm sure they have some around here." She stood and looked around as if someone in the restaurant would have it.

Cami kept whispering about the curse and said a bit louder, "We don't even know where the third stone is. This is never going to stop."

Third stone? What? There were three stones in my mother's story too...

Delilah turned toward her. "Remy has a lead. Have faith."

Have faith they will find a third stone that's cursed? The connection was clear. I could've, but didn't, tell them that the third stone was standing right in front of them, or rather, the woman who had it in her bag was.

Cami ran from the dining room, Delilah close behind. Will and I stared after them. He glanced at me. "Am I the actor or...?" He shrugged.

I couldn't say for certain, but then Delilah rushed back toward us, put her hands on my shoulder and said, "Be on set at 4 am." She looked at Will. "You too, Captain." She added a wink.

I watched her walk away because Delilah Bradbury had a walk that demanded it be watched. When she was out of sight, I turned back to Will.

He had an eyebrow raised. "Did you just use all this,"—he motioned with both hands to my face, chest, body as a whole. —"To trick me into playing a pirate in a movie I'm trying to stop from filming?"

"I'm sure I have no idea what you mean." I was trying for humble coquette. It felt right in the moment.

"I'm sure you know exactly what I mean." He smiled.

I smiled back because I wasn't the one with pox and he was standing in front of me looking every bit the fantasy I was having. "I'm certain I don't." Maybe I wanted to hear him say it. After all this time, I deserved that kind of thing. Clay wasn't big on compliments.

His tongue slid across his lower lip, and I was envious of it. Trying to figure a way to take my turn, licking his lips. He pulled that lower lip between his teeth. "All your pretty and that curviness."

I could've swooned, and only part of it was from the alcohol.

He could say what he wanted, and I loved that he said it, but he was the pretty one. His hair was curly, a little too long, dark, satin, and my fingers itched to run through it. His cheekbones were high, lips full, eyes like melted milk chocolate. Oh, holy cannoli, the arms. The chest. The ass. He was an entire package of deliciousness, and I wanted a nibble.

"Do you want to eat?" We had a table. Presumably a waiter.

"With you?" When I nodded, he smiled. "Yeah."

This guy was a whole vibe. When we sat down and I was facing him head on, I was captivated, struck dumb. I wanted to ask him to be naughty. I wasn't a naughty kind of girl. Never.

I shook it off. I wasn't going to start acting the fool now, or at least I hoped not. I cleared my throat and smiled at him. "Are you related to the Remington who's about to marry Cami?"

I had whittled down the information I'd gleaned from the conversation.

Will nodded. "I presume he's Ethan Remington. His dad and my dad are cousins."

"Oh." I knew his father was still alive. It was why Will was suing me and the hospital. "I'm really sorry about what happened with your dad."

He nodded. "Truth is, my dad was freaked out for a minute, but he loves telling that story." After a second, he nodded. "I'll drop the lawsuit."

"Thank you." I nodded. "Incidentally, my mom broke her hip, that's why I'm here and she isn't." I didn't bring up the curse of the stones. I wasn't sure he would be receptive to the idea, and I wasn't certain I was quite the true believer the others seemed to be.

He chuckled. "I would be having a very different conversation."

"Oh yeah, you would." I laughed. "My mother would've had you in a séance by now, trying to contact everyone's favorite pirate."

"I doubt Renegade was a favorite. The real history isn't as romantic as everyone makes it out to be." He spoke as if he had information the rest of the world wasn't privy to.

I was intrigued. "How so?"

He looked down into his drink, swirled it in the cup, then glanced up at me. "It was some grand love story that started out underneath a starlit sky or a seaside sunset. Ariya Thornbridge started as his prisoner." Well, he had all the names right.

"How do you know?" I knew first-hand about a journal that had been found. Written about things that no one but Ariya could've known.—I'd read a copy once, because my mother forced me to, although it was just a few pages—but what I had read was actually quite compelling. What he was saying contradicted what I'd read.

"They're my family." As if that explained it.

"Mine, too." We were connected by the pasts of those who came before us. "Are we relatives?"

"Not necessarily. Probably much in the same way everyone is related to Adam and Eve?" There were a lot of threads, and I didn't want to waste a lot of time trying to untangle them.

"Are you sure?"

He cocked an eyebrow. "Does it matter?"

It did if I was the kind of girl who wanted to take him into the bathroom for a quickie. It turned out I was that kind of girl. What I wanted to do and what I actually did varied by several measurable degrees. Maybe there was a compromise?

"It does if I ask you to come up to my room." Oh, I was brazen. I was bold. I was shaking.

"Are you? Asking me?" Now he looked at me from beneath those long, black lashes that, if I was a slightly vainer person, would've made me jealous.

"If I had a room, I would. A shower..."

"I have a room with a shower." He smiled again. "If you're interested."

"If we're not related..."

"Not more than I am to the bartender. Trust me, I've studied my family line. Interested?"

I was interested. Very interested. I didn't want to give myself away, so I nodded and took his hand when he stood, walked around the table, and offered it to me.

For the first time in a very long time, I wanted something, and I wanted it badly.

Chapter Eight

It's a Pirate's Life For Me

HIS ROOM WAS what I assumed mine would look like. A bed—king sized—a walk-out with a balcony that overlooked the sparkling, blue Caribbean, a small fridge, a shuttered-door closet, and a bathroom. I didn't care about much more than the man and the bed. He walked to the French doors that led to the balcony and pushed them open. A gust of ocean air blew the curtains into the room, and I breathed it in.

When he turned, he crooked his finger. "Come here."

I liked a man who took charge and who knew what I wanted without me having to ask. That he was handsome enough to take my breath away was a bonus.

Unfortunately, I still felt gross from my dip in the ocean. "I was promised a shower..."

He sighed and pointed to the bathroom with a wicked smile that made my knee wobble. "Make it quick."

I did. Using the hotel-provided soaps and shampoos, I cleaned every inch of my body as fast as humanly possible, dried, and slipped back into my unpleasant clothes. Briefly staring at my reflection in the mirror, I combed my fingers through my hair and stepped back out, hoping I didn't kill the mood.

He was still on the balcony, or maybe he'd just gone back out, I didn't care either way. I made a beeline for him.

The arms I knew would be strong wrapped around me. He pressed me closer. I rested one hand on his chest—I had to make sure this was real, and it so was—and laid the other hand on his shoulder. I used my finger to caress the side of his throat.

He smiled. "That's nice."

"You should feel it from where I'm standing." That was no exaggeration. Every inch of this guy was pure perfection. I'd never been so hyper-attracted to someone before.

"I want to kiss you."

Oh, and I wanted him to. "Okay." By okay, I meant now. *Puh-lease.*

He lowered his head and brushed his mouth over mine. It was soft and almost tentative, for a couple of seconds. I slid my hand into his hair, and I was lost. Lost.

He walked me backward until my ass hit the edge of the mattress. He lifted me so I was sitting on the bed. He did it without ever breaking the kiss. I'd never felt particularly dainty before or small, but he lifted me like I weighed nothing.

This man kissed like he was born to do it. He crawled up beside me as he nudged me backward, then lay beside me, still kissing, still holding me, his hand on my hip now.

He lifted his head for a second. "Is this okay?"

"Oh yeah." It was okay in eighty languages. I nodded and pulled him in for another kiss. This one was more intense than the last, but that couple-second break was all it took to let the doubts in. I didn't know him. Yesterday, he wanted to sue my pants off.

I pulled back. "Will..."

He nodded and breathed in slowly. "Yeah." He lay back beside me, so we were both staring at the ceiling.

"What now?" I still didn't have a room, but I was more than willing to leave.

"I could finish telling you about Ariya and Renegade." He turned his head to look at me. "Just don't go."

His voice was silk against my skin, against every single one of my senses. If this acting thing didn't work out, or he tired of construction, he had a real future in reading books out loud or giving speeches or any occupation that required a sexy, warm tone of voice.

I nodded. "Okay."

He turned to his side and stared at me. A slow smile slid across his face, and he laid his hand on my stomach. The shirt hadn't ridden up—dammit—so he wasn't touching skin, but my heart rate increased to about ten times its normal speed. I'd never been so alive.

Some curse.

He breathed out slowly and propped himself on his elbow to look down at me. Even at this angle—which usually distorted features, made them appear longer and more awkward —he was the most handsome man I'd ever seen.

"Ariya worked in a town along the eastern seaboard in Massachusetts. She sold potions and was generally thought of as a healer." He smiled and the fingers on my belly dragged my shirt in tiny circles. "This was a while after the witch trials. Not that she wasn't in danger, but..." He shrugged one shoulder. "She didn't care. When they came for her, to burn her or hang her, whichever the court of the time decided, and they would decide, the Sea Queen—Renegade's stolen ship—had docked at the harbor. He was walking through the town with some others of his kind."

Oh, this man knew how to tell a story. "He rescued her."

"Yes. Some people said they fell in love at first sight, others said he dragged her kicking and screaming to the boat and had to hold her captive in his cabin." He leaned in for a soft kiss. It was quick, almost nothing, but I felt it in my stomach. "I like to think he had to rescue her. That something about her was... calling to him and he couldn't stand the thought of leaving her behind."

"I like that."

"He brought her here. Back then there was no hotel, just an uninhabited island, a place where they could fight it out and fall in love. Make a life." He made it sound romantic even though he'd told me it wasn't.

"Sounds like they found their paradise." I tilted my head, and he kissed me again. This was the kind of thing I'd never experienced before. I'd had plenty of sex. For god's sake, I was forty years old. It wasn't like I was some love-struck virgin, but this was next-level intimate. Or maybe it was just an effect of the alcohol.

"Yeah. It took them a while to get there, but it was their place."

I pulled him down for a kiss this time, and let my hands explore under his shirt because he might be a gentleman, but I wasn't sure I was a lady, and I wanted to feel his skin. I dragged my mouth away from his and down the side of his throat. He breathed out a groan, and it was all the encouragement I needed. I grabbed a handful of Remington rear-end and it was glorious. Divine. Just like I knew it would be.

It wouldn't have taken much to roll on top of him, to grind my hips into his, to feel what I could only assume was his massive manhood. In my mind, the assumption made sense. Every other thing about him was as close to perfection as one could get, so I chose to believe that was too.

He was restrained and that said something. I pulled back. "How old are you, Will?"

He was younger. I could tell. I couldn't tell by how much. He had an old soul. Didn't seem like a player, though. His skin was untouched by time. He wasn't a child either. There was a tiny scar near the end of his left eyebrow and a dimple on his chin.

"Thirty-one."

I pulled my hands back. That was only nine years younger than me. "Oh."

"I meant thirty-one plus five?" I wasn't buying it. "How old are you?"

"Too old to be lying on a bed making out with you." I only found out last week that Netflix and chill meant sex. I was old.

"Thirty-five?"

He was guessing low. “Forty. I’ll be forty-one in...” Oh God. Three weeks.

I sprang off the bed like I had, for lack of a better word, a spring attached to my back, and I paced, albeit unsteadily, from one edge of the room to the other. “Are you sure you’re only thirty-one?” Maybe he’d meant to say forty-one. Or something a bit more age-appropriate.

He was on his feet in front of me. “I can be whatever you want.” Like he’d heard himself, he shook his head. “I’m so cheesy. I might as well be made of milk.”

“You’re young.” It made me sad. Sadder than I’d ever known.

“Not that young.” He had full mastery of sultry and sexy which was not helping this specific situation one bit. “I’m not a virgin.”

“Oh, thank God.” What was I supposed to say to that?

He laughed, and I stared at him like he’d grown a third head. It occurred to me as a ridiculously bad time for humor. I hadn’t gotten to know the first two that well yet. I laughed and then sobered, hiding a second giggle behind my hand. “I’m sorry.” I was being inappropriate in my head.

The moment was gone. I wasn’t some sexually neglected forty-year-old doctor. I was just a woman in a room with a guy and we were laughing. It was nice.

This kind of thing didn't happen for me. I couldn't remember the last time I'd laughed. Or the last time I'd wanted to.

"Do you know about the stones?" We were back to that. Anything else would've led somewhere I wasn't prepared to go.

He nodded. "I do."

"The curse?"

He nodded again. Somehow, we were pressed together again from mouth to hip to toe. I didn't know how it worked because his legs were longer than mine and he was taller.

"It's actually what brought me here. That and the fact that Mass Gen isn't excited about having me back. I would like to blame the curse on what happened with your dad. Or the nurse. The truth is, I think I messed the numbers around and the herbal Viagra..."

He shook his head and chuckled. "Dad's a very... active guy."

"Obviously." Because I hadn't, in almost forty-one years, outgrown my awkward, dork stage, added, "Good news for you, right?"

He smiled down at me and brushed my hair back, tucking it behind my ear. "Could be good news for you, too."

I laughed. "Are you proposing marriage?"

"You're a Thornbridge, and I'm a Remington. We'd be finishing this once and for all." He grinned. Whatever he saw in my face wiped his smile away. I stepped back, and he stepped back and then I shook my head, and he shook his head and held his hand out. "No, no, no. I was only kidding." Softer he added, "I think."

He moved closer again, this time I held out my hand. "No, just... no."

"I don't know what's happening to me right now, but I know that I don't want you to go." He talked faster as he moved in again. "You don't have a room or luggage. I could lend you something, sweats maybe or," he sighed and raked his hand through his hair. "Don't go."

Not only because I didn't have anywhere to go, but because I didn't want to leave. I nodded.

This time when we lay together on the bed, we didn't touch. "Can you believe we're working on a movie set tomorrow?"

I wasn't even sure he heard me because now he was snoring.

Chapter Nine

You're Not Famous Until My Mother has Heard of You

HOLY GRASSHOPPER GOO. I didn't think there was a way Will could've looked better than he had when I saw him the first time, but that was only because I hadn't seen Will in a pirate get-up. Oh my, what a sight he was. He had the hat. The tight pants. The ruffled shirt.

We were at a standstill. I looked at Delilah. She was hissing and cursing, sending a couple of bits of spittle flying.

I was standing beside one of the assistants. "What's going on?"

She rolled her eyes and took a bite of the muffin she'd taken from the "craft" table. I didn't know what a craft table was, but since I'd not finished last night's dinner and I was awake before sunrise, I was very glad for said table.

"The actress who's playing the witch, you know her. She was in that movie with all the arrows and the guy..." She snapped her fingers and rotated her hand in a big circle as if she was trying to get me to remember.

"Oh, right yeah. What about her?" I didn't have any idea who we were talking about, but I wanted to know what the holdup was and how it pertained to her.

"She won't come out of her trailer. Her agent promised her that she would be doing love scenes with the guy they fired and now she's got her princess panties in a twist because she doesn't want to kiss some 'unknown.'" On the air-quoted word, she widened her eyes. "If you ask me, she's way too big for her princess panties."

She had to be blind. I was wearing one of his shirts and it smelled like him. All I could think of was his bare chest as he'd handed it to me.

The assistant wasn't finished dishing the dirt, or was it called spilling the tea? I didn't know, but I was tuned in. "This chick's been a problem since she's been in Hollywood."

"Well, she doesn't know what she's missing. He might be unknown, but he kisses like a leading man." She turned to me, and I nodded. "Like look out Brad Pitt. Will Remington is coming for your job."

Heads turned and people looked. Will, too. I shrugged as heat burned in my cheeks and embarrassment added another couple of creases to the collection at the corners of my eyes and on my forehead.

Like she'd heard me—I didn't realize I'd been standing at the corner of her trailer—the door flung open and the problem actress herself poked her head out. "You want to kiss him so badly, you can wear the wig"—she yanked it off her head and handed it to me, then reached inside her corset dress and pulled out a pair of fake boobs—"and the tits and this god-awful sage necklace." She tossed it at me, too. "You can smack lips with him and bump nasties and whatever else with him. You're as much a nobody as he is."

She stomped off. Through the sand. Barefoot.

Every eye on the beach was on me, but only Delilah seemed to be surveying. "It's not a bad idea."

"Oh, no. It's a bad idea." I held up my hand and shook my head. Then Will was there. Smiling. "You were Sandy in Grease."

"How do you know that?"

"You told me on the plane." Some parts of that flight had dissolved into a black hole of my memory. "It doesn't matter how I know. You're a Thornbridge. I'm a Remington. It's fate that we're the ones telling their story."

He looked at Delilah, who had stopped sputtering and was staring at me. She put her hands on his arms and moved him, so we were standing together. "I could be the next Cameron. Making stars." She nodded at Will. "I'm going to get a camera. You're going to kiss her and we're going to see if this works on film." As she turned away she probably didn't mean to say it aloud. "Oh, God, please let this work."

It took a couple of minutes but then there was a camera and she positioned us this way first then that way, his arms at my waist first—not romantic enough—then his hands pushed into my hair, his palms on my face. She nodded. "Kiss her."

Sweet honey on toast, he did and when he pulled back, I smiled. "Definitely a leading man kind of kiss."

Delilah Bradbury, my hero, my idol before the moment I decided she was losing her mind to cast me as Ariya Thorn-bridge, clapped. "Can you imagine the press on this one?" She was salivating. She turned to the assistant. "Get her into the makeup tent, get that costume back from Jessica Rabbit, and get the good doctor fitted. We're rescheduling until nine a.m." She nodded and people fluttered into motion.

I chased after her, kicking up sand, and stumbling forward. "Miss Bradbury?" She kept moving like she didn't hear me. She did it with elegance and speed. Much speed. "Delilah?"

She wheeled and it caught me by surprise enough that I stum-bled backward. Her assistant caught me. "You've been promoted. You're going to be a star. Pirate movies are really in right now."

"I'm a doctor."

"Opportunities don't come along like this very often." She was right, of course.

"I don't have movie experience." What I did have was a tough-pitched, shrill tone that drew looks, so I lowered my volume. "I don't know what to do."

She patted my shoulder. "I do and I'll be right here with you every minute. Don't worry." She smiled and gestured at Will. "You made this all happen. Or the stones did." She said it like I was unaware of the stones. I wondered how much she knew about them. I had a vague, kind of foggy recollection of one of them mentioning the curse in relation to Cami's hives.

Right now, that wasn't the most concerning part of my day. This was. "I didn't mean to."

"Of course you didn't." She smiled. "It's done. Let's make the best of it."

I sighed because Delilah had walked further away and was talking to the man who'd been with her last night–Ricky I think she called him–and at the award show and on the cover of many-a-tabloid of late.

Her assistant walked over to me. "We need you to sign your contract."

“My contract?”

“Are you opposed to full frontal nudity?” She had a clipboard and was busy writing things I couldn’t see.

“Full frontal what?”

“Have you ever had any sexually transmitted diseases?”

“What? No.” I couldn’t keep up and it was kind of important now that I did because she was off and running. She held open the flap of a tent and waved me inside with her clipboard.

An hour later, I was Ariya Thornbridge. I was the spitting image of the picture of her that was hand-drawn and hanging in the corner of the mirror, to the point that it was unsettling.

“All right.” Delilah Bradbury stood behind me, nodding her approval.

I stood and she motioned for me to turn. I did a full circle. “Sign the contract?”

I shook my head. “Not yet.”

She handed me a script. “Read this while we get the contract ready. Can’t work without one.” She was calm.

I, on the other hand, was trembling. Right up to the moment Will came into the tent and stopped. Stared. “Wow.”

My skin flushed with pleasure. He smiled, too.

Delilah nodded. “I can see chemistry isn’t going to be a problem.”

She didn’t know the half of it.

Chapter Ten

Onyx is a Girl's Best Friend

It was after dark before we stopped for the day. There were first takes and second takes and eleventy-seventh takes. They were not because we'd done badly—actually, it had gone well—but because Delilah wanted the scenes shot from various angles. I didn't question it because I hated when anyone played Monday morning quarterback after one of my surgeries. If she said we had to reset and do it again, I was going to do it again.

It was fun. Mostly. Hard work, holding a pose, trying to remember exactly where I'd been holding my head or my hand. She'd assured us we were kicking ass.

I was tired, but it had been a good day.

I wasn't sure where Will had gone, I'd had two scenes after he'd finished. He stayed around for a bit, but when I looked again, he was gone. I chalked it up to his being as tired as I was and getting a head start on his sleep.

I'd had a break this afternoon and went to the desk to make sure everything was straightened out with my room. It had been straightened out yesterday, but I'd had a lot of other things on my mind.

Tonight though, as I walked through the lobby, Art stopped me. "Doctor Thorn? The airline delivered your luggage."

Yes. I hitched my bag—the one I'd refused to let leave my sight except when I was filming because it had the stone in it—higher on my shoulder and reached for my suitcase.

I could've hugged Art. My shampoo and conditioner were in this bag, and my panties and clothes that fit.

Art snapped his fingers and another man—this one wearing khaki pants and a flowered print button-down—reported to the desk. "Yes, sir?"

"Please help Doctor Thorn to her room." I could've kissed Art, had I not been too tired to leap over the counter.

"Thank you, Art."

He nodded and shot me a wink. "We take care of our VIP guests."

I was almost giddy as I walked to the elevator with the bellman. "We turned your bed down and there's a complimentary bottle of champagne from the resort in your room."

If this was VIP service, I never wanted to be anything else ever again. "Thank you."

He nodded. I liked that he was a man of few words. Today had been one of those sensory-rich days. The silence was a luxury I was never going to take for granted again.

At my floor—the third, and just down the hall from Will's—the bellman took my key and opened the door, motioning me inside ahead of him. At some point, I'd dropped my bag from my shoulder to my hand, and as I walked, the purse somehow got tangled up in my feet. I went down, my belongings went sprawling and the box that the necklace was in slid out, opened and the necklace skittered across the floor.

I was relatively unharmed, except for a skinned knee and some bruised pride. It didn't stop me from picking up the necklace and turning. I wanted to apologize to the bellman for my clumsiness and try to save some face in a ridiculous situation, but when I looked at him, he was frozen mid-step.

No way. This wasn't real. He was toying with me. I walked closer, snapped my fingers in front of his face, and he didn't even blink. I poked his shoulder, but he didn't move.

"Whoa." When I looked at the old-time bell on the top of the clock, the second hand wasn't moving. The ocean waves weren't rolling in onto the beach. They seemed to be standing still. Waiting. The dust wasn't settling. As eloquently as I could, I said, "Whoa," a second time.

I put the necklace down and the clock started ticking behind me. Waves crashed. The bellman put down my suitcase. I picked up the necklace again. Once more, everything stopped. Time itself quit moving.

A third whoa would've been overkill, so I went with, "Holy crap."

I put the necklace down again. Some crazy things were happening. Things that lent credence to the details my mother had recounted, to the legend I'd heard all my life, to the power of witchcraft. I had no other excuse for it. Especially when it continued over and over again. I slid the necklace back into its box and put it in my purse.

This was... insane. Or maybe I was insane. I'd never believed in my mother's magic. Never trusted that it existed. Maybe it didn't but if I didn't believe her, then I couldn't believe anyone else, and now—thanks to the necklace and the irrefutable proof I'd seen with my own eyes—my whole belief system was on its ass.

I felt like I should call and apologize to her. First, I tipped the bellman, brought the necklace and its box into the bathroom, and took a long, hot shower. The water pelted my skin, and I should've been luxuriating in the basket of scented soap and lotion on the counter, compliments of the hotel, but I couldn't stop wondering about the necklace and what it could do. I wanted to take it out for a spin.

When I finished my shower, instead of drying my hair, I piled it in a messy bun, put on a pair of jeans and a t-shirt then left the necklace in the box and walked out of my room with the box clenched in my hand. I was hungry. I was more than a little bit tired, but there was no way I was going to be able to sleep until I proved to myself that this was a fluke or a product of my over-tired imagination.

I walked down to the restaurant. The place wasn't very busy, but there were a couple of tables and the maître d smiled at me. "Dr. Thorn. A table for one?"

"Yes, thank you. Somewhere quiet." I followed him to a table in the corner. "Perfect."

He nodded and smiled, then silently handed me my menu, and walked away. It was only a few minutes before the waiter approached. "Good evening, Doctor Thorn. Can I start you off with a bottle of the house red? It's a robust blend with notes of plum and mocha. Or if you would prefer, we have a delightful chardonnay with a creamy, buttery flavor that is slightly fruit-forward."

I wasn't a connoisseur of fine or any other classification of wine. I was more of a tequila shooter kind of gal. I had to be back on set in a few hours—I felt so important thinking that way—so I needed something of the non-alcoholic variety. "Just water." As he took my goblet from the place setting and used the pitcher he'd brought with him to fill it, I pulled out the necklace. The water stopped, mid-flow, the waiter's mouth stayed open mid-sentence, and conversations quieted until I put the necklace back into its box.

This was probably the coolest thing I'd ever seen. I was tempted to call my mom and find out if there were more details about it that she hadn't told me, but I'd been a jerk to her about the magic. My memories were full of arguments over her magic. I should've been better to her.

Maybe my being in the "family" movie would be enough to make it up to her. I hoped so. She deserved so much better than the way I'd treated her.

I pushed the regrets away. I would revisit them another time, but right now, I had to get a nap in before I went back to the movie set. I ate a grilled chicken salad with smoked pineapple and then went back to my room.

When I returned to the room, I had an idea. It wasn't a great idea. I wasn't sure if it would work, but once I thought of it, I was powerless to ignore it.

I slipped the necklace out and watched the clock again. It had stopped. I had to be back at two a.m. but if I could catch up on my sleep, and be refreshed, tomorrow would be an easier day. I was hopeful.

I slid under the blanket and fell asleep.

When I woke, the necklace was still in my hand and the clock was ticking. It was one-thirty, and while I had time for a shower, if I shampooed, conditioned, and blow-dried, I was going to be late.

Apparently, there was a time limit on how long I could put a pause on things. It was an interesting tidbit of trivia, but I didn't know if there was a way or if I even had time to try to figure it out. I only had a half hour before I had to be in the makeup tent, and I didn't want to be late.

Chapter Eleven

That's too Coincidental to be a Coincidence

EVERYTHING WAS GOING WELL. I kept the necklace with me, using it to stop time because despite my almost photographic memory, I'd had a couple of issues with lines. It had held everyone up, and I didn't want to be responsible for it again. It hadn't been a big issue, not big enough anyone complained—if they did that sort of thing, and I didn't know one way or the other—but big enough to be bothersome to me.

My corseted witch dress—a garment I wasn't sure fit the time period, but who was I to question—had a pocket, and I shoved the necklace in so that when I needed it, I could put my hand in and grab it instead of bringing the necklace out.

Maybe it was a fluke, or maybe it was because I hadn't done much to find the answer to how to return it to the pirate.

That should've been my primary focus since it was the purpose of my trip, but so many other things had happened, plus I'd learned about the necklace's magic power, so I hadn't been in a hurry to give it back. In any case, it was like the damned thing was trying to escape and fell out of my pocket. As someone who consistently looked for the rhyme and reason behind the magic, I was fairly certain it had more likely caught on the lace at the edge of my sleeve and fell out, but these days, it could've gone either way.

Delilah looked down at the necklace and then up at me. "Is that one of the stones?" Her voice was an excited whisper, which made it louder than a whisper, but there was no one around, so it didn't really matter.

Instead of waiting for my answer, she pulled me toward the makeup tent. She looked at the two women inside the tent. "Get out."

When they were gone, she stared at me. "Where did you get that?"

I sighed. There was no reason not to tell the truth. "My mother." She was still at home recuperating from surgery. "She couldn't bring it because she fell and broke her hip. I said I wasn't going to bring it, but then I lost my job and my boyfriend." Although I cared more about the job. "My apartment was flooded with raw sewage and by the time all was said and done, she convinced me that it was the curse."

"You don't believe her?" She cocked a brow.

"Well, my plane didn't crash. I didn't have to pay for my stay at the resort and my luggage has been found." I didn't mention Will or the fact that I was now being paid to kiss him.

"Did it occur to you that the curse is... on a break, so to speak?"

No. It hadn't. "Not really."

"You'd better sit down." I did as I was told. Partly because she was my boss, partly because the shoes I was wearing had been fitted to an actress with freakishly small feet and my new ones hadn't arrived yet, and partly because I couldn't believe I'd told anyone about this.

She sighed. "I have one stone, and Cami has the other. Now all three are here on the island."

It was still a lot to believe. It ranked right up there with Santa and the Tooth Fairy. I shook my head.

"Okay, think about it." She sat in the chair opposite me. "What are the chances in a world not dominated by this weird legend, that a doctor would be cast as one of the lead roles in a major motion picture?"

"Well, that other girl was... kind of spoiled." I sighed. I didn't want to rub salt in what had to be an open wound but, "Word in the lobby is that the movie with her as the lead was horribly over budget and chances were that it wasn't going to get finished."

She nodded. "Maybe, but now it's under budget. There are other things, too. Things that can't be a coincidence."

This I had to hear. "Such as...?"

"Well, what are the chances again that you, a Thornbridge by birth, a descendant of the witch herself, would meet a Remington, one of Renegade's brood, at just the moment you were coming to the island? What are the chances that said Remington would bear such an incredible resemblance to our buddy Renegade?" Okay. Those were valid points.

"Very true, but..."

"Maybe they want their story told." She shrugged this time. "Maybe that's why Cami got hives and not me. Something bigger here is at play than just coincidence. We're here for a reason and since nothing horrible has happened to the production of the movie, I have to assume the pirate and the witch are okay with the story we're telling."

"The pirate and the witch?" I supposed if I bought into any of it, I would have to believe that maybe they were behind all of it. It was hard to wrap my head around any of it, to undo years of doubt and disbelief. "For God's sake, my mother would love this place."

She cocked her head at me. "You said she broke her hip?" I nodded, and she tapped her finger on the arm of the chair. When she needed to think, she tapped, whether it was a foot, or a hand, or a finger. "How?"

"She tripped over her cat. Truth be told, she could've just as easily broken it rollerblading through the park at midnight on a Tuesday, even though she's never rollerbladed before in her life." I shrugged. There had been a lot of coincidences these last few days. I could give an idea some thought, and give credit where credit was due. Even if the idea sounded like something out of a movie. Maybe she was onto something.

"Are you insanely attracted to your Remington?" I didn't know that I would call it insanely, but I did think about him a lot more than I'd ever thought of Clay and I hadn't wanted anyone in my life the way I wanted him.

I shrugged. "I suppose I'm attracted."

"More than usual? More than to any other man in the history of men? If Brad Pitt came to the table, sat down, and told you he had to have you, would you still be thinking Remington?" She smiled, and I didn't have to answer. "I thought so. The fact is, fate, the witch, or even the dead pirate brought us all here for a reason."

"He wants his jewels back." I blew out a breath. "He told me so."

"He told you so? He, being Renegade?" When I nodded, she gave a slight head shake. "I think he wants his happy ending with Ariya. I think we have to reunite them." She shook her head. "I know it sounds insane. I didn't believe it myself, but Cami and I have been here, and strange things... her rash, the necklaces have power..."

I nodded. I was well aware of what we were dealing with. I only hoped we could figure out a way to deal with it before things spun completely out of control.

Chapter Twelve

Dear Diary...

THE MOVIE SET was full of big-named actors, A-listers, B-listers, comedians, a musician who was writing the soundtrack, some guy who'd been living on a prayer since the eighties but had contacted Delilah to be a part of the production because it spoke to him. I didn't know if he meant it in the literal or figurative sense, but he was always quick with a joke, a laugh, or a smile. He sang. A lot.

This was a Delilah Bradbury movie and despite her epic and very public fall from grace, the stars had come out in force for her.

As I was walking past the makeup tent, an actress I'd only seen playing the receptionist in low-budget films said, "I think it's great that there are unknowns playing the lead parts."

She'd been super supportive in explaining the process and helping me run lines. She was a part of Ariya's on-screen coven. We had scenes together.

"I don't understand it. She's like ten years older than him." The makeup artist who has a crappy habit of snapping her gum, snapped her gum. "She's a doctor. Not an actor."

I wasn't really eavesdropping. I was walking past. The one thing I didn't need to hear was how unsuited I was for Will. I always knew it. I was too enchanted to walk away.

Every day he was more the part. Although things on set weren't flowing as well as they had been. The ship they'd built for the interior shoots still hasn't passed the safety commission. There was a safety commission. Also, by now—well into shooting—Cami's pox were bigger and there were many more of them.

We were operating under the assumption that the movie wasn't the pirate or the witch's main concern. They wanted their necklaces. We had to wait for the right day–the new moon or full moon, I couldn't remember.

In today's market, they weren't worth much. The sapphire was probably the most valuable. Not that it mattered. If it was truly ghosts, and I was only prepared to say it might have been, the value wouldn't matter to them. What were they going to do? Not like they could walk into a pawnshop or spend the money. This was a sentimental issue.

Most days, I didn't remember anything specific about being on the set. I was never going to tell anyone that or the fact that I had felt, more than once, like I was outside my body watching someone else act the part. Maybe Mom's brand of crazy was rubbing off on me, but that didn't mean I was going to brag about it.

There were three love scenes that had to be shot, but we weren't shooting two of them because they were on the "boat" set, and it wasn't ready, and the other was on the beach, but someone mentioned a sensitivity coach, so we were waiting for one to arrive.

Today was a rainy one, so Delilah called off shooting altogether and gave everyone the day off.

She found me in the dining room of the restaurant, stuffing my face with glazed donuts that were fresh from the grease. If there was one thing I could do with enthusiasm, it was snarf donuts.

Cami stood behind her, a scarf wrapped around her face and head. She glanced at me. "We need to talk."

I nodded and put my donut on the plate in front of me, then wiped my hands. I was wasting time, and I had no real idea why. "Okay."

She pulled out the seat next to mine and slipped into it. "We need to figure out if we are just tossing the jewels back to sea or if Delilah is right and there's a ceremony, a process of some sort."

"How do we do that?" Wasn't like we could just make a call. Unless maybe my mother knew, but I wasn't at the point where I was ready to use the last resort to phone the crazy relative option.

"There's a Captain Renfro Remington museum. Right here on the island. If we're going to figure it out, that's the place we're going to find the answers." Cami's words were garbled under the scarf she was wearing, but I understood why she needed to wear it because I knew she was hiding her pox.

I reached for my donut, then saw them both staring at me. "Oh, you mean *right* now?"

Delilah lifted a brow. "Yeah, this would be the best time. We can figure out the stones and not delay the movie with our search for information."

Okay, she was right about that. I guess the rest of my donut would have to wait.

Cami's man wasn't back from wherever he'd gone off to. Delilah's was playing cards with some of the camera operators, and I didn't have a man to check in with, technically, so we left.

"Bring your necklace along." Delilah glanced at me, one brown eye cocked as if she thought I was going to argue with her.

I didn't even bother to ask why. Of course, it wasn't an issue anyway since I never went anywhere without the necklace these days. Although instead of its box, I kept it in a heavy velvet pouch inside a thick leather cross-body bag. I patted the purse. "I have it."

We took one of the resort golf carts because the island didn't have cars, although it had roads. Even though the route we took wasn't much of a road—narrow, cobbled stones, rough—but fortunately, the museum wasn't far.

Delilah drove because she'd been here before. She'd used this place for research. The museum itself wasn't much more than a house that had different memorabilia in different rooms. It had white siding that needed a good paint job, probably from its beachside proximity, but it looked sturdy and sound. It was a couple of stories tall with blue shutters and windows that had been replaced at some point or possibly added as they were modern vinyl with grids inside the glass.

The front door was rounded with heavy metal embellishments and a small cut-out in the center. On the roof, a pirate's skull and crossbone flag waved in the wind.

We walked inside and just in the foyer, there was a painted portrait of Renegade, and to say he looked like Will or Will looked like him would've been an understatement. They could've been twins. Same eyes, same broad shoulders, same half smirk-half smile. There were some good genetics in that Remington gene pool.

We stayed together as we walked through, although I dragged a few steps behind because I wanted to absorb it all. I owed it to my mother, who would've loved all of this so much and I wanted to recount it all for her.

There was a chair inside the "famous guests" section that had a gold etched plate that said, "Elvis Presley composed one of his number one hits while sitting on this chair in the veranda of this museum, according to some locals."

I hadn't seen a veranda, but who was I to question it? It was just a piece of trivia. Although my mind focused on the "according to some locals," part, and the fact that it didn't say which song.

A typewriter sat on a desk and a plaque beside it read, "Novelist, Margaret Milan wrote the prize-winning and much-lauded novel, Daydream Sailor, about Renfro Remington's childhood at this typewriter."

The paintings of Remington throughout the house were all signed by Arthur Thornbridge. A cousin maybe.

We came to a room dedicated to Ariya. Her clothes. A painting of her. A book. The diary my mother had bought copies of pages from.

It was the clothing that matched my costumes for the movie that caught my eye while Cami and Delilah fawned over the diary.

"Wow. The clothes in the movie..." I looked from Delilah to the dress and back.

She nodded. "Right? Cami had a dress designer for her daughter's wedding. Dionne. She's fabulous. I hired her. Now since I'm not paying that rotten little girl actress, I can afford her, too." She wagged her eyebrows once, then went back to staring at the diary.

She, too, had a bag on her shoulder, but it was huge, big enough to hold a book similar to the one inside the glass case.

"What are you doing?" Cami went to the door and shut it.

"We need this diary," Delilah said with no hint of remorse. "We have an idea."

"An idea?" They were both smiling at me. I could tell it was both of them because Cami's eyes crinkled at the corners. My stomach churned. Delilah looked at my bag and tilted her head. "You want me to use my necklace to steal the witch's diary?"

"It probably says in there how to return the jewels."

"If it doesn't?" I used the necklace nefariously.

"We're going to return it. We just need to make a few photocopies." I wasn't sure I could do this. It was wrong. Theft.

"My mom bought pages of it online. Couldn't we just check there?" I really didn't want to add theft to my resume.

"Look at Cami." Like they'd planned it, Cami removed her scarf while Delilah continued talking. "Her pox are getting out of control. The movie is... my last-ditch effort at saving my career. I've worked hard on it. If I have to steal a diary—"

Well, that wasn't quite right, was it? "It won't be you."

"If you have to steal a diary, then in my opinion, the risk is worth the reward." She was certainly passionate, and although speaking quietly, and using her hands for emphasis.

The risk. Like the curse coming back and ruining more of my life. Maybe even me never getting to be a doctor again, getting sued, and losing any chance to connect with the man I really needed to stop thinking about.

I nodded. I could be a team player. If the museum people caught me, or us, then one or maybe all of us would point out that this movie would only help their tourism. Increase their donations. Delilah was certain to put a card at the end of the credits telling people where to donate.

"All right." I opened my bag and pulled out the velvet pouch. "Let's do this."

Chapter Thirteen

Love Needs No Language

IT WAS AN HOUR LATER, although it felt like much less, but I'd figured out how to keep track of time. I had to wear a watch.

We were on the beach reading the diary. The air was heavy and damp, but the rain had stopped, and we were all barefoot in the sand. We were down the beach from the resort, where we could still be seen but far enough down that anyone could tell what we were doing. For all they knew, we were playing witches and brewing a spell. I laughed a little at the thought, but it was on the outskirts of the truth.

Delilah was holding the book because until we knew for sure that Cami's pox weren't contagious, none of us were touching anything Cami touched. She was standing on one side of Delilah, and I was on the other.

“Look at that handwriting.” It was pristine. The kind a third-grade cursive teacher would have loved. Uniform. Beautiful. To have been written by a feather, very neat.

“Sold a batch of valerian root to Master Whipple. He calls me a witch behind my back, but he’d be first in line to buy my sleeping potions. I have been tempted to add some hawthorn and dandelion, but he would know.” Delilah read in what I would have called an Irish accent, and she made the words sound perfectly charming.

“Why would she add hawthorn and dandelion?” Cami asked and when I chuckled, they both looked at me.

“They’re diuretics.” My mother had been known to add some to her potions. I wasn’t defending her, but sometimes, revenge was sweet.

Delilah laughed. “Old Ariya had a sense of humor.” She turned a few pages. “Oh, look at this.” The writing was the same, but the language was different. “What do you suppose that is?”

I pulled out my cell. Opened the search engine, typed in a few words. “It doesn’t recognize.” The only person who would know about this was still the one I didn’t want to call. Now, it was time. “I could call my mom. She might know.”

Part of the reason the internet wasn't cooperating was because this island had spotty service. I would have to wait until I was back at the hotel to use a landline. I moved three paces and had full service. "Oh, let me have the book for a second. I have service." I took a picture of the page and sent it to my mother. "If she recognizes it, she'll call."

Not ten seconds after the picture showed the sent icon, my phone rang. I loved this woman. "Mom."

"Where did you get that?" She was in her shop. I could tell by the deadness of the sounds. "That's Romani."

"Do you know what it says?"

She sighed as if she didn't understand why I would be questioning her knowledge of a language Google didn't recognize.

"Of course I know what it says. " She huffed out another breath. "It says she met her love in the dark of night, under a moonless sky where the water rolled onto the beach like a soft blanket." This time, she sounded as if she was ready to cry. "I have failed you so badly, Ember. All Thornbridge women know Romani."

"It's okay, Mom. I have you." I hated when she was upset like this.

"Do you need me to come to the island?" She sniffed and blew her nose.

"No. You concentrate on getting well so we can come to the island together when you're better." This was a trip I would treat her to a thousand times over. "I love you, okay? And... this place is magical. You were right."

"Don't sound so surprised," she was teasing me, but there were still tears in her voice.

"Right now, we're reading through her diary..."

"You need to go. I understand. Focus on breaking the curse," she didn't sound as upset, still, I could tell she wished she were here with me.

"I'll call you tonight." Because I couldn't hang up with her being so upset, I said, "You can sign me up for Romani training when I get home."

"Deal." I could almost hear her smile. "Ember, I love you."

"I love you, too." When I hung up, maybe too quickly, because I was excited about the diary and what she'd said, she was still talking. Instead of calling her right back—partly because my service died again—I slid the phone into my pocket. I would speak to her tonight.

I turned to Delilah and Cami and told them what my mother said about the passage.

Delilah flipped a few pages. "It looks like whenever she talks about Renegade, she speaks in Romani."

We spent the afternoon reading what we could of the journal. It was mostly a record of her sales, a couple potion recipes—one to soothe a troubled infant that was made of lavender and chamomile, one made of honey and rose petals she called a love potion and sold to "the old hag Helter," and one for obedience to the poor mother of Atticus Hart—and some poems. When she spoke of Renegade, her love, she spoke in Romani.

Although we had no idea what any of it meant.

As we stood on the beach, a storm rolled in from the water

I took the journal back to my room with me because I was going to send pictures of the pages to my mother so she could translate them for me, and because I'd been the one who was going to end up in jail if we got caught so I called dibs.

I had no idea what the words meant in the Romani entries, but I read them aloud, loving the way they sounded. The interwebz were absolutely no help. Possibly because of the storm outside, but I had no phone service whatsoever. Even the resort phone was down when I tried it.

Instead of trying to decipher or translate, I just read it. All of it. Aloud.

As far as I could tell, there was no word on what to do with the jewels, not from what I read in English, anyway.

Until I finished with the journal, I'd never wished to know anything as much as I wanted to know all the words I'd read.

Chapter Fourteen

Stop Driving Me Crazy I Can Walk From Here

I HAD no idea when or how I'd gone to bed. Last I remembered, I'd been watching the waves, thinking they were so volatile even though the rain seemed to have stopped and the storm had cleared.

Instead of worrying about it, I looked at the clock on my phone. It was only 7 am, and we weren't due to shoot any scenes until nine, so I had some time to myself, and I felt like I hadn't had any in a while. I walked into the bathroom and looked in the mirror. I had something green and gooey in my hair and I looked as if I'd crawled into bed in wet clothes. I was wrinkled. I was flawed. I was... a mess. It made absolutely no sense.

If I wanted to enjoy a leisurely breakfast like the star of an upcoming movie should've been allowed, I had to get a move on. I took a world-record fast shower and washed my hair but didn't take the time to deep condition, then stepped out to grab the complimentary resort robe from its hanger. It was gone. My room hadn't been cleaned in two days because I'd hung out the sign to keep housekeeping out, but someone had taken my robe? Maybe it was a laundry thing. I didn't know.

Instead, I wrapped myself in a towel and didn't waste time sitting around air drying. The robe being gone was probably a good thing. Although I knew I'd hung it there. I distinctly remembered doing it.

I dressed and made my way down to the restaurant. I was famished. Probably because I'd been too engrossed with the journal to remember to eat before I went to bed. In any case, I eyed the buffet line and the made-to-order omelet station with the same adoration I might've eyed a Birkin bag or a diamond bracelet.

I didn't even get a table before I filled a plate and then looked around. Will was sitting at a table alone and he looked up as if he knew I was staring at him, then he waved me over.

He stood and pulled out my chair. It was gentlemanly and unexpected, and I smiled at him over my shoulder. I smiled, and he smiled back and a woman in the corner of the restaurant photographed us with her cell phone—the flash went off, plus she wasn't trying to hide it—and the waitress sat a glass of water in front of me.

"Hey, I thought you couldn't swim." No one knew better than he did since he'd had to jump in and save me on our first day here.

"Um, I can't." Nothing had changed since that day. A week and a half ago.

He laughed. "I saw you in the cove last night."

"I wasn't swimming in the cove. A, I can't swim and B, I'm smart enough to never go out in the ocean alone, and certainly not at night." I'd seen Jaws, Jaws 2, Jaws 3, and a whole bunch of other movies that made the idea of a moonlight swim just seem dumb.

Even as I said, an image flashed in my mind. I'd been swimming. With... Will in the moonlight. Once again—like the incident with the seaweed earlier—all I could think was... what?

He shrugged, but there was a thought or what might have been a memory nagging my frontal lobe. "Were you there?"

He cocked his head to the side as if he was experiencing the same thing. It was kind of like a reverse déjà vu, like a memory we were trying to have but didn't. "Were you there?"

It wasn't like I was pressuring him to have the same thought I was, but he shook his head. "I don't think so, but also, I feel like I might have been, for all the sense that makes."

It made perfect sense to me because I felt the same way. "Can you beat waking up with seaweed in your hair?"

He pursed his lips. "I didn't have boxers on when I woke up."

"Did you go to bed with them?" Now I was sitting at the table with a bacon and egg omelet, and I was picturing Will in his boxers… and not in his boxers.

He nodded. "Yeah, but I thought…" He waved a hand, dismissing this line of thought. "It doesn't matter what I thought. I woke up without them on."

We finished breakfast silently and there was nothing that said leisurely movie star, less than sitting across from a man choking down an omelet while I thought of him naked. Repeatedly. I couldn't look at him.

I looked at the floor, my plate, the fork in my hand, the other people eating, and finally, the door.

Delilah stood just inside the dining room, her eyes narrow, lips pinched. This woman knew how to glare, how to be angry on a whole other level. She cocked her head and waved to us. Not in the 'hello, how are you way', more in the 'get your ass over here before I kill you' way.

I pushed my chair back and stood, hurried like a minion toward her. That was when things started getting weird. Weirder.

Chapter Fifteen

But Did You Die?

IT TOOK an hour for hair and makeup to get us ready. I sat quietly, getting my hair curled as Delilah tapped her foot behind us. "We talked about this last night. How do you forget in the space of six hours?"

I had no idea what she was talking about. "Did you call me? Did I sound like I was asleep when I answered?" Maybe I'd answered the phone and forgotten it.

"No. I saw you when you were coming back in from the beach, all sexied up with boy wonder. He was wearing some artfully placed seaweed, and you were wearing your pajamas, soaked to the skin and hiding nothing." She tilted her chin and her eyes narrowed further. No way could she see. She sighed. "Look, I get it. You're the pretty people. You want to make more pretty people." What? "Or at least do the thing that makes more pretty people. What you do in your own time is absolutely your business. This is my time. My camera people were here. My makeup people were here. My extras were here. Romeo and Juliet, the pirate version, were nowhere to be seen. All this idle time costs me money."

I understood, but I had no recollection of speaking to her, walking wet through the lobby or anywhere else in my pajamas, or being "sexied up" with Will.

I did the only thing I could do. "I'm so sorry." It wouldn't have mattered to me if we were in Massachusetts, and this was a shift I'd been late for at the hospital or if I was on a Caribbean island filming a movie. A job was a job. My responsibility was to arrive on time.

"Aye, me too."

He was already in character, and I was barely laced into my corset, but ever so grateful Delilah wasn't the one pulling those cords today.

Finally, we were camera ready, and the safety crew had cleared the "boat" set. Not for the first time, I marveled at the authenticity with which we were operating. As I had the thought, a voice in my head chuckled.

I chalked it up to my subconscious finding me amusing, and I looked around the boat. It was all dark wood and fabric, and the floor moved as if it was rolling with the swell of the waves with each step so I was disoriented. I did not have sea legs.

I sat heavily on a chair and waited for Will. He was "above" checking a mast, whatever that meant. The camera guy was positioned on the "fourth wall" side of the set and his brow furrowed.

"You okay, Ember?" His concern was comforting but didn't do much for my nausea.

I would've answered him with more than a nod, but my head was spinning.

I had a vague feeling of frustration, but I didn't know why or what had caused it, so I concentrated on breathing in and out, trying to calm my stomach.

The entrance from "above" was a ladder and instead of coming down the way a painter, or a construction worker—as he said he was—would, he came down daredevil style, with one foot on each side of the rungs, he slid down, hands-free.

"Woah." He brushed his hands down his pant legs then stood upright and smiled. "Hello, my love."

He was using the Renegade accent, and the Renegade smile—it wasn't quite as broad as Will's, but equally potent and more smirk-like. He was going full method, and this was the first time I'd seen him do it this way.

The words, “I’ve missed you,” came out of my mouth with little to no assistance from my brain. My hand, of its own volition, reached to brush his hair back, to stroke his jaw, to creep around and tangle in his hair, to tug him close. His smile was the last thing I saw as I sank into a kiss I didn’t mean to start.

Now that it was happening, I wasn’t wholly unhappy about it. It was wrong, and I pushed my hands against his chest and stepped back. My body was fighting me. One hand lay flat on his chest, pushing, the other curled into the fabric over his heart and hung on.

“What are you doing?” I asked the question, but I had no idea who I was talking to.

“What are you doing?” It was Will, sans his Captain Renegade persona. “You kissed me.”

Technically, he was right. It was my mouth, my tongue. It was me. Not me.

I nodded. “Yeah, but if I said I’m not sure it was me, would that make sense to you?”

He pressed his lips into a tight line, stared, and nodded. “I think so.”

Delilah had been right. There was something bigger at play than any of us realized.

“How do we keep it from happening again?” To me, the question was reasonable.

"Do we not want it to happen again?" He tilted his head, and the accent was back. "Because I would like to make certain otherwise. I quite enjoy your mouth."

I stared at him. For a second, he was the full Renegade. The changes though, were visible. His forehead crinkled. His eyes narrowed. His lips thinned. "What the hell is going on?"

I had an idea, but I didn't think he was going to like it. It turned out that didn't matter because Delilah was ready to start.

We were an hour into shooting when it occurred to me I had no memory, no recollection of any kind of the last forty minutes at least. My hand lifted, my voice spoke, and I was in control of none of it.

"That's not what we said." Delilah stood. She was behind the camera guy, watching us through a screen, but she came out from her spot and stared at me.

"I-I-I... erm." Whatever was going on in my head grew louder, shriller, a yell, or a scream. My mouth fell open. "I don't feel well." I had to get myself under some sort of control.

To say I didn't feel well wasn't a mis-statement. Neither was it an understatement. Honest to goodness, I wasn't in any shape to work today. Not until I figured out why the hell I sounded like some kind of diva and why I had absolutely no control over my mouth or, apparently, my body.

I rushed away and headed straight to my room. It was the only thing I could do.

Chapter Sixteen

What's the First Sign of Madness?

I WAS in *oh my god* mode. As in, "Oh my God. Oh my God. Holy funky farmland."

I paced from one side of the room to the other and back again. Over and over.

"Oh, settle down."

The words came out of my mouth, but this wasn't me giving myself a pep talk. This was the voice in my head. Not my voice.

"You're acting like an infant." She tutted at me. Or rather, I did.

I wanted to call my mother. She was the one person I knew who might understand what the heck I was dealing with. Actually, I probably needed an exorcist more than a witch, maybe a voodoo priest. Someone.

"Where is my thought book?" My voice was quite demanding.

Thought book? The journal.

"Where's Renegade?"

That one didn't take a whole lot of explanation.

"Ariya?" I asked because I wanted to make sure I was fully over the edge.

My voice sniped back at me. "You're not altogether sharp, are you?"

To anyone outside of our conversation, anyone who wasn't me, anyway, it would only look like I was talking to myself, but I had a whole other person in my head.

"Am I possessed?"

"Dramatic, aren't you?" I shook my head. Or she shook my head. "You aren't possessed. You are bonded." She paused and a bolt of triumph covered me. Her triumph. "To me."

"Bonded?" I didn't know what it meant. A girl in this situation could never have too much clarification.

"I didn't know if it would work." I was smug. "It was such a bold idea." I could feel her pride.

"What does *bonded* mean?"

She threw my head back and laughed. There weren't words created to describe this sensation of having her thoughts in my head, her emotions.

"It means you read a bonding spell aloud. You called to me." Once again, her triumph felt like a bolt in my belly. "Here I am."

I wondered if she would be receptive to the idea of giving me the unbinding spell.

"I would not."

Wonderful, she could hear my thoughts. Interesting. Fair, too, I supposed since I could hear hers.

"Yes."

"You blocked me, didn't you?"

She laughed. "Because you're a prude. I wanted to fornicate."

Fornicate? "With Will?" Now I was seething. "You had sex with Will and blocked me from it, used my body and I… have no memory?" How rude.

"You're so crude." She shook my head at me again and sounded properly aghast. She was the one doing the deed and using my vagina to do it. I felt cheated.

It made me petulant. "You're the one who brought up fornicating." This was not the amusing fun time it might have sounded. I was irritated.

Things would've gotten louder had we not been in my head and had there not been a knock on my door.

It wasn't Delilah, but Cami who called out. "Open the door, Ember. It's us."

"Us?"

It wasn't me talking in my head this time. "Get rid of them, or I'll turn them into toads."

"Fine." I hissed at her, then opened the door. Cami brushed past me, then Delilah came in, slower, quieter, without Delilah's dramatic stomp of heels, or her loud huff of breath.

"What's up?" That was me asking, but the disapproval in my head was loud and mimicking me, answering *with the sun, the sky, the number of poxes on that woman if you don't get rid of them.*

Cami's brow pinched. "What's up?" She looked at Delilah. "Where's the journal? Have you talked to your mother?"

There was no way to get word to them, to let them know that I was being held captive in my own mind—or maybe it was my mind being held captive—by a dead and somewhat sarcastic dead witch I'd bonded with thanks to the fact I'd read something aloud in the journal that I shouldn't have.

I couldn't give them the journal because we could all end up bound to a critter we couldn't get rid of.

"I haven't been able to talk to my mother." When they both stared like I'd just confessed to armed robbery, I added, "She's on a lot of pain pills right now."

She wasn't. She didn't even believe in them, but Delilah and Cami didn't need to know it.

You lovely little liar, you. Get rid of them.

Ignoring her, I looked at Delilah and put my hand on my stomach, before making a face. "I'm really not feeling well right now."

I walked closer to the door, but Delilah eyed me. "You're still in your dress and corset."

Looking down, I kicked my leg out from beneath the skirt. "The boots." I probably hadn't needed to announce that but... This was a weird day in a collection of weird days, and I wasn't thinking clearly.

I stayed by the door, thinking that if I didn't move further into the room, they wouldn't, and I could get them out of there. I was wrong. Delilah made herself at home, sitting on the edge of the bed, legs crossed, one swinging up and down.

"What are your symptoms?" She asked me, her leg swinging like she was a Rockette.

"Terrible nausea." I held my stomach with one arm and covered my mouth with the opposite hand.

"You seem fine." She narrowed her eyes.

Cami nodded, then moved to look at me. "Not pale at all."

I shook my head. "I think it's the curse. My stomach is rumbling. It feels explosive."

At the word curse, Cami's eyes widened. "Oh, f-f-s."

Delilah rolled her eyes. "Pardon her. She's trying not to f-bomb."

"It's effin killing me." Cami widened her eyes.

I nodded. I was never big on swearing, but these last few hours could've made a priest cuss. "You guys should probably save yourselves. The smell…"

The voice in my head guffawed.

Cami moved toward the door, and Delilah followed. Thank goodness.

"I'll see you tomorrow."

I shut the door as soon as they were out.

"I need you to do a spell with me."

"No." I hadn't meant to do the first one, and I certainly wasn't doing one voluntarily until I knew what I was dealing with. “Unless it’s going to send you back to wherever you came from, forget it.”

“I can make you.”

“No, you can’t.” I didn’t know that to be true. I had no idea what she could do. While I also wasn’t itching to find out, I wasn’t giving in to her.

Ariya Thornbridge had other ideas. She smacked me with my own hand. I couldn’t even fight back. Not when she slapped me a second time. When she grabbed my hair with one hand, I pulled the hand under her control away with the one I controlled.

We were wrestling. “Stop it.” Thrashing one way, then the other as we battled for superiority inside my body.

“You will do as I say. You’re a peasant.” She was using my voice to shout at me.

“You’re a witch, not a queen. Peasant? Get out of my head.” I was holding one wrist, and she was fighting me for control. My body shifted and jerked. We, or rather, *I* crashed into the dresser, then the wall. I bounced off the door and sent the single chair in the room toppling.

There were going to be bruises all over my body and there was nothing I could do. This witch was tough. Was I? It was my body.

I would've finished it, but another knock sounded. "Doctor Thorn? Is everything okay?" It was Art from the front desk.

The answer was subjective, depending on his idea of okay. Certainly, the truth wasn't going to help anything.

I was still holding my wrist in my opposite hand. "I'm fine." My voice was high-pitched and thin because we were even fighting for that. I was winning the battle. Barely.

He knocked again. "Are you sure? Because if someone was in there holding you hostage. I think he would tell you to tell me that you're fine." Well, he certainly had a point, didn't he?

"I have to open the door." I whispered the words. "He's never going to go if I don't."

The pressure fighting my grip eased, and I dropped both hands, blew out a calm, slow breath, and opened the door.

Art smiled at me, then widened his eyes.

I smiled back at him and pushed the door open. He walked in, checked the bathroom, the closet, and under the bed.

When he stood and wiped his hands, I shrugged. "See? All good."

I caught a glimpse of myself in the mirror. My cheeks were ruddy, and my hair was matted on one side, sticking out in a clump. "You caught me changing is all. This dress is a bitch."

He cocked his head. Moved the door so he could look behind it. "Aha." He jumped into a karate position of feet spread to shoulder width, palms flat and perpendicular, and shoulders twisted to the side. When there was no one for him to pummel into next week, he straightened, smoothed his shirt, and glanced at me. "I think you're safe now." He said out loud as though he'd run the madness out of my room, but he had no idea what I was dealing with. Probably be better for both of us if I kept it that way.

I shut the door behind him and Ariya—in my head, using my voice—started in again. "I want to see my Renegade."

"He's not your Renegade." I assumed she meant Will. I was still burnt from her using my body to... *do* the man she thought was Renegade. I wondered—briefly because I didn't want her to know how much it bothered me—if Will had been himself or if he was bonded to Renegade, and if he had a memory I didn't.

She wasn't listening. She was chanting in my head. *Renegade. Renegade. Renegade.*

As if she'd summoned him, Will was the next one to knock. I smoothed my hair before I answered this time.

It wasn't me who pulled him into the room, who locked our mouths together.

Not that I fought it.

She pushed him onto the bed. Pounced to straddle his hips.

I jumped back to stand, and he sat up. "It isn't me, Will."

He nodded and smiled, pulling me close. "Aye."

I had a feeling it wasn't Will, either. "What have you done with Will?" I wasn't sure which one of them I was talking to, but it wasn't like either was going to answer. They were making out again.

He went for the skirt, moved one layer, then a second, and I slapped his hand. "Will?"

Me mangav tut. *Say it.*

"No." I could've screamed it for all the listening anyone in that room or my head was doing.

Say it. Me mangave tut. *Say it.*

If I ever saw this broad in person—like if she jumped into someone else's body and I knew for certain it was her—I was going to punch her in the face.

Say it. Say it. Me mangave tut.

"*Me mangave tut.*" She was winning the voice battle now.

As soon as she spoke the words, his kissing grew deeper, and the hand pawing at the costume's full skirts—plural, as in more than one, more than two, and more than three—became more persistent.

When his hand touched my skin, I was aware he had no idea it was me, and part of me was wounded. The other was excited, lusting, grinding my hips into his through four layers of cotton and polyester.

"Stop." That was me.

"Shut up." That was her.

Will, or maybe it was Renegade, looked up at me. "My love."

That was all it took. She shoved me to the far recesses of my mind. I couldn't see or hear or feel any of the things happening at the moment. I clawed—in my mind—fought, screamed inside my head, and still nothing. She cried out. Sensations took my body—a scream, a pleasure so intense I curled into it—or I thought I did.

The line between us was blurring. I clung to it for a second because the sensation was incredible, and could've easily become an addiction, but I had to figure out how to unbind myself.

I yanked her control away—had no idea how I did it—when Renegade came out from under my skirt, unfastening his pants, I put a hand on his chest. "Whoa, big boy."

He grinned with Will's face. "I am no horse, lady. Although," —his grin morphed to a smirk—"there are similarities that canna be denied if you care to have a look."

I shook my head, not caring to point out that any similarity between his body and a horse's was thanks to Will, not Renegade. I didn't think Renegade would care for the logic. "Thanks, but no."

"I'm gonna have to ask ya to bring my Ariya back and be gone. I need release." He gave a hip thrust and leered. "Or you can stay, and I'll be happy to please ya again and again and again." His grin widened. "Again."

I didn't know if it was arrogance or confidence or truth, but I was in control of my body now, and there would be no pleasing anyone. Instead, and to give myself a moment to get my head straight because Renegade's words from Will's body were potent, I adjusted my skirt. It also kept my hands busy, so I wasn't tempted to push him back onto the bed. "Sorry, big fella. You're going to have to take matters into your own hands. I'm in charge here now." I looked up.

There had to be a way to get Will back.

There isn't.

"Shut up." I muttered the words and rolled my eyes, then walked closer to the pirate, put my hands on his shoulders, and looked deep into his eyes. "Will, come back. It's your body."

Maybe he doesn't want to come back.

This time, I ignored her and repeated my words to Will. It took a couple more times and a few solemn shakes of his shoulders, but his eyes cleared, and I could see Will again.

"Is it you?" Because I wasn't certain, but I was hopeful. "Will?"

He nodded and sighed, swishing his finger in his ear. "He's singing in my head. How do I make it stop?"

Oh, how I wished I knew. "I think you just have to learn to tune it out."

He rolled his eyes. "Great."

It wasn't, but he would figure that out on his own. He wouldn't need me to tell him.

Chapter Seventeen

Don't Blame Me My Alter Ego Made Me Do It

At first, I thought we would be better off staying together. One room where we could remind each other to fight the powers inside of us that were trying to root us out. After he flirted with me the second time, I reconsidered the logic of it all.

He was alluring in ways women weren't meant to resist. That voice... whether it was his words or the pirate's, they lit a fire in my belly.

"What are we going to do?" Will asked, using the butt of his hand to rub his right temple. "I can't live like this." He shook his head. "How do I get him to shut up?"

If only I knew. Which I didn't. "I think you have to figure out how to ignore him until we can figure out how to get rid of them."

He sighed. This wasn't what either of us wanted to hear, but we were in a real situation. As unreal as it was.

"You're a beautiful woman, lass. How about we put those wide hips to use?"

I glanced at Will's body. "Fight him, Will, because he just called my hips wide, and even if he's the one who keeps talking, *you're* going to be the one who gets a black eye." I wasn't threatening him. I meant it.

"Oh, now, Lass. Wide hips are a sign of good breeding. Somethin' a man can curl his fingers into while he's getting his sword wet." He gave a solemn hip thrust of his own as he acted as if he was holding onto a pair in front of him.

"Will, I don't want to have to gag you. Fight harder." I was standing beside the small table in my room and Will-the Captain was sitting in the desk chair looking at me. I flipped through the journal. I was sure the answer was in this book, but I had no idea which one. Even if Google managed to translate it accurately, I doubted a witch, crafty and patient enough to get a descendant of hers to say it, would put the cancellation spell in the same book. If she did, she sure wouldn't label it for me.

"What are we going to do?" This time, it was Will.

I thought so anyway. I shook my head at him. "Maybe we should just let them go at it. They can get it out of their system." It wasn't the worst idea I'd ever had. "In my experience, once the guy gets the sex, he goes away, gets bored, forgets to show up." Whether that was everyone's experience, I didn't know. It had certainly been mine. "Maybe the pirate will get bored."

"What the hell kind of guys have you been with?"

Now it occurred to me how it sounded. Shameful. Embarrassing. "It doesn't matter." I shook my head. The only way out of this conversation was just to pretend it hadn't been said. In a matter of a couple of seconds, I'd told him we should have sex—as the pirate and the witch—then revealed how crappy I must be at it if I couldn't keep a man interested once it was over. Not my most shining moment for sure.

I tried to ignore the heat rushing to my cheeks. I didn't want it to acknowledge the heat that went with it either, but my entire body was warm, and I fanned myself with my hand. "Anyway, we should figure out how..."

He was smiling at me. Not the pirate's smirk, but Will's smile. "I would take one for the team."

Oh. Admissions like that certainly weren't going to help my focus or the temperature in this room. "We can table that issue for now." It was good to know. Maybe not knowing he thought of it as... taking it for the team. I cleared my throat like I would be able to clear my mind so easily. "Maybe we can reason with the witch and the pirate." It was an idea, one that was mostly unformed, untested, unfinished.

"What do we have to offer them?"

I shrugged. "We could let them tell their story to Delilah, make the movie authentic." Somehow we were standing close again, and I took his hand and put it over my heart. "We have them here."

He swallowed and looked down at his hand on my skin, where the dress pushed my boobs up. To his credit, he didn't get grabby. His fingers didn't even twitch. "Is that you... or Ariya?"

I thought it was me, but I wasn't generally the kind of girl who would put a guy's hand on my body. "Maybe it's both of us."

"Why would Delilah believe that there's a witch living inside of you, or a pirate inside of me?" In his defense, he didn't know everything about the jewels.

Delilah did. She knew they existed outside of the story. Plus, whatever it was the journal said to summon the ghosts of the dead to live inside of us. She had seen the jewels in action. She believed that the afflictions that Cami was currently facing were going to come around again and would possibly aim their power at her next.

This probably wasn't any more unbelievable than that.

Chapter Eighteen

Dead Witch Dating Service: Where Do I Sign Up?

I MANAGED to escape the room without succumbing to either the pirate's charms or Will's. Whether it was my feelings or hers, Will was looking better and better with every minute I was around him.

There was no defense to how appealing I found him, how attractive he was, which was ten times more striking than any man I'd ever seen before. At least, there were no defenses I knew of. I wanted to explore all that pull because I wanted to explore him. Whether it was me or Ariya directing that desire, I was the one in charge of it and it seemed I agreed.

I had managed to change out of my costume without falling into bed with Will, and I had a new respect for the women who'd lived back in earlier centuries, simply because they had to carry around all those layers of clothing. There was no way to hurry without exhausting myself, and I had to hurry. It felt like it anyway. Every minute I wasted was another where Ariya could figure out how to take control again.

The place was busy—it was resort season, *and* we were filming a movie—Eventually, I found Delilah and Cami in the restaurant. My mental well-being depended on getting this all done as soon as possible.

Delilah looked at me, almost surprised. "Hey. Are you alright?"

I nodded, even though I wasn't completely sure it was true. "I think the diary is mostly not useful. If used incorrectly could bring on catastrophic events." I had a witch living inside me, so I didn't think using catastrophic was an exaggeration.

"Did you get the pages sent to your mom?"

We'd agreed that we needed those Romani pages translated, and I had sent pictures. "I haven't heard back from her yet." She'd responded when she received them, but then she'd gone radio silent. Now I couldn't get a hold of her. I hoped she and her coven weren't out "bonding" themselves to whoever they could possibly summon. God only knew what my mother might have been doing with the pages if not. She'd been unpredictable for the sum of my entire life.

I looked at Delilah. "I think we ..."

In my head, Ariya was chanting again. *Renegade. Renegade. Renegade.*

Cami's brow was pinched. "Are you all right?"

I looked at her as the voice in my head continued. *Renegade. Renegade. Renegade.*

I gave a slight head shake like I could unhinge Ariya or knock her off her train of thought. When that didn't work and the chanting continued, I tried placating her. *If you shut up, I'll take you to Renegade when I'm through here.*

Still, she chanted. *Renegade. Renegade. Renegade.*

I didn't have anything else to bargain with but Will, who was still in my room because he didn't want to go to back to his until he knew how to stop the pirate—whose name was over-mentioned these days in my opinion and didn't need me to speak it—from taking over his body. Plus, I didn't mind him being there.

"I have to go." If they found my behavior erratic, there wasn't much I could do about it. The chanting was at a crescendo. At least, I hoped this was the peak because I couldn't take much more.

I hurried back to my room and was only moderately surprised that it was empty. Will and I had discussed sticking together until we got this worked out, but it wasn't like we'd pinky swore or anything. I shut the door as the chanting in my head continued.

“What do you hope to accomplish?” I was talking to no one.

“I want you to have what you want.” My own voice answered because I wasn’t fighting her handle on it.

“What is it you think I want?” She had access to all my private thoughts, probably my dreams, my desires. Plus, she had access to my body. My heart rate, my sweaty palms, my damp… other places. There was no keeping her out. I didn’t really know the point in asking.

“You want the pretty little rich boy. The young Remington.” My face smiled, although I didn’t do it. “See? Just hearing his name, or saying it, makes you warm, makes your heart glad.”

My heart had nothing to do with it. “It’s funny, that you think, you know, what I want.” I didn’t even know.

“What you *desire*.” She said the word like it had an entirely different meaning.

“Well, he-he’s-he’s…” She was right. There really wasn’t much to say or a reason to argue. Especially since she was inside my head.

“You should have him.” The voice was mine, though I was *almost* certain she was the one talking. “Maybe if you lifted up your skirt for a minute and let your pretty boy crawl under it every once in a while, you might not be so uptight.” She spoke with the haughtiness of her century, the vernacular of mine, and the confidence I sometimes wished I had.

"I don't even know if I'm what he wants." A man who looked like Will, was kindhearted like Will, and had a body like his could have any woman he wanted. While there was no denying I wanted him, there was also no way I was ever going to be courageous enough to ask for it.

"When a man looks at a woman with such lust and desire in his eyes, there's no denying what he wants."

I sighed because there was nothing I wanted to believe more.

As shameful as it was, I was about to ask the witch in my head for advice on men. Thankfully, before my desperation overloaded my vocal cords, someone knocked on the door.

I sighed and walked around the end of the bed and twisted the knob, then stood back as my mother, in a wheelchair, rolled into the room followed by a nurse.

Because things just weren't quite bad enough.

Chapter Nineteen

Don't Be Afraid to Steal: Steal the Right Stuff

SHE ROLLED IN, but it was like a breeze. She had that effect on rooms. When my mother was in a place, the air was lighter. She claimed it was her aura. It was more.

"There's a presence in this room, Ember." Apparently, being from Boston and having that accent was not good enough for my mother. Now she'd switched it up. Romani was the accent of the day.

"A presence?" I had spent most of my childhood smelling sage, so much I could hardly eat Stove Top stuffing. I wasn't going to tell her anything until I had to. I needed to find out what she knew and how to get rid of the witch's voice in my head.

My mother looked at me, waved me closer so that I leaned down. “Does she know what I did?”

I sighed and looked up at the nurse. “Has she had pain medication?”

The nurse shook her head. “She says it clouds her vision.”

I really wasn’t one to throw stones since I was the one sharing headspace with the ungrateful dead, so I glanced at Mom. “What did you do, Mom?”

If it was something that was going to require legal advice once we returned to the United States, it was better I found out now. I did better when I worked under pressure, when the to-do list was piled high with unchecked tasks, when there were multiple issues that needed to be handled. At least that’s what I told myself, partly because the number of things I had to worry about was getting a little steep.

She sighed, sucked in a long inhale, and blew it out slowly. “I stole the Remington jewels from the museum collection.” She cocked her head. “I had them stolen.”

My mother, the mastermind of a jewel heist? No. That kind of thing didn’t track. “What now?”

“I needed money.” She cocked her head. “*We* needed money.”

Of course, it stood to reason I was going to take some of the blame.

“You ripped off a museum?”

"Technically... yes." Technically. It was her excuse word. Technically, the milk was only a day past the expiration date when she served it to me for breakfast. That was her kind of thing. "I'm here now to make it right."

Well, there was that. I nodded. "Thank you." The chanting in my head was loud. Romani. Growing louder by the second.

She closed her eyes and bowed her head. "The stones have to be returned to the sea in the handle of the dagger."

"Does this mean anything to you?" I stared at Mom as the words repeated again. "*Tace gura sit ace mintea. Păstrează secretele a tot ce găseşti...*" Ariya went silent except for the laughter.

I glanced at my mother. She'd gone silent, stared blankly at nothing, her mouth slightly agape.

"What did you do?" I spoke the words into the silence of the room, the silence that should have been full of my mother's accent—the real Boston one or her new Romani one—as she explained the meaning of whatever I'd just said.

Ariya laughed again.

The woman who had come in with my mother, looked at me and, like she was in a trance, she said, "Silence the mouth and silence the mind. Keep the secret of all that you find."

Just my luck. The witch in my head was the Doctor Seuss of spell casting.

"Undo it, or I swear, I will never touch Will again." Suddenly, she didn't have anything to say. I could've heard a pin drop in my mind. I knew she was there, I could still feel her.

I walked toward Mom, put my hand in front of her, and snapped. Once. Twice. She didn't even blink. "Shit." The nurse was standing near my medical bag. "Hand that here."

The bag was black and leather, had a gold, quarter-moon shaped clasp that slid into a rounded loop on top, it had all my instruments—stethoscope, reflex hammer, otoscope, tongue depressors, portable blood pressure cuff and sphygmomanometer, an O2 sensor—diagnostic tools that could be useful in an emergency. Every doctor had a bag stuffed with these things. Mine was the old TV prop kind. Mom found it —or possibly stole it now that I thought on it—from an antique store.

I listened to her heartbeat, checked her reflexes, and took her blood pressure. All was normal. I was willing to bet that while I was hearing voices in my head, my mother was trapped in her own wondering why she couldn't hear anything but her own thoughts.

"Ember?" She looked at me. "What are you doing?"

She flicked a finger at the stethoscope hanging around my neck.

"Uh… are you okay?"

"Of course, I'm okay. I'm..." She looked around the room. "Where am I?"

"Pararey Island." I cocked my head and looked at her, because sometimes I thought the world might look better with my head tilted. That wasn't true, but I didn't know why my head sometimes cocked. It was medical or physiological. Maybe it was mental. I wasn't sure but thinking about it in that second made me feel less crappy about whatever had just happened to my mom.

"Did you or I win a vacation?" She looked back at the nurse. "Who is that?"

"That's your nurse, Mom. Remember? You fell and broke your hip? At some point, the two of you decided to come here." She looked at me, then again at the nurse who had her hand raised.

"I'm not a nurse. I'm Raine. From the coven." Again, she sounded like she was in a trance.

Of course she was. Raine from the coven. Why would my mother bring a nurse when she could bring another witch wannabe?

Raine looked at me. "Your mother is my friend." It had to be a speech quirk because she still spoke in a very low monotone and didn't look at me as she spoke.

"Oh. Okay."

"I am also a nurse." This whole speech thing was weird, but probably not the weirdest thing in the room right now, so I didn't comment.

I would deal with her later. Instead, I looked at my mother, smiled and pulled out my phone, typed some words into the search engine, then into Google Translate, and prayed there was enough signal strength for this thing to work. "Mom, do you know what *Sar čo anav?* means?"

She shook her head. "No, should I?"

She should have. "Maybe."

"It means 'what is your name?' in Romani." The nurse smiled like she had passed my test.

Mom looked at me, her confusion visual in the pinched brow and narrow eyes. "How did I break my hip? Was I baking a pie, at least?"

My mother had never baked a pie in her life. "Baking a pie?"

She shrugged. "I don't know. I just feel like I was baking a pie."

I didn't want to ruin her Martha Stewart daydreams, but the idea of my mother baking a pie was as out there as normal mothers casting spells. "You weren't baking a pie."

If I ever got my hands on Ariya Thornbridge, I was going to find a way to punish her, ensuring she could take it back to the underworld with her.

In my head, she laughed. "Such a temper for a healer."

"Shut up." Instead of quieting, she laughed louder—cackled—in my head.

My mother's head whipped toward me. "Em?"

I held up a hand. The last thing I needed was for my mother to figure out exactly what was going on with me. "It's fine, Mom." I glanced at the mirror and saw Ariya staring back at me, with her expression on my face. "You're had now, sister."

Mom was still staring at me like I'd lost my mind. "Honey, do you need to see Dr. DuLong?"

I hadn't seen Dr. DuLong since I was eleven. "Why would I need to see a child psychiatrist?"

My mother widened her eyes and pursed her lips. She remained silent. I could feel her judgment. Since it was a first—in my entire life—I stared for a second. "I'm fine, Mom. Thank you, though."

The key to all of this was in the journal and there was only one person I knew who could help me figure this out, the only person, aside from her coven, none of whom I knew or trusted, who spoke fluent Romani. I just needed her to remember that she could do it.

When I handed the journal to her, she ran her fingertips over the cover. "I can feel it."

"Feel what, Mom?" I shook my head, and it must've been muscle memory. There wasn't anyone in this room who believed more in magic than I did. I had it *living* inside of me. Aside from me, my mother was the most magically endowed and to see her without her power now was sad in a way my heart couldn't comprehend. I watched her, and she looked up with tears in her eyes.

"Power, love, grief."

I hadn't felt any of that, but I wasn't as intuitive as my mother. "Can you find a way to help me?"

"Yes." She was confident. Because of course she could. When I needed something, anything, then this was what she did. She came. She assessed. She fixed. Without fail. She had magic inside of her, whether she remembered it or not.

She opened the book, and I laid my hand on the page. "Don't read anything out loud."

She nodded. "Of course."

"I'll be in the bathroom." I walked in and shut the door, went straight for the mirror. I liked seeing who it was I was yelling at. Especially when that someone lived inside of me. "Let my mother go."

"I cannot. She's here to unsettle my plans."

Unsettle? My mother was going to expel this evil from my body, send her to that great big witch trial in the sky. Or lower, probably.

If Ariya wanted to go with *unsettle,* we could use her word. "You can't just take over someone's body."

She laughed. I was tired of hearing it, but I couldn't stop her. "I can. I did. It's your own fault." Hard to argue when she was right. "You stole the thought book. You read It." She smirked at me with my own face. "Aloud."

I didn't like this woman. Couldn't wait to be rid of her.

"You're no prize either," she practically hissed. "There were others before you, better ones, you know."

"You've done this before?" There was really no reason for me to believe that I was the first, but I had believed it wholeheartedly. Now I felt foolish.

"The woman who was called upon by the museum to authenticate the journal also read it aloud." She shook my head. "Curiosity seems to be a genetic flaw."

"How the hell do you know about genetics?" I shot myself a glare, but I could vaguely see Ariya behind the mask of my face, so it counted.

She cocked my head. "I have had many a hosted bond. For two centuries. I learned things."

Oh good. "Like what?"

"Like how to blend in when I was in control." She sounded proud. "How to make men bend to my will. How to research and find my jewels." She sounded so full of herself, I wanted to smack my own face. "I'm not going back into the darkness. I'm staying and my Renegade is staying. I will never let the magic that has brought us back together go free."

If she thought that was the end of it, she had another thought coming.

Chapter Twenty

My Demons Don't Play Well With Others

I DIDN'T WANT to call Delilah or Cami, since it was after midnight when my mother finally fell asleep. Plus, I sounded like a crazy woman. Of course, any one of us who told our story to anyone who wasn't one of us would sound crazy. We were all in this together, but theirs wasn't necessarily the comfort I wanted. Or needed.

Instead, I waited until my mother fell asleep, snuck out like a teenager breaking rules. Specifically, like one who was sneaking out to see a boyfriend. Not that *that* was what I was doing. I wasn't.

I was, in fact, sneaking down the hall to Will's room, looking in front of and behind me like I'd been cast to replace Tom Cruise in Mission Impossible 27.

My hands were shaking. Could've been adrenaline. Could've been anticipation. I pushed it back long enough to knock.

When he answered, he was wearing a t-shirt and a pair of knit pajama pants. I didn't mean to stare, but I did. I couldn't help it. I'd seen him mostly in the pirate garb these last few days, so this was a nice change. Super sexy.

I shook off the thoughts, unsure if they were mine or *hers*. "Hi."

"Hey." He smiled and my heart pitter-pattered. "Come in?" He stepped back and held the door open wider.

I walked past him and tried not to inhale the scent of his soap or his cologne. At the last moment, I breathed in and could've swooned. He smelled clean and fresh and edible.

I wasn't here to lick him. Although the temptation was real.

When I was inside and he'd shut the door, Ariya was pushing me to run to him. At least it felt as if I should be running with how hard she was trying to get me to move. Instead, I planted myself against the desk and held onto it. This was my body, dammit. We weren't doing anything that would compromise my...

I stood and took a step.

We were *not* doing this again.

"Did you just come to visit?" He'd moved to stand within groping reach, and I curled my fingers around the edge of the desk.

The word yes was clogged in my throat. You should just lick him. Go ahead. Lift his shirt and run your tongue over his nipple. Men like that, too.

Now I was getting sex advice from her. I shook my head. "Can you ask Renegade if there's a dagger I should know about?"

The words sounded strangled from my throat. Ariya was fighting hard for control, probably because Renegade was bonded in his body. Or at least squatting there and she'd figured out how to call him forth.

Before I could explore the theory, or Ariya could take control and force the exploration of the theory, Will smiled up at me. "Of course there's a dagger." Will widened his eyes and held up his hand. "Uh, that wasn't... me."

I nodded. "That's okay. I kind of need to talk to him, anyway." I smiled when Will nodded. The change happened quickly, and I wondered if it was as visual to others when Ariya took over. "Captain? Renegade?"

"Aye." He reached for me and pushed his hand into my hair, held me in position as he lowered his head and brushed his mouth over mine. "Where's my love?"

"I need to talk to you." I pulled back. Ariya wasn't just fighting, she was brawling inside of me. I was expending a lot of unnecessary energy.

He nodded and crossed his arms, stood with his feet apart like he was about to stand at the bow of his ship and direct the guy running the wheel. Well, that was how it looked in my head.

"Can you tell me about the dagger?"

"It was mine before... the mutiny. I was forced to walk the plank." His accent would've sounded odd had I not been listening to it every day as we filmed. "There were three stones in the hilt. A blue sapphire, a golden citrine, and black onyx."

"Could you draw it?" If there was a drawing for me to show around, maybe I would be able to find someone who'd seen it. There's certainly been no mention of it in the journal.

"Aye. Get me a quill."

A quill? I turned to the desk and slid the drawer open. Just like my room, Will's had a pad of paper and a pen, each with the resort logo. He gave the pen a look and put it to paper. I took it, removed the lid, and handed it back.

He drew for a couple of seconds. He was quite good. Even with an ink pen rather than a quill. "Does the dagger have anything to do with putting the stones back to the sea?"

"I don't know."

Then Renegade moved toward me again. "I've missed the company of a woman." He reached for my breast.

I slapped his hand away, but Ariya pushed my chest out. "You just banged... Ariya the other day."

He reached for the other breast this time like I'd been unsure based on which side he was grabbing. "No, lass. She fornicated with the body I'm in. I wasn't there yet."

Please. I'll be kind to you for the rest of the day. Just let me kiss him. Let me feel his body against mine.

I was having a weak moment. Had to have been that because I nodded. Let her throw herself against him. She moaned and ground my body against his. I tried to ignore it, but I could feel the sensations of his hands, and his... erection against my belly.

It wasn't Will kissing me or me kissing him. It was them in our bodies and as progressive as I was, as in touch with life, I couldn't let this go on.

"Stop." I moved back, and held up a hand when Renegade-Will tried to pull me close again.

I grabbed the picture he'd drawn, turned to the door, and walked out. When I was in the hallway, I fell back against the wall and tried to catch my breath, but it took a minute.

When I moved to go back to my room, Cami came walking toward me.

"We need to talk. All of us," I told her because the sooner we all had the information, the quicker we could finish this and get back to what and who we were before we all got caught up. Well, as soon as the movie was finished filming.

Chapter Twenty-One

Can't Get You Outta My Head

Delilah, Cami and I met in Delilah's suite. It was bigger—she was the director of the movie being shot at the resort where we were all staying—and full of premium amenities. Namely alcoholic beverages.

Delilah had a screen set up and linked to her tablet so she could view the dailies. It was new terminology for me, as I had no idea what a daily was, or why she needed to view them, but she had her script open and was making notes.

Her hair was in disarray, as though she'd run her fingers through it over and over. She looked up. "The card they used on camera 3, all the freaking closeups of everything shot today is on a dead card." Her voice was shrill, angry. She was Delilah

Bradbury, and she had a dramatic tone to play. "It's all going to have to be reshot."

Cami, whose hives seemed bigger today and who had what looked like a bad case of pink eye, looked up. "It's the curse."

"More likely an incompetent camera operator." She muttered under her breath.

"What is the emergency?" Cami ignored Delilah's explanation and looked at me.

I pulled out the drawing and handed it to her. She stared for a second, then passed it to Delilah.

Delilah glanced at me, her brow pinched. "What's this?"

"The dagger that we need to send the stones back into the sea with." In the category of statements I never thought I would say, that hit the list. "Have you run across it at all?" She'd done research for the movie.

"No." Cami answered quickly. "Remy might know." She shrugged. "He's still on the mainland."

Delilah sighed. "I might know someone who's seen it." She worked an eyebrow and stood, swiping her hands down her pants legs.

She walked to the bedroom, disappeared behind the door, returning quickly with her hot Cajun boyfriend.

I handed him the picture of the dagger and he studied it, staring until I was almost certain he'd stared the ink off the paper. When he handed the page back to me, it looked fine.

In my head, Ariya was going on. On. On. *It's him. Him. Him.*

Because they hadn't all seen my crazy yet and didn't know I'd used the journal to rent space in my head to Ariya, I didn't ask her what she was talking about. I very seldom got a straight answer from her anyway.

"I haven't seen it before. It wasn't with the jewels when..." He stopped abruptly, like his words had crashed into a wall. "It wasn't with the jewels."

In my head, the noise was overwhelming. Loud.

Marcel. Marcel. Marcel. Marcel. She was screaming the name over and over in my head. *Say it. Marcel. Say it. Marcel.* Louder and louder, her voice rang through my head. *Marcel.*

I tried tuning her out, but she was persistent. *Marcel. Say it.*

When she bellowed again, I shouted, "Marcel, dammit."

All other sounds in the room stopped. Didn't fade. *Stopped.*

"Who's Marcel?" Cami finally asked though she was looking at me with her one good eye like I'd lost my ever-loving mind. Maybe I had, but that was a problem for another day. We had to get through this day first. Right now, I had to figure out why Ariya wanted the world to know who Marcel was.

While I was waiting for Ariya to answer, the hot Cajun cleared his throat and looked at me.

"Marcel Devereaux is the treasure hunter..." He paused, and took a long, solemn breath. "The treasure hunter my crew stole the jewels from."

"You stole the jewels?" I hadn't meant to say it out loud, but he nodded.

"There was no dagger, though." He shrugged like he hadn't just confessed to grand theft.

These stones had brought us all here and now Ariya had her claws in deep, and I didn't know how much more I could take.

I pulled the onyx from my pocket and opened the tissue paper so that time stopped. That was just fine because I needed a minute alone with my inner witch, and I wasn't talking about the metaphorical one.

Inside me, though, before I could find the words to question her, panic swelled for any number of reasons.

I had voices in my head.

To send the jewels back to the sea, to the pirate, we had to have a dagger and had no idea where to look for it. It could've been anywhere in the world.

My mother was counting on me to bring her back—even if she didn't know it. Right now, though, I needed her to know it.

"You worry too much," Ariya said to me in the mirror.

"I want you out of my head." I hissed the words in a distraught whisper because I was a hundred percent distraught.

"Not a dream for me either," she tutted in my head. "I barely understand a single thought you have and you're so *loud*."

"Well, excuse me, but you're the interloper in my head space."

As if I hadn't spoken to her, she continued. "You don't ever have a fun thought at all," and like I might've missed the word the first time, she added, "Ever."

"By all means, go." I shook my head, tilted it to the side, and tapped the side facing up like maybe she would just fall out of my ear. "You've done it before, so go find someone new to torture." Although I would feel immensely guilty for passing this witch along to anyone else, I also thought it was probably guilt I could learn to live with.

"If only I could."

"Use the wishing stone." Why hadn't I thought of this before?

Maybe I could work out a switch with Cami.

“Doesn’t work that way.” She sighed like I was the one testing her patience. Like I was the one with the annoying voice. “Only a specific person can activate the stones. The stones chose you. They didn’t choose me.”

“Chose us?” This was new information.

“I might have assisted, but I was running out of time.”

“Helped?” She wasn’t the only one who was having trouble understanding.

“My last body was dying, but she was smart. A Thornbridge by birth, and she had a gift. She taught me things. Control. The internet. How to manipulate a situation.”

I wasn’t buying it. “She couldn’t have known Cami’s daughter would choose to have her wedding at the resort or that Delilah would buy her award show jewelry at a flea market, or that my mother would trip over the cat and break her hip.”

“Of course, I knew. I’m Ariya Thornbridge.” Perfectly haughty. Perfectly insulted.

I wanted more. I wanted the *how* of it. “How?” No better way to learn, than to ask.

“I put the spell on the stones.” However she’d done it, she wasn’t going to tell me. She would just keep walking me in circles until I gave up.

"How long do you plan on keeping this arrangement with me?"

My shoulders shrugged under her power, not mine. "It's only temporary."

"How. Long?" Temporary was too abstract. I needed the numbers.

"Twenty years at the most." She almost sounded sad. "It seems like once I make it in, everyone's in a big hurry to get rid of me." She wasn't what I would've called remorseful. She was more perplexed by it.

I was never going to survive twenty years with this woman talking in my head. "How do I get you out of my head?"

"Last one died. One before that killed herself." Now she was remorseful and the power of it brought a tear to my eye. "I liked her, enough that I tried to stop her."

None of this was good news for me. "I can't do this for twenty years, Ariya."

I walked back into the living area of the suite and looked at Cami, Delilah, and her man. I put the stone back in its tissue paper.

"We have to find that dagger," I told them. It couldn't happen soon enough.

Chapter Twenty-Two

I Want to be Invited, but I Probably Won't Come

While Will and I went to work on the movie with Delilah and her boyfriend, Cami, Remy (who'd shown up overnight), Penelope, and Arthur all went to the museum.

"Last night." Delilah handed Will and me each a few pages. "I wrote these. Obviously, we need to find the dagger, but if we don't, then in a couple of days I'll have the prop department contact someone on the mainland. For now, just focus on this, these lines replace the end." She said, indicating the pages she had handed us.

I nodded because what else was I going to say? The only part of it that concerned me as far as the movie was concerned was the new pages I had to learn and if I was honest, I didn't have to learn them.

We ran scenes for the day... discussed them, blocked them, tortured each other with "put your hand here," and "no, you're blocking her light," and "for god's sake, people, this is romance, not porn. Put the girls away."

It was that kind of day on set and all the while, I had Ariya in my head.

Unfasten his trousers. You won't be disappointed.

And...

Remington men are skilled at pleasing women.

There were more, but the others were bawdy and filled with innuendo. I tried to tune her out. I focused harder on listening to anything but her. I made sure my hands were busy and never near the flap of his trousers.

Will smiled at me. "Sorry you signed on now?" He was adorably bashful at the moment, and I'd never seen anything or anyone so attractive, and it had nothing to do with the leading suggestions Ariya was making in my head.

There was no way I could do a love scene right now. Not without embarrassing myself. I looked up at him and smiled back. "No. It's actually"—except for the annoying witch in my head—"been pretty great."

He nodded and shoved his hands in his pockets. I crossed my arms, but my closet top was weird today and my boob slipped up and out again.

I didn't notice it right away.

"Your..." He cleared his throat and pointed, then looked up at the ceiling—we were on the boat. "You're hanging out."

I looked down and with all the grace of a worldly doctor who'd graduated top of her class, muttered, "Oh shit," and tried to put the damned thing back in its cup.

The voice in my head guffawed. "Seriously? Was that you?"

I was talking to her, but Will held up both hands and backed away. "No. God, no." His refusal bordered on insulting. I cocked my head, and he shook his. "I mean, no. I didn't, not that I wouldn't like to." He crossed his arms, then gestured again to the runaway boob. "I would. They-they're nice."

Nice?

I would take nice. "Thanks?"

He sighed. "My point is, I don't just go around touching breasts. I like to be invited."

"Invited? Like with calligraphy and a card?" I grinned because it was nice not to be the only one who was embarrassed.

"I prefer embossed invitations. Sent in advance." At least he was playing along. He sighed again. "As you might have always guessed, I'm not the smoothest guy in the room." He nodded toward Nicky. "That guy is smooth."

"Man crush?"

"I believe the term is bromance." He nodded at Nicky. "I'd probably be smooth if I could speak the language of love."

He might not have been able to speak it, but he had the smolder, the look. I could've stared at him all day.

Of course, Delilah wasn't having that. She tapped me on the shoulder so both Will and I looked at her. "Brilliant day. Letting the girls out today was kind of brilliant, so you're not shy tomorrow, but tomorrow the set will be closed."

She thought I'd done it on purpose like I was some kind of exhibitionist. I wasn't. Not until the next shoot anyway.

"All right, kids." She wasn't that much older than me, but I let it pass. "Tomorrow is love scene day. Now we're only gonna see a bit of Will's ass, to about here"—she drew a line low under his waistband, "and some of your side boob." She reached and lifted my arm to indicate. "Unfortunately, you'll be mostly naked for that, so we can get the shots we need. If it needs shaved, shave it. Plucked, pluck it. Lotioned, lotion it." She smiled. "We have to film the scene from about twenty angles, so we don't want any whisker burn or chafing if you know what I mean."

"They plucked and shaved back then?" I asked, not because I cared, but because she'd been a stickler for authenticity since we started.

"Probably not like we do now, but no one wants to see that in a movie." Delilah laughed. "It will all be very tasteful, I promise. You won't be embarrassed to have your mother watch it." One of the assistant directors or producers brought over a paper she had to sign, so she paused to do it, then looked back at me. "We'll use soft lights and smudge the edges, maybe view it through a bent lens. Don't worry. You guys are going to look great."

I nodded, although I doubted a soft light or a bent lens would hide the fact that I wasn't a model and I liked carbs. I didn't care much, but the public I'd heard and seen could be brutal.

Delilah looked Will up and down. "You guys have a chemistry that is burning up the screen already. The first kissing scene was..." She shook her head slightly and blew out a quick breath. "I'm just saying..." Now she fanned herself. "We need more of that tomorrow."

She waggled her eyebrows at me and then walked away, so Will and I were staring at each other. At the same time, we turned away from one another and walked away. I returned my costume to the tent. They would take them to the room inside the resort, that was reserved for them.

I went back to my room and Mom was sitting in her wheelchair reading a copy of the script. "Isn't it funny, Em? We're

Thornbridges and you're in the movie about Ariya Thornbridge."

If I ever got my hands on Ariya Thornbridge… I had a thought. My mother would've had to do some research on the stones to know that they had to come back here. Some family research.

"How did you know that… *do* you know that?"

She chuckled and put the script in her lap. She had read to near the end, so the pages were curled around the back. "Oh, dear. Back when Aunt Charlotte and I were in school, she had to do a family tree project. She discovered it. Has the whole family traced back to England in the 1600s." She shrugged. "You should call her. Maybe she'll know something about the stones."

I wondered why she hadn't told me all of this in the beginning. "When's the last time you talked to Aunt Charlotte?"

Mom shrugged and waved a hand through the air. It was her new thing when I asked her a question she couldn't answer. "I don't know."

If she had talked to Charlotte recently, it had to be connected, and that was also why she couldn't remember it. Maybe Aunt Charlotte had told Mom something that had made her decide to come to the island, broken hip and all.

I picked up Mom's cell and looked at her history. She had called her, the day before she arrived on the island. I pushed the button to call her again. It rang five times and went to voicemail.

"Hi, Aunt Charlotte. It's Ember. Please call me back as soon as you get this, either on Mom's phone or on mine. Thanks." I hung up. She wouldn't call back. My mother and my aunt were the worst people in the world as far as callbacks. I would have to try again later.

I listened for the voice in my head to chime in, but she didn't, which was odd. "You in there?" I never really initiated conversations with her, but then again, I never really had to. She had opinions about everything. Knew everything. It was like having a teenager running around in my mind.

She didn't answer, and I looked at Mom. She'd been cooped up in the room all day because her "nurse" wanted to sightsee, and Mom didn't. Much of the island was dedicated to the movie right now. Mom said it wasn't worth the hassle of dragging her chair along.

The guilt was real. "How about dinner?"

She smiled and marked her page by folding it in half. It was why she wasn't allowed to borrow any of my books, but it made me smile. It was one of those things that I would always remember about her.

"I would love that." She said it as if she was surprised I'd asked.

It wounded me because it said I hadn't been a stellar daughter. Maybe it was because we had such very different belief systems. Or maybe it was because I thought I was better than her and now this trip had shown me that I wasn't.

I was definitely going to make it up to her.

As soon as we were back in Boston, I was going to take time, to be with her more. I only wished it hadn't taken me so long.

Chapter Twenty-Three

Hey Diddle Diddle

I WOKE in the morning with the sun on my face. Slowly, because I was never too quick when I first came awake, I realized that I couldn't have been in my room and been able to see the sunrise. My room faced the sunset.

My powers of deduction were also limited before my first cup of coffee, so it took a minute to figure out where I was. I figured it out because I reached behind me, over the blanket.

I felt the warm, hard, and bare chest of a man. I didn't have to check to know I was naked. I could feel the sheet against my skin. All of my skin.

This was one of those *what have I done* moments. I had no recollection of anything past eating dinner with my mother, going up with her in the elevator, going into our room, changing into my pajamas, and falling into bed exhausted.

It was a lot of work filming, memorizing lines, mystery-solving—or trying to—and having a second person with no off switch in my head. At all times.

I turned to look at him. No way had I been so asleep that the witch in my head had been able to take over my body and, for lack of a better way to phrase it... do Will.

He cleared his throat, and I met his gaze. "Will, um, good morning." When he went to answer, I held up my hand. "Did we..." I waggled my eyebrows, but he didn't answer. He was going to make me say it. "Have sex?" I whispered the word *sex* like we were in the 1960s and even people who did it didn't talk about it.

He looked under the blanket, lingered a second longer than made me happy and I yanked more of the duvet to my side. Which revealed that he was wearing as few clothes as I was. I tossed the blanket over him because I didn't need a repeat performance of whatever I didn't remember about last night. Naked Will was more than I could resist.

"I guess so? Maybe?" He breathed out. "Probably."

I was only forty. He was... I couldn't even think of the number, but it was a decade—an entire decade—younger. While my uterus wasn't optimal for childbearing anymore, it was still possible. "Do you think we used a condom?" Heck, I should have asked myself the first time we had sex if I'd been thinking properly.

"Not unless you brought one with you." We were both staring at the ceiling now. This was as awkward a morning-after situation as I'd ever been in.

"What do you remember?" Maybe he knew what happened. I tried again, searching my mind, but it was a great big black hole.

He shook his head. "Not much really." Didn't that figure? "I remember you came to my room in your robe. It was pretty sexy." He turned toward me, smiled that charming and adorably bashful smile that I so liked. "Maybe if we do it again, it will refresh our memories."

Shamefully, it took a glance at the clock—we were late—for me to make up my mind. I sprang out of the bed. "Delilah is going to kill us."

He nodded and leaned up on his elbow, staring at me. "It isn't like they can start filming the love scenes without us."

"Love scenes?" Oh, Lord. I'd forgotten. Hadn't shaved or plucked or lotioned. "I have to go get ready."

He grinned now and flipped the blanket back on my side so the spot I'd just vacated was uncovered. "Or we could rehearse some more."

I growled like I was a bear in the woods, then snatched the robe I had so far been unable to locate from the lampshade. I slid it on and tied the belt in a knot in case temptation tried for another shot at me. "I'm going to my room to shower, and I'll meet you downstairs."

He nodded, and I was out the door. Staying one more second, looking at him, wouldn't do more than make me reconsider—again—leaving.

I hurried down the hall, which was an obscene distance from my room since he'd had to switch for a plumbing problem. I held the top and the bottom of the robe closed as I went.

"For heaven's sake, Ariya. There's no way we are doing this crap for twenty years." I angry-whispered the words at the air. "You can't be using my body to diddle the pirate, who isn't the pirate, by the way. It's Will." A woman and man exited a room near mine, and I smiled at them like I wasn't batshit crazy and talking to myself. They would never believe I wasn't, and I wasn't sure I cared anymore. I was at that point. I just wanted this witch out of my head.

"He certainly *diddled* like Renegade." She was making fun of the word.

"For God's sake, did you at least use a condom?" It was a big deal. He didn't know my history. I didn't know his. Again, the pregnancy issue was still front and center in my mind.

"What is a condom?"

If ever there was a question that would make my mother's eyes spring open, it was that one. "Honey, we had that talk when you were twelve." As perplexed as she was, she didn't do much more than sigh and close her eyes again.

I walked into the bathroom and shed the robe then stepped into a shower.

"A condom is birth control. It also prevents diseases," I hissed at the shower head, trying to be silent but not sure I wasn't screaming. In my head, everything was loud.

"Birth control?"

I couldn't have this conversation with a Lady Schick in my hand. Maybe once I was shaved—I concentrated hard on that one—I could finish it, but by then I had to hurry and get to the set.

"I don't care what I have to do, I'm going to get you out of my head."

It took a second, but Mom knocked on the bathroom door. "Honey, who are you talking to?"

I sighed again, lower, from deeper in my lungs. "No one, Mom. Sorry. I'm just working on my lines."

When I finished my shower and was dressed, almost out the door, I looked at Mom. "Would you call Aunt Charlotte and ask if she has any information about Renegade's dagger?" She still didn't remember anything, but that was all the information she needed to get the details from Aunt Charlotte. Not that I had much more to say about it, because I didn't know more about it, and what I did know, I wasn't going to share with anyone outside of this island.

"I assumed you knew all about that already." She chuckled. "You got yourself all dolled up last night and walked out in that skimpy little robe, said you were going to see the pirate king. I assume you got to know his dagger quite well, considering your outfit and the fact you said not to wait up."

Oh, God. I'd told my mother—or Ariya had implied to my mother, anyway—that I was going down the hall to get laid.

I nodded and walked out, humiliated as much as I'd ever been, although I wasn't sure why.

On the bright side, it had been a long dry spell, well, since I'd had good sex, and I'd finally gotten lucky. There was that.

Unfortunately, I didn't remember it. I just had the witch's word that it was good… even though I believed her.

Chapter Twenty-Four

The Voices in my Head Have Been Drinking

I WALKED onto the set and Delilah didn't look at her watch or tap her wrist or make mention that I was late. She was either sick or had seen me traipsing to Will's room in my robe —it reached barely past the lower edge of my ass—and had decided we'd gone method with the acting and should have been given a pass.

She waved me over, and I was almost sure that my good luck had run out, but instead, she thrust a grainy photocopy of a grainy portrait of the captain. "Okay, so it occurred to me last night that I had done months and months of research, had pictures of the captain and the ship and the witch and the others that we used to create the sets and the ship and the costumes."

I pulled the picture closer to my face for a better look. If it was an accurate depiction, the resemblance between Will and the captain was incredible. Same hair. Same chin. Cheekbones. Lashes. Stance. "Yeah. Stone cold fox that one." I handed the picture back.

She scowled. *Scowled*. Deep and with narrowed eyes. "Look at the photo."

I took it back and looked again. "Okay. What am I looking at?"

She sighed like she was tired of dealing with idiots. I couldn't blame her, since I felt like the town idiot, but inside my head, there was some singing going on, and I was having trouble concentrating. Then Ariya, in my mind, said, "That man makes my thighs tremble."

"The dagger," Delilah told me, pointing to it in the picture. It had three colored jewels in the hilt.

"I'll be damned." I pulled the photo in again. "I'll be damned." It deserved to be said twice.

"There is a dagger." She pointed to the photo on the back side.

It wasn't that we didn't believe there was a dagger, we just hadn't found any proof of it until now.

I had to tell them about Ariya now. Especially if she could help us find the dagger. Even if she didn't want to. We would have to figure it out.

I'll never help you. I'm not going back to the way it was.

Oh yes, she was. Somehow. Some way. Didn't matter what I had to do.

"Well, you're not strumpetting your way through *my* life."

Delilah looked up at me. "What?"

Yeah. I said it out loud and she was staring like I'd grown a unibrow or a third breast that would radically screw up the costumier's job.

"We have to talk." I had to tell them now. I needed their help.

"We have a full schedule today." Yeah. I was aware. Love scene Day.

"After that. We'll talk *after*. You, me, and Cami." I couldn't stress enough how important it was, and I was prepared to beg because I had to be free of Ariya.

She nodded, then waved me back to the photo. "Look at the dagger."

"Yeah. I've committed it to memory." I handed the photo back as Will walked onto the set. "Let's do this."

By let's do this, I meant he looked very doable. Doable enough that from the first kiss, the first touch of his skin, I wasn't going to let Ariya have control. Not now.

The struggle between us popped the buttons off Will's trouser flap, gave him a bloody nose when my head thumped it in a particularly staunch battle to be the one who kissed him.

After we finished shooting, he walked with me to the costumier's tent. "You okay?"

"I'm good." I was still vibrating with need, and because I couldn't be sure if it was my desire or hers.

Before we got to the tent door, he pulled me around the side of the canvas and against him. "I have to go, Will. I have to talk to Delilah and Cami."

"You guys are pretty chummy." He smiled and brushed my hair. "Can I see you later?"

I didn't think it was a good idea. There was no guarantee that I would be able to control the witch inside me, and history had already shown that I was having difficulty in that area, so there was no telling what would happen, but maybe that wasn't such a big deal either.

If I subscribed to my mother's way of thinking—prior to the whole bad spell from the witch anyway—and the witch's, maybe Will and I were fated to be on this island at the same moment, at exactly the time Delilah was making a movie about our ancestors and how in love they were. Maybe history was destined to repeat itself.

Now you're talking. Unfasten those britches and get to business.

He lowered his head and kissed me. Soft and deep, his lips soft and gentle against mine. When he parted my lips, his hands came around my waist, and he pulled me in. When he lifted his head and opened his eyes, I breathed out slowly. "Was that you or... someone else?"

He smiled. "That was all me. Why, have you been going around getting kissed by other guys dressed like pirates?"

Either he was teasing me, or something about the spell made him forget. Regardless, I wasn't about to explain to him that there was a pirate in his head. "No." Maybe I could check what he knew and didn't know. "Do you ever feel like we're slipping away, and the pirate and the witch are taking over our lives?"

I didn't mean the question to sound like I was being possessed. Thankfully, he didn't do more than grin. "I don't care who takes over so long as I get to kiss you again." He did.

"You did what?" Delilah glanced at me, eyes wide, mouth half hanging open.

Cami, on the other hand, cocked an eyebrow. “She summoned one of her ancestors who apparently has some serious magic bones and now said ancestor is living in her head.” She said it as if she didn’t have a single question.

“Right.” I wanted to communicate with them that I needed their help to get rid of the aforementioned witch, but I couldn’t say it without alerting Ariya and I was already exhausted from a day spent trying to wrestle her for control. “She cast a spell on my mom that removed all memory of her magic, of who she is. She’s upstairs right now reading recipes for pineapple upside-down cake. If you knew my mom, you would know that just isn’t her.”

“And?”

“And... I want my mom back.” I sighed because the pain in my heart was real. “You know, I always thought her hippy magic stuff was annoying, but without the hope of her magic, I’m... lost.” It came to me, and I tried not to think about it. “I have to go and talk to... the witch.”

They’d heard my issue. Now I needed to go talk to Ariya. As soon as the elevator doors closed and I was alone, I smiled. “You know, I’ve always counted on my medicine to help my patients. One time, there was a boy who came in. He was young. Ten. Someone’s son.” I was trying not to think, but I continued talking to myself through the mirrored door. “The medicine failed him. Failed me. He was going to die, I’d done everything I could. Tried everything I knew to do, and it was for nothing. He got worse." I swallowed hard. His name was Jeffrey Parker. "I went home, and I cried to my mother."

Is there a point to this?

"I had given up. All that was left for me to do was to tell his family he wasn't going to make it." It had been the worst day of my life. "When I got to the hospital that morning, my mother was there. She asked me to hold her hand, to chant with her." I hadn't known what the words meant, but she was trying to help, and it was just another example of all the times she'd been there for me. "An hour later, he woke up. Today he is a bright and happy 14-year-old. Thanks to my mother and the family bloodline."

Your story isn't going to work. I know you're only telling me this so you can take my body back and send me to the darkness. I won't go. I won't.

I hoped those were famous last words, but I had a really bad feeling.

Chapter Twenty-Five

Never Let a Fool Kiss You, or a Kiss Fool You

LATER, while my mother had dinner with Penelope, Arthur, and the pig, I was still in my dressing room on the set—which was just one of the cabanas on the beach.

The cabana itself was round, with a pointed top and enough room for me to dress and undress and a rack to hang the clothes. It had a vanity and a couple of chairs, a small refrigerator that was plugged into a power strip that was plugged into an orange extension cord that ran under the wall of the cabana. There was a flap on each side, and unless I was changing, I kept the seaside open.

I could see the "ship" and watched it rocking. That gentle motion had been nice today, soothing. The water was choppy tonight, and there were whitecaps on the tops of the ripples farther out.

Further down the sand at the cove, the water crashed against rocks covered in green and black slime and sprayed onto the wall of the cliff above. There was something about this place that seemed magical more than the witch inside me and the stones that were infused with her power.

Will, still in his costume, stood in the doorway. "Knock, knock." He came walking somewhat drunkenly inside and pulled his chair closer to mine. There was always something beautiful about him, but tonight he was different. I couldn't imagine why he was still in his costume, but it didn't really matter what he wore. He looked good.

He grunted and sat hard beside me. "You're not my Ariya."

I straightened because the conversation had barely started and already we'd taken a sharp left turn. "Excuse me?" His Ariya? Oh, God.

He tipped back a flask of what I could only assume was something alcoholic, swiped the back of his hand over his mouth, and smiled at me. Breathed out heavily.

Oh yeah. That was alcohol. I didn't know what kind, but I could smell the sharpness of it.

"My Ariya." He put his finger in his ear as if he thought by cleaning out his ear I would hear better. I didn't have a problem hearing. Mine was more with comprehension. Jiggling the ear wax wasn't going to solve that.

His voice was deeper, his posture more relaxed. The accent wasn't American. "Will?"

"Will? My name is Captain Renfro Remington." His smile was wide, definitely one of Will's, but a little sharper. "You don't sit straight enough to be my Ariya."

I straightened. Looked at him. "I wouldn't know." It wasn't the kind of thing I paid a lot of attention to. I was more set on figuring out how to get her out of my head.

"I would like for you to pour me some rum." He held out his flask as if I should take it.

"There is no rum." I wasn't a waitress, and certainly not his.

"There's always rum."

"Not today." Ariya is fighting me.

Let me hold him.

I pushed her back.

Please. Please.

He turned sideways on his chair, pushed his legs apart, and pulled my chair closer, so it was between his legs. I could've swooned because he looked like Will and he wore Will's cologne, and for all intents and purposes, he *was* Will.

Ariya was begging inside of my head, and she was purring in between. More so when he slid closer, rested an arm on the back of my chair so his hand was dangling over the side, and then used his free hand to turn my head toward him, threading his fingers into my hair.

This was a pirate with moves. I was… captivated. Maybe because of Ariya. Or Maybe not.

"Captain?"

"Aye."

We were both speaking softly, almost breathlessly. "Ariya is…"

She won the battle and pressed our-slash-my mouth against his. His fingers massaged my scalp, and he pulled me closer until I was on his lap.

When we pulled apart, I smiled because I was back in control. "Well, now I know what the fuss is about." Pirate or actor, this was a guy who knew how to kiss.

"Aye."

He kissed me again and this time, dragged his mouth from mine over to my jaw and then down my throat.

"Oh." I couldn't manage more than that right now.

"My love…"

Please.

"Take me to my dagger, Ariya. I want to be done with this bumbling oaf's body." He put his hands on my shoulders and she got control again because his touch weakens me.

I pushed her back. My will is strong because I needed to stay in this conversation. "What are you going to do with it?"

He smiled and smoothed my hair on both sides. "I'm going to take us back to the sea. We can be together there for eternity."

"No." It was her again. "I'm not giving up the body until..." She stopped.

Even the white noise I assumed was her fault, which always seemed to be ringing inside my head, had gone silent.

Chapter Twenty-Six

Well, Well, Well. If it Isn't the Consequences of My Actions

I WAS a little slow on the uptake, a little annoyed that I hadn't figured things out sooner, and that I had to stay awake to keep Ariya from using my body for her nefarious, sleazy behavior.

Of course, the more I tried to stay awake, the more tired I became, the heavier my eyelids. I was tired of waking in strange places—not so strange since it was Will's bed, and I was working really hard to not look or sound like it was a place I wanted to be found again. I couldn't let her have all the midnight powers over my body.

I stretched again and listened to my mother sleeping in the bed next to mine. She was snoring softly, and it reminded me of how much I missed her being the way she was. Not that this version of her was bad. Right now, she was the mom I'd always *thought* I'd wanted. She wasn't her. She wasn't the spell-weaving, incense-burning, sage-cleansing mother I'd always known.

At this moment, her snoring sounded musical. It was the one thing that connected this version of her to the other. It lulled me. In and out. Peace and quiet broken only by her chainsaw-sounding breaths.

I was so tired. My eyelids fluttered. Closed. It was only for a second. I flipped them open. Somehow the light of a new day was outside my window.

I was in my bed with pajamas on. I hadn't put pajamas on when I was sitting in the chair beside the window last night. I hadn't even set them out on the bed. Yet, I was wearing them. I'd washed my face—I could smell the astringent—and I was lying on my bed, under my blankets, in my hotel room. At least in my blackouts, I was hygienic and this time, I was chaste. There was that.

I only had a few days left of shooting and I would be finished with the movie. Delilah had mentioned that there would be some post-production work, but it wouldn't require me to stay on the island.

We had a night shoot coming up—a new moon night shoot. It was also in a few days, so the timing was all coming together to finish the movie, return the stones to the sea, and break this curse. Now, all we had to do was find the dagger and turn Mom back into herself.

Taking a deep breath, I got dressed and ready for another day of acting... and probably keeping the witch inside me under control. Before I could leave the room, my cell rang, and it was a Boston number. There were only a couple of folks who would be calling me.

When I picked up a voice said, "Dr. Thorn, please hold for Dr. Warren."

I never understood why people did that kind of thing. Had a secretary make the call when they needed to speak to someone. Especially if it was about termination, which undoubtedly it was.

A second later, he came on the line. "Dr. Thorn, the investigation into your misconduct is complete and you have been reinstated as a physician at Mass Gen."

Hmm. I'd been suspended. Now investigated and then reinstated. "Thank you, Dr. Warren."

"Do you have a prospective date of return? I need to get your reinstatement papers filed."

I had no idea what was involved in post-production, but I figured I had at least another week on the island and then everything was up in the air because I hadn't had anything to go back to. "I'm going to have to check my schedule. I have some obligations that I need to see through to their finish." He didn't need to know everything. "I can phone you when I have a concrete date in mind."

"See that you do," was all he said before he hung up.

Quite the day I was having.

After I'd taken another deep breath and felt ready to face the day once more, and whatever repercussions my witch had caused the night before, I walked down to the dining room and sat at a table. Delilah and Cami were a couple of tables over and Cami waved me over.

I took my orange juice and walked over. "Did you guys have any luck figuring out how to return my mom's memories? Or how to get Ariya out of my body? Anything about the dagger?" I wasn't so concerned about getting the Captain out of Will since Will didn't seem to mind and the Captain was intent on going back to the sea.

Delilah shook her head. "There wasn't anything in the research or at the museum. Our only hope seems to be the diary unless the witch has a suggestion." She cocked an arched brow at me.

"My little predator seems pretty content with her host body." That didn't bode well for me. I *needed* this information. Like

I needed my next breath. Like I needed my body back. Like I needed her out of my head.

Before we could brainstorm, Arthur from the front desk walked over, and stood behind Delilah until she looked up at him, then he bent at the waist and whispered something to her.

Like he'd just told her that all the films we'd spent the last month or so shooting had just been stolen, Delilah pushed her chair back, didn't speak, and followed him out of the dining room. I glanced at Cami, and she shrugged.

I hadn't served myself breakfast yet but was still enjoying my OJ when they returned with Penelope. "Miss Thorn, we have urgent news for you waiting at the mainland."

That meant another boat ride. I was fine with the one that I had to be on for filming, the stationary of the pirate's ship. Not so much with the live-action version, especially if the pig was coming along. I didn't have anything against him as a pet, as a pig, even, but I didn't care for him as a co-passenger in the boat I was riding in.

Instead of driving us toward the mainland, she circled us around the island to the cove and shut off the motor. "Miss Thorn, this is the exact spot where the ship of one Captain Renfro Remington succumbed to the harsh waters and rocks of this cove."

If that was true, I wasn't so certain I wanted to be in the cove on a boat driven by a woman who'd dumped me out once, even if it was on a previous trip and now we were at a rocking standstill.

Penelope stood and pointed as she spoke. "Do you see those cameras?" I looked to where she had mentioned and saw the glint of something catching the light. "We put those up a while back because people kept diving for the boat. We were overrun with treasure hunters. Not that much of the boat is left."

It was all nice, but I didn't know why I hadn't been allowed to eat breakfast instead of hopping in this glorified kayak with a motor. The cameras were rather artfully hidden, and if Penelope hadn't pointed them out I wouldn't have noticed. "Okay?"

"We watched the video from the night you went swimming in the cove."

"I went swimming in the cove?" I woke up one morning with seaweed in my hair.

Penelope nodded. "Yes, dear. You swam out to this very point in the water and dived." She cleared her throat. "Spent a few very long minutes under the water before you surfaced."

"I don't remember that." I had no recollection of that swim. Especially considering as *myself*, I couldn't do it.

In my head, Ariya was silent, but I had a serious sense of uh-oh going on under my surface, only it was her *uh-oh* not mine.

"What did I do when I surfaced?" Maybe there were clues. Certainly, they didn't just bring me out here to show me where I swam to.

"You went to the basin at the near side of the beach and buried something in the sand." She shook her head. "The light wasn't so good there, so the cameras in that location can only see the shadow of you. Looked like you were digging."

Now, Ariya was yelling in my head, doing a full Fa-la-la-la-la at top volume. "Is it the dagger?" Oh, my goodness. "Do you have it?" Hope burned inside of me.

Penelope smiled as Ariya tried to attack the old woman and use my body to do it.

Ariya had underestimated the old woman. She was fast and tough and spry, delivered a karate chop to the back of my neck that crippled me long enough she could move away.

Then Penelope jumped from the boat like her ass was on fire. Took off on a jet ski that was at the back of her boat.

That was okay. I could drive a boat. Maybe. Possibly.

Or not. Penelope had taken the boat key. I couldn't blame her. We were alone. I'd attacked her. Or tried to, anyway.

My choices were to sit there and wait to be rescued or to swim for it and hope that Ariya kept me afloat.

Before we dove in, I wanted to make sure we were on the same page as far as keeping me alive. “Ariya, if you let me drown, you die, too, and…” Now I was going to try to reason with her. “We have to make this right again. I need my mom.”

Fine.

“I’m going to need a little more than that.” We weren’t exactly working with mutual trust here. I was going to have to take her word, but before I could do that, I needed her to give it.

I won’t let you drown.

I probably wasn’t going to get better than that. I sat at the edge of the boat for a few seconds, afraid to jump, and then I gave Ariya control.

This time, I was the voice in my head. *You love Renegade?*

“More than a poet loves words or a pirate loves treasure.” I liked not having to worry about swimming, that she was in control. She made it seem easy.

You’ve had your chance with life and love. Talking to her made the swim take a lot less time and when she took a break and looked back for a few seconds, we were about halfway between the boat and the shore.

“I wish you could have known Renegade. He was a gentle soul despite being a pirate. Sweet and tender. A lover like no other.” She spoke with such fondness. “My heart was consumed by him.”

I'd never known that kind of passion. Not even with Clay.

"Are you going to marry your Remington?" Her voice was soft now and she was swimming faster.

Things are different now than they were back when you were... alive. I don't know him.

"I know some of the ways things are. This isn't my first time back." We reached the shore, and she walked us in. "He's a good man, and you could do a lot worse than a good man."

For once, I thought she might have a good point.

"What about you?" I asked. "Do you think that you and your pirate can be together forever?"

She was silent for a moment, but it almost felt like I could hear her thinking. *I know nothing lasts forever, but we lost each other so young. Never had children. Never had a life together.*

"Can you have that now? Through us? Would it give you back what you lost?"

Silence again, and then, *when I made the spell, I never thought it would be like this, and then I had nothing else to hope for. These last few days back together, the best that it can be between us, I realized it's not the same. Wonderful. Not the same. Not when we aren't ourselves. Not when Remy wants to return to the sea. Each night he's tried to convince me that I have to let this dream go, but I...*

When she didn't finish her thought I did. "It's hard to let go of a dream." Like my perfect life as a doctor, without magic in my life, without a younger man who I want to be with so much it hurts.

Maybe it's time.

She didn't say any more, and so I didn't push her. Hopefully, she was realizing the right thing to do on her own.

Chapter Twenty-Seven

Everything Ends

When I got to the beach, the girls were there with Remy, Nicky, and Will. My mother was sitting near the beach on the sidewalk that separated it into sides, and she was reading the journal.

I stopped and stared as they all chatted. Ariya tried to keep me from walking toward them, but when Will came closer in his costume—or maybe it was Renegade in full regalia—he held out his hand, and Ariya took it. I smiled though I didn't know if it came through on my face or if it even mattered.

When I was standing near them, I looked at Cami and Remy. "If we send the jewels back to the sea, what about Remy's job?" He's been hired by an insurance company to find the jewels and return them to the collection they'd been stolen from years ago.

Remy smiled. "This is important. The insurance company knew it was a long shot." He shrugged. "They belong to the sea, not to a collector. They're Renegade's, not Marcel Devereaux's."

I nodded because that made perfect sense to me. Ariya, remarkably, remained silent. I could feel her sadness, though, and it touched my heart for her.

Delilah touched my shoulder, then handed me a piece of paper. "It's the script."

It wasn't until then that I noticed Garrett and Nate with cameras and another couple of light stands set up on the beach, I paused. "Can you guys give me a second?"

Delilah cocked her head as if she found my question a taxing one, but Cami nodded. "Take your time."

I walked a few steps away and pulled Will with me. "I can only give you a couple of minutes, but if you want to say goodbye to Renegade, now is the time. You have to go peacefully."

Ariya sighed and the breath escaped my body. "Okay." I turned control over to her. She walked a few more steps down the beach with Will then stopped and turned to him. His arms went around her waist and though I could feel them, I knew this wasn't for me.

Ariya leaned in and kissed his cheek. "Thank you for everything. For holding me last night, for letting me believe you were Renegade." She tugged his head down for a kiss. A hell of a kiss. One that made my toes curl in the sand. It was the kind of kiss dreams were made of. My dreams anyway. I heard her words. *For letting me believe you were Renegade.*

When the kiss ended, he was wide-eyed, and shook his head like he couldn't believe that kiss. I knew how he felt. It had been... something. Soft and sweet, fraught with emotion and passion. A goodbye. A thank you. He smiled and leaned his forehead against mine-hers.

Then Ariya gave me control. "Can I have one more minute, Will?"

"You bet." He smiled, kissed my cheek, and walked back toward the group waiting for me to finish this.

You've been the best one, the best host. No hard feelings?

Well, she'd had sex with my body, and I hadn't been a part of it. I hadn't even gotten the memory of it.

I didn't have intercourse with your Remington.

I stopped walking. "What?"

I love Renfro and I've tried and tried, waited years for him to come back to me. Your Remington was convincing, but he wasn't my Remington. Although, he looked out for you. For me.

"When did you know?" Not that it mattered. Probably mattered that she knew, and I didn't. It hardly seemed fair that she'd been able to keep her thoughts from me, but she'd known mine. It didn't really matter, now.

The night he tried to get me to take him to the dagger. I can't bring Renegade back. I don't have that kind of magic.

She sounded sad. I could feel it inside of me.

"I think I saw him. When I was drowning." I wanted her to have her happy ending. Maybe then she would stop trying to come back, and live her eternity with him.

Maybe he's out there waiting for me to come to him. A second later, she added, *I hope so.*

I walked back to the spot on the beach Delilah had marked and then we fit the stones into the hilt of the dagger. A second boat—the smaller version to the one Penelope had left me on out at sea—was waiting at the dock. We fit into the boat, Me, Delilah, Cami, Remy, Nicky, Will and Garrett, the cameraman, and this time Remy drove.

My mother stayed behind on the beach, but she'd given us the words we needed to say. It translated to love and light and resting in a peaceful slumber surrounded by love.

When we were near the other boat, Remy dropped the anchor, and Delilah, Cami, and I formed a small circle, hands clasped together at the hilt of the dagger as we spoke the chant. The boys passed out, but we continued until a light blinded us, and one by one, we went down, too.

Chapter Twenty-Eight

I Need a Six Month Vacation...Twice a Year

I LEARNED a few things from my time on the island. First, magic was real. All those years I'd thought my mother was a little bit crazy, she'd been telling the truth and even if she hadn't been, there wasn't anything wrong with believing in some magic.

Second, if there was a paparazzi photographer outside the house, I couldn't take for granted that they were good people. It made changing clothes a challenge since my mom's house was full of windows. Said photographers would make my work situations unbearable enough my only choice was to quit. Something I *probably* should have thought about before agreeing to act in the movie, not that I regretted my role.

Finally, missing someone the way I missed Will started in my soul and worked its way into my bloodstream so that I was a mopey, depressing excuse of a human.

"We're going to miss you, Dr. Thorn," Dr. Warren said, though he'd been none too unhappy when I turned in my notice. It had been too hard to work with reporters and photographers following me.

I appreciated the sentiment, but Dr. Warren had already hired my replacement.

Perhaps one of the most frustrating parts of it all was the fact that the reporters all asked the same questions—every single day. They could've just sent one guy and then borrowed his notes like chem class, but they sent an army of them. It was overwhelming and finally too much.

I put in my notice.

What else could I do? I was too big of a distraction at the hospital which meant I needed to go somewhere new. Or somewhere old. Like a Caribbean island that didn't have a physician's office.

Maybe.

First I had to go to New York and do some postproduction work with Delilah. Later, there would be a press tour. I felt so important saying it. Although, my hospital family had decided to give me a going away party—with gifts. So far, I'd opened dark glasses, a black fedora, a trench coat, and a big black bag. It was my disguise to get out of Boston without all the papers following me.

It made me cry.

They'd given me an autographed photo album of our time together.

More tears.

The thought that had me holding it together was Will. If I had work to do still, so did he since most of our scenes were together. I was nervous about seeing him—hands shaking, mouth dry whenever I thought of him made me kind of nervous. Those butterflies were welcome. I wanted to see him. Thought about him a lot.

He hadn't called. Hadn't tried to get a hold of me. We'd been off the island for more than a month and went home, but still, nothing.

The door to the staff room of the hospital opened and a breeze rustled the paper napkins on the table. "There she is. Famous movie star, Dr. Ember Thorn." Delilah Bradbury walked toward me with the new Mrs. Remington—Cami Danes-Lacroix-Remington.

We hugged, air-kissed, and hugged again. I didn't even know how they knew to come here since I hadn't told my mother where I would be, but here they were. My sisterhood.

"Who wants to see a little sneak peek of Dr. Ember Thorn as the witch Ariya Thornbridge in her debut film, *Eternal* ?" A cheer from my colleagues and friends at the hospital went up. Not like a Bon Jovi concert kind of cheer, which would've been nice, but more a quiet kind of chorus of *yeah* and some scattered applause.

Delilah held up a DVD and gave a, "Hell, yeah," when someone brought in a player.

It was a DVD projector we used for presentations and seminars and meetings in the hospital. It projected onto a wall, but today it would be projecting my romance with Will. My debut as an actress. A flashback to one of the strangest times of my life. I had no idea what it would look like.

I watched the scene, watched Will, and remembered every second of what I saw until the final scene. I hugged Delilah. "It's incredible." They'd only been short scenes, a couple of minutes each, but there was one at the beginning, one in the middle, and one at the end. No love scene, although I remembered that one as well as any other. I remembered fighting Ariya for control so I was the one kissing Will. It had been so... awe-inspiring.

Speaking of... "Have you talked to Will?"

Delilah nodded. "He's been working on the island for a bit to make sure that any treasure hunting doesn't happen inside a five-mile radius of the island. I think he just finished that and will be meeting us in New York." She smiled. "He made sure the jewels are safe there now."

"The journal?"

"Returned to the museum. They weren't even mad we took it." Cami grinned like we'd accomplished some great coup. "They were just thrilled that Delilah is adding a card at the end of the credits that directs people to the museum with questions about the history of it all. Delilah promised to donate the costumes and the replica of the ship for tourist attractions. All is well."

"How is your Mom?" Delilah asked. They'd bonded over stories of Hollywood and leading men. My mom was a movie buff and she'd seen every Delilah Bradbury movie ever made at least twice.

"She's good. Selling love potions from the journal now." Of course, she still had her photocopies. I wouldn't have dreamed of keeping them from her.

Cami looked at Delilah and Delilah nodded her head. "We have a present for you."

Who didn't like presents? I certainly did. I took the black velvet box. It was a necklace box, and I flipped the lid up. Nestled inside was a gold necklace with a three-stoned pendant—a citrine, a sapphire, and an onyx. "It's beautiful." It was. Intricate and on the back of the pendant it was inscribed *ECD SoS*. "SoS?"

"Sisterhood of the Stones." Delilah had an identical necklace as did Cami.

Now we really were a sisterhood.

"We have one more surprise." Cami nodded to the door, and it took a second, but it opened and Will—dazzling in a stormy blue shirt that matched his eyes and a pair of jeans that hugged his legs—walked in.

Delilah and Cami disappeared, or maybe they walked away to get a piece of cake. I couldn't be certain because I was distracted. By Will.

"You're here."

"Yeah." He smiled. "I missed you too much to stay away."

He pulled me close, cupped my face with his palm, and kissed me until we probably needed to get a room. Not really, but I wouldn't have minded getting a room. When he pulled back he smiled and leaned his forehead against mine. "Do you know that I was rooting for Renegade and Ariya throughout our entire time on the island? I thought that if they worked out for eternity, we would, too. Same genetics, same happy ending."

I didn't know a guy as perfect as this one and it was all I needed to know. "You know that Renegade was killed by his men and the witch killed herself when she walked into the sea, right?"

He grinned and I could've stared at him all night. "Our story won't be exactly the same, but it's going to be a good one."

I couldn't have agreed more. "Aren't you glad you didn't stop the movie?"

He nodded and kissed me again, softer this time, shorter, but just as perfect. "Oh yeah. Really glad." One more kiss later, he held out his hand. "I think it's time we get started on our own happily ever after. You ready?"

I really was. "I can't wait."

More Paranormal Women's Fiction

Witching After Forty https://laboruff.com/books/witching-after-forty/

A Ghoulish Midlife

Cookies For Satan (A Christmas Story)

I'm With Cupid (A Valentine's Day Story)

A Cursed Midlife

Birthday Blunder

A Girlfriend For Mr. Snoozerton (A Girlfriend Story)

A Haunting Midlife

An Animated Midlife

A Killer Midlife

Faery Odd-Mother

A Grave Midlife

Shifting Into Midlife https://laboruff.com/books/shifting-into-midlife/

Pack Bunco Night

Alpha Males and Other Shift

The Cat's Meow

Prime Time of Life https://laboruff.com/books/primetime-of-life/

Borrowed Time

Stolen Time

Just in Time

Hidden Time

Nick of Time

Magical Midlife in Mystic Hollow https://laboruff.com/books/mystic-hollow/

Karma's Spell

Karma's Shift

Karma's Spirit

Karma's Sense

Karma's Stake

An Unseen Midlife https://amzn.to/3cF3W54

Bloom in Blood

Dance in Night

Bask in Magic

Surrender in Dreams

Midlife Mage https://amzn.to/30MFNH3

Unveiled

Unfettered

An Immortal Midlife https://amzn.to/3cC6BMP

Fatal Forty

Fighting Forty

Finishing Forty

About Lia Davis

USA Today bestselling author Lia Davis spends most of her time writing racy romance and witty women's fiction, the majority of which takes place in fantasy worlds full of magic and mayhem. She prides herself on her ability to craft strong and sassy heroines, emotionally intelligent alpha heroes, and rich, expansive universes that readers want to visit again and again.

She is the mastermind behind the bestselling Ashwood Falls Series and the co-author of the beloved Witching After Forty Series.

She currently resides in Florida where she's working on her very own happily-ever-after with her supportive husband and spends her free time doting on a pack of feisty felines and her loving family.

Follow Lia on Social Media

Website: http://www.authorliadavis.com/

Newsletter: http://www.subscribepage.com/authorliadavis.newsletter

Facebook author fan page: https://www.facebook.com/novelsbylia/

Facebook Fan Club: https://www.facebook.com/groups/LiaDavisFanClub/

Twitter: https://twitter.com/novelsbylia

Instagram: https://www.instagram.com/authorliadavis/

BookBub: https://www.bookbub.com/authors/lia-davis

Pinterest: http://www.pinterest.com/liadavis35/

Goodreads: http://www.goodreads.com/author/show/5829989.Lia_Davis

Check out the official Davis Raynes Merch store on Etsy: https://www.etsy.com/shop/davisraynesmerch

About Lacey Carter

Lacey Carter writes paranormal women's fiction and cozy mysteries with humor, adventure, and a little romance. Her stories are sure to make you smile, laugh, and maybe even cry. But don't worry, she's always sure to give her readers a happy ending for her brave heroes and heroines.

As a USA Today bestselling author, Lacey is always working on another story. She thrives off of the adventure both in her books and outside of them, while raising her three beautiful children, with her amazing husband. She also writes steamy romances under the name Lacey Carter Andersen.

So if you're looking for fun and adventure, dive into one of her worlds today!

About L.A. Boruff

L.A. (Lainie) Boruff lives in East Tennessee with her husband, three children, and an ever growing number of cats. She loves reading, watching TV, and procrastinating by browsing Facebook. L.A.'s passions include vampires, food, and listening to heavy metal music. She once won a Harry Potter trivia contest based on the books and lost one based on the movies. She has two bands on her bucket list that she still hasn't seen: AC/DC and Alice Cooper. Feel free to send tickets.

L.A.'s Facebook Group: https://www.facebook.com/groups/LABoruffCrew/

Follow L.A. on Bookbub if you like to know about new releases but don't like to be spammed: https://www.bookbub.com/profile/l-a-boruff

Printed in Poland
by Amazon Fulfillment
Poland Sp. z o.o., Wrocław